The Jinn and the Sword

A Tale of Mystery, Suspense, and Romance in the Sixteenth Century Court of Suleyman the Magnificent

ROBERT TRUSS PEACOCK
AND SARA LAWRENCE COOK

Library of Congress Control Number: 2017918144
ISBN: Hardcover   978-1-5434-6897-7
                Softcover   978-1-5434-6898-4
                eBook   978-1-5434-6899-1

Print information available on the last page.

Cover Design: Katelyn J. Cook and Sara Lawrence Cook with Xlibris
Book Interior Design: Sara Lawrence Cook and Katelyn J. Cook
Book Editor: Rebecca L. Cook

Author Photos: Robert Peacock: Anne Peacock
               Sara Cook: Suzy Chandler

Rev. date: 01/24/2018

To order additional copies of this book, contact:
Xlibris
1-888-795-4274
www.Xlibris.com
Orders@Xlibris.com
771106

Contents

DAY FOUR

DAY FIVE

A FEW DAYS LATER

Dedicated to the memory
of our parents, Francis
and Amelia Peacock,
whose generous love,
encouragement, spiritual
and secular guidance have
firmly framed our lives.

Preface

By great good fortune, I was assigned to Turkey as a freshly minted Air Force JAG officer. I had spent much of my childhood and young adulthood living in Europe, but Turkey was a stimulating, new cultural experience. I was inspired by the generosity and kindness of the Turkish people, the richness of its past, and the exhilarating feast for the senses one experiences walking the streets and alleyways of Istanbul- its exotic history, sounds, smells, calls to prayer, music, color and artistry. Strolling among the ghostlike ruins of Ephesus, Troy and other coastal settlements of the ancient Greeks and Romans, also provided fertile ground for the imagination and senses. I was captivated and the genesis of our story began there, in those unforgettable moments. That was nearly forty years ago. Life intervened. I delighted in my career, the raising of my twin daughters, Mary and Anne, watching them grow, proud of their many athletic achievements and scholarship as they earned doctorates in veterinary medicine and human rights. My time hearing and mediating cases and writing decisions as a federal judge consumed the hours. I also co-authored a book on the Contract Disputes Act and authored law review articles and monographs on government contract related matters. Years passed and I found myself refocusing on those ancient and mysterious places where I had lived early in my career. Plot and character development began, set against the backdrop of 16th century Istanbul-Konstantiniyye- centered on mysteries and intrigues surrounding the fascinating Imperial Court of Sultan Suleyman, the Magnificent, and the Ottoman Empire. I approached my sister, Sara, approximately a decade ago asking her to enrich the characters and scenes, paint beautiful word pictures, and participate in developing this novel. The timing wasn't right. Again the demands and vicissitudes of life interfered. She was managing her successful interior design business, caring for our aging mother, and raising her wonderful sons Zachary and Joshua, often while her husband, John, was serving in the Middle East. Sara promised she would reconsider when she found "peace." I muddled along without her but never was sufficiently inspired or energized to complete the work. Sara was true to her word. After a grueling recovery from cancer and a move to the northern Great Plains (she now refers to herself as a "High Plains Drifter") she reached that place of "immeasurable peace." She passionately immersed herself in a new creative effort, taking on our project in late 2016. We endured numerous co-edits of the evolving manuscript, predictable sibling spats about creative differences regarding the direction and tone of the novel and countless hours spent "word-smithing" before finally producing our book that we now humbly place before you, dear reader.

Robert Peacock

Prologue

It was Spring with the promise
of renewed life.
The holy days of Ramadan
and the celebration
of Eid having ended,
the great emperor,
the Sultan Suleyman Kanuni,
"The Lawgiver,"
known also as "The
Magnificent," directed the
captain of the Beyliks, his
elite palace guards,
to meet the new envoy from Venice.
The envoy's caravel was to arrive at the
Golden Horn, that stunning
convergence of
land and sea, where the "sweet waters"
of Europe and Asia meet
beneath the Seraglio Point and
walls of the Yeni Saray.
To the eyes of a young warrior then
and his fading vision now, it was the most
beautiful setting he believed
he would ever be
blessed to see. The beauty of the
familiar vanishes quickly for some, perhaps
revived only after absence
or new perspective
refocuses memories on the splendors
that have been known.
But the beauty of a
moment…a second…
can also live forever.
In the remembrances of
a long ago glance.
In a scent. In a caress. In a kiss.
This is a tale of this time and place…
a few days worthy of being written…
A few days affecting the fate of empires…
And a humble warrior's soul.

It was the Year of the Prophet 937 in
the city of Istanbul- The City of Intrigues-
where deep beneath the
ancient cobbled and cacophonous
streets, in the moments just after
midnight, the mysteries were
manifest and multiplying.

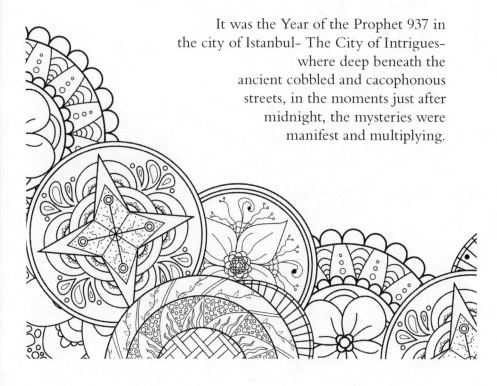

Day One

Birinci Gün

Born of the Smokeless Fire

he faint light of the torches carried by the two janissaries was scarcely sufficient to break the gloomy darkness that engulfed them as they exited the Harem and made their way into the deep stygian crypts beneath the city of Istanbul. Guards to Sultan Suleyman the Magnificent, they were inebriated and in violation of not just their sworn allegiance to the sultan, but the obligation of sobriety as devout Muslims. Mehmed, the brutish *Kizlar Agha* and Chief Black Eunuch, waited as each dropped silver *yirmiliks* into his outstretched hand. The third highest ranking official in the sultan's government, he was bestowed with considerable powers as the overseer of the Harem. The corrupt "Keeper of the Girls" had provided the debauched janissaries with the "favors" of odalisques in the Harem. If caught, Mehmed's risky and illicit enterprise was punishable by death. Hefty recompense was expected from those using his services. On this night, he grunted at the penurious offering for the risks he had taken.

Mehmed and the janissaries descended staircase after staircase, crudely carved out of the substratum of earth and alluvium beneath the Topkapi Palace and laid in a deliberately haphazard and confusing maze, before reaching their exit. He pushed open the concealed door, camouflaged and carefully carved from the stone, leading to secret passageways and cisterns. The janissaries would be required to navigate the well-memorized labyrinth through the subterranean crypts and ultimately well beyond the grounds of the palace, exiting into the streets of Istanbul.

The flickering torches illuminated the amber tones of the ceiling of the Basilica Cistern, incised with delicate carvings depicting eyes and tears—homage to the wretched existence and deaths of the slaves who had constructed the cisterns during the time of the Romans. The ceilings were double-vaulted, buttressed by columns resembling rows of meticulously planted trees, mostly adorned with Corinthian capitals, designed to support and ornament the vast underground complex. The cistern imbued eerie and unsettling sensations, its water squalid and murky and its darkness capable of hiding not just depth but other recondite mysteries.

"Drink!" Mehmed demanded of the janissaries, stopping them before exiting. The oafish cretin thrust cups of steaming liquid at them as he stood sucking food from between his teeth, revealing black, rotting holes in two of his central incisors. "If you are caught, the tea will help cover the stench of too much fig wine."

The janissaries drank the acidulous tea. "Do not draw attention to yourselves. Also, chew this to help your breath," he ordered, offering them peppermint leaves. "Fools! Remember your tasks are not completed! You are to meet Kareem and Jamal at the appointed place, just before the sun is to rise. If you fail, we all will be in peril! You must act exactly as I have instructed or your demise is near! Now straighten your backs and keep your mouths shut!"

"We won't be caught. As often as we've come, we know our way. Only a chosen few know this path," Adem, the less intoxicated of the janissaries, assured.

"Don't worry, Mehmed, you old prick. Uh, well, I guess I can't mean that literally," Baris laughed at his insensitive joke at the expense of the castrated eunuch as he retreated into the maze. Mehmed grunted, watching the dissolute warriors exit.

He shook his head in disgust as they disappeared into the shadowy aphotic gloom, their steadying arms slung across each other's shoulder, engaged in nonsensical chatter and drunken laughter. Mehmed was worried. He reflected on those he had recruited for great treachery, his clandestine league of miscreants and his head hung heavy in contemplation of the consequences of their conspiracy. Within the walls of the Topkapi Palace shortly after midnight, the corrupted warriors had carried out the instructions that Mehmed had given them. Mehmed hoped they would just as scrupulously complete the last of their tasks and meet their co-conspirators before sunrise as planned. Their condition however, caused disquiet and reason for concern. Mehmed now stood witness to the consequences of the janissaries' unfettered access to the orgiastic activities he had provided as partial reward for their compliance with his orders. Mehmed had corrupted them completely. He realized that those so easily corrupted could be just as easily swayed to treachery against him. So few knew of his felonious enterprises. These two had knowledge that could compromise him. As he listened to the echo of their footsteps before closing the heavy door to the secret passageway, Mehmed uttered a short prayer to Allah that they would not be caught, thus allowing him to keep his head firmly attached to his shoulders.

Continuous drippings from water collecting on the walls and ceilings fell on the janissaries' oil-soaked torches as they leaned on one another in their stupor, making their way deeper and deeper along the dark and narrowing path. Their torches insufficient to light the way, they relied on memory to navigate the twists and turns taken so many times after their frequent visits to the Harem.

"I think Mehmed dislikes us because we know too much. We would be wise to pay him more next time," Baris opined, reflecting on their tenuous relationship with the *Kizlar Agha*. "*Baksheesh, baksheesh!* Bribes! He bribes us to do his bidding and then we return the bribes for more favors in the Harem!"

"Damn these cistern flies—they are everywhere," he waved his arms, batting them away from his face. "I don't remember there being so many of them. And when it gets hotter in the summer," he continued, "the mosquitoes down here will be as big as horseflies with an appetite for blood to match. We'll have to cover our faces to keep from being eaten alive."

Adem nodded, slapping his face in an attempt to kill one of the annoying and biting flies. "Let's hurry and get out of this stinking hole in the ground!" he encouraged.

Baris lagged slightly behind Adem in order to navigate the narrow pathway and avoid falling into the cistern waters. "Yes, yes!" he slurred. "I hate this place!"

They quickened their pace. Their circuitous route had taken them from the Harem of the Topkapi Palace through the crypts and cisterns, past an intersecting corridor that led under the *Has Oda*— the place of sacred relics. They wended their way under the revered *Hagia Irene*. They intended to exit beyond the first court of the palace.

Upon reaching their destination, the janissaries would make their way back to the palace above ground, giving the appearance to any who might notice that they were simply returning from time spent in the city.

Succumbing increasingly to the considerable drink they had consumed, Adem and Baris were becoming more disoriented on a path ordinarily familiar to them. Seeking relief for their parched throats, the flagitious janissaries touched their tongues to small, moisture retaining, cuplike protrusions in the crudely carved cistern walls.

They too were worried, having acted in treasonous concert with Mehmed against the sultan. Consumed with renewed apprehension, unable to forget the gravity of their acts even in their inebriated state, they also sensed a strange, unsettling eeriness—something was not right.

Adem watched a panic-stricken Baris grasp his throat. "Damn! Something just stung me and it stings like hell! They're everywhere!" Baris grabbed his neck and swung his torch in an attempt to keep the flies at bay.

"Damn! *Bok!* I was just stung too." Adem grabbed his neck as he felt an excruciating pain. "What the hell?" He pulled something from his jugular, but there was no time to examine what he held in his hand.

An unexpected rush of air caused their flames to flicker. The janissaries were blanketed in a sudden and ghostly silence. Alarmed by a play of shadows and a menacing hissing utterance, their bodies shuddered, terror seizing them.

"What in the name of Allah was that?" a petrified Baris sputtered.

Baris' question would forever remain unanswered. A barely discernible shadow, which had previously eluded their bacchic eyes, took form and held them spellbound as it moved before them. As if to rid themselves of hallucinations, the janissaries blinked, shaking their heads in disbelief as the frightening apparition came to life, seemingly emerging from the carved stone walls. Confined to the narrow pathway with nowhere to flee, they watched, trembling and transfixed, as the sinister specter materialized and took shape. Drunkenly attempting to escape, they stumbled over one another and found themselves staring up into the face of a demon, cloaked and hooded.

Looming large, it engulfed them in a morbid and ghastly embrace, its cloak flailing and flapping around them. Their muscles weighted and paralyzed, breathing became increasingly laborious. An apocalypse of terror flooded over them as the seasoned warriors helplessly and unwillingly succumbed to their terrible fate, held captive and overwhelmed by the putrefying, suffocating stench, the foulness, of the Jinn—the evil Ifrit—the ghoulish and dreaded demon of the darkness. Born of the smokeless fire, the Jinn engulfed them. Unleashing long, sharp, and deadly talons, the deev began slashing them to pieces. Their skin shredded and hanging, the helpless janissaries were still grasping at their throats as they met with excruciating and agonizing death. The demon howled—its devilish and horrifying voice descending from a high piercing screech to the emoting of a deep, guttural hissing. As the mutilations ended, its utterances transformed into a fiendishly crepitating grunting, ending finally with sounds of deep, sated gratification as it stood over its kills.

The feckless and corrupted warriors lay on the floor of the cistern, bodies convulsing, bleeding, as they grasped at the tightening inferno in their throats. Their blood-curdling screams reverberated deep and loud through the cisterns echoing into the crypts, their bodies struggling for breath and clinging to a whisper of life. As they died, the accursed stench of the Jinn still upon them, Adem and Baris stared petrified into the menacing and gruesome face of the gorgon Medusa etched into a cistern column, partially submerged in the glaucous waters.

Topkapi

The Topkapi Palace, the Palace of the Cannon Gate, was more than the residence of Sultan Suleyman and the imperial family. It was a center for art and education as well as administration of the Empire. Topkapi Sarayi had been constructed over the old Byzantine acropolis. The palace complex included hundreds of rooms and chambers, discrete areas separated by four major courtyards. Nearly 4,000 people lived within its walls. The entire structure was built with the sultan's private quarters on the highest promontory, the Seraglio Point, for the most spectacular views of the Bosphorus and the Golden Horn. It was, from a distance, an awesome sight to behold, positioned imposingly on a distant hill, inspiring wonder in the observer by its silhouette and the shining, opalescent quality it radiated. It was equally capable of inspiring fear. Approaching the formidable towers, walls and series of gates imbued a sense of trepidation—a disquieting dread—knowing that upon entering through the massive and heavily fortified gates, there may be no return.

The palace had grown rapidly under Sultan Suleyman. A dramatic expansion had been ordered to fulfill administrative and housing requirements necessary to superintend the exponential growth of an empire flourishing under the leadership of The Lawgiver. Suleyman's architect, the venerable Mimar Sinan, designed and oversaw the construction of this and many projects the emperor desired. The palace had a mint, kitchens, stables, copper works, an armory, hospital and a mosque—the *Hagia Irene*—everything required for a virtually self-contained, vibrant, and thriving Islamic city. The Topkapi Palace was in and of itself, a city—autonomous—with little unavailable to its inhabitants.

Entry was made through a series of gates into each of the courtyards. The Imperial Gates allowed entrance into the first courtyard housing the *Hagia Irene*. Traveling deeper into the complex, visitors passed into the second courtyard through the Gates of Salutation, beautifully inscribed with Koranic verses and royal monograms, all in exquisite calligraphy. Within the gates was the Divan Square, housing a park filled with peacocks and gazelles. It was here that courtiers politicked and viziers and pashas gathered to discuss business before meeting with the sultan. The Square also housed the Fountain of the Executioner, where after decapitating the doomed, the executioner washed his hands of the blood and, symbolically, of the deed.

Only the sultan and his family were permitted entry into the third courtyard through the Gate of Felicity unless authorized by the sultan himself. The Audience Chamber, the *Arz Odasi,* was situated within the third courtyard. The chamber's furnishings were lavish, including the elevated and elaborate gem-encrusted 24 karat gold throne, upon which the sultan sat while dispensing his will. Dignitaries, too, were often granted audience in the square building, the *Kubbealti*—under the dome—with its ornate green, gold, and white ceiling, and its weight supported by twenty-two columns of marble, feldspar, and quartz. A latticework-screened mezzanine above the dais allowed light from the marble loggia into the building. It was a place of surreptitious eavesdropping by the sultan's advisors, the concubines of the Harem and, on occasion, even by the sultan himself. The luxuriant brocade cushions of the golden throne, were ornamented with pearls and emeralds, and covered the seat upon which Sultan Suleyman sat.

Above the throne, the ceiling was lacquered in shades of deep blue and decorated with gold leaf stars. Near the entrance to the throne was a fountain intended, by the sound of its rippling waters, to muffle conversations, preventing them from being overheard. The inscription on the fountain read, *"The Fountainhead of Generosity, Justice and the Sea of Beneficence,"* homage to Sultan Suleyman us-Selatin. The mosaics and Iznik tiles covering the floors and walls were resplendent in their patterns and shades of blue, turquoise, and white. Finely knotted handmade carpets representing provinces throughout the Ottoman Empire covered the floor. Opulent fabrics, often with intricate hand-detailed needlework, covered the cushions used for seating.

Above the door to the visitor's entrance was the inscription, embossed in exquisite Arabic calligraphy, *"In the Name of God, the Compassionate, the Merciful."* Visitors who pleased the sultan were often showered with titles and gifts. Some, however, never left and, upon a displeased sultan's orders, were strangled by deaf and mute eunuch assassins. Deliberately and cruelly reduced to their condition, the eunuchs could neither hear the cries of those they tortured and killed nor speak of their deeds.

Occasionally, musicians welcomed visiting dignitaries. Court musicians, the *cematt-i-mutriban*, played on bamboo flutes, and a plethora of membranophones, including small kettle drums, trumpets, a zither, a timpani, a harp, and a lute. Exotic fragrances comingled and wafted through the air—amber and musk, violet, lavender, rose, jasmine, and magnolia—in the form of perfumes and incense. Sultan Suleyman was known to favor sandalwood. Visitors entering the throne room were struck by the sumptuous and splendid sensory feast creating an indelible memory of dazzling, inestimable richness.

Amid the lush gardens beyond the Gates of Felicity lay the residential and private rooms of the royal family, and the *Has Oda*, or the privy chamber. The greatest treasures of the Ottoman Empire were kept in the *Has Oda*—the sacred relics of Muhammad. The Harem and its protective eunuchs, including the *Kizlar Agha*, and the *agas*, the boys who were in service to the sultan, made their home in the third courtyard.

Reliquaries of such exquisite artistic and spiritual value, destined to endure and resonate over the centuries were displayed in the *Has Oda*. The palace treasury was also a repository for resplendent objects gathered from countries conquered by the Ottomans, gifts from kings and queens, as well as finely crafted treasures of inestimable value, created and gifted by artisans and sovereigns. The Topkapi Palace was a spectacle of splendor, a kaleidoscope of changing colors and patterns and fragrances intended to delight every sense. Precious gems, astonishing in size and variety, gold and gem-encrusted jewelry, and regalia that included thrones—one with over nine hundred topazes and over five hundred pounds of gold were housed in the repository. Crowns and scepters of astonishing opulence, compotes and cradles crafted of 24 karat gold, pearls of massive size, diamonds, emeralds, and rubies were among the palace treasures.

Persian miniatures were particularly revered, the figurative and non-figurative ornamental illustrations, some in single sheets and others bound into *muraqqas*—beautifully embellished albums. Particularly prominent among them were the strikingly beautiful works of the artist Kamal ud-Din Behzad, the most prolific and renowned of the illuminators. Ancient Korans and a 4th century Bible were housed within the fortress walls along with religious relics that included the staff of Moses, the sword of David, and a saucer belonging to Abraham. The relics of John the Baptist—his hand and skull fragments—were also among the reliquaries maintained within the treasury.

Even with the abundance of riches contained within the Topkapi, treasures that rivaled those of the fabled Ali Baba, the most venerated and protected were the priceless relics of the Prophet Muhammad. In the *Has Oda* were the Prophet's cloak, protected in a golden case embossed with verses from the Koran, the Prophet's bow, swords, and scabbards, hair, a broken tooth, his footprint, and standard—all sacred and carefully guarded. The richness of material and spiritual wealth was rivaled nowhere else on earth.

Sacred Relics

Almost indiscernibly, a section of the intricately laid mosaic tile floor of the *Has Oda* was slowly raised. A small portion of the floor had been deliberately and carefully excavated allowing access from below for the two thieves. Dressed in black to conceal themselves in the dark ambiguity of the morning twilight and just a few hours after their co-conspirators Adem and Baris had dug out the section of floor, they moved nimbly but cautiously into the most sacred area of the *Has Oda*. They quietly made their way to the holy objects of the Prophet. Each had a mission and each took treasures—one quickly grabbed Muhammad's cloak from its golden casket, the other his standard and a sword wielded by the great Prophet. Bounty in hand, they quickly exited back into the hole.

"Here, stand on my shoulders while you reseal the floor," Kareem instructed Jamal. "You are not as heavy. Here is the sealant we are to use." Kareem reached into his sash and handed his partner a small jar with a creamy, paste-like compound. He then stooped down to allow Jamal to climb on his shoulders.

"Hold steady," Jamal cautioned, as he carefully lifted the portion of the floor needing to be reseated. After a few moments, Jamal jumped down from Kareem's shoulders. "I think that is good enough. If I use too much it may not dry by the time the relics are discovered missing."

The thieves removed their black garb, revealing themselves as janissaries, unfaithful to their oaths and their sultan. They had precisely followed instructions provided in a message from Mehmed delivered by a young eunuch and now felt relieved that the first part of their mission had been completed. The theft had been accomplished timely - with stealth, precision, and without detection. They were soon to be rewarded for their efforts, and once their bounty was paid, the two thieves had made plans to flee the palace before the thefts of the priceless relics were discovered.

"Where are Baris and Adem?" Kareem asked his accomplice, holding the Prophet's sacred cloak. "The morning sun will soon be up. I cannot believe they are not here, because this is the spot—just before we leave the cistern. We followed their clues. The shaft in the ceiling of our passageway was in exactly the right spot. Lifting the tile floor was easier than I thought it would be." Kareem was anxious.

"I know they understand what is at stake here. They could ruin everything." Jamal, the second thief, paced nervously.

"They did the work that was required of them when they were on their shift today so that we could finish the job. They knew they were to meet us. Maybe the cowards ran away. Don't they realize how dangerous this is? The need for precise timing is crucial."

"I haven't seen them since they completed their shift and Adem reported their work was complete. That is when he told me to look for the shaft protruding from the ceiling because it marked the spot where we should lift the floor to gain access to the repository." Kareem fiddled with the small rod in his hands, not forgetting to leave it behind as evidence.

Waiting for their seemingly incompetent co-conspirators, the thieves were suddenly confronted by Qais, second-in-command of the Beyliks. His appearance was haggard, his deeply wrinkled and tanned visage making him appear at least a decade older than his captain. His hooded eyes glared at them. Qais was a vengeful man consumed by festering resentments.

"Where is Mehmed? He was supposed to meet us, not you," concern evident in Jamal's question.

"Shhh!" He commanded in a low hiss, his sneer broadening across his leathered face. "Quiet! It does not matter. Mehmed could not be here so I am here. Do you think I would know to be here if he had not sent me? Shut up! There is still danger! Here," Qais growled, "give me the relics!"

The janissaries handed the treasures to Qais. He moved slowly down the passage, feeling and meticulously examining the wall. He stopped, his fingers outlining an indentation in the stones. He pushed his hand firmly against the area and it opened, revealing a secret chamber. He carefully placed the cache of religious relics inside.

As they watched, there was uneasiness, a sense of anxiety that came not just from the extreme danger associated with the theft of such precious relics, but an irrepressible feeling they were being watched. As Qais loaded the relics into the chamber, Kareem and Jamal exchanged worried glances as they heard a slight shuffling not attributable to Qais' movements.

They had good reason for concern. The demonic Jinn was in fact watching them, just as it had watched their missing co-conspirators. Its ghostly presence was camouflaged and undetected against the stones, as it waited patiently and silently.

"Where are Baris and Adem?" Qais demanded.

"We don't know, we were just wondering ourselves," Jamal answered, his head slightly lowered to avoid Qais' glower.

"They are unreliable idiots. It is late—the sun will soon cast its full morning light—and we can't wait for them." Qais paused, his lips muttering a barely audible prayer. "I have worked hard to make arrangements. I should never have selected *them* for this job," Qais grunted disgustedly. "I would have expected Mehmed to tell me if they were unreliable. This cannot be tolerated!"

"Why are we hiding the relics so close to the *Has Oda*?" Kareem asked.

"They are fools—all of them," Qais sneered. "The last place any of them would look is under their noses. They would never think to search this close to the repository. Besides, there are only a few of us who even know of the secret passageways, much less this hidden chamber. Quit worrying and behaving like blithering morons!"

"But if we deliver the relics now, we can get the rest of our payment," Jamal insisted urgently. "The longer we wait, the more chance we will be caught. I don't like this."

"Stop with your questions, I said!" Qais snarled. "We will do as we are told. The plans are well laid. You will be paid! We should not leave together. Besides, I have other, more important plans to finalize. You stay here until I am gone and then get out and keep your mouths shut!" Qais commanded them as he moved toward the secret exit.

The chastened thieves obeyed and as they watched Qais' flickering light disappear, the intensity of their anxiety grew knowing they were required to obey Qais and wait a bit longer.

The seriousness of their crime began to loom large in their minds and a chill deep within overwhelmed them, urging them to get out of this place of a thousand eyes. The heightened sensitivity that had alerted them to the shuffle heard previously continued to cause great apprehension. Their instincts were right. Suddenly, as if having been touched with the fiery finger of the devil, each experienced a searing pain in their necks in quick succession. Seized with terror and confusion, the thieves watched as the wall before them inexplicably came alive. The Jinn slowly turned revealing its horrifying visage. They screamed as its cloak and stench was upon them. The demon would be merciless as it wreaked its mayhem. Kareem and Jamal would suffer no less than their co-conspirators as they succumbed to the howling and hissing creature. The Jinn had been patient as it watched and waited to work its sinister and diabolical evil in the tenebrous depths of the cisterns.

Cavalcade

Kemal Bey, Captain of the Beyliks, the elite personal guards to the sultan, passed the heavily fortified and imposing Theodosian walls and the lush vineyards and abundant apple orchards surrounding the city of Istanbul as he led his contingent of janissaries from the Topkapi Palace toward the sea walls along the Bosphorus Strait. The strait, a long and heavily trafficked waterway, connected the Sea of Marmara to the south and the Black Sea to the north. The port of Istanbul had been a thriving place of commerce for centuries—a place where the East and the West met, where Europe and Asia merged. Before falling to the fierce and determined Ottoman Turks, the city—referred to as *"Konstantiniyye"* by the Ottomans—had been known as Constantinople, after Emperor Constantine, the first Christian ruler of the Holy Roman Empire. Yet even through all the political and social turbulence it had remained a place where peoples from the known world came to share, trading in goods and knowledge. As the decades passed, it became even a place of tolerance for the cultural and religious differences of its multiethnic populace. There was as much a sense of intrigue and mystery that surrounded the city, as there was a sense of enlightenment. The streets teemed with pulsating masses, pausing only momentarily, to make way as the powerful and formidable janissaries, mounted on their majestic horses, headed to the water's edge on a mission for their sultan, Suleyman the Magnificent.

Fishmongers, shopkeepers, craftsmen, merchants, artisans, and their customers were all equally at ease in the great crowds that assembled daily in the streets and near the sea walls in the majestic city—the seat of the Ottoman Empire. Armenians, Jews, and Greeks migrated from their quarters of the city and mingled to craft and exchange their goods. Children with their tiny, nimble fingers sat in open doorways hunched over looms, weaving and dexterously knotting intricately designed kilims and Ushak, Keysari, and Konya Ladik carpets.

On this day, there was an obvious joy in the surging swells. Ramadan having ended and Eid celebrated, there was a vibrant frenzy of excitement and new energy that was palpable and pervasive. Their bellies once again full and having atoned for their sins, there was certainty among the faithful that Allah would find each deserving of reward for enduring such long and arduous sacrifice. Even the Jews, Christians, and other infidels celebrated and shared in the Muslims' uplifted spirits.

Kemal loved the mesmerizing allure of the city and knew it well. He spent any free time walking its streets and back alleys, sharing stories and tea while mingling with the shopkeepers and studying the city's antiquity and architecture. A journey within itself, Istanbul always revealed new discoveries with each visit. To cross from one side of the street to another was to walk through the centuries. The thundering clap of their cavalcade and Kemal's commanding presence sent people scurrying out of the way as he rode expertly on his coal-black Arabian. A beautiful, powerful horse seventeen hands, it had been a gift from Suleyman, upon Kemal's promotion to commander of the Beyliks.

Kemal was a renowned warrior who had proven his mettle fighting alongside Malcocqlu Bali Bey during the Ottoman siege of Belgrade in the Prophet's year 927. Although he had only been a youth during the siege, Kemal's prowess as an expert swordsman and archer, as well as his high intellect distinguished him. The formidable paladin had earned his rank despite his youth. He had risen quickly and deservedly to this appointed highest honor at the age of 26.

Kemal's uniform dolman was scarlet and his shirt, made from the cloth of Salonica, was dyed turquoise—the color of the Turks. He wore black trousers and a gold sash. His soldiers wore gold coats with a turquoise sash. Along with a few personal possessions and scimitar, his most prized, was tucked into his sash—a dagger encased in a gold sheath and encrusted with turquoise and lapis nuggets. His turban was of fine linen and wrapped into a spherical shape, distinguishing him further from the other janissaries whose turbans were globular.

Venetian Splendida

The late morning sun determinedly broke through an opacus sky. Kemal watched a scavenging of seagulls circle the vessels that had docked, screeching and landing on decks, searching for and stealing any tasty morsel. He caught his first glimpse of the *Venetian Splendida* just as the ramp had been put to solid ground. It was impressive—a caravel about 75 feet in length, with three pole masts, lateen-rigged with triangular sails. Designed to be at sea for up to a year, it could carry a cargo up to 60 tons and had a double tower at the stern. Kemal knew this was the personal vessel of the famed Vincenzo Lupo—Il Lupo, the Wolf—and was impressed that such a thing of beauty could navigate its arduous, long journey. The caravel was capable of sailing at 6 knots per hour. With a distance between Venice and Istanbul of over 1500 nautical miles, the journey would have taken approximately twelve days under optimal conditions. At its bow, a deeply carved, majestic, heraldic plaque stood in place of a figurehead. It was framed by crossed rapiers at the top and bottom with a large wolf—*Lupo*—at its center, crowned with a coronet of pearls, the French designation for a Count. The family motto bordered the edges. *"Per Vires Arte, Doctrina ac Spiritu"* which Kemal translated to read, "Strength through Skill, Scholarship, and Spirit" and believed it to be an apt representation of Il Lupo's renowned and respected pedigree.

"Hurry, Francesca! Our escort awaits!" Il Lupo urged his daughter, observing the arrival of Kemal and his entourage from the porthole window.

"*Padre*! I am hurrying! I am having increasing difficulty disguising myself as a boy!" Francesca replied with irritation as she struggled with the linen bindings designed to conceal the burgeoning size of her breasts.

"Men will never understand the difficulties a woman must endure to compete in a man's world!" she hissed under her breath. She threw on her shirt and ran her fingers through her dark, loose curls—recently and deliberately cropped into boyish fashion to aid in her deception.

She gazed briefly into her mirror; her reflection was that of her beautiful, olive-skinned Borgia mother. Her cerulean blue eyes were vibrant and intense, so different than those of her fair-skinned father. She was no longer the ingénue of even a few months ago. She reflected for a moment, wondering how long she would be able to secrete her feminine identity.

"Remember, try not to act like a lady! Although that should be no great challenge!" Il Lupo commented wryly with a smile. "And for this advice I beg your blessed mother to forgive me!" Il Lupo turned his eyes heavenward, his hands clasped in mock prayer.

"And you must remember *mia Padre*, not to be over protective. *That* will be *your* challenge!" Francesca replied with equal sarcasm.

Two months previously, Vincenzo Lupo had received a message from the great Sultan Suleyman requesting his services in Istanbul. Suleyman was aware that Il Lupo's *Academia Artum Militarum Venetiae*—Martial Arts Academy of Venice—was held in high repute throughout continental Europe, its fame extending even to Britain and the Orient. Il Lupo possessed a fabled prowess with the sword and other weapons, as well as in the martial arts. His skills had been acquired and honed during his extensive travels and learned from warriors from around the world who visited his academy, seeking tutelage from the great master. The Venetian Doge, Andrea Gritti, entrusted Il Lupo's academy with the training of his elite palace guards for the *"Most Serene Republic of Venice."* However, Suleyman's invitation to Il Lupo was based on other reasons for his fame—more pertinent to Suleyman's needs and summons. Il Lupo was equally renowned for his erudition, scholarship and, in particular, his astute skills in detection and the unraveling of mysteries.

Suleyman's message indicated he was troubled by rumors circulating within the palace of a deep restiveness within the janissary corps and a recent, possible attempted poisoning of a favorite concubine. He did not believe the intrigues to be trivial and groundless and solicited Il Lupo's assistance, offering to pay him handsomely. Vincenzo Lupo accepted the sultan's request and immediately immersed himself and his daughter in the requisite study of the Ottomans before setting sail to Istanbul. It had been agreed that he would be arriving ostensibly as an official Venetian envoy to avoid speculation as to the true purposes for his presence at the Imperial court.

Vincenzo Lupo's name had not fallen on the ears of Suleyman by chance. Il Lupo had gained particular repute after his recent exploits resolving plots involving the French and Prussian courts. During a war between France and Spain in 1526, Francis I had been taken prisoner by the Spaniards in Parvia, near Milan. He was later released based on an agreement entered into under duress to relinquish claim over several duchies, including Burgundy and Artois. Once freed, Francis reneged on the agreement. War ensued and there were rumored plots and attempted assassinations against him. At the request of Francis, Il Lupo was called to thwart a plot, purportedly conceived by the famed Andrea Doria. The rumors had in fact proven true. Il Lupo successfully uncovered and quashed two attempts on Francis' life. The first attempt involved tainting Francis' favorite, succulent grapes from the Champagne area of France with poison-grapes customarily served at his table. The second attempt involved an insurrection by a small faction of his military to depose him. Both schemes were, fortunately for Francis, timely discovered just before their successful execution. A deeply grateful Francis I survived. Without Il Lupo's shrewd assistance, the outcomes would likely have been very different. Francis I rewarded him with a chateau and land just outside Paris and bestowed upon him the honorific title of Comte. While the title of Count had been bestowed on Il Lupo by King Francis, the Venetians took great pride in the acclaimed celebrity of their native son and Vincenzo Lupo became known as Conte Vincenzo Lupo de Venezia.

Again, in 1528, Albert, the Duke of Prussia from the House of the Hohenzollern and the 37th Grand Master of the Teutonic Knights, sought Il Lupo's aid. Albert was a wise political administrator, politician, and patron of Erasmus; his support for the arts and learning was widely acknowledged. A fervid supporter of Martin Luther, Albert established the first Protestant duchy in Europe. He had joined the League of Torgau and was openly and ardently opposed to the Catholic Church and the Holy Roman Empire. Albert's support for the Protestants and his rebellion against his adversaries led to the Estates vote to cast him aside as Duke and to replace him with Walter von Cronberg as Grand Master. The decree was unenforced and Albert's ouster unsuccessful in large part due to the need to quell widespread unrest throughout the duchies. An intransigent Albert ignored demands to relinquish his authority and he too became a target for assassination. One plot was suspected to have been masterminded by von Cronberg. Il Lupo concluded the plot by von Cronberg to be unfounded, but foiled a second. His fame for resolving intrigues surrounding troubled royal courts of the time grew.

A grateful Albert richly rewarded Il Lupo not solely with gold and gems, but also four stud stallions and eight mares from experimental breeds imported from Lipica on the Karst Plateau. Experimental breeding had become an obsession of the royals of Europe who sought to enhance and reproduce traits, such as stamina and musculature, essential for horses to be used in war. Cross breeding began using Andalusian, Barb, Arabian, Neopolitan, and other horses in an attempt to create a superior warhorse. Il Lupo could not have known that the breeding stock he was given were predecessors of the famed Lippizaners, valued above all others for their stamina, strength, and astounding ability to be trained as warhorses. Not to be outdone by the king of France, Albert bestowed one more priceless gift, a first printing of the Gutenberg Bible. Albert was covetous of his collection, having five of the original two hundred in his own library, but decided Il Lupo's service was worthy and deserving of the extraordinary reward. Il Lupo added the volume to his extensive library of books and manuscripts, which now included three of the Bibles.

Vincenzo Lupo was held in the greatest esteem and had deservedly earned the patronage of the powerful. He was enigmatic, but not deliberately so; it was simply his genetic construct. For all his fame he remained a modest man, possessing a great deal of humility. Cultured and worldly, he was an accomplished, sophisticated patrician, esteemed equally for his wisdom as for his sword. His mastery of the sword was, however, unrivaled. His integrity and reputation were unquestioned and he possessed a certain savoir-faire without any air of pretension. He was vigorous and physically muscular, strong, and formidable yet enormously graceful, refined, polished, and even elegant. The Count possessed a wry sense of humor, which was often self-deprecating. Fair-skinned with riveting hazel eyes and thick, slightly-wavy, dark hair, he could just as easily have been mistaken for an English aristocrat as a Venetian nobleman. A Count "by the letters," neither he, nor the elected Venetian *Doge,* had been born to nobility. He had earned his status and wealth through his own acumen, skills, and exploits. He was accustomed to moving adroitly among the powerful, practiced, scholarly, and famous personages of the era.

Vincenzo was a widower, his sadness masked from the world as, even after seventeen years, he still mourned the loss of his beloved wife who died shortly after giving birth to Francesca. Women frequently attempted to enthrall him, often with brazen and unapologetic flirtation, but he found only those of keen intellect and humor most appealing. He was sensual and deeply passionate but never perfidious in his affairs, rather highly selective and exceedingly discreet when it came to the fulfillment of sensual desires. He remembered...each name...each face of the women he had known. While desirous of loving permanence and companionship, he was cautious, having witnessed enough the too often failed promises of relationships.

Although highly sought after, he accepted social invitations infrequently, avoiding large gatherings except where diplomacy or business required. His acceptance of a dinner invitation was a coup for any host, but offers were usually politely declined, having little tolerance for what he considered the predictable shallowness, gossip mongering and vagaries of the Venetian milieu. He chose his friends based on qualities of sharp intellect, wit, demeanor, general righteousness of character, and accomplishment, never solely based on their political or noble pedigree. He sought to surround himself with those of diverse backgrounds, ethnicities, expertise, and religious beliefs, particularly those with intellectually challenging, stimulating, and varied opinions. He was of the firm belief that soundness of knowledge and insight derives most powerfully from such diversity. It was in those social settings he found most pleasure, preferring his small circle of well-trusted friends with whom he enjoyed robust intellectual debates, comingled with the savoring of fine wines he uncorked for enjoyment. An Arneis Bianco from the Piedmont and the Chianti produced by the Ricasoli barons of the Florentine area were his favorites, although he kept dozens of bottles, if not hundreds, in his wine cellar, gathered eclectically from near and far in his travels. He was learned and fluent in six languages and while not a dedicated scholar, well versed in the intellectual disciplines of the arts, sciences, and philosophies of his times.

Grace of a Gazelle

Kemal watched as Il Lupo and Fran appeared on the deck of the *Venetian Splendida* and was impressed with the mutual, egalitarian ease and respect shared with the crew as they laughed, spoke warmly with one another, and slapped shoulders upon conclusion of their successful voyage. Catching Il Lupo's attention, Kemal saluted, letting him know they had arrived.

Just as he intended to dismount, a skillfully thrown knife flashed before Kemal's eyes, narrowly missing him. An astonished Kemal recoiled, realizing the dagger had found its mark, pinning the hand of a thief who had been plundering a trunk unloaded to the dock. Shrieking in pain, the thief's eyes bulged in their sockets, as he attempted to free his impaled hand, cut nearly in half from the force of the throw.

Amazed by the agility and accuracy of the strike, Kemal stared at Fran as she yelled, "Stop them, they have our jewels!"

Seizing upon a momentary lapse in security during the unloading of Il Lupo's belongings from the *Venetian Splendida*, five more quay-dwelling thieves were also ransacking the contents of several trunks, snatching, among other things, a hefty pouch containing some of Francesca's most personal and prized possessions—her mother's jewelry.

Fran immediately drew both her sword and another knife as a stunned Kemal and seemingly unperturbed Il Lupo watched. With the ferocity of a Samurai and grace of a gazelle, Fran catapulted from the ramp onto the dock. Kemal was held in awe at her spectacular skill and power, while Il Lupo appeared surprisingly unconcerned as she, dashing and expert in her swordsmanship, wreaked mayhem on the thieves. With uncanny precision, Fran expertly threw the knife, a *jambiya*, hitting another thief directly in the thigh, disabling him and causing him to fall, overturning a cart of unloaded fruit from an adjacent ship. With daunting expertise, she quickly slashed and disabled a third with her sword. Simultaneously and fluidly with her other hand, she removed what appeared to be a simple braided, leather necklace, adeptly loading it with a solid brass ball. With remarkable dexterity, she used the woven ornament as a sling, hurling the brass missile with impeccable accuracy, hitting a fourth escaping thief directly on his forehead, rendering him unconscious. Though she had single-handedly and quickly dispatched four of the thieves, the remaining two successfully broke away to make their escape.

Kemal, no longer temporarily dazed, sprang into action, shouting to Fran while tipping his dagger to his turban. "Wait here, *kucuk uzman*! Let me have them!"

"Finally, a little help, now that most of the job is done," she yelled at Kemal sarcastically.

Kemal did not acknowledge the implicit insults Fran had hurled his way. Letting the braided leather reins fall loosely to the side, Kemal reached for his bow. Kicking his steed, they galloped after the thieves, while he easily and nimbly drew two arrows from an intricate and elaborately hand-etched leather quiver. His arrows flew in rapid succession and, as if pulled by magnets, expertly found their marks in the backs of the two escaping thieves. Kemal's proficiency made the exercise look as easy as lancing a stationary quintain. All thieves having been dispatched or disabled, he pulled out his scimitar, using it to lift the velvet pouch of jewels from the cobblestones. The crowded dock had become nearly silent, onlookers having watched in spellbound astonishment the dazzling exhibition of skills displayed by Fran and Kemal.

Francesca, admittedly impressed by Kemal's horsemanship and mastery of the bow, was equally irked at her father. Hissing under her breath, she looked at her father, eyes questioning and wide with astonishment. "No help for a lady in distress?"

"You said not to be an overprotective father. And, you forget, you're no lady!" he jested, with an underlying tone of caution that she not forget her disguise. "You also weren't in distress," nodding in direction of Kemal returning to them after having chased down the terrified remaining thieves. "Those brigands—*they* were in distress!"

"Are these yours?" Kemal smiled looking directly at Fran while he playfully dangled the retrieved embroidered purple velvet pouch in front of her. He was immediately struck by the beauty and intensity of her blue eyes. She flashed them at him, grabbing the pouch from the end of his saber, her mouth in a tight grimace. Fran pulled the blue silk cords and untied them, her fingers searching within the velvet folds for the possessions from the material world that she most cared for—the jewelry that had belonged to her mother.

"Yes, everything is here" she sighed with relief. "Thank you." She looked at Kemal, deciding that a display of gratitude was appropriate while she inspected her treasures, the intimate objects worn by her mother.

"They belonged to my wife," Il Lupo interjected, stepping in front of Fran, saving her from an explanation. "I am in your debt for their safe return."

"It is the least I could do. My sincerest apologies for not recognizing the danger sooner. Are you injured?" Kemal asked, trying to downplay his admiration for Fran's remarkable prowess.

"No and you've recovered everything. I am Vincenzo Lupo and this is Fran Lupo. Thank you for your assistance. Rarely have I seen such superb horsemanship and skill with the bow." Il Lupo complimented sincerely, stepping forward and crossing his right arm over his chest as a salute of gratitude.

"And I have never seen such daring and expertise with knives, the sword, and sling. My compliments, Fran! From now on to me, well, I will call Fran *kucuk uzman*, 'young expert.' I am quite impressed. I thank you for your generous words. I owe much to *Siyah*, my horse. He has been superbly trained. We work well together, as one. He senses the subtleties of my movements and responds perfectly. He is a beauty, is he not?" Kemal gently slapped the horse on its glistening black croup. "There is not another like him!"

"He is extraordinary indeed!" Il Lupo complimented. "Perhaps one day you will see the fine breeding stock I have in my own stables. They are smart, strong, and fast, but just as spoiled children, perhaps a little undisciplined. They could benefit from the expertise and training of someone like you."

Somewhat unsettled by the events that had just transpired, Il Lupo continued. "What has happened here was unfortunate. You must realize based on Fran's obvious expertise, had Fran's intention been to kill the thieves it would have been accomplished. But our lives were not in danger. Fran has bested far more formidable adversaries than these hapless thieves. Fran's skills cannot be understated. Fran was merciful. You, however, did not have an option since your targets were fleeing with no other way to stop them before they disappeared in the dense crowds."

"I trust you are correct, Il Lupo. My eyes do not deceive me. Fran has astounding skills, unmatched in my experience! I do not, however, apologize for killing those thieves. It is against all laws and traditions of Islam to steal and, as you say, I could not risk their escaping with your belongings. As your escort and guardian, I am charged by the emperor to ensure your welfare." Kemal explained his actions without guilt or remorse. His reaction was instinctive and his justification unapologetic.

His serious tone quickly changed and he flashed a genuinely warm smile. "And now, allow *me* to introduce *myself*. I am Kemal, captain of the Beyliks. Sultan Suleyman has sent us to escort you to your residence. It is good to meet you, Count and Fran," tipping his dagger once again to his turban. "Praise be to Allah—*AllahAl Mu'min*—you are unharmed."

"Yes, thank you, Kemal. I see you are referring to Allah by one of The Ninety-Nine Names. You have praised Allah, The Giver of Security, I believe?"

"Ah! Yes," Kemal answered. "You have more than a passing understanding of Islam. I am quite impressed that you understood this is the Allah I have praised. Yes, I am thankful for your security and must in turn thank He who provides it."

Feeling a flush of warmth covering her, Fran conceded that there was no denying Kemal was not only dashing in his skills, but also immensely handsome. She breathed in deeply and then sighed, slightly enamored of Kemal, while even more impressed with his horsemanship. She marveled at the way he and his horse were as one single, breathing machine, insinuating each to the other. His stallion responded to his movements, however slight, slowing, turning and surging as he shot his arrows, as though the steed understood the surge was required to propel the arrow faster and straighter. Even to her remarkably well-trained eye, Kemal's horsemanship was rare and expert.

Kemal ushered Il Lupo and Fran to their horses, their saddles made from tooled leather resting on saddle cloths embroidered with arabesque flourishes in vivid shades of turquoise, copper, and gold. Both mounted their Arabians as the janissaries loaded their trunks and boxes onto sturdier breeds. At Kemal's direction, two carts were commandeered and shopkeepers ordered to take the bodies of the slain thieves to the mosque for burial while the wounded survivors of the melee were loaded onto the second cart to be taken to the palace where justice would be rapidly dispensed.

"Again, my apologies for your rude introduction to our beautiful city," Kemal offered sincerely. He was genuinely displeased by the unfortunate welcome they had received. "We were unexpectedly delayed by the need to discipline restless janissaries and our late arrival allowed time for the local riffraff to spoil your first impressions of us."

"Oh," Il Lupo replied with feigned surprise. "That is unfortunate. Restless janissaries?" He was unsure he should reveal to Kemal just how much he had been told by Suleyman. It was clear that Suleyman trusted this young warrior enough to appoint him as his closest guard, but Il Lupo was protective of the secrets that had been shared with him. He would watch Kemal carefully and decide when and if he could be completely trusted. Il Lupo suspected that Kemal was equally wary and protective of the sultan.

"Janissaries are trained and paid to fight. We have had a tedious peace and with no wars on the horizon, no spoils of war for the janissaries." Kemal's frankness impressed Il Lupo.

"Peace in our time is rather fleeting. I doubt it will last and spoil their fun for long," Il Lupo quipped.

"You know, Count, we must be careful what we wish for," Kemal responded wryly, waving his troops forward. Although Il Lupo had not used his title in introducing himself, Kemal thought the deliberate omission a sign of admirable humility and decided the nobleman should be addressed, accordingly.

Konstantiniyye

There was no direct route from the sea walls to the villa of the Venetian Ambassador where Vincenzo Lupo and Fran would reside. The villa was cloistered among massive stands of Persian Silk trees and Mediterranean Cyprus lining the waters of the Bosphorus but shops, markets, and architectural wonders lay between them. Kemal led them through the crowded Jewish quarter—the *Balat*—and *Ayvan Saray*, the District of Faith—and passed by the *Hagia Sophia* with its splendid dome and four glittering minarets. To their west, they watched as workers toiled on the massive doors of a new, impressive building under construction and caught a glimpse of the Hippodrome. Weary men hobbled by, carrying the burdensome weight of handmade carpets on stooped backs, inducing permanent pain and disfigurement.

The persistent sun emerged from the clouds causing the waters of the Bosphorus to glisten a brilliant smaragdine, as if in competition with the lustrous emeralds filling the Topkapi treasury. Kemal was imbued with a sense of pride, an ownership, of the beautiful vistas he shared with his guests as they were guided through the crowds parting before the procession. He felt he was sharing intimate secrets with his guests. Closely watching their reactions, he was pleased as they visibly admired the scenic splendor, inhaling the excitement and energy of the masses as they passed.

Rising temperatures intensified smells and aromas emanating from street vendors' goods as the procession entered the meat markets, flies clinging to the freshly butchered meats that were hung on massive hooks. The stench was lessened only by the tantalizing and exotic scents of clove, cassia, cinnamon, ginger, and coriander wafting from the spice market nearby. Meandering through tiny, cobbled streets filled with fruit and vegetable stands, they passed merchants shouting *"taze simit,"* pleading for takers of their fresh and aromatic salted pretzels. Emerging from the din and hum of the metropolis, they finally arrived at the iron gates of the magnificent and palatial home of the Venetian Ambassador.

"As you are aware, you will be the honored guests of your friend Giovanni Contratini. You will reside here for the duration of your visit to Istanbul. My guards will ensure that your belongings are safely delivered inside the villa," Kemal instructed, pulling his stallion alongside Il Lupo and waving to his guards to begin the unloading.

"Tomorrow morning I will escort you to the Topkapi Palace, but this evening you will be the honored guest at a reception in the residence. I hope you will not be too tired from your travels for the occasion," Kemal continued courteously.

"Fran and I are honored to be the guests of our friend for our stay. I hope that you too can attend the reception this evening as my guest," Il Lupo offered generously, deciding that he liked Kemal and wished to cultivate a potentially valuable ally. Il Lupo was a good judge of character. He was impressed with what he saw in this spirited, young man—this warrior and diplomat—who had the makings of perhaps much more.

A smile broadened across Kemal's tanned, handsome face. Genuinely honored by the unexpected invitation, he quickly responded.

"It would be my pleasure! Until this evening then!" Putting his forearm to his chest in a gesture of respect and with his broad smile still lighting his face, Kemal kicked his heels into the sides of his stallion. With a swoop of its long black, majestic tail, *Siyah* turned, and together the finely tuned and unified machine galloped toward the heavy cast iron gates, exiting the villa's grounds.

Palazzo

Fran and Il Lupo, relaxed, refreshed, and ready for a pleasurable evening, descended the circular staircase that led them from their assigned bedrooms to the common areas of the villa where the guests were gathering. Kemal greeted them at the bottom of the stairs and together they proceeded to the *Grande Allee* that led to the opulent main gallery of Giovanni Contratini's home and the waiting party. Even in the early evening, the villa was suffused with a beautiful light. Polished to a shimmering luster, the floors were laid with Rosa Duquesa, a richly colored marble with terracotta field and steel blue veining, acquired from the recently discovered marble pits in the New World. The home was illuminated by spectacular Murano and Venetian multi-tiered, glass and crystal chandeliers, adorned with hand-cut festoon garlands and bobeches designed to catch the dripping wax from the countless dozens of candles. Teardrop and crystal ball prisms played with the natural light of the fading day and mixing with with candlelight, created rainbows throughout the room.

The villa stood in ostentatious contrast to the more refined and restrained Venetian palazzos in the home city shared by Il Lupo and his host, where excessive displays of wealth were considered tasteless. It was by any measure extravagant, palatial in adornment and appointments if not in size. Giovanni Contratini had wasted no expense flaunting his wealth and success as a merchant. Every area entered presented its own unique and evocative vignette. Carefully crafted upholstery was covered in sumptuous velvets and jacquards, in deep, saturated jewel tones. Embroidered Chinese silk curtains draped from every window, each deliberately framed with the luxurious fabric and treated as though it was a dazzling piece of prized art. Tapestries and portraiture of the illustrious from Central Europe hung salon-style, one priceless piece atop the other. Inlaid marble floors not deliberately left bare to reveal the artistry of their inlays were covered with intricately detailed and tightly knotted silk and wool Turkish and Persian carpets. The furniture ranged from those crafted of elaborate veneers and insets of Dutch and Italian marquetry to heavier, hand-carved oak bookcases from Flanders and England designed to carry the weight of voluminous, intellectual collections and illuminated manuscripts. The library also contained a vast collection of timepieces, some small and portable, including several from the renowned Nuremberg clockmaker Peter Henlein. They were not just the fashion, but functioned to replace shadow clocks and hourglasses. Il Lupo also carried a timepiece from the famous clockmaker.

No niche or corner had been left neglected, each containing foliage or statuary and on narrow walls, art and Venetian glass mirrors had been hung. Walls that were not papered were painted in marmorino—superb, classic Venetian plaster—and ceilings adorned with frescoes rivaling those in any monastery or cathedral. The library frescoe depicted dozens of figures on land and vessels at sea, recounting Venetian-Genoese naval skirmishes from previous centuries. While not carefully edited and arranged for precise and balanced display of the objects, the rooms were warm and welcoming, inviting a guest to pause and admire the beauty and craftmanship of each individual piece. The air was refreshing and scented very subtly by the savory herbs used to prepare a reception feast of hor d'oeurves and sweets, including baklava. The mood was festive and Il Lupo and Fran were anxious to engage in the delights associated with a communion of convivial, intriguing people.

Kemal had changed to his formal dress uniform, one reserved only for the captain of the Beyliks. His dolman was made of scarlet velvet decorated with gold beads at the edges of the sleeves with complimentary beading on his turquoise shirt and gold sash. Both Il Lupo and Fran were dressed in the debonair fashion of the day with blackwork embroidery on the ruffled sleeves of their shirts, velvet pants, and doublets with billowing sleeves made of heavy and intricate jacquard—Fran's with silver detailing and Il Lupo's with gold. Their stockings matched their black velvet shoes and breeches and each wore gold chains—Il Lupo's gifts from dignitaries he had served, and Fran's less weighty, from their family coffers.

"Vincenzo! My friend! How good to see you again! And Fran, very nice to meet you!" An effusive Giovanni, attempting to ingratiate himself to his guests, grabbed the Count by the shoulders, kissing him on both cheeks and then unctuously doubling back to kiss him again.

He greeted them at the door in an emerald green caftan, contrast lined with a striped duponi silk in shades of green, royal blue and gold and in keeping with the fashion of the Ottomans. While the caftan might have been in keeping with fashion, its color was not in keeping with Ottoman sensibilities and tradition. Emerald green was considered sacred – the color of the Prophet Muhammad and reserved to be worn only by the sultan. Kemal was taken aback by the insensitivity for Islamic custom. The new ambassador to the Ottoman court, he felt, should have known better. Upon brief reflection, he decided, while it was tactless, it was not egregiously so since the garment was worn at a private gathering. He dismissed his reservations regarding Giovanni's breach of Islamic etiquette as simply poor or perhaps, uninformed judgment.

"And this is your guide and protector? The Captain of the Beyliks? Quite an honor, Vincenzo, for the sultan to place you under the protection of his most trusted warrior!" Giovanni smiled as Kemal gave a stiff but polite bow.

"Come, let me introduce you to my other guests. Lucia! You must remember Vincenzo, don't you?" Giovanni beckoned to his cousin.

"Of course I remember Vincenzo. What woman would not?" she said looking demurely at Vincenzo as she unfurled her hand-painted fan. "I, as are many, am a great admirer of the Count. News of his exploits reach us far and wide." She looked directly at him and smiled flirtatiously.

Lucia was exceedingly beautiful—even more so than Vincenzo had remembered. He detected a coy twinkle in her eye as she gazed at him. Her long, dark hair was pulled up and braided slightly off her face with a few tendrils falling loosely and deliberately out of place, adding to her provocative allure. She was wearing a heavily structured, embroidered pink silk bodice and skirt that was becoming to her complexion. Il Lupo wondered if the pink tint on her lips was natural or intentionally dyed and designed to generate a more sensuous and enticing mouth.

While she was undoubtedly quite stunning, Fran was taken aback by Lucia's overly ostentatious fallalery, finding it gauche. Her earrings were tiered with pink diamonds and around her neck was a necklace of white diamonds with a large, pink diamond in the center. Even her lips and cheeks were stained to match her dress. Venetian custom and in some cases law, forbade tasteless public displays of wealth—a custom Lucia had clearly discarded when she left Venice—perhaps the influence of the Spanish court she was known to frequent. Nevertheless, Fran grudgingly conceded that a man might find her captivating, detecting her father's interest despite his restrained, calm, and refined demeanor.

She watched her father as he walked away from Lucia and wondered, *"I am in no need of a mother, but perhaps my father is in need of a wife. I hope it is not her."*

Despite Fran's youth, she was disciplined and perceptive beyond her years. The importance of strong character and morality had been instilled since childhood. She had studied rigorously under her father's tutelage, and was proficient at an early age in the contemporary arts and sciences of the Renaissance, fluent in four languages and considered expert with knives, slings, swords, and other weapons from many parts of the world. She quickly excelled and ranked at the top of Il Lupo's students. Even more important than her physical adeptness and prowess, however, Fran also had mastered how to maneuver socially and adeptly interact publicly in a complex and political world—a man's world—a valuable but essential feat especially for a girl posing as a boy. She studied people and quickly developed an innate sense of their worthiness and integrity. She had rare intuitive gifts and was invariably prescient when dissecting and studying individual behaviors and motives. She was intensely protective of her father who seemed to be too easily accepting at times of the motives of people he encountered—women in particular. Unlike her father, Fran was not. Even so, she was usually courteous and diplomatic—unless provoked to behave otherwise—and was always simultaneously studying the nuances, innuendo, and subtleties of social interactions. This night, surrounded by all manners of society—noble to obsequious—Fran intently studied. She trusted her intuition. Tonight, she was not at ease; some things, she felt, were amiss.

Her thoughts were interrupted by Giovanni. "I would like to introduce our new envoy, the famous Count Vincenzo Lupo of Venice—Il Lupo, 'The Wolf,' and Venetian patrician to be sure! And, they say, the finest swordsman in Europe!" Giovanni announced to other gathered guests, who applauded the introduction.

Il Lupo bowed, and quipped, "Only one parry away from being the second-best—not to mention, dead, Giovanni! There is always someone better. Knowing this helps keep me alive. It is only divine generosity that has allowed me to be here to thank you for, and be the recipient of, your compliments and gracious hospitality!"

"May I introduce, Fran, who may soon make me second-best. And our guide and protector, Kemal, Captain of the Beyliks." Both Fran and Kemal bowed their heads and Fran noticed that Kemal's head was slightly tilted toward her. He winked at her and she blushed.

"I wish he wouldn't do that! Why is he doing that?" she thought, again feeling a slight flush in her cheeks.

Giovanni escorted the three toward the group. "Allow me to introduce you to the Marquis and Marquise Valois, the Ambassador from Francis I to the imperial court. And Hassan Pahlavi, the Persian envoy."

"Vincenzo! My friend, it is wonderful to see you again!" Antoine Valois greeted Il Lupo, extending his arms to greet him in a fraternal embrace. Antoine's blue eyes were a near match to his blue velvet jacket finely detailed with the French fleur de lis. "If not for you, I would not be here to enjoy your company once again! Everyone! This is the man who saved my life by the simple act of preventing me from eating a grape!" As Antoine spoke, Colette Valois stepped forward, accepting a kiss to her hand from Il Lupo.

"What a story that is! He must tell you—come Vincenzo—share the experience that binds us together for all time and for which I will always be indebted to you. Before he begins his recollections, I must tell you that before this encounter I had never met the Count and he was not yet even a Count! It was a most infelicitous moment and as you will hear, one never to be forgotten."

"Ah, yes, it is an interesting story," Il Lupo began as the group gathered to hear his tale. "I was invited to the court of Francis, for reasons you may now know—he was under threat. We uncovered one plot to depose him by none other than Andrea Doria. You all know of him. An opportunist and mercenary—first a Genoese allying himself with France, but ultimately betraying Francis by supporting Charles V. I presume everyone knows that when his deceits were discovered, he escaped before justice could be dispensed. There were other threats as well.

"On the occasion referred to by Antoine I was to attend a light afternoon banquet. The finest French cheeses, sweetmeats and pastries, foie gras, pate and the succulent, king of grapes—the *Cote de Blanc*—as well as the king's favorite wines from the Burgundian and Champagne areas, were to be served. These fetes were always a delight and attended by participants in meetings of the King's Council. As I arrived, just outside the door of the banquet room, a servant lay dying on the floor. I knelt and spoke to him. Most fortunately for us, he was still lucid enough to provide information. Just before delivering a platter of grapes, I learned he had sampled the forbidden Cote de Blanc grapes—which were reserved only for Francis and his invited guests. Francis' guests on that day were those in his closest and most trusted, inner circle of advisors. Entering the room just as Antoine was poised to partake I grabbed his wrist, preventing him from eating the tainted fruit. He was of course astonished—incredulous—irate in fact, at my audacious act. I am forever grateful that he did not kill me on the spot. I explained my actions to an initially, quite perturbed marquis and the assembled guests. This was our first and most fortuitous encounter. We are now bound to one another in great friendship."

"Vincenzo discovered that the grapes had actually been tainted with wolfsbane just before entering the palace kitchen," Antoine continued. "Wolfsbane and nightshade are favorite poisons used to quickly dispatch those targeted. He found that the purveyor of the grapes had sent his servant with the delivery in haste just before the fruit was to be served and so it would be placed on the platter without tasting. His servant surreptitiously sampled the fruit. The poisoning was traced to the purveyor, who had been paid by forces aligned with Charles V. So you see, the famous Il Lupo saved not just the great King Francis and our country, but me as well and all those assembled on that day who would also likely have consumed the grapes. We are all indebted to him. The king, of course, has rewarded him not just with his honorific title, but lands and a chateau near Paris." The audience was dazzled by the retelling of the incident and the exploits of the storied legend, Il Lupo.

"Individually and on behalf of France and Francis, we are all grateful and we toast your name!" Antoine encouraged as the assembled raised their glasses, each taking a sip of Antoine's fine champagne.

"Thank you, Antoine. It was providence that brought me to that moment and nothing more. I am now the grateful recipient of your valued friendship. We are most fortunate, for while war and treachery beget great pain, brutality and loss, they also create no greater brotherhood, my friend," Il Lupo answered the toast with humility. "As for the chateau and lands, however, you are always welcome and I will assure you that the wine flows untainted and as freely as the wild boar run. Join me there soon for the hunt, my friend."

"But Vincenzo tell us, for we are all curious what intrigue brings you here—perhaps more plots against kings and sultans? You are equally renowned as the solver of great mysteries and intrigues as for your mastery of the sword? What brings you to Istanbul and Topkapi Palace that requires your skills?" Lucia looked at him quizzically, although she felt certain that Il Lupo was likely there for those very reasons.

"Imagine—intrigue here in Istanbul? Intrigue so great as to require the service of the great Il Lupo? Please share with us, Vincenzo!" Giovanni urged. "We here are your friends and can keep any secret!"

"I am Hassan Pahlavi," the Persian introduced himself, moving closer and situating himself between Giovanni and Il Lupo. "And yes, it is true. We have all been speculating," Hassan laughed. "Perhaps he has just come here for a respite from the beautiful city of Venice? The consensus is, we think not!" he smiled, realizing it would be unlikely Il Lupo would reveal his true reasons.

"But on the improbability that you are looking for an escape from the exquisite city of Venice, I might suggest our beautiful city of Qum with its turquoise skies and copper roofs. I guarantee you will never receive such a rude reception there as you have here! We Shiites know how to welcome a legend! We have heard of the unfortunate events at the docks this morning and I wish to inform you that not all Muslim countries allow their visitors to suffer such indignities," he smirked, looking directly at Kemal, a Sunni Muslim."I hope the remainder of your trip is less eventful."

Kemal bristled slightly over Hassan's intentionally impudent remark but remained stoically silent, impressing Il Lupo with his restraint. A lesser man might have responded with contempt or hostility.

Giovanni injected, attempting to change the subject. "My sources tell me, Kemal, that the janissaries have grown more restive, which may not bode well for Suleyman."

"Yes," Kemal retorted defensively. "As always, we have our share of disciplinary issues." His concern heightened—*how was it that Giovanni knew of unrest among the janissaries?*Kemal believed that such knowledge was confined to the janissary corps itself or, at most, within the walls of the palace. What he found most worrisome was that the Venetian ambassador treated it as public knowledge.

"Allow me to introduce myself," a ruddy cheeked, robust looking gentleman moved forward, inserting himself into the group.

"I am Ambassador Gregor Zabatny. I am proud to represent my mother country Russia and the Crown Prince Vasili III Ivanovich and his beautiful wife, Elena who, by the grace of God, has given our prince two sons, Ivan and Yuri." Gregor beamed with patriotic pride.

"This is my lovely bride, Nadia. Most formally, she is Contesă Nadia din casa lui Drăculesti. However, we shall dispense with formalities and any references to her grandfather, Vlad III – Drăculea. You can believe she inherited no blood lust – only a lust for life! Is she not the most sumptuous morsel you could imagine to possess? She is my sweetest *kotyonok*." A pretty, rubenesque Nadia stepped forward and gave a slight curtsy, holding her fan to her face, enormously pleased that her husband had announced publicly that he found her so appealing. The pair seemed a good match—both rosy-cheeked, rotund and jovial—their smiles genuine and rather endearing.

Gregor summoned a servant carrying a silver platter of etched Murano crystal glasses. "And now, to ease the pain of your trip and your rude welcome, may I invite each of you to toast Il Lupo with our famous Russian vodka! Can you imagine our peasants were

clever enough to have discovered such a wonderful use for potatoes!"
It was clear Gregor had already consumed considerable quantities of
the fruits of the Russian peasants' labor. He was in a most convivial,
loquacious mood.

Il Lupo found Gregor affable and amusing, his hearty laugh
infectious. He was unlike so many of the pretentious cockalorums
who strutted about the stifling and often effete royal courts of Europe
where great attempts were made by the many to curry favor with
the few holding at least momentary power. He found Gregor's
unassuming, gracious demeanor refreshing.

All but Kemal and Hassan, whose religion forbade the consumption
of alcohol, took a glass and sipped the bitter liquid.

"Oh no!" shouted Gregor, "*You* drink it like *this!*" Gregor
demonstrated by throwing his head back and quaffing the biting,
clear liquid with great gusto and all at once."It is best this way. A
little burn for just a moment in order to enjoy the warmth that will
sustain you!" he insisted.

Everyone smiled at his instruction, and for the sake of diplomacy,
complied by downing the remains of their glass in one gulp as
Gregor toasted, "*Nostrovia! Nostrovia!* Russians—we love a party and
especially one with such distinguished company!"

"And to your resourceful Russian peasants and a new fondness for
potatoes!" Vincenzo offered, enjoying the warmth of his welcome
and the surprisingly quick and relaxing effect of the vodka.

"Tell me, Vincenzo, what *really* brings you to the imperial court
of Suleyman the Magnificent?" Lucia asked, resurrecting the earlier
line of questioning. "Giovanni is quite a capable representative and
has no intentions of soon departing," waving her arms at the grand
surroundings. "You are here as an envoy? If so, why? We have been
speculating—all of us here, before your arrival. You and Fran—what
are your plans?"

Giovanni continued nattering away, the vodka taking effect and
adding a slight slur to his words. "There is always idle talk regarding
the imperial courts. Anyone here can attest to that! But I can also
attest to the fact that not all talk is idle—that there are ever-present
threats and plots and perceived slights to be avenged by the aggrieved.
Suleyman is the supreme and omnipotent ballast of the Ottoman
Empire, but even he would be unlikely to survive a wide-spread

insurrection among the janissaries. There is no isonomy in the Ottoman court, and Suleyman reigns supreme. But he may have to quash insurgencies to maintain that power." He turned to Kemal, hoping for a response and valuable insight into the intrigues at court.

Despite the directness of Giovanni's disturbing speculations aimed at Kemal, Il Lupo was grateful he had once again interrupted the conversation, deflecting the conversation from the reasons for his presence in Istanbul.

Kemal attempted to put matters into better perspective. "Janissaries are often restless, often easily vexed by the smallest trifles. This is nothing new. A tale as old as the first warriors. Rather than honing their skills, they are prone to succumb to laziness and complacency and engage in idle but usually benign gossip. But talk of overthrow of a most noble and good emperor? I find this very difficult to believe. What leads you, Ambassador Contratini, to believe that the emperor may be in danger from insurrection?" Kemal asked uneasily, his brows furrowing. He was barely able to conceal a growing anger that internal rumors of the Imperial Court had become fodder for gossip at a dinner party hosted by this infidel. "You understand that what you are suggesting has consequences, do you not, Ambassador? The restless janissary will be disciplined, but the rebellious will be executed?"

"I do not wish to alarm you with idle gossip and speculations about intrigues at court, but you must be aware that this is common knowledge bruited about all over the the Continent," the quidnunc continued coyly, deliberately implying that he was privy to information about the janissaries that Kemal was not. Both Vincenzo and Fran knew there was more ground for concern than mere idle speculation.

"So long as our lucrative trade with the Ottomans is not affected, you janissaries can riot to your hearts' content. I'm certain the Doge and Il Lupo understand the importance of our trade with the Ottomans and the need to protect it," Giovanni grunted.

"Giovanni, you surely realize that those trained for wars, especially those with the fabled skills of the janissaries, understandably grow restless—to use your word," Il Lupo countered. "Even the vicissitudes of war are preferable to many—especially janissaries—over the interminable transience of peace. War games for planning purposes even during times of extended peace are common in many courts. War is a constant companion and one to which a warrior's individual identity is inextricably tied."

Il Lupo continued, deftly changing the subject to Giovanni's passion. "Yes, Giovanni you are most certainly correct when it comes to understanding the importance of trade and commerce!" the Count complimented, hoping to brighten Giovanni's mood. "We are fast entering a time when merchants may become more powerful than kings and money more potent than the sword. We are witnessing a time when the spiritual confronts the secular. We can only pray that nothing is ever more valuable than truth and wisdom, for if we make the wrong choice, I fear we will all be doomed," Il Lupo cautioned his host.

"Vincenzo, you are not just expert with the sword; your words show you are a wise man of learning and letters—an attribute for which you are equally known. Your words are true, and we must heed them. Trade and diplomatic relations are critical to civilization and stability, and yet so fragile," Antoine contributed.

"I believe it is important to have a fast ship ready to sail at a moment's notice," Gregor injected. "Hassan, how are relations between Persia and the Ottomans?"

"I am still alive, Praise be to Allah, and so relations are at least tolerable!" Hassan responded with a shrug.

"Please, anyone, tell me more about Suleyman. I know of him as the 'Lawgiver,' which speaks well," Vincenzo solicited.

Antoine offered his thoughts. "He is not only powerful, but wise. His private life is quite complex, as you may know or will certainly learn. He has five living children by two women. Mustafa is his son with Gulbehar, Suleyman's wife. Do not let her name, which means 'Spring Rose' fool you. She is difficult, to say the least, and comes equipped with thorns that she plucks and flings with deadly accuracy at the hearts of her enemies. It is said she considers Mustafa her 'whole joy.'"

Antoine continued. "But the state of affairs at court is complicated because Suleyman has had five children with his favored concubine, Roxelana: three living sons—Sehzade Mehmed, Sehzade Selim, and Sehzade Bayezid. Another son, Sehzade Abdullah died at the age of three from unknown causes, which has caused great speculation in the court. Suleyman also has a daughter with Roxelana, Mihrimah, and it is suspected that Roxelana is now with child, although this remains unconfirmed. Unlike monarchies to the West, any of the sons could inherit the throne upon Suleyman's death. There is no rule of primogeniture. The younger son could become emperor. Which son will eventually ascend to the throne, by which woman, is a question that looms large at the court. The reign of any sultan and his legitimacy is, however, dependent foremost on his acceptance by the elite janissaries."

"When Suleyman's father, Selim I, died, Suleyman raced to Istanbul first and gained the support of the janissaries," Gregor added.

"However, Suleyman's Grand Vizier, Ibrahim, runs the daily affairs of the empire. He wields great power," Hassan continued warily. "His influence with Suleyman is great. I personally find him dour and overweening, interested mainly in his own self-aggrandizement. In most cases, he is a man of few words, except when he chooses to speak in platitudes. It is most irritating."

"Ibrahim is not shy about taking the credit for Ottoman successes. He maintains the perpetual hauteur of the arrogant. He is not pleasant to deal with, I must warn you," Antoine continued, his advice taken seriously by Il Lupo, who trusted his friend. "But this is often the case when lesser men serve greater men. They long for accolades that they did not earn and would be incapable of earning."

"The Ottomans maintain their power and expand their empire by taking the best, most skilled, and brightest boys from lands they conquer to train in the elite janissary corps," Giovanni pronounced. Kemal shifted his weight from one foot to another at the unsettling statement, knowing too well its veracity.

Antoine explained, "One-fifth of the bounty taken by the Ottomans in lieu of gold is the most promising young boys and men. Enslaved and converted to Islam, they are trained as janissaries in the palace school to become administrators, scholars, and warriors. Ibrahim, the Grand Vizier, was a product of that training." So too, was Kemal. Il Lupo knew fully well of the barbaric Ottoman practice of enslaving the finest young boys, tearing them from their families during invasions, and training them for the janissary corps.

"Then, of course, there is the Harem, the 'restricted area.' Depending on the month, Suleyman has 250 to 300 concubines, including Gulbehar and Roxelana," Gregor chimed in. "When romance is no longer in the air, concubines are simply retired to the old palace, never to be seen again!" he chortled. "Put out to pasture. Pensioned off to a palace."

"Better to be retired or pensioned than beheaded as is done in some countries!" Il Lupo responded, reminding the guests of other, more permanent and painful means of disposal for those unfortunate enough to have been found undesirable or obstacles to power in other Imperial courts.

"That's because to men, a woman's head is a useless appendage! It's our other parts men appear to be more interested in," Lucia interjected sarcastically.

Turning to Il Lupo, Lucia coquettishly unfurled her elaborate fan to cool herself. She continued snidely, "Why don't you all seek appointments to the court of the Chinese emperor? They say he has 10,000 concubines. There's an enterprising emperor for you!"

"I have learned that the number of Harem concubines, wives, or consorts is more a symbol of wealth rather than sensual appetite," Il Lupo remarked, adding further insight and understanding of the custom—a custom shunned by the royal courts of the Continent.

"In my estimation," Gregor exclaimed, "we may have much to learn from Islam and perhaps the Chinese. Women keep their appendages and men get new women!" Nadia gave him a hard nudge, suggesting she did not find everything he said quite as amusing as he did.

Gregor added with emphasis and pride, "But now Suleyman has himself a Russian as his favored concubine, and it is unlikely he will tire of a Russian. Roxelana—the Russian—his consort and mother of sons is the one who carries the greatest influence. And we Russians are known for our relentless pursuit of the object of our desires and our unfailing stamina in this and in *all* other matters."

"Gregor! *Mysh!* Stop!" Nadia protested, blushing once again. "You will embarrass the guests with such risqué innuendo!" she chastised. The guests laughed, equally amused by Gregor's remarks and Nadia's attempts to curtail his enthusiasm for indelicate insinuation.

Her father taught her well. Francesca studied all evening, certain that her father was doing the same. She listened carefully, searching for insights in the conversations and actions of the guests as to their character and motives. There were many. She noticed that Giovanni and Hassan stood speaking quietly in a corner and that Gregor had playfully patted Nadia on her derriere, a plump posterior made more prominent by layers of petticoats. She saw Hassan's body language change and stiffen at Gregor's intimate gesture, his sensibilities offended. In contrast, she noted a faint smile pass over Kemal's face as he witnessed the playful Gregor. She too found the love tap sweet and endearing. Again, with relief, she noted that Lucia had left the room for several minutes, reentering with her cheeks a deeper pink-either from flush or blush. She was followed by her fragrance and a servant carrying a platter of glasses filled with white wine. Francesca watched as the vixen approached her father, thinking, *"Oh, not her again!"*

"Vincenzo, look what I have especially for you! Your favorite—the Arneis—and enough to share with the guests!" Lucia gushed, openly flirting.

"Thank you, Lucia! Most thoughtful. Please everyone, have a glass of my favored elixir—one I turn to in moments requiring the greatest contemplation. How did you know, Lucia?"

"I make it my business to know what delights a man who delights me!" Lucia pronounced boldly, unembarrassed by her undisguised and brazen pursuit of Il Lupo's affection.

"I find it goes especially well with melon wrapped in prosciutto. Bring a tray of the melon!" she ordered one of the servants.

Each infidel took a glass from the tray and began to sip the delicious, slightly dry white wine. Hassan's cup of tea remained tightly clenched in his dark hands.

Il Lupo, raising his glass toasted, "Gregor! I love your vodka but *'in vino veritas.'* To truth!" After drinking, Il Lupo continued, "They say that wine is excellent for the health. Perhaps, if we drink enough we can achieve immortality?!"

Il Lupo was pleased that the conversation had shifted away from the reasons for his presence in Istanbul. Maneuvering further, he motioned sweepingly to the villa and its beautiful furnishings. "Judging by your surroundings, Giovanni, trade with the Ottomans has been quite good to you. You have a better appreciation of the importance of trade than most, a merchant who recognizes quality and moves to possess it."

Giovanni nodded in self-satisfied agreement. "You are right Vincenzo. As a matter of fact, please, all of you, join me in the library to view my newest acquisitions. They are absolute treasures—two small volumes of illuminated manuscripts—one of prayers and one of the Gospels. The words are divine and the art exceptional." The coterie of guests turned and walked toward the library.

Anoesis

Fran remained behind, beckoning to Kemal to join her rather than follow the other guests into the library. "I would like to view the Bosphorus and escape the stifling warmth and conversation of the villa. Come and join me."

Kemal remained troubled by Giovanni's speculations of uncertain provenance and was slightly ill at ease leaving Il Lupo's presence. He paused, assessing the situation, and decided there was no threat to Il Lupo in the home of Giovanni. He joined Fran who had thrown open the terrace doors. He relished the irresistible sparkle of her blue eyes as she again beckoned him to join her.

A breeze emanating from the Bosphorus rustled the gold and green damask draperies, providing instant cooling and welcome relief from the now nearly suffocating interior of the villa. The candles lighting the chandeliers flickered while the crystals danced, tingling in the breeze. The garden was in full spring bloom and the air scented with a bouquet of jasmine, roses, and magnolias—the comingling of their fragrances intoxicating. One could believe it was nature's deliberate conspiracy to draw them into the tranquil, fantasy-like beauty of the garden, tempting them to seduction in the misty and soft moonlight. Both were held captive in a momentary state of anoesis.

The terrace presented a beautiful harmony of sensual textures. The same marble used in the interior had been extended outdoors, but in its natural and unpolished form; exposure to the elements and debris enhanced its depth of color. A colonnade of marble balustrades and stone railings formed a semi-circle, extending the terrace seemingly to the edge of the waters below. The terrace was surrounded by fully blossoming Persian silk trees, each nearly forty feet tall and blanketed with voluptuous pink and white flowers. Peacocks flaunted their exquisiteness, strutting through the surrounding grounds, unfurling their plumage. Fran believed she heard the cooing of doves settling into the evening and felt like an interloper, a voyeur, intruding and eavesdropping on their intimacy. The evening sky was translucent and bright with the underside of heavier clouds glowing in painted butterscotch—the result of reflections cast from the setting sun on the terracotta roofs of the city.

For Kemal too, the terrace and gardens were magical; his demanding and arduous life rarely provided opportunity for contemplation and enjoyment of the ethereal or sublime. Even burdened with the worrisome conversations of the evening, he was ready for a mental respite and eager to become better acquainted with the *kucuk uzman*.

Fran breathed in the refreshing, cooling air and turned to Kemal. "Even in my short time here, I find this city vibrant and stimulating. Does your city cast its spell on all who visit? Has Istanbul always been your home?"

"Yes, I agree. Istanbul is magical. Its enticing textures intoxicate all the senses. But, no, I am not from this city. I am from Palestine. My parents were Jews. I was taken by the Ottomans when I was young—eleven in fact—during their invasion of Palestine fifteen years ago. I am from Safed in the Galilee. I was brought here to be trained at the palace school and learn the skills of the janissary." Kemal was somber, his answer succinct, disquieted as he recalled his past life. He never shared his feelings with anyone, finding the only way to deal with the tribulations was to suppress them completely. He had done so quite successfully until now and somehow he felt a certain relief—a wisp of hope—that he might perhaps have found someone to share the burdensome weight of his past. He continued, returning to a subject he loved.

"But yes, Istanbul is magnificent and exhilarating. It has cast its spell on me. I love to wander through its streets. I could compare them to a well-known friend. I am glad you like it, even if your welcome was less than hospitable, which I greatly regret. I again offer my apologies."

"It was not your fault, Kemal, and of course I accept your apology. Yes, I can see why you would love the city. I hope that I will have the time to explore it more. Perhaps you can be my guide at some point!" she invited, hoping he would be tempted.

"Indeed, I would welcome that. There are so many places an ordinary visitor would miss, and it would be my great honor to escort you and your father around the city on a private tour, if time allows," Kemal responded enthusiastically. Fran's delight was diminished only by the thought she might have to share her time with Kemal with her father. She had been observing him throughout the evening and found herself drawn to his manner and intellect.

Fran continued. "It is the practice of the Ottomans to take the best young boys from the kingdoms they conquer to train them to be scholars and the best soldiers in the world. Personally, I find the practice abhorrent, but it appears you are content. Am I wrong?" Fran asked inquisitively, her head slightly tilted toward him, enabling her to better see his expression.

She could not fathom how painful his memories must be. She wondered whether he ever reflected upon those memories and how deeply buried they were. She also wondered whether he harbored resentments.

"That is a difficult question to answer since this is the only life I know. It is not the only life I remember, but it is the one I have lived. I am among the most fortunate," Kemal stoically replied.

"One's station within the janissary brotherhood is based on talent and ability. I was given opportunities to excel and was noticed by the teachers and elders in the Enderun School of the palace, who would determine my fate. It is a better life than most experience, to be sure."

What Kemal could not share with Fran were his deep yearnings. Fran was a child who he doubted was capable of understanding the conflict and complexities of his life. He believed he could discern that Fran would be a willing and compassionate listener, but he feared the revelations. For all his devotion to the sultan, for the sultan's graciousness, trust and generosity toward him, Kemal remained haunted by memories of his loving family. His father was a rabbi and baker. Kemal remembered the *pesaha appam*, unleavened and served on the Passover, and the richness of the sweet *challah* bread, lusciously braided, one braid on top of the other, sprinkled with sesame seeds and yellowed from saffron. He sometimes imagined it not nearly as sweet as he remembered, thinking his mind played tricks. So on occasion, Kemal would send a servant to the Jewish quarter to buy a loaf of *challah*. He savored each bite, briefly satisfying his hunger for his lost life. Indeed, it was as sweet and delicious as he recalled.

His mother's face was kind, always in a pure white apron covering her humble clothing, humming softly and melodically under her breath, generous with her love—always providing a kiss to his cheek. His father would ruffle his hair and often leave remnants of flour, dusting Kemal's hair white. Kemal attempted desperately to rid himself of the memory of the day he had been taken . . . stripped naked for examination and then torn from the home he loved. He could not rid himself of the memory of his father's pleadings to the janissaries to spare his son—his only son, and his mother falling to her knees, clutching the clean, crisp apron to her face to stem the waterfall of tears. His mind could sometimes only barely cope with the horror of having been ripped from his bucolic life, and so he had tutored himself to suppress his thoughts, controlling them. What would his life have been had he stayed with these good and loving people? Would he too have become a rabbi, a man with a wife and family to love?

These were his torments, juxtaposed against one another: the life he had as the most faithful servant to his master, arguably the most powerful man in the world, and the deep aching for the life he might have had. He felt it hopeless to explain his life to this unworldly boy in a way that might be understood—no matter how good or comforting a listener—so he avoided the subject or, if necessary, glossed over it evasively and briefly. Fran could never comprehend the depth of that pain. His janissary training had been arduous, demanding, grueling, and sometimes even cruel. Nevertheless, Kemal had some degree of contentment with his life if for no other reason than there was little to which it could be compared. He was a warrior, a trained assassin, and equipped with an iron will, his mettle tested. He excelled at his profession. And now, in conversation with his young friend, he was faced with exposing what still resided within his soul—his unresolved needs.

Kemal reflected. "I find myself wondering if things will ever taste as good as they did in my childhood or if the air I breathe will ever smell so sweet. Things I try to avoid thinking about." He was serious and Fran intuitively sensed a deep longing within him.

"I understand this, Kemal. I try not to allow my thoughts to go to places that can only cause despair. It is a struggle, to be sure."

Fran turned and moved slightly away, pretending to look over the edge of the terrace. Kemal, in an effort to guide the conversation, unknowingly moved from an uncomfortable subject for him to an uncomfortable subject for Fran.

"Tell me, where is your mother? Does she remain in Venice while you and your father travel abroad?" he asked, innocently.

"No, my mother died from childbirth fever when I was born. It is difficult for me to reconcile in my own life that my birth was the cause of her death."

"I am so sorry to have asked such an insensitive question, Fran. I did not know—how could I know?" Kemal answered, distressed. "Forgive me."

"Kemal, we are getting to know each other." She reached out impulsively to touch his hand in comfort. Kemal watched as she did so and found her touch…. her caress…to be extraordinarily delicate for such an accomplished warrior.

"You asked your question as innocently as did I when I inquired about your painful past," she smiled at him gently, reassuring him that she had not been offended. She tried to comfort him without revealing her femininity and she was finding it a struggle.

"I have come to terms with it. It has after all, been seventeen years. My father has told me she would sing to me before I was born when I was restless in her belly. '*Fa la ninna, Fa la nanna, Nella braccia della mama…, Nella braccia della mama.*' Fran softly murmured the old Venetian lullaby, in a whisper, hardly audible under her breath.

"Small things like this provide some comfort. It may seem trivial, but she sang to me because she loved me even before I was born. Sometimes I think I can remember her singing to me—but no, that would be impossible," Fran finished, dismissing her thought.

"But you, Kemal. What you have endured is more difficult. You have memories of your mother and I do not. You are good and kind to forgive those who ripped you from your home. I could not be so noble. I believe it is a gift from God to be forgiving. You have been blessed in this way."

"As I have said, I am more fortunate than most and I have great devotion to the sultan. He has treated me very well, and I am humbled by his confidence in me. I focus on my duties and how to improve my service to him. It does no good to dwell on things we cannot change. My life is not without many rewards," he reassured her, struggling with the sincerity of his words.

"But something you have said I find so interesting," Kemal moved on. "One of the things I remember the most about my mother was the way she was always humming. It is unusual, would you not say, our mothers' singing, humming intrigues and remains with us so? It is, after all, such a small thing, Kemal responded, understanding Fran's feelings.

"Yes, that is remarkable. I never saw my mother, of course. She was renowned for her beauty—a Borgia. Yes, I know it is a notorious name—the papal Borgias. My father has told me that she possessed none of the characteristics of her infamous family; rather, she was blessed in abundance with the qualities of goodness and kindness. He told me she was generous and loving, possessing what he called, 'an exquisite intellectual curiosity' that challenged him always. We gratefully have a striking painting of her. *Mia Padre* had it commissioned by the famed Luca Signorella of Cortona in Tuscany. My father carries a miniature of her, also done by Signorella. It has been almost eighteen years and he has never remarried. I think it is too late for me to need a mother, but I am sometimes beginning to think he has great need for a wife. I feel there is a quiet loneliness that I cannot fill even as much as he loves me. He once told me he would rather be alone than lonely and I have come to understand his meaning. He would rather spend his time alone than with one he cannot share a full and complete life. To be paired with the wrong person in lifelong matrimony would surely be to sentence him to loneliness. I loathe to think though that he is never to find someone with whom he can share the end of his days. I pray for his complete happiness."

Attempting to again shift the conversation to another, less painful subject, Fran complimented Kemal. "Your Latin is excellent. Do they always teach warriors languages?"

"Again, another fortunate opportunity for me. I was given special training in the palace school. I am fluent in Arabic, Persian, Latin, Aramaic, and Spanish, as is required to command the Beyliks," Kemal answered, but his thoughts lingered on their previous conversation.

He could not help but feel sympathy and some empathy for what Fran had just revealed to him. He also found himself entranced by Fran's demeanor, her spirit. He lingered on her strange attractiveness, thinking that Fran's mother surely must have been beautiful judging by her stunning offspring.

"*Kucuk uzman*! You and I have more in common than we first knew!" Kemal proclaimed, trying to lighten the mood. "We even look a little alike. Sorry, that's no compliment to you." He ran his hand through his dark curly hair and reached over to do the same to hers. "Except, of course, that I am older and more mature. Also, you are in possession of the most magnificent blue eyes, while mine are dull and brown."

Fran playfully slapped his hand away, but welcomed his attempt to bring levity to their colloquy. She smiled. "Kemal! There is nothing dull about *you*! In fact, I think your eyes reveal depth and kindness. Sensitivities that you are perhaps required to keep hidden, but are not hidden from me. I see more than you think and I am very perceptive. Thank you though. It is said I have my mother's eyes. It is sad that we do share some things in common—the loss of parents. To lose parents, or a parent—no matter how they are lost—is a tragedy for a child. I have the sadness of not knowing, but you bear the sadness of knowing. Yes, I agree, we do have similar features, but just because you are older does not mean you are more mature or wiser," Fran challenged.

Francesca was keenly aware that she had likely revealed her femininity to Kemal. Both were highly intuitive and she could not imagine he had not realized she was no boy. In fact, she decided, it was the way he looked at her—the way a man looks at a woman. She was not dismayed that he may have discovered her secret, even though she was filled with conflict and confusion over her feelings. She needed to believe that her secret would remain safe but that her abilities would not be underestimated by Kemal, merely because she was a woman. Francesca would not, however, overtly disclose her identity, even if her secret was no secret at all.

Kemal too, was perceptive. With every piece of new information gleaned from their extended conversation, he was more and more certain that Fran's disguise could not conceal what he believed to be true—that Fran was a girl.

Fran looked at his quizzical expression, dismissed it, and continued her inquisition.

"But now, Kemal. I want to know more about you." She was also concerned that perhaps she had revealed more of her feminine side to Kemal than she had intended. Her concerns were justified. Kemal would not easily be fooled and she believed he was sizing up more than just her conversation. "I was very impressed with your skills this morning on horseback and with the bow. It is said that the janissaries are the best fighting force in the world."

Kemal shrugged. "You have impressive skills with the knife, sling and sword—especially for one so young. Quite remarkable. The rapier, is it? And your arsenal of weapons! I am impressed! Perhaps you would be able to teach me some of your skills!"

"Yes!" Fran responded with delight. "This I can do, but only if you will teach me to ride like a janissary in return! You and your horse, moving together in unison, are a thing of beauty—a prized skill to master." Fran felt slightly more relaxed, believing it unlikely that he had detected her femininity, particularly in the remembrances of her mother.

"How did you learn such skills?" Kemal looked at Fran seriously, but noted that her shoulders and hips were nearly the same width—an odd shape for a young boy. He was finding the child, and the shape, equally beguiling.

"*Mia Padre* established a martial arts academy in Venice—*Academia Artum Militarum Venetiae*—just over twenty years ago to teach the art of fencing in particular. Warriors from all the known world attend, even from as far away as China. *Mia Padre* and I pride ourselves on mastering their techniques and the use of their weapons, just as they are intent on learning ours," Fran related, justifiably proud of her father's accomplishments and renown.

"This is of great interest to me. Please tell me more about a school where someone as young as you has learned to be expert in so many martial disciplines! Perhaps I can convince Suleyman that I need to attend this illustrious academy!" They both lifted themselves to sit on the wide, flat railing of the marble colonnade. Fran's feet dangled loosely over the edge, but Kemal's height allowed his feet to rest just above the ground.

"There is a great deal to tell. I will start with the three 'S's'—the premise of the martial arts portion of my father's program. Actually there are five 'S's' but the last two pertain to the scholarly and spiritual training. I will describe those later. The first requisite for success is that there must dwell in each of the students, a fire, a burning, deep in the belly, for excellence in each of the disciplines—an insatiable desire to excel. *Mia Padre* demands that intensity and dedication. It is not something that can be taught or feigned. It exists or it does not. Success requires mind and body preparation, perseverance and, perhaps most importantly, perspiration.

"Now, back to the three 'S's.' They are Speed, Strength, and Stamina. To build speed for example, we run sprints two days a week. One day a week we do the same, but we race uphill, which concurrently builds greater strength. Twice a month we run a quarter marathon. In each of the runs we are required to vary our intensity, sometimes even adding weighted sacks to our backs. These runs also strengthen our core and build stamina and endurance. Twice a year, we run a half marathon, and once a year, a full marathon.

"For strength, we primarily lift weights, building all the important muscle groups. Weights are carved from rock from a local quarry by our stone masons to our exact specifications and, while somewhat crudely fashioned, they are highly effective. We also use barrels and buckets loaded with water. *Mia Padre* is very inventive and creative to ensure the training never becomes boring. We pull carts laden with stones up hills and use ropes for jumping and climbing. Only when our speed, strength, and stamina are sufficient do we embark on extensive martial arts training. Daily exercises and training take place in the mornings—just immediately after sunrise. We eat well-managed diets prepared by our kitchen staff, and then in the afternoons we are immersed in the scholarly disciplines. To attain basic competence, completion of a rigorous six-month course is required before advancing. Then we begin cross training." Fran paused.

Kemal urged her on, anxious to hear how this school compared to his own arduous training. "My training is targeted and intense, but your descriptions of what is required in your academy are astonishing."

"M*ia Padre* did a great deal of traveling before I was born to acquire the skills he has. Since I was a child, I have accompanied him on his trips and now am well adapted to the adventurous life we now share. I am grateful that he was wise enough to know that exploring the wonders of the world would only increase my desire to know more and wanted me to view the world as the greats have seen it. For example, our trip to China was long and quite arduous, by water and land. Our journey took us along a portion of the Silk Road. It was there that my father told me that we might be standing on the very cobbled path where Alexander stood, or perhaps touching a wall that Aristotle of Sagria, his tutor, may have touched. He has challenged me to imagine the thoughts of those who have come before us. We even saw the Buddhas of Bamiyan, and they were astonishing in size. It is inspiring to view each moment from this perspective. Our travels have increased my desire for knowledge and I have witnessed so much. We learn from the world, Kemal. I have also learned that in order to become a true expert—and you as an expert will understand this—one must never shirk the drills and training no matter how physically or mentally demanding they become. I have learned that I can push myself far beyond the limits I believed I was capable."

"Yes! I have worked so hard that I have physically retched after I completed my training goals. It is arduous and painful, but the results so worthwhile. I also understand the value of your journeys. I would love to travel the world as you have done."

"I agree!" Francesca was eager to share with a kindred spirit. "We returned from China a few years ago. We were privileged to be students of the formidable Shaolin warrior monks, who extended our knowledge of the martial arts. Their focus is on spiritual, as well as physical training, self-control, and self-reflection. They taught us to better appreciate and respect the solitude of silence, for it is in the quiet that answers often lie. The body will perform at its best when the mind is focused and clear. An uncluttered mind is necessary and integral to the mastery of the martial arts, and with spiritual dedication, greater self-knowledge and control is attained. Kung Fu disciplines, when required in self-defense, are much more likely to be effective when in possession of a focused mind.

"We were fortunate to convince two monks to return with us to Venice. They have refined and now oversee significant portions of our martial arts training. The techniques they teach are truly impressive and, when used properly and with the requisite skill, can stop any aggressive force. There are many specialties falling under the umbrella of Kung Fu. They also teach selective skills, such as *Waijia* which focuses on physical strength and agility through the use of explosive and fast movements." Fran paused. There was so much to tell and she could see the eagerness for more in Kemal's face.

"Kemal, perhaps one day you will visit or, as you have suggested, come to the academy as a student! I think we agree this is an excellent idea! Let me tell you a little about our dexterity and training with the blades. The most important aspect is repetition—we engage in exhaustive practices. We repeat our drills hundreds of times, perhaps thousands, with each weapon and with each hand. The repetitions are intended to make our actions second nature, so that our muscles respond unthinkingly with great speed. For example, I am not ambidextrous by birth. I have been taught. It is our belief that the full body should be capable of defense and sometimes it is required that each hand work together simultaneously. No part of the body should remain idle. This is crucial. Today I had to use both hands and with great precision to stop the thieves."

Kemal interrupted. "Yes, that was quite impressive. Rarely have I seen such swashbuckling in anyone other than myself!" They laughed together.

"Yes. There is such variety in the skills and lessons taught at the academy. We are trained in the use of many weapons. Of course, swords and knives. My favorites are the *jambiya* and *kard* for throwing. I like their weight. The rapier is part of our heritage, but we are skilled in all the known swords, even the exquisitely forged blades of the Japanese samurai. In fact, Kemal, before we came here, we were immersed in intensive training with the use of the scimitar, again with both hands. Better to take advantage of any defensive weaknesses of your opponents, as well as doubling the lethal force brought into the fight. I will have to show you sometime! We can also fight and protect ourselves even if one of our hands or another part of the body is injured. Other weapons include the bow, javelin and other spears, axes, maces—I am proficient with the use of the mace, but have had no opportunity yet to use it in combat."

"And, of course, the sling! Now your display today—*that* was impressive!" Kemal could not help interrupting. Anxious for another display, he asked, "Could you do that again? Prove to me it wasn't just luck!" he challenged.

Never one to pass up a challenge, Fran removed the leather sling from the pocket of her doublet. She put a lead ball in the pouch and asked, "Lemon for your tea, Kemal?" She took aim at a solitary lemon tree in the far corner of the yard and in one swift movement knocked a single, juicy lemon from its branches.

"I got the lemon. If you want it for your tea, you will have to retrieve it!" she laughed. "I hunt, you gather!" Kemal tried not to gape open-mouthed at her expertise and precision.

"You have convinced me beyond a reasonable doubt. From one warrior to another, I bow my head in respect." He made an exaggerated low and impressive bow.

"Just in case I should meet my Goliath," Fran smiled. "It is an underappreciated weapon, but it can be lethal as history has taught us. You know it is not usually our intention to kill. While our training enables us to be lethal, we prefer only to subdue, unless provoked to act to save our lives or the lives of others. You saw that today and it has been discussed."

"You are correct, Fran. It depends on the circumstances. I am trained to kill—that is not just a mere avocation. I am most often the aggressor. In battle, I have no choice. It might do me some good to come under the tutelage of those Shaolin monks of yours, as you have suggested. Perhaps I need a little attitude adjustment." Kemal chuckled.

"I should tell you a bit about our intellectual and spiritual training," Fran continued. "It too is arduous, but I find comfort in the studies. There is a quiet peace in scholarly learning, and I value it greatly. It is why, just as you, I have been tutored in languages. It is *mia Padre's* requirement that we completely immerse ourselves in a language a month at a time. Also, I might be required to speak in German and answer questions *mia Padre* asks of me in French. It is a most interesting way of conversing. I am also fluent in German, Spanish, English, and French and understand the histories and philosophies of those who have shaped the world we now know.

There is transcendent comfort in the great silences of reading and absorbing knowledge."

She loved talking to him, but decided she dare not look him straight in his face. Sitting so close to him, their bodies touching, she was worried that the telltale warmth she felt flooding her body would make its way to her cheeks, shining them a deep pink. It was a new feeling for her. Nothing had prepared her for a time such as this. This *kucuk uzman* was suddenly and woefully lacking in expertise. She found herself profoundly inadequate.

Il Lupo suddenly appeared on the terrace. "This is a lovely setting," he noted surveying the terrace and gardens. Il Lupo had found the two engaged in their own coze, apparently oblivious to the sudden change in weather. The obvious growing affection between the two did not escape the protective father's notice.

"Don't you two realize it is starting to rain? I believe that is a sign it is time to end the evening. We have had a wonderful reception and it is good to see the two of you must have found common ground and shared interests."

"Yes, indeed we have," Kemal was quick to respond, as Francesca jumped to the ground. "I have heard so much now about your academy and would consider myself most fortunate if I am somehow able to visit, or even better, become a student!" His eyes shone with excitement.

"Yes, *mia Padre!* Would that not be wonderful? Such a visitor to the academy, or as a student? We would welcome it, do you not agree?"

"Of course we will welcome Kemal! It must be arranged! However, now we must all rest. Tomorrow is an important day. Thank you, Kemal, you have been an exceptional escort. We look forward to seeing you tomorrow. Come Fran, or should I say, *kucuk uzman?*" Il Lupo teased. The three laughed, even Fran, deciding that not only did she very much like Kemal, but that he had deemed her worthy of the complimentary sobriquet.

"It is truly an honor, Count. I will come for you and Fran in the morning to escort you to your audience with the emperor." They walked through the garden to the villa's front entrance where Kemal's horse had been brought around from the stables. Kemal put his hand to his chest in salute, swiftly mounted *Siyah* and departed.

Cryptic Communications

During the lively evening gathering, other mysteries were unfolding. A hooded messenger waited as the lock of the heavily carved side door of Giovanni's villa clicked and opened slightly. A gloved hand extended a small leather roll tied with leather strings. The message delivered, the door was quickly closed again and locked. Moving surreptitiously around the thicket of Mediterranean Cyprus, the courier scaled a wall and jumped to the grassy area just outside the villa's grounds. Hurriedly vaulting onto a horse tied nearby, he made his way to the narrow and cobbled streets of the city, glancing over his shoulders repeatedly to ensure no one had followed. Finally arriving at a predetermined drop point, he dislodged a stone in the Theodosian wall, slid the leather package in the hollow, returned the stone to its proper position, and left as silently and swiftly as he had arrived.

Watching and waiting a few moments, a second cloaked and hooded messenger arrived, this time on foot. Retrieving the missive, he jogged through the twisted alleyways of the old city, stopping and covertly placing the message behind an urn planted with the boisterous blooms of a hydrangea.

A young turbaned eunuch stood for a few minutes, nervously pacing and surveilling the area. Once certain he was not under observation, the eunuch swiftly grabbed the leather roll, placing it in his waist sash. He made his way directly into the Harem quarters of the Topkapi Palace undetected.

"You are certain no one saw you leave or reenter the Harem?" Mehmed demanded of Omar, his young servant. He grabbed the minion by his ear. "If I hear that you have been recognized, you will lose this ear or maybe your tongue," Mehmed assailed Omar, his face twisted and menacing. Mehmed was a massive, hulking man, his rotting teeth complementing his rotten temper.

"I am certain, Mehmed! No one saw me. I was very careful. I am completely confident I was not observed. Please, you are hurting me!" Omar grimaced, pleading to be released, convinced that Mehmed did not make empty threats.

"Wait here. I will need you to carry this back when I finish," Mehmed instructed as he entered the privacy of his room. Mehmed scribbled his answer to the cryptic message and returned with the rolled leather package, handing it to Omar.

"Return this message fast, imbecile!" he hectored, roughly grabbing Omar's ear again. "And be sure no one sees you." Mehmed threatened, his fetid breath enveloping Omar's face, causing him to gag.

"I will be careful and fast!" Omar assured his inveterate abuser frantically. With that he turned and quickly departed, Mehmed's message in hand, grateful to escape his foul breath and foul mood.

Awakenings

The rain of the early evening had intensified from a soft drizzle to a waterfall, rhythmically pulsating against the leaded glass windowpanes in Fran's bedchamber. She had finished her daily elocution rituals designed to control the pitch and modulation of her voice from rising above that of an alto. She was concerned that her voice might betray her. Despite her most ardent attempts, she was occasionally unable to maintain strict control, especially in stressful situations when her voice could rise to the level of a coloratura soprano without concerted discipline. She exercised daily enunciating each word as she deliberately lowered her speaking voice, finding the lowest tone to ensure her voice would be comfortable and convincing. Her growing fondness for Kemal was surprisingly stressful, for reasons she found herself struggling to comprehend. So on this evening, she extended the time spent practicing.

Finished, she sighed, loosed the bindings she had painstakingly tied that morning and felt instant relief as her breasts were freed from their constraints. She admired her figure in the Venetian looking glass—a large mirror framed with cut and incised pieces of Murano glass. Francesca gazed at her body. She was six inches taller than five feet, lean but wiry strong, which assisted in her necessary disguise as a juvenile boy. Her hips and her breasts were ample—not voluptuous, but her shape, without bindings and disguises, was unmistakably womanly. The morphing contours of her body and voice control caused apprehension. She sighed in resignation, quickly pulled on her chemise and jumped into her heavily carved tester bed. Large and comfortable, it was draped in layers of luxurious brocade and velvet. The rain continued and she found herself strangely contented; a true pluviophile, she found emotional comfort in the melodic tapping of water on glass.

Alone within the confines of her bed, her thoughts turned to Kemal as her hands slowly moved intimately over the curves of her womanly body. Her thoughts had previously turned to the opposite sex only occasionally, and she had always dismissed them as jejune. Now, however, it was decidedly different. Kemal was fascinating, handsome, and unlike anyone she had ever met. He was an artisan warrior, and she felt there was a Pierian quality to him—poetic in his words, actions, and physical beauty. She was bewildered by his swift and invasive intrusion into her mind, a sort of plundering of her thoughts, as though he had deliberately tricked her. She did not yet suspect it, but she was no longer an ingénue. She could not help but think of his muscular legs wrapped around his magnificent stallion, and how he looked in his shirt made from the beautiful cloth of Salonica. She found herself anguished and conflicted, delighted by thoughts of him and angry with herself for allowing them to flow so freely and unrestrained. Feelings unique and unknown enveloped and transported her to a complete and novel state of limerence. Agitated by the way he penetrated her thoughts, she felt she was losing control, the ambiguity of her feelings pervasive. Francesca Lupo was panicked. Heretofore, she had always maintained control.

"By my own sword," she hissed, sitting straight up in bed, her arms crossed defiantly across her chest. "I will not have it! I am Fran and cannot be Francesca in this world. I cannot *feel* like a woman. I must *think* like a man!" she chastised herself.

The same rain that comforted Fran pounded down on Kemal as he made his way back to his quarters at the court. He too found himself warmed by thoughts of his new friend. He was having difficulty coming to terms with his feelings. Fran was pleasurably perplexing and filled with passion that he had not seen in another. He felt a compathy with his new young friend over the shared loss of parents. Their conversations had filled Kemal with nostalgia, his suppressed yearnings for his homeland and past life now in the forefront of his mind. He had vowed never to wallow in melancholy reminiscence; rather, he had been determined to accept that his longings could never be fulfilled. It had been years. Now memories resurfaced in a most unexpected way. The lid of his Pandora's box had opened, even if not completely. But hope was loosed.

"Hsss," he muttered to himself, arriving at his quarters. "No time to waste pondering a juvenile—especially a boy—albeit unlike any I have ever met. I have more pressing business to attend to."

Annoyed with himself, Kemal shook the rain from his jacket as his aide took *Siyah*, guiding it toward the stables. He walked toward his room continuing to reflect on this child, this *kucuk uzman*, and found himself slightly unnerved over the arrival of such new and unanticipated feelings. How was it that Fran had seized such control of his thoughts? What spell had been cast? How could his senses have been so assailed? He entered his room and lay down on his bed, cradling his head in his hands. Unable to rest, he rose to write thoughtfully in his journal:

> *Fran.*
> *Grace.*
> *Inconnu.*
> *This child is no child...*
> *This boy, no boy...*
> *I am intrigued...*

He closed his journal and returned to his bed. He lay quietly for a few moments before closing his eyes and smiled. His imagination refocused on his alluring new friend, feeling renewed confidence in his instincts—instincts that had always served him well.

Shaitan

Mehmed meticulously followed the directions he had received in the message delivered earlier in the evening by Omar. He departed the Harem and arrived at the place designated in the message at the exact appointed time. It was now shortly before midnight and the streets were quieter, the normal bustle of the evening in Istanbul having subsided. His nervousness rose in fear of the dreaded rendezvous to come. He paced back and forth anxiously, his eyes twitching and darting in every direction. His hood and the darkness of the evening partially disguised his features. He fretted, knowing so much depended on strict adherence to the directions.

As he approached an alleyway, Mehmed caught whiff of a sickeningly sweet smell coupled with a repugnant foulness—a suggestion of decomposing magnolia blossoms mixed amongst rotting corpses—causing him to cover his mouth and nose with the sleeve of his cloak. Instantaneously he realized that there was someone— or something—emerging from a recessed opening in the building where his instructions had told him to come. Mehmed stumbled back, nearly falling to the ground, as out of the darkness a hooded wraith slowly raised its head revealing its hideous countenance. A terrified Mehmed gazed into the distorted and grotesque face of the Shaitan, its wildly flashing eyes exuding a phlegethon of malice and drooling mouth filled with sharp, cuspidated teeth.

He knelt in front of the demon as if to beg for his life and sputtered, *"Allah beni kurtarmak! Allah beni kurtarmak!"* pleading repeatedly for Allah to save him.

The Shaitan emitted a guttural hiss, "I trust all has been completed and *everything* has been accomplished exactly according to the instructions! If you deceive me, I will know!"

"As you have instructed, my lord; everything is completed according to your strict instructions. The initial work required was completed just after midnight and the final actions just before the sunrise," Mehmed whimpered, cowering.

Certain he would be killed on the spot if he divulged the full truth, he deliberately did not tell the demon that he had not participated fully as had been instructed. He had been unable to leave the Harem without drawing suspicion and so Qais, another conspirator, had been sent in his place.

The gnarled skeletal fingers of the Shaitan opened, revealing a handful of precious, glittering gems. Its thick, twisted, and sharp fingernails clicked over the colored stones. "As agreed, half now and the other half on the final delivery. There will be nothing more until I have what I want."

The gems were placed into Mehmed's outstretched and trembling hands. Although the number of gems was hardly paltry, Mehmed's greed briefly overcame his fear.

"My lord, there are so many with whom these need to be shared. There is extreme danger and I will need more to convince them to keep their mouths shut!" he boldly blurted out to the Shaitan.

"*Aptal esek! Seni domuz!*" The Shaitan vituperated, shrieking at Mehmed, its foul spittle covering his face. "I am the Shaitan, and a messenger of Iblis! *You* do *not* question! The one who needs convincing is you! I will expose all your crimes should you fail me! You tell them, if they dare to question, it will be with their last breath! They will accept what they are given and what *I* decide they deserve!"

The Kizlar Agha recoiled at the threatening attack. No one had ever dared call the powerful Mehmed a stupid donkey or a pig and he knew too well that he would lose his head should his felonious enterprises be discovered. He was stunned and terrorized into compliance with the Shaitan's demands.

"Of course, of course, my lord! It—everything, will be done just precisely as you command!" Mehmed stepped back, servile and cringing as he bowed deeply.

"For now, you will cease all your other illegal business affairs. No more bribes and Harem prostitutes for the janissaries. The *ask melegi*—the angels of love—the prostitutes and your bounty as their bawd must wait. I demand this!" the Shaitan sibulated. "The success of the plan is jeopardized. And, from now on, use only Ali to carry messages and not that sniveling Omar. Is all this understood?"

"Yes, my lord, completely. I will follow your instructions exactly. You need not worry," Mehmed offered meekly.

With those words, the hideous Shaitan, its stench now overwhelming, disappeared as a phantom into the night and into a blackness as dark as its soul.

Day Two
İkinci Gün

Expletives and Insurrection

 iovanni Contarini, along with the envoys and ambassadors who had been his guests the previous evening, arrived at the Topkapi Palace to be received by Sultan Suleyman at an official state reception. Although already known to the sultan, the occasion marked Giovanni's formal introduction as the new Venetian Ambassador to the Imperial Court. The entourage included other diplomats and Conte Vincenzo Lupo de Venezia, ostensibly as an envoy. Fran, also in attendance, was once again convincingly, disguised as a boy.

Kemal escorted the dignitaries but paid particular attention to his charges, Count Vincenzo Lupo and Fran. A rare privilege afforded to few, all would be allowed through the Gates of Felicity and into the inner sanctums of the palace. Such a large assemblage with direct accessibility to Suleyman breached important security protocols, creating an understandable need for precaution. While Kemal knew there would be a thorough search for weapons of anyone entering through the Gates of Felicity, he remained ill-at-ease. The leaked rumors regarding restive janissaries he had heard the previous evening elevated his anxiety.

The dignitaries were dressed in their finest fashion and uniforms. Fran and Il Lupo had both chosen heavily embroidered doublets. The billowing sleeves had inverted pleats revealing a contrast silk lining—Fran's in red and Il Lupo's in a royal blue. Each of the sleeves was heavily boned—the ornamental contrast welting on the edges provided significant structure to the garments. They had worked carefully with their tailors in Venice who had skillfully embroidered flower heads laced within the design of the detailed jackets that allowed camouflage of the grips of knives. Incorporation of the weapons into the clothing was achieved by substituting knives for the boning in the garment, which was ordinarily placed in long, thin linen pockets within the lining of the clothing and which assisted in its shaping. Il Lupo had commissioned the finest clothier in Venice, and together they frequently designed garments that allowed concealment of weapons within them. Il Lupo was resourceful and thoughtful, and rarely allowed himself or Fran to be without protection. Given the unsettling rumors regarding potential dangers to Suleyman from within the janissary corps, lack of preparedness would be grossly negligent. Understanding the potentially dire consequences of discovery of the knives during the anticipated search, Il Lupo had cleverly arranged for their concealment for himself and Fran.

"My janissary guard must search you. I apologize for this intrusion, but it is our duty to protect the sultan and no one is exempt," Kemal explained, somewhat apologetically. "Please understand. No slings today, Fran?" He smiled, noticing that her lethal leather necklace was not hanging from her neck.

"No, Kemal, not today. I am certain I will not need it—the sultan surely has plenty of lemons to offer to his guests for tea and sufficient numbers of hunters and gatherers." She returned a warm smile. Kemal nodded and laughed at their shared joke.

Il Lupo removed the leather binding that held his sword. "We are not offended. It is customary for the courts in Europe as well."

The guards patted them down with some roughness, one of them pausing at Francesca's waist, her boned jacket hugging her just above the hips. Stopping, he suspiciously repeated the search, causing momentary concern for Il Lupo. He was unsure if the guard suspected she was not the boy she represented based on the curves he might have detected in her hips, or perhaps he had felt a hidden blade.

Il Lupo turned to Kemal and the guard. "It is the fashion of the day in Venice. Not comfortable, but we sacrifice much to be fashionable!" Il Lupo smiled, trying to discourage a continued and more thorough search. The guard also smiled, stopped frisking Fran, and moved on to the Count.

After the mandatory searches were completed, Il Lupo and Fran were relieved that their knives remained undiscovered. Kemal collected the entire entourage and led them to a large room guarded heavily on all corners and at the entrance by janissaries. As he approached, Qais, his lieutenant, gave a cursory bow to his captain.

"That was Qais, my second-in-command, my lieutenant," Kemal explained to Il Lupo, who noted the cold, perfunctory greeting between them. "A sour man with an extremely unpleasant disposition. He has seniority in the corps. It was only by Suleyman's direct intervention that I was appointed Captain of the Beyliks instead of him."

Kemal watched as Qais then stepped back to speak to Mehmed. Ever alert, Kemal noticed apparent friction between them, wondering why there was any need for them to engage in conversation. Also observing the hostility between the two, and intent on eavesdropping, Il Lupo moved slightly closer to them, feigning interest in the ceiling, marveling at its artistic qualities.

As he passed them, Il Lupo heard an agitated Mehmed utter, "I said *wait*! Not today!" to Qais. Qais cowered slightly as he backed away from Mehmed.

"Who is that—the person speaking with Qais?" Il Lupo asked Kemal, tilting his head slightly in Mehmed's direction.

"That is Mehmed. He is the Chief Black Eunuch, Keeper of the Girls, and favorite of the sultan's wife, Gulbehar." Il Lupo nodded, watching the eunuch suspiciously as Mehmed distanced himself from Qais. Becoming increasingly apprehensive, Il Lupo noticed that Fran was regarding Mehmed with suspicion as well, as she turned her attention to Qais, Kemal's lieutenant.

"*Padre*, those men are a concern. Something is not right," Fran whispered to Il Lupo, feeling the hair on her neck stiffen.

"I agree. We must be alert."

They were in awe of the extravagance of riches of the Ottoman Court as they passed through the Imperial Gates, Gate of Salutation, and finally the Gates of Felicity into the third courtyard of the palace. The dignitaries entered the *Endurun*, the inner palace in the third court, and were ushered into the magnificent *Arz Odasi*—the Endurun's Audience Chamber. They marveled at the inscription over the entrance door of the kiosk "*In the Name of God the Compassionate, the Merciful,*" the sultan's monogram and the stunning Arabic calligraphy. The bright sunlight illuminated the ultramarine ceiling and gold-studded stars, and highlighted the azure and gold mosaic walls that glittered in the reflected light. The abundance of windows ensured that the room would always be sparkling in the constant and diffused light.

At the center of the Audience Chamber was an elevated gold and gem-encrusted throne sitting beneath a large canopy. The floors were covered with a spectacular assortment of Turkish carpets in rich, vibrant colors and intricate, hand-knotted designs—some with woven inscriptions reminding the faithful of their spiritual obligations. Pillows covered in brilliant fabrics and festooned with tassels were stacked around the perimeter of the room and made available for seating. The spectacle of wealth was overwhelming and intended to inspire respect and admiration in the beholder and even fear of the power behind the wealth. All of the visitors were well acquainted with the splendors of royal courts, but the stunning artistry of the Topkapi was unparalleled. Il Lupo and Francesca had often been guests at the *Palazzo Ducale*—the Doge's Palace—in Venice, which was filled with treasures including art of the Renaissance era, and the royal courts of Europe. Still, they marveled at the grandeur of their surroundings.

As was often his practice, Sultan Suleyman once again disregarded quotidian protocols of the court. On this occasion, he had arranged to have his wife Gulbehar and mother of his son, Mustafa, as well as his favored concubine, Roxelana—"the Russian" —and mother of three living sons and a daughter, in attendance. Roxelana was also Suleyman's closest confidant. Gulbehar and Roxelana were both seated on the dais. Suleyman knew there would be gifts specifically for them and, as a gesture of his kindness, allowed them to join the festivities. Suleyman's reputation for breaking traditions often caused great consternation and chagrin among his advisors.

The two women sat on low, pillow-covered chairs to his left. Never before had a sultan shown such favor to a concubine publicly such as Suleyman displayed for Roxelana. The court was rife with speculation that he would take her as his wife and most recently, that she might again be with child, Gravida VI.

Even though they remained unmarried, the relationship between Suleyman and Roxelana was unique and their devotion to one another was constant fodder for court gossip. Suleyman could not disguise the depth of his love for Roxelana. They had been together for many years, and his relationship with her engendered renewed energy and excitement in his life. He did not tire of her, this Russian concubine.

Roxelana was known as *"Hürrem"*—the cheerful one—a name affectionately given to her by Suleyman. Born near the Sea of Azov, she had been captured and enslaved by the Tartars of the Golden Horde, in the Tauric Peninsula, in Crimea. Her father had been an orthodox priest. Ibrahim brought her to the court of Suleyman as a concubine, and Suleyman quickly took notice. She was fair, in contrast to many of the concubines in his Harem, and her hair was long and Titian red. He found her captivating and intoxicating with a stimulating, intriguing intellect. Initial infatuation and friendship grew into a deep mutual affection.

Vulpine in appearance, Suleyman's wife Gulbehar sat in sharp contrast to Roxelana's beauty and demeanor. Her face and nose were long and tapered, her lips thin, and pinched into an unattractive pout. As many others in the Harem, Gulbehar was olive skinned, with dark hair, small and gaunt in stature. Gulbehar appeared peevish, her black hair pulled back into a tight, structured bun away from her face, drawing attention to her large, pointed ears, thus magnifying her foxlike appearance.

While approximately the same age, the two powerful women were otherwise completely dissimilar. Out of respect for Suleyman and for the sake of appearances, they kept their rivalry in momentary check. One could not help but observe the stunning difference as Roxelana sat voluptuous, her long hair flowing about her shoulders, a soft smile on her sensuous lips.

Both women were beautifully dressed, wearing conical-shaped hats draped with a delicate, gossamer silk. Roxelana's was trimmed with braided cording in lavender and gold. Her caftan consisted of layers of shimmering silk—the outer layer a delicate, gossamer lightweight silk and the under layer a silk taffeta. When she moved, the garment captured light, changing colors from a delicate pink to a deep purple. Gulhebar's headpiece was similarly shaped with flowing silk fabrics and embroidery in shades of melon and gold; her caftan was a more heavily structured and embroidered brocade with a flourishing leaf motif.

Sitting cross-legged on his golden throne, Suleyman was indeed "The Magnificent," his countenance distinguished. He had an angular face and markedly muscular body, manly and robust. A perfectly groomed moustache framed his mouth and drew attention to his dominant, strong jaw. His visage was formidable yet calm, with green, deeply penetrating eyes that surveyed those assembled. While he was not handsome, there was a refined and sensual composition to his face, which added greatly to his mystique.

The sultan was luxuriously adorned. His trousers and shirt were constructed from turquoise and silk taffeta, creating a light-capturing, shimmering effect—complementing the garments worn by Roxelana. At his waist was a gold brocade sash covered in tiny seed pearls. A dagger in a gold sheath with an ornamental and massive emerald at the hilt, was tucked into his sash. His undercoat was a lightweight gold silk robe with wide ribbon borders embroidered in the colors of copper, turquoise, leaf green, and poppy red. The brocade outer caftan was finished with prominent embroidery, mimicking that of the silk robe, while his gold, silk shoes matched the delicate embroidery on the edges of his lightweight robe. The exceptionally intricate needlework was interspersed with gold and silver threads creating an even more lustrous appearance. Resting on his head, and worn in lieu of the crowns of European kings, was a turban of gold taffeta with a wide diamond and seed pearl border and two jeweled aigrettes. Adorned with the vestments of the emperor, he presented an unforgettable reflection of the splendor and power of the Ottoman court.

Standing to his right was the Grand Vizier, Ibrahim, solemn and unamused by the spectacle. He loathed the breach of the rules of decorum of the court by Suleyman. His mouth was pulled tight, giving the appearance that it was incapable of forming a smile and altogether giving the impression that he was burdened with the pain of distasteful duty. His nose was prominent—an exaggerated aquiline with a beaked appearance—beneath which sat a bushy and rather poorly manicured moustache. Il Lupo recalled Antoine's description that Ibrahim possessed the "hauteur of perpetual arrogance," believing it to be completely accurate as he watched Ibrahim pompously scrutinize and appraise the reception attendees.

Flanking the dais were two janissaries, completely trusted and appointed by Kemal. The room was filled with other janissaries in ceremonial dress, and viziers and court attendants of various rank and function, adding further color and finery to the setting. Music played in the background and, while layered and polyphonic, its strains were sharp and hollow without the robustness of the more harmonious music of Europe. Dignitaries were summoned forward, one by one, introduced, and given opportunity to present lavish gifts to the sultan. Each audience ended with the obligatory kiss of the hem of the sultan's caftan.

Giovanni Contarini was especially pleased with the gifts he was to present to the sultan, Roxelana, and Gulbehar. His need to impress the sultan was imperative; his success as an ambassador and merchant could be strongly influenced by the impression made in this initial reception.

When summoned forward accompanied by two janissaries, Ambassador Contratini's first gifts included masterfully carved rosewood boxes, lined with turquoise blue velvet, designed to carry dozens of colored and etched Murano glass perfume bottles. Each was a singular work of art containing equally exotic fragrances, carefully blended and bottled. Giovanni had two boxes made for each of the women—each uniquely carved, but with identical contents. Diplomacy dictated that the wife and the favored be treated equally, understanding that Suleyman expected, even demanded, that his *Hürrem* was never to be slighted. Each of the presented chests was filled with mixtures of the finest flower and spice fragrances. The massive chest carved for Suleyman contained musk and sandalwood-based colognes and required the assistance of two janissaries to lift and convey to the dais.

With elaborate flourish, Giovanni clapped his hands and ordered, "Bring the rest of our offerings for Suleyman the Magnificent!" Janissaries came forward carrying massive filigreed, silver cages filled with large exotic birds, setting the cages at the foot of the dais.

"For you and your family, Your Majesty," Giovanni bowed deeply, his arms flaring out to his sides.

"Allow me to tell you about these birds from the New World. They are all the rage on the Continent. I have been importing them, and *these* spectacular specimens have been selected especially for *you*. Two pairs of Scarlet Macaws and one pair of the Rainbow Toucan. Majesty, if I may, they are the most enchanting birds. As you can see, the beaks of the Toucans are colored with turquoise—the color of the Turks and your empire. May I humbly suggest that you keep the Toucans for yourself? You see, they do not speak, thereby keeping your secrets close. They will never repeat a word you say," Giovanni concluded with a smile.

The exotic birds piqued the emperor's interest. Suleyman moved from the dais and walked around the cages, examining the toucans. Their overall turquoise beaks were beautifully accented with red tips, predominantly orange sides and several shades of green, one shade flawlessly blending into the next. The feathers were black, with the exception of yellow feathering on the neck and chest. Suleyman was clearly pleased.

"They are most exotic. Not as beautiful as the macaws, but you tell me these do not talk. What does that mean? Do the macaws talk?" Suleyman was not sure he believed Giovanni.

"Yes, Your Majesty, the macaws can be trained to repeat short phrases. They also listen well and are known to repeat what they hear spoken—very amusing, even embarrassing, at times. In fact, they have an uncanny and sometimes unwelcome knack for repeating risqué phrases and secrets they hear spoken. You wouldn't want vital state secrets spilled by a bird, would you?" Giovanni laughed.

"These currently speak only in Latin and are surprisingly fluent in Latin expletives. No telling what the precocious birds may pick up in the Harem."

Suleyman concurred. "I see your point, Ambassador Contratini. These," he pointed to the toucans, "will keep my secrets. Very thoughtful advice—advice I will accept. And the matching pairs of macaws—they are for *Hürrem* and Gulbehar?" Those in the audience could not help notice that Suleyman had used his affectionate name for the concubine. "If so, they will hear a great deal of chatter in the Harem, perhaps some not worthy of sharing in polite company," Suleyman chuckled.

"They are quite exquisite," he remarked circling their cages. "Come, *Hürrem* and Gulbehar! Welcome your new companions!" Suleyman beckoned and the women joined them, delighted by the brilliant red plumage and light blue tails.

"Look here, Gulbehar," Roxelana pointed to the vibrant feathers. "See how the blue is almost iridescent and there is yellow and green also within the folds of the wings." The rivals stood for a moment of shared wonder at the beauty of the birds. For at least that brief moment, each was so enchanted that they forgot their mutual loathing.

"Thank you, Ambassador. They are beautiful!" Roxelana graciously offered, accepting his gift. Gulbehar gave Giovanni a simple smile.

"*Damna Dogem! Damna Dogem!*" One of the macaws suddenly screeched just as the three had turned to resume their seats on the dais.

Stunned by the spewing of Latin expletives, everyone who understood the language was initially shocked but unable to repress their laughter. Even the great emperor found amusement in the slander of the Venetian Doge, and those lacking understanding of Latin took his lead and added to the chorus of laughter.

"Apparently the bird dislikes the Doge? Profane birds in the Harem? Ambassador Contratini! They should be right at home." Suleyman facetiously scolded Giovanni.

"Sultan Suleyman, I must apologize!"

Before Giovanni could continue in his apology, and upon hearing the word, "Suleyman," a second bird, not to be outdone, shrieked, "*Solimannus! Solimannus! Futue Solimannus! Futue Solimannus!*" It shrieked Latin expletives suggesting the commission of lewd acts on the emperor.

Many of the assembled again broke out in laughter, finding continued amusement in their outrageous antics and assuming the bird was just once again spewing Latin expletives. The audience grew quiet however, when Suleyman stopped, turning his head back to the cages, his face stern.

"Oh Your Majesty! My deepest and most sincere apologies!" Giovanni sputtered, understanding fully well the seriousness of the insults hurled at the emperor. "I swear to you I do not know where the bird could have learned or even heard such a thing. Perhaps in the hold of their ship—I cannot even imagine where?" Giovanni stammered, his voice faltering as he quickly tried to regain the sultan's pleasure.

"These birds have never heard such words from my mouth and have never spoken these words while in my presence. In fact, I rarely spend time in the presence of these creatures. Had I attempted to teach them anything it would have been only to sing your praises. I beseech you to believe me. I am at a loss for words and humbly seek your forgiveness," an embarrassed and terrified Giovanni protested, fearing his attempts to ingratiate himself to the emperor had failed and his tenure as ambassador short lived. Even in his panic, Giovanni imagined he might just be one more official who, upon displeasing or insulting the emperor, never left the Topkapi Palace, instead meeting the executioner or the dreaded assassin eunuchs. He wiped his brow with his lace-trimmed handkerchief, looking for any sign of absolution from the emperor.

"Your birds need to learn some manners, Ambassador! However, I am not immune to the knowledge that expletives are hurled my way—just not usually in my presence. I believe this is a first. Foul from fowl! How fitting, actually. I will try to find some humor in it. I hold no ill will against you, and you are forgiven. Sending them to the Harem is best. I would perhaps lose my temper and they their pretty little heads as the result. I would not like to be remembered through the ages as the sultan who beheaded birds! Take them to the Harem and the toucans to my chambers!"

A shaken Giovanni had lingered to kiss the hem of Suleyman's caftan. The cowering Venetian Ambassador muttered, "Thank you, thank you. You are gracious and merciful…" his voice trailed as Suleyman returned to the dais.

During the presentations, Kemal leaned in to Il Lupo. "The sultan usually leaves matters such as these presentations to Ibrahim. Those given audience today should feel honored. Ibrahim would gather the gifts and the ones deemed worthy, would be presented to the sultan. What happens to those deemed less worthy is not known. It is rumored that a visit to the Grand Vizier's home might resolve that mystery. We will soon be summoned."

Nodding toward the elaborate goldleaf, lattice fretwork above the dais, Il Lupo whispered to Kemal, "We are being watched." Kemal agreed but did not look up, not wanting their observation to be noticed by the secreted onlookers.

"Yes, that area—the mezzanine—is used frequently by senior members of the Harem and sometimes even the sultan himself, to observe the day's business. Judging by the amount of rustling, there is much interest and curiosity in today's ceremonies. If they make too much noise, they will be removed by the eunuchs. Hmm, perhaps my role as your guard is generating interest as well—it is very unusual to not be at the sultan's side at all times and so you may well be the object of their interest. Ah, Ibrahim has signaled us to approach. It is our time."

Called forward by Ibrahim, who motioned they stand in front of the sultan, the two approached the dais. Kemal accompanied the two janissary guards who flanked them as they moved forward. Before leaving Venice, Il Lupo and Fran had thoughtfully selected the gifts they were to present.

"Vincenzo Lupo—the renowned Vincenzo Lupo! I had heard you were coming. Welcome!" Suleyman smiled warmly, continuing his ruse to cover the true purpose of Il Lupo's presence at court. Suleyman had apparently decided that their arrangements would remain, at least for now, confidential. Suleyman began speaking in Latin; he had spoken his native Ottoman Turkish for the previous audiences.

Turning his gaze to Fran, "You, too, of course are most welcome!"

"We thank you for the great honor you have bestowed upon us by granting us audience in the reception," Il Lupo graciously replied, he and Fran both bowing. "I will have much to report to the Doge regarding the kindness with which we have been treated and the splendor and unsurpassed wealth of your court."

Their presentation began with a treasure trove of intricate, handcrafted Venetian masks for Gulbehar and Roxelana—each one a unique and remarkable piece of art. The sultan graciously studied each of the masks presented, nodding his approval and holding them up to show to those in attendance, who responded with well-deserved *oohs* and *ahhs*. Passing them to both women, each briefly lifted the artistic creations to cover their faces. It could not be overlooked that the great Sultan Suleyman, not hiding his preference for "the cheerful one," had passed each mask to his favored Roxelana first. Gulbehar's displeasure was not difficult to detect as she ruckled her lips tightly, repressing her repugnance over the special treatment of Roxelana. The artfully crafted masks seemed to distract her and improve her mood slightly.

"Your Highness, we hope you will find a place in your library for these," Il Lupo said, next handing Suleyman a book of illuminated manuscripts from the Richenau Monastery on Lake Constance, the *Bodensee.*

"Your library is renowned and I believe that we share the view that life is barren without the illumination of learning." With near reverence, the sultan took the book carefully into his hands relishing its beauty and texture while examining the exquisitely detailed art held within its hand-embellished pages.

"It will indeed be a wonderful addition to our library. Thank you," he said, smiling, casting a regal gaze at both Il Lupo and Fran. "Yes, I fill my library with stories of the tragedies of those who have lived, the comedies of those who have laughed, and the fables of the fictitious. Books and learning bring pleasure and their contents are filled with the distinctions that are critical to wisdom. The treasures of learning must always be defended."

"Your Majesty, we have one final gift. It is a gift of the new age—the Gutenberg Bible. We know that as a scholar, this is a gift your library should have," Il Lupo said, handing him the massive volume. Its binding was made from richly tooled, embossed leather with heavy, hammered brass fasteners.

"Ah! The Gutenberg Bible! I value this greatly! I could not be more pleased. It is magnificent. As my ancestor, Mehmed the Conqueror, who took Istanbul in the last century, I too have always valued manuscripts more than gold. It is here, inside the volumes, we receive knowledge from far beyond our times and borders. Within such pages, we can find understanding and truths. Life without knowledge and understanding is bleak and desolate." Suleyman's thoughts resonated strongly with Il Lupo who shared his sentiments and the same thirst for knowledge and learning.

"Westerners have much to teach us about the art of printing en masse. We have much history and tradition here, but we know that we can learn from the West as well. I am most grateful. Now I have two new beautiful volumes to peruse in my leisure time." Suleyman was clearly pleased, turning the pages with a gentle admiration, passing his hands reverently over the art and the words, as if through the mere act of touching them knowledge would be absorbed. He appeared briefly lost in contemplation and then blinked, lifting his gaze from the pages.

"Such printed manuscripts may also bring an end to the sufferings of scribes, rubricators, copyists, and the scriptoriums for which the Christian monasteries have so rightly been famed. Their sufferings have allowed for the preservation and expansion of knowledge. Progress? Perhaps the new publishing techniques will prove that to be true. I still wish to never lose the magnificent work of those artists and illuminators. They glorify our humble existence." Suleyman closed the heavy book, his long, artistic fingers lingering over its embossed bindings.

"Your Majesty is wise. Knowledge and learning, coupled with compassion and tolerance, are the only hope for a civilized, peaceful world, and perhaps, for its salvation," Il Lupo observed.

"Indeed, we are again in agreement, Vincenzo Lupo! Such salvation may take many lifetimes to achieve. One hundred, or surely perhaps in five hundred years, the world will have learned from the collective wisdom of the ages, and there will be a peaceful coexistence and tolerance."

"At some point, Your Majesty, it is my fervent hope that we may have the opportunity to share conversations regarding these very matters. I would be honored if you have time during our stay in Istanbul for scholarly exchanges. I would greatly benefit from your wisdom."

"Indeed, we shall, Vincenzo Lupo! I shall see to it!" Suleyman promised, putting the weighty Gutenberg Bible to his side.

During the sultan's inspection of the masks and even through the duration of the conversations at the dais, Kemal, Il Lupo, and Fran had become increasingly uneasy. Each noticed subtle, nearly indiscernible hand and facial gestures among the janissaries and Qais. The gallery balcony above the throne had been emptied and whisperings could no longer be heard. Just steps from Suleyman, Qais stood with the janissaries who had escorted Il Lupo and Fran to the dais.

The audience with the sultan ended, their escorts resumed their places at the foot of the dais. The subtle and increasingly suspicious communications among the janissaries continued. Moments before backing away from the sultan, Il Lupo turned his head toward Fran and looked at her, his glance conveying that something was severely amiss—they stood in the midst of very real danger. Both were on high alert. Il Lupo hoped that Kemal sensed the peril too.

There was no time to ask. Within seconds, there was a commanding shout, "Now!" Qais ordered, his face twisted into a menacing grimace. Roaring thunderously, he aggressively charged the dais.

The janissaries who had escorted them turned on Qais' command and vaulted on to the dais. They seized Kemal's two loyal and unsuspecting janissaries standing guard at either side of the sultan and violently slit their throats, causing near decapitation. With murderous intent, the malcontent mutineers advanced toward Suleyman, determined to assassinate him.

Instinctively and instantly, Il Lupo and Fran leaped into action. Adeptly pulling their deadly knives from the folds of their intricately embroidered doublets, they threw, striking two of the murderous janissaries in the neck. Sprinting, their feet hardly touching the ground, they leaped onto the dais, grabbing scimitars from the dead janissaries, fighting off the onslaught of at least a dozen more, along with Qais, their apparent leader. The sultan, lionhearted and as if in a choreographed dance with Il Lupo, pulled his jeweled sword as they fought, side by side. Fran nimbly flipped a second scimitar to Kemal after ripping it from the belly of a slain assassin, while pulling another stiletto from her doublet. Using his hidden weapons and those acquired in the onslaught, Il Lupo moved in rhythmic, powerful strides, wreaking havoc as the knives and his slashing sword left five more rebels dead in his wake.

Within moments, other janissaries loyal to the sultan joined the melee. Chaos reigned and screams echoed in the great hall. Blood spilled over the great throne, over the pristine mosaic floors, and sprayed onto the bodies, hair and clothing of Roxelana and Gulbehar, who sat frozen and stunned. Unable to give chase as she fought, Fran watched as two of the attacking janissaries managed to escape. In minutes, all the others were dead but Qais. Il Lupo was holding him by the shirt, his unwavering sword held threateningly to Qais' belly.

"Time for a little chat?" Il Lupo quipped, dryly. A quivering Qais had no time to reply, even if he had so desired.

Moving toward them, purposefully and with great calculation, Il Lupo saw Mehmed emerge from the crowd with scimitar in hand.

Suddenly, a small object flew by Il Lupo causing him to instinctively recoil, realizing that Qais had been struck by a dart, delivered with masterful precision into his jugular.

With events happening so swiftly, Il Lupo was unable to prevent Mehmed, the hulking Keeper of the Girls, from raising his sword, and delivering a deadly blow, cleaving Qais' skull with his scimitar. Blood, tufts of hair, and cerebral matter gushed from the gaping wound created by the brute force of Mehmed's attack on Qais, spewing over Il Lupo as he released his grip of Qais' shirt. Despite his blood-blurred vision, Il Lupo was certain he saw, for a fleeting moment, an apparition in the latticed balcony above the dais moving quickly away from the light. Though momentarily surprised, Il Lupo considered possible motives for Mehmed's actions. Had he simply been emboldened to protect Suleyman, albeit after the plot had been crushed? Or were there more sinister reasons for Mehmed's intervention? Mehmed stood grave, his deadly scimitar in hand, he too covered in Qais' encephalon. He wiped his face with his sleeve and moved toward the exit of the *Arz Odasi*.

"Are you all right?" Kemal rushed to Il Lupo's side as Fran removed one of her waist sashes to wipe her father's face.

"Yes. Where is the sultan? Is he unhurt?" Il Lupo asked.

"He has been removed to a safe place. Those with him we are certain can be trusted. He is unharmed. I was amazed at his fighting skills. They have not been tested for some time. And I continue to be astounded by yours! I knew something was seriously amiss, but had no weapon to use. I had to jump into the fray empty handed, grabbing scimitars from the dead and Fran. How did you know?" Kemal registered his astonishment at Il Lupo and Fran's uncanny ability to sense trouble was near.

"Instinct, Kemal. From the moment, Fran and I saw Qais and Mehmed together. It was their posturing, along with subtle hints from Qais and rebellious janissaries during the course of the ceremony. It is our job to be vigilant. We both intuitively sensed the insurrection."

"For your instincts, I am most grateful. While it is providential that this time you were armed, in the future we will need to perform more extensive searches of our guests. The protocols will have to be revisited. Your intervention in this case, however, ensured our sultan is alive. We are all indebted to you," Kemal finished with a grateful nod.

"Good, I'm glad the emperor is unhurt. We will discuss my suspicions later." Il Lupo nodded in the direction of the dais. Ibrahim was approaching. "Yes, perhaps your search protocols need to be adjusted, but not all would come prepared as we have."

With an accentuated froideur, the Grand Vizier, Ibrahim, approached. He was known as Pargali Ibrahim Pasha—the Westerner and Makbul Ibrahim Pasha—the Favorite and had been appointed Grand Vizier by his childhood friend, Suleyman the Magnificent. Ibrahim had been a Christian slave, who converted to Islam and been chosen to be schooled alongside Suleyman. When Suleyman seized power, Ibrahim rose along with him. He had served his master for years and amassed a fortune in doing so.

His lavishly detailed caftan flowed behind him as he approached—his face scowling. It was clear he disliked them—they were infidels and had managed to smuggle in weapons. There would be no pretense at disguising his feelings, his disdain prominently on display.

"Suleyman desires your company over dinner tonight." He glared malevolently at Il Lupo and Francesca and nodded to Kemal indicating he too was invited, his haughty head tilted slightly backward as if to avoid breathing the same air.

"Make sure this time there are *no weapons*." He continued, addressing Kemal. "You will also be dining with his concubine, the Russian. She makes nothing but mischief for this court. I am sorry I ever gave her to him. Before it is finished, she will have taken down the entire empire and its coffers." Ibrahim made no attempt to hide his disrespect and his contempt for "the cheerful one."

Giovanni chimed in, "Are we not invited? After all, I am the Venetian ambassador and the Count and Fran are *my* guests." Giovanni looked hopeful, but any illusions of dining with the sultan were quickly quashed.

"No," Ibrahim sneered. "Only the three." Giovanni appeared miffed at the perceived diplomatic slight, but gave a quick bow, hiding the expression of elevated dudgeon covering his face.

"Thank you. We will be honored," Il Lupo accepted graciously. Ibrahim backed away. As he moved, the back of his caftan flared in a dramatic flourish. Then Ibrahim stopped abruptly and turned back, looking at Il Lupo with narrowed eyes.

"Do not think because we share a heritage that I can trust you," Ibrahim sneered, before turning to leave. Il Lupo knew exactly what he meant. They were both Venetians.

Il Lupo could not be certain but believed he had heard Ibrahim mutter the word, "*gaiours*," an offensive slur against the infidels who he obviously held in contempt. Il Lupo found his loathing of the infidel perplexing; he and Ibrahim not only shared a Venetian heritage, but before Ibrahim's conversion, Roman Catholicism as well. Il Lupo wondered at the irony of how such an intolerant man could have risen to become the Grand Vizier—the closest advisor— to a sultan widely acclaimed for his tolerance.

"Well, that was certainly a warm welcome," Il Lupo observed dryly. "Something is amiss here, but we must believe that the sultan knows best who to trust," Il Lupo said, turning to Fran and Kemal.

"Surely Ibrahim is sagacious, but I am unsure whether he is truly loyal. While he may be quite capable and skilled in statecraft, he requires tutoring in the art of diplomacy. It is my fervent hope, for the sake of Suleyman, that we do not find that Ibrahim is involved. The situation cannot bode well for him as it is; he could suffer grave consequences as a result of today's assassination attempt. No doubt, he will be reprimanded for failing to uncover the conspiracy and breaches of security. Hopefully there is nothing more nefarious here."

Blasphemous Brushstrokes

Despite the intrigue and chaos of the day, Fran and Il Lupo found time to luxuriate in baths scented with sandalwood and musk to wash away the residuum of the day, rest, and prepare for dinner with the sultan. As a gesture of gratitude, the sultan's guests had been invited into the inner sanctum of the palace, a place where few had ever been honored to join him. Fran and Il Lupo spoke little of the shocking and brutal circumstances of the day, including the unvarnished hatred in Qais' murderous attempt on Suleyman, choosing instead to dissect the events and arrive at their own conclusions. There would be time later to share their thoughts. They traveled quietly to the Topkapi Palace with janissary escorts, each in personal reflection until arriving at the gates of the palace, where they were once again greeted by Kemal.

"It is an extraordinary, in fact unprecedented, honor that you should both be asked to attend a private dinner with the sultan, but the fact that I too have been invited to this momentous occasion will live forever in my memory!" a beaming Kemal welcomed them. "I am filled with humility!"

"Despite our good fortune today, I am very troubled about today's events and anxious to learn your thoughts concerning the plot to kill the great Suleyman. This has caused the greatest alarm. We must discuss this soon, perhaps even this evening," Kemal shared as he led them to the private chambers where they would dine with the sultan.

They passed through a small forest of massive and ancient fig trees, some hollowed out from disease but still standing, sharing life sustaining roots intertwined with adjacent trees. Seeing Ibrahim just ahead and waiting, Kemal quickly shared more information.

"Ibrahim is most disturbed that infidels, who managed to smuggle in weapons to the ceremonies, would be rewarded by an invitation to dinner. Adding further insult to existing traditions, Suleyman has invited you into his private dining room and has asked his favorite concubine to be in attendance! Ibrahim is furious. The ill-tempered man is most indignant this evening. Be prepared."

"Perhaps it would be in Ibrahim's best interest to spend time in reflection that there are no protocols or policies unless Suleyman declares them so. It is not up to Ibrahim to pass judgment on the decisions of the emperor. He would be wise to remember who has elevated him to his exalted rank," Il Lupo responded philosophically.

Waiting to escort them to the intimate chambers of the royal family, Ibrahim watched as the guests approached. Predictably, there was no friendly greeting. He remained implacable, merely turning as he guided them to a door guarded by two heavily armed janissaries. Their long axes were crossed barring entrance. Ibrahim waved his arms impatiently, instructing them to open the heavy, brass doors.

Ibrahim broke his cold silence without apology for his brusque manner. "Follow me," spitting out his instruction through gritted teeth.

Il Lupo viewed Ibrahim as intransigent, completely unwilling to find any good in an infidel, particularly one in a position to influence Suleyman. Il Lupo's relationship with Suleyman was on the threshold of mutual confidence, respect, and perhaps friendship. They would be sharing the emperor's deepest concerns and thoughts to solve the mysteries that surrounded the assassination attempt—an attempt that Ibrahim had failed to identify and prevent. An alliance in pursuit of the truth would be formed between Il Lupo and Suleyman. Il Lupo was a potential provocateur who could endanger Ibrahim's influence, power, and authority in the royal court.

The three guests could not restrain their amazement at yet one more breathtaking spectacle hidden beyond the doors of Suleyman's private chambers. Despite the grandeur of portions of the Palace they had previously admired, this dining room was opulence beyond compare—a room of created floribunda. Ornamental and intricate mosaic inlays and paintings of fruits and flowers covered every surface. A stacking of splendidly elaborate crown moldings interspersed with the detailed mosaics lifted the eyes to the coffered heights where fig-leaves painted in gold leaf and flowers with jeweled centers dressed the ceiling between the coffers and beams. Standing to the side of the room was a magnificent fireplace reminiscent of a *mihrab,* slender and topped with a gold-encrusted onion-shaped dome, mimicking the minarets found on the astonishingly beautiful mosques of Istanbul. Supple, soft upholstered divans flanked the edges of the room, beckoning fortunate guests to sink into their sumptuous comfort. The intricate creativity that permeated the room was enhanced by artistic restraint, as though the artists understood instinctively and precisely when one more tile or jewel was unwarranted to convey their vision. The three stood in momentary, stunned, and awestruck silence.

The Sultan Suleyman studied them for a moment. He was pleased by the obvious admiration his guests found in his home. "You are pleased?" Suleyman queried rhetorically in the Latin he knew to be Il Lupo's native language and spoken during his audience at the diplomatic reception. Suleyman required no answer, knowing the response by the look on their faces.

"It is pure perfection. Astonishingly beautiful, Your Majesty," Il Lupo responded sincerely.

"Beautiful, I agree," Suleyman answered, "but not perfect. Let me show you," as he led Il Lupo and Fran to an intricate tile and gem mosaic.

"Look, what do you see?" Suleyman beckoned Il Lupo forward. "Surely you see the flaw, but perhaps your good manners prevent you from identifying it?"

"Yes, I admit I do see it. There is a piece missing." Il Lupo ran his fingers across the small, empty space. "Why? Did it fall off, and if so, why has it not been replaced?" Il Lupo asked, perplexed.

"Yes, there is an emerald missing from this flower. It did not fall off, nor was it stolen, and there is nothing to replace it. It was deliberately omitted by the artisan who created it."

Puzzled, Il Lupo asked, "But why? It is hardly noticeable—I would not have seen that it was missing until you pointed it out to us."

"It is out of respect for Allah. In our religion, we believe there is nothing that is perfect but that which is made by Allah," Suleyman explained. "In the making of any object, imperfection is essential to art. In a rug from Keysari for example, in the field of azure blue, you might find a white thread, put there deliberately by the weaver. It could easily be snipped out but it is necessary to remind us that we are incapable of creating perfection and to show Allah that we recognize it is only He who can do so."

"What a humbling thought. Beautiful. We could all do well to remember that while we attempt to achieve perfection. We are incapable of it." Suleyman was pleased with Il Lupo's answer.

"Yes and one must remember that perfection is the enemy of very good! Beauty does not require perfection. We will discuss other matters of religion perhaps later, but now, please be seated." He gestured to a low table in the middle of the room.

The table before them was just one more feast for the eyes. It was rosewood, inlaid with ivory and mother of pearl, with a motif of lavish gardens, people lounging, animals, and musicians. It was so finely crafted that even the tiniest of grapes depicted had depth and individual definition. Plush cushions provided seating.

"The table is a depiction of Paradise—an earthly imagining of how life will be when we are called," Suleyman explained as he watched his guests visually feast on yet one more of his possessions.

"As is the entire room, Your Majesty, the table is exquisite."

Roxelana was already seated. "Here, come sit here next to me," she patted the cushion next to her and beckoned Fran. "I'm taking care of you tonight. I will make sure you get the most savory food if you sit here—even if it means I must steal it from Suleyman!" she laughed.

Suleyman was seated across the table from Roxelana and motioned to Il Lupo to sit next to him, on his right. There were four armed janissaries in the room and two eunuchs, including Aziz, a formidable-looking, tall and heavily muscled African guard and Roxelana's most trusted eunuch.

"*Sevgilim*—my darling—you won't mind if I take a choice morsel from your plate to share with our guests, will you?" It was apparent she had complete control of the sultan, her lover. He smiled and shook his head.

"Of course, Roxelana, my *Hürrem*." He looked at her lovingly, reaching over to touch her hand.

Fran could not help but notice, thinking to herself, *"Ah, to be loved like that by a man."* The ingénue felt a covetous flush sweep through her body, captivated and enchanted at the display of outward affection. She quickly glanced at Kemal and found that he was staring at her with an expression on his face she was unable to read. She immediately looked away but wondered if he had seen the glow within her rise to warm her face.

"Now it is time to become better acquainted. I am intrigued at your prowess with your daggers and the sword—and Fran is, especially for one so young, remarkable in the art of swordsmanship. Words are inadequate to express my deep gratitude for your alertness and the swiftness with which the two of you and Kemal moved to save my life today." The expression on the face of Suleyman was serious, the sincerity in his voice obvious.

"We have much to talk about tonight. Before we begin however, I have a test…" his voice trailed off.

Fran and Il Lupo looked at one another, not quite understanding what the great Suleyman intended. They could not know Suleyman suspected, during the assassination attempt, that they understood and spoke fluent Ottoman Turkish. To confirm his suspicions, Suleyman had prearranged an experiment to verify his assumptions regarding their linguistic ability.

Suleyman nodded to Aziz. In Ottoman Turkish, he commanded, "It is time. Slit the Venetians' throats!"

Suleyman's suspicions were confirmed. Understanding the order completely and before the tall, well-muscled Aziz had even moved, Fran bolted from her seat, emitting a high-pitched curse. She knocked Aziz's legs out from under him and sent him sprawling. Aziz's massive size was no match for Fran's quickness and agility. In the next instant, she jumped on his chest, pinning his arms, with the full intent of administering a crushing blow to Aziz's windpipe.

Watching the mayhem unfold, Il Lupo, amused once again, calmly remained seated, drinking his tea and dabbing his lips with a napkin.

"Stop!" Il Lupo ordered Fran. Her fist froze in the air directly above Aziz's throat, poised and still ready to strike. "The sultan wanted to test your linguistic skills, not your martial arts skills. I think he has already seen a masterful demonstration of the latter this afternoon!"

A shocked Fran dismounted an even more stunned Aziz. Breathing heavily, Fran ran her fingers through her hair and shook her head. She could see that all in the room, with the exception of Aziz, were smiling at the melee they had just witnessed—and at her expense. She returned to her seat next to Roxelana with a slight harrumph to express her frustration while a recovering Aziz managed to get up, attempting to regain his composure along with some dignity.

"It appears, Your Highness, that we now know each other a little better," Il Lupo turned to the sultan, speaking in fluent Ottoman Turkish. "Our lives are always in your hands." Suleyman nodded his approval.

Looking at a still flustered Fran, Il Lupo explained, "The emperor had no intention of having Venetians for dinner. He could have us executed without ruining his meal." He smiled at her. Miffed and resenting that she had been the brunt of a joke, an impetuous Fran sat in stony silence, grinding her teeth. After the earlier events of the day, she thought this was hardly the time for a test in the form of a potentially deadly practical joke.

Suleyman turned to Il Lupo continuing to speak in his native tongue rather than Il Lupo's Latin. "Now that I know you understand, it would be best that we speak in my language. Tell us how you have come to learn it."

"Of course," Il Lupo responded affirmatively to his request. "It would be best for everyone to converse as you have suggested. As to your query, when we received your request for assistance, we immediately called upon tutors and immersed ourselves in study of your language and customs before coming. Your language is derived primarily from Persian and Arabic. Fran and I both have reasonable fluency in Arabic and so it was with the Persian we had a little more difficulty. We would have come unprepared had we not done so, even though you are a renowned linguist and fluent in Latin yourself, Your Majesty. To best serve you, it was essential to increase our understanding of Ottoman society and culture. Your language is enriched with nuance. Meaning and intent are often dependent on voice inflections and facial expressions. Even the raising of an eyebrow can change the meaning of a word. Subtle differences in the tone and modulation of the voice may convert words that would be acceptable speech in polite company into insults or slurs. I tread carefully and hope you will forgive and correct should any such ignorance of these subtleties arise. I also much prefer the speaking of your language to the writing of it because of the complexities of your diacritics."

"Yes, the diacritics are complex and sometimes puzzling when studying the language. However, you appear to believe, as do I, that it is the responsibility of the scholar to be well versed, if not fluent, in many languages?"

"Your Majesty, fluency is important if for no other reason than to understand the customs, traditions, and thinking of those of other countries and cultures. Since few translations exist among even the great theses and manuscripts of our time, as well as the great works of the past, it is incumbent upon us to study languages if we wish to truly understand and perfect our world. Yes, I agree, Your Majesty."

"Your reputation has preceded you. As you have proven today, it is well- earned, as you are not just a warrior but a scholar as well. I have of course also heard of your talents solving mysteries and that is why you have been called here. Allah works in mysterious ways, does He not? How providential it has been that you arrived when you did. Ah, and now I am equally impressed with your wisdom.

"You of course realized that the eunuch Aziz had been instructed beforehand not to hurt you," Suleyman explained, offering his reassurance that he had not intended harm.

"And now before us we have the bruised egos of Aziz—who was nearly killed by the child —and Fran, who believes this has been some sort of bizarre practical joke. Wisdom will come and Aziz will recover his dignity. He is usually formidable and quick on his feet, but since he did not believe there was any threat to him, he moved more like a lazy house cat than a tiger. Had he been instructed differently, there may well have been an altogether different outcome," Suleyman shared candidly.

"I can agree that it has indeed been providential that we were here today. The designs of the Almighty are often difficult to discern. I must, however, and in all candor and respect disagree with Your Majesty regarding your language 'test'. I will tell you that out of all the hundreds of students we have trained in our academy, I have never yet met one more expert than Fran. I have not yet met the man who could best Fran in a fight. Had I not intervened, Aziz would be dead."

Il Lupo continued in his assessment. "As for Fran's actions, there is a brashness and impetuousness in youth. Just as we have studied to understand the nuances of your language, Fran, while a master of the martial arts, is only just learning to let the head control the instincts in certain circumstances. We can often not control what we feel, only what we do in reaction to our thoughts and emotions. This is not just part of mastering the martial arts and diplomacy, but necessary for mastering life. This will come because the intellectual and emotional capacity is there. There is work for all of us in this respect, not just Fran. Nevertheless, I am pleased with Fran's remarkable skills and accomplishments."

"That Fran is undefeatable sounds like a challenge I would ordinarily accept. But based on his feats today, outnumbered by seasoned and trained janissaries, yet emerging the victor—I will allow that challenge to stand. I will not be the one to dispute his prowess!

"Now that we have that out of the way, let me ask you—and I ask for honesty—what do they think of me in Venice?"

Il Lupo paused. He wanted to be honest and diplomatic; relations between the city- state of Venice and the Ottomans had not always been good.

"We are fortunate, Your Highness, to be living in a time where peace and respect exists between us. As Venetians, we understand that this is in substantial part due to your wisdom and beneficence. Venetians believe that you are the wisest of the Ottoman emperors. After all, you are known as *Kanuni*, 'the lawgiver.' We know too, that you are a scholar and a fierce warrior, which you have again proven today as we fought side-by-side. We know of your successful campaigns and exploits throughout Europe in Belgrade, Rhodes, Mohacs and even recently, the Guns—the great German campaign." Il Lupo answered directly, not mentioning the failed siege of Vienna. "Venetians believe, Your Highness, that you honor your namesake, Solomon."

"This is most gratifying to hear. You are proving yourself to be a true diplomat. I have attempted to be fair. I am proud of the unique multireligious, multiethnic, and multicultural empire over which I preside. Ottoman wealth and power flows from that tolerance and diversity. In Istanbul, for example, I allow diversity of religions and opinions, for therein resides certain contentment for my subjects. This is not a theocracy. Diversity of thought and creed thrives and keeps us prosperous and contented. Can you imagine the tumult of the people and disruption of trade if I were to demand every citizen of Istanbul convert to Islam? While I have very devout personal beliefs, I believe it is best when one is allowed to follow their conscience and true self. We gain in knowledge from those with whom we disagree. If we surround ourselves only with those who share our opinions, where is the growth? Where is the challenge intellectually? I demand the best from my subjects in service to the empire regardless of their diverse beliefs and backgrounds. We have forged the greatest fighting force in the world out of diversity.

"For example, under Bayezid II, the son of Mehmed Fatih, the conqueror who seized Konstantiniyye in 1453, the Sephardic Jews who were exiled from Spain following the Catholic Reconquest in 1492, were given refuge by the Ottomans. This is the tolerance that is expected and shall continue as long as I am the emperor. It is a belief that I shall pass to my sons.

"My religion asks that I conquer and convert, but I have some disagreement with that. While I am dedicated to my faith personally, I am also the sultan of millions. I am not a firm believer in orthodoxy, per se. Nor am I believer in inquisitions such as the Spanish prefer to enforce perceived religious 'correctness' and orthodoxy, dependent of course on those secularly defining it at the time. It is my fervent hope that all within my empire will follow Islam, but I believe it is better to seduce them with the beautiful strength of our message than convert them by force. If by force, you cannot know what truly lies within their hearts and minds; if by choice, they will follow. This is the best way." Suleyman's voice had a commanding resonance, adding further gravitas to his words.

"Let me provide you with another example. We waged war on Rhodes nine years ago because of their persistent provocations in the Levant. I invaded with 100,000 troops and 400 ships. We established complete control. I did not force conversion of the populace to Islam. I allowed the Christian Knights Hospitallers twelve days to leave— to gather all that was important to them—their icons and relics— anything they valued. Further, I allowed three years for islanders or infidels to leave without harassment. I promised no desecration of their churches. Those who chose to remain under Ottoman rule, and convert to the Islamic faith, were rewarded with no payment of taxes for five years. As I have stated, my conviction is that forcing one's belief is not the best way to convert, a conviction for which I am often greatly criticized. It may also be a principle for which I may be required to atone when my time comes in paradise. It is my hope that I shall meet with Allah Al-Ghafur—Allah, the Much-Forgiving, who will mercifully understand," Suleyman reflected, using one of the Ninety Nine Names.

"Like the varied hues of an artistic masterwork, each person I appoint offers his unique, vivid, intellectual palate of experiences, creating a unified, harmonious whole far more beautiful, rich, and dominant than the sum of its discrete parts. A perfect example of this is our illustrious and brilliant court architect, Sinan, who is a Christian. Without his contributions, the harmonious whole would not be as vivid and vibrant."

"One more reason why you are revered in the West," Il Lupo was moved by Suleyman's sincerity. Suleyman smiled and nodded, accepting Il Lupo's compliment. "So long as we focus on and emphasize the differences in our thinking rather than finding the commonality, there will be no end to strife and wars."

Suleyman turned to Francesca. "And you, Fran—how do you find the city?"

"Your Highness," Fran began, "I have been here thirty six hours. In that time, I have defended myself from thieves, helped saved your life, and been attacked by Aziz. Where is the world-renowned hospitality of Islam?" Fran was defiant, and even in the face of such power, if her hands were not throwing daggers, her eyes were. She felt she appeared young and foolish in the eyes of those seated at the table. Her youth and inexperience in the subtleties of diplomacy had been exposed, and she was intent on defending her honor and her dignity. In so doing, she also hoped to enhance what she worried might be a somewhat diminished opinion of her in the eyes of Kemal.

"Fran!" Il Lupo admonished her for her unabashed response.

"No. Fran is correct. The words are spoken freely with the honesty of youth. There is integrity and character here," Suleyman smiled, his graciousness at Fran's audacity calmed the room.

"Now, I will attempt to change your opinion and offer you the antidote to such an unfortunate welcome. Now! Ottoman hospitality!"

Suleyman clapped his hands and the doors opened. Servants holding overflowing trays of food flooded ceremoniously into the room. Musicians took their cue and began playing. The music was exotic, reminding Fran of the music earlier in the day, reminiscent variations on the individual monophonic calls to prayer five times each day. She watched as a musician nimbly plucked at the strings of the baglama.

"It is not the usual custom for my favored concubine to dine with dignitaries. However, it was impossible for me to refuse her request. She was insistent on helping entertain and welcome those who saved my life. How could I deny her? It seems a fair request." Suleyman looked across the table at Roxelana. Her head was tilted slightly downward with her eyes peering up at him in a most flirtatious gaze. He was clearly dazzled.

"*How romantic!*" Fran thought, calming down, allowing herself to once again muse over the transparent and passionate romance between the sultan and his Titian-haired beauty.

The table set before them was a cornucopia of abundance, a sumptuous feast for the senses: savory pies filled with chicken and grapes in a clarified butter sauce; roast lamb with mint; and leavened and unleavened breads and pilaf. Fruits of all shapes and flavored yogurts, in small compotes and large, were interspersed between the courses offered on heavily laden platters. Sauces in embossed gold gravy boats, sweet pickles, and olives were served on small trays in front of each of those dining as well as yogurt. Chutney in fig, mango, and peach varieties were set onto the table in gold and silver compotes with tiny spoons. Beverages of lemonade and exotically flavored teas were offered, as well as hot steaming coffee, served from an elaborate samovar-a gift earlier that day from Gregor Zabatny. The place settings were each slightly different, but shared a theme of gold charger plates topped by silver and copper-etched dinner plates. Suleyman boasted of his recent acquisition of cutlery—two pronged forks, spoons, and knives—all with jade handles with arabesque designs in gold and silver inlays, sanded and polished smooth to the touch.

The conversation was lively during the dinner and it was apparent that there was a growing mutual respect developing between Suleyman and Il Lupo. The genial atmosphere was conducive to more cheerful and personal conversation without the formalities and structure of a diplomatic dinner.

It was also becoming apparent to Roxelana that the person sitting next to her was *not* a boy. Just as Fran, she was intuitive and trusted her instincts. Roxelana noted that Fran had lost control of her normally well-modulated alto voice during her altercation with Aziz. Her shrieked curse was quite within the range of a mezzo soprano. This, the perceptive Roxelana thought, was not the cracking voice of a young boy, but that of a young woman, recognizing the feminine lilt of her voice.

She quietly chuckled to herself, pleased with her discovery, and wondered if any of the men, usually much less attuned to such things, would have also noticed. She could barely contain her delight. Her playful nature was anxious for an opportunity to let Fran know she had been found out and to use this revelation to her advantage.

"Your Highness," Il Lupo looked at Suleyman. "I have one more gift for you. This one, I was unable to present during our reception today. May I ask that it be retrieved?"

"Another gift? I am delighted. I have deduced that since you were unable to smuggle it through the inspection at today's ceremony or tonight, it must be a large weapon. A sword, perhaps?" Suleyman posited, enjoying his brilliant deduction.

"You are indeed correct, Your Highness." Il Lupo smiled. "May it be brought in?"

"Of course!" Suleyman clapped his hands sharply. "Bring me the gift!" he commanded. Aziz briefly left the room and returned, handing the sword directly to Suleyman and not to Il Lupo. "Merely a precaution. Aziz will not feel comfortable with this in your hands."

"My gifts earlier were for the scholar and seeker of knowledge. This gift is for the warrior whose skills were very much on display today," Il Lupo offered, watching as Suleyman marveled at the craftmanship and beauty of the rapier he held in his hands. The hilt, emblazoned with the coat of arms of Venice, was crafted from exquisite cloisonné, and embedded with tiny diamonds. Its blade, forged of the finest, highly polished Toledo steel, was inscribed with the sultan's titles, including "The Magnificent" and "The Lawgiver" on one side and on the other, his monogram.

"It is indeed a marvel," Suleyman offered, impressed with the beauty of its craftmanship and feeling its perfectly balanced weight in his hands.

"I am certain that your personal armory must be filled with blades from the entire world. We have all seen the swordsmanship displayed by you and Fran today and your illustrious school has a justified worldwide reputation." Suleyman continued, "I thank you for the generosity of all the gifts you have presented to me this day. I will find great delight in them for many years to come and will reflect on remembrances of this historic day—a day my life was saved—each time I look at them or hold them in my hands."

"Thank you for your generous words, Your Highness. We are pleased that you like your gift. It is a double-edged rapier and crafted to my precise specifications by the finest Venetian armorers," Il Lupo continued.

"Fran and I will also never forget the events of this day. We feel privileged beyond words for your hospitality and are only grateful that fortuitously we were present and able to help thwart the attack." Il Lupo put his hand to his chest in a display of respect. Fran, taking her father's lead, nodded her head deeply and humbly to the great sultan.

Suleyman in return crossed his arm to his chest in the Islamic sign of brotherhood and respect. "Your visit, as I have said, has been providential for me. Praise to Allah that you were here on this day. And now, I have a few gifts for you and your Doge in Venice. The gifts to you are given in well-deserved gratitude, and the gifts to the Doge out of respect for his high office and our alliance. There is a difference. One I give to a new friend. The other to a Doge." Aziz again brought a cloth- covered tray and set it down next to Suleyman.

"First, for *His Serenity,* Andrea Gritti." Suleyman handed Il Lupo a copy of the Koran, its cover spectacular in ornamentation and its pages edged in gold. Il Lupo received the book and opened it, admiring the exquisite calligraphy of the Arabic script. It was truly stunning.

"The Doge is also known to be a scholar, as is your majesty, and has an extensive library in the palace in St. Mark's Square. The Ottomans are known for the flawless beauty of their art. I can assure you he will be overcome by the magnificence of your gift. I thank you on his behalf." Il Lupo ran his hand across the pages that felt like silk even beneath his calloused fingertips.

"It is true, Il Lupo, that the Ottomans excel in the arts. What is not true is that the art is flawless. As I have told you, nothing is perfect but that which is created by Allah. So, once again, there are deliberate mistakes or flaws hidden within each of the beautiful pages. We must constantly be reminded to consciously avoid attempts at creating perfection, with the exception of striving for it perfection in our souls. The way we live. The way we treat one another. Perhaps we might even convince the infidel Christian that you are, or the Doge, that there is value in our strivings." Suleyman was serious.

"Yes, I understand and am respectful of your beliefs, Your Highness," Il Lupo responded carefully. "As you know, it is the Christian ethic to be more 'Christ-like,' and we are called to act with kindness and treat the least among us as we, ourselves, would wish to be treated."

"Oh, we Muslims have great respect for the Christians. We share many common beliefs—did you know that we too, believe in angels?" Suleyman continued, striving to find common ground in their religions.

"And if you have the opportunity, you must visit the *Hagia Sophia*, a most revered mosque. It was built by the Christian Emperor, Justinian, when this city was named Constantinople. It is here where Christianity became the official religion of the Roman Empire under Constantine. Justinian's *Hagia Sophia* is covered in mosaics of your great prophets, Jesus the Christ, and John the Baptist. When it was converted to a mosque, those images were never destroyed out of respect for Christians and their beliefs. Islam does not permit the making of images or icons—idolatry is forbidden—of the Prophet Muhammad or of Allah as an artist might perceive Him to be, but we have respected our religious differences and allowed the images created by Christians to remain. It is our obligation to honor our histories. I will add that it is still my hope that we can convince you heathen Venetians that Muhammad is the true Prophet of the one

God we both worship. And, we can agree that we both believe in one God—Allah—spoken only by a different name," Suleyman mused.

"Yes, I understand," Il Lupo acknowledged. "We are grateful for that respect." Il Lupo believed that Suleyman possessed an impressive equanimity. He felt a growing comity between them. Suleyman was a genuinely sincere man, Il Lupo deduced. When he smiled, his face warmed, with the smile radiating from his eyes.

"Now," Suleyman said, smiling at Il Lupo and turning to Fran. "Gifts for my new friends and protectors." He reached down to the tray at his side.

"For each of you," he said offering each of them miniature caskets, boxes made with silver and gold gilt and inlaid with ivory carvings and jade, their closures made with delicate, filigreed brass. Fran and Il Lupo opened their boxes together and both uttered a small gasp at their contents. Each contained dozens of loose, precious gems—emeralds, rubies, sapphires, and diamonds. Each glittered when removed, put to the light and admired individually.

Astonished at the preciousness of the gifts, Il Lupo shook his head in disbelief, a deep sense of humility flooding over him. Nearly stammering, he caught himself. "Your highness, I...I..., these are truly wonderful and extravagant... we feel unworthy."

"There are not enough gems in the world that could repay what you have given me today and that is my life," Suleyman responded.

"However, that is not all." Again he reached to the tray, bringing forth three daggers, each identical. Encased in embossed gold sheaths with emerald cabochons on the tip of the handle, they were very similar to the sultan's dagger kept in his sash, but with smaller emeralds and less elaborate, incised etching of the metal.

"I offer one to you, Il Lupo, one to you, Fran, and one to my faithful and devoted Kemal."

Kemal, who had been silent throughout the evening, was astounded. "Your Highness! You have already been so gracious and good to me. This gift is far too valuable for a humble servant. Surely for their actions, Vincenzo Lupo and Fran are most deserving. But I need nothing more than your continued health and happiness as my reward."

"Kemal," Suleyman responded to Kemal's gratitude. "Today you have learned one of the most difficult lessons of life. It is also a lesson you may encounter many times before closing your eyes for the final time. Today, you learned about betrayal and the shocking and devastating impact it has on those betrayed, by those whom you have trusted. Qais betrayed us, and the entire empire. It is a painful lesson and we are to learn caution from it. Betrayal should not make one cynical, rather careful, drawing knowledge and wisdom regarding when, and upon whom, to bestow trust.

"Is it not true, Count Lupo? Betrayal is written of in Dante's *Inferno*. He assigns the betrayers to the ninth circle of Hell—the most tortured of all the circles. Those who commit the betrayals are doomed to eternal pain—a place where the Judases of the world belong.

"Before we leave the subject of gifts, I have something I wish to tell you. As you know, we are plagued with fanatical clerics and there is deep unrest between the Shi'a and the Sunni. I am the leader of all Islam. Therefore, there are obligations I have to ensure that nothing that would be found to contain blasphemies or heretical insinuations come to our library." Suleyman appeared quite serious. "You surely realize this.

"Your gifts are magnificent, Vincenzo—may I call you Vincenzo—but of course I must first ensure that these beautiful books pass muster with our cleric and *Hodja* art critics." Suleyman smiled, but feigned seriousness.

"Finding the ungodly and impure in art and new convention is a robust enterprise among the rabid cleric and Hodja zealots. Keeps them in *yirmiliks* and popular with their devout and unquestioning flock. To them, Vincenzo, apostasy lurks in each new style. It is imperative that the books be inspected for heresy so as not to be an affront to Islam. Titillating temptations! Blasphemous brushstrokes!" Suleyman spoke sardonically.

"One heretical image or word, whisperings begin! Fingers point. Admirers of the newly discerned satanic temptation unwittingly risk being mired in sin, barred from the gates of Paradise, and subjected eternally to suffering the torments of the damned! We must all pray to Allah that we be spared!" Suleyman's audience was mesmerized by his satirical monologue. His distaste for preachers of dogma and radicalized militants could not be overstated.

Il Lupo watched those at the table, eager to absorb the words and philosophy of the esteemed lawgiver. In particular he eyed Ibrahim, who remained stone-faced, his jaw noticeably tightened, their muscles twitching, as Suleyman spoke. It was apparent that Ibrahim did not agree with the sultan on these subjects, but at least had the momentary wisdom to remain stoically silent and mired in disgust for anything even remotely blasphemous. Perhaps he was even engaged in his own hunt for the heretical.

"We live in a time where turmoil is rife within the Ottoman Empire, the Holy Roman Empire, throughout the Continent and in England. It is a place and time for zealots to seize on the weaknesses and imaginings of the ignorant, exploiting their fears to their benefit. It is a dangerous time, which requires caution. Change must never result from fear or ignorance. The masses need to be educated so that they are equipped to understand and reject militant, intolerant thought. This is especially true when religion is usurped by zealotry. Intolerance and zealotry are a poisonous concoction too often forced down the throats of the feckless and uninformed for nefarious purpose or self-aggrandizement, leading to internal chaos, if not war. Those who stand against such militants are labeled impure and are targeted with malicious intent as heretics. Intolerance is the enemy of the advancement of knowledge and all that is good," Suleyman concluded. The room remained quiet for a few moments.

"Indeed, Your Majesty," Il Lupo broke the silence. "These issues are great questions of our time and deserve the attention of those who can facilitate access to knowledge for all. The words of God should not be considered so cabalistic in content that the common man be denied the right to read them for himself. Words of God should not be deemed so esoteric and lofty as to be reserved only for high priests to construe and often misinterpret to further their own goals. Even as a Roman Catholic, I can see that there is good in educating the populace to read the word of God themselves, as Luther demands. And in the doing, knowledge obtained creates opportunity for a more personal relationship with the Almighty."

Suleyman sat calmly and smiled at Il Lupo, feeling him to be a kindred spirit and worthy of friendship. "You and I will have much to talk about as opportunity provides. Thank you, Vincenzo."

Revelation

Turning his attention to the assassination attempt, Suleyman continued, "Ibrahim has already begun an investigation into the extent of the insurrection among the janissaries. It is only by the grace of Allah—peace be upon Him—that Il Lupo and Fran were at the reception and accompanied by Kemal."

Roxelana interjected. "You saved his life. The leader of the Ottoman Empire. We are forever appreciative and grateful. You, Vincenzo, and your daughter have saved the sultan's life and I am forever in your debt." Just as quickly as Roxelana realized her unintentional mistake of revealing Francesca's sex, all the men at the table registered simultaneous shock. All heads whiplashed toward a now very red-faced Francesca, who sat mortified.

Ibrahim and Suleyman appeared particularly unsettled.

"Is this true?" Suleyman asked sternly. Without waiting for a response, he continued, "I can see by the color of your face that it is true." Suleyman looked at Roxelana and this seemed to calm him, making him less discomfited. Aziz was initially wide-eyed, with his mouth agape, but quickly regained his composure, raising his eyebrows and nodding his head as if with a certain respect. After all, he was an accomplished warrior and he had been humiliatingly defeated by a woman—a young girl at that.

Kemal's reaction was one of relief. While surprised by the inopportune outing of her gender, the revelation was not surprising to him, as it was to Suleyman and Ibrahim. He emitted an almost audible sigh of relief; Francesca had dominated his imagination and daydreams since the day before, almost at their first meeting. "*Praise be to Allah! I knew it! It had to be!*" he thought to himself. "*That this beautiful woman could have actually been a boy would be impossible! I knew it!"* He was elated and had to restrain himself, suppressing his desire to jump up from the table and rejoice. Kemal beamed at Francesca and he could see that his broad smile unnerved her more than the revelation that she was female. She looked at him briefly and just as quickly cast her beautiful blue eyes downward.

"More deceptions! Regardless of the outcome, this deception should not go unpunished!" Ibrahim fumed, his scowling face grimacing in fury. "It is forbidden for a woman to dress as a man and to use that deception to gain access to the sultan is unpardonable. Even your own religion forbids it! Joan of Arc was burned not for her zealotry and preachings, but for dressing like a man." Ibrahim remained predictably obdurate. His imperious demeanor was irritating to Vincenzo and unacceptable to Roxelana.

Roxelana bristled and unable to contain her anger any longer, jumped to Francesca's defense, lashing out at Ibrahim.

"It is *you* who should be punished, Ibrahim! Janissaries under your command almost assassinated the emperor. This would not have happened had Kemal not been carrying out other duties for the emperor. *You* were the one in charge. *You* are the one who should be held accountable. If not for the action of the so-called 'deceivers' this morning, the mutiny would have succeeded. I think we should look no further than *you* to find our villain, Ibrahim!" Roxelana accused, her renowned fiery temper and passionate protection of her sultan prominently on display.

Roxelana moved slightly closer to Suleyman, reaching her hand out across the table toward his. "Man or woman, you owe not just Vincenzo, but this remarkable young woman your life also, my love. I realized immediately after she defended herself against Aziz's attack that she was *not a boy!* Quite frankly, I am astonished that none of you men realized this 'boy' was an alluring young woman!"

Kemal made no comment. He had no clear proof that Fran was indeed, a girl. He was slightly vexed having not been the one to reveal his suspicions to Francesca personally and in private. He must tell her at some point that he had never been completely fooled.

"During our conversations this evening, I have been thinking and believe that I have conceived a plan to turn this to our advantage," Roxelana pleaded.

Addressing Kemal, Vincenzo, and Francesca, she continued. "Very few know that there has also been a recent attempt on my life. It is well- known that the emperor has shown favor to me, his concubine, and it has angered many. I have few allies. There are many reports of strange events in the Harem. On the night of the attempt on my life, I was called unexpectedly to Suleyman's chambers. When I returned, the eunuch guarding my rooms was found strangled with a bowstring. Had I been in the rooms as was normal, no doubt I would have been a victim also."

Roxelana paused, her expression revealing that her predicament within the Harem caused her pain. "With all these unsettling events, I ask permission, my dearest, my master, that Fran—uh, it is rather, *Francesca*, I believe—stay in my chambers with me for my protection, disguised as a new concubine. I will feel much safer knowing I have her at my side while the investigation continues and until answers are found. She could also be of great assistance in solving these mysteries. This is, of course, with the Count's permission and Francesca's acceptance of my proposal." She turned and placed her hand on Francesca's. Francesca nodded her acceptance, turning to hear the sultan's thoughts.

Suleyman was quiet, apparently giving the suggestion due consideration. He looked inquiringly at Il Lupo. "It is a clever plan, *Hürrem*. But then, why am I not surprised? You are always so creative in your solutions to problems. Vincenzo, would you permit us to borrow Francesca in this capacity for a few days? It would give not just Roxelana peace of mind, but me as well. I must keep my love safe too."

Il Lupo smiled wryly at Suleyman. "A few days as a Harem slave just might do wonders for her." There was laughter from all except Francesca who managed a faint smile acknowledging the amusement at her expense.

"Then it is settled. Aziz will make the necessary arrangements for you to be picked up in the morning from the home of the Venetian ambassador," Suleyman commanded, nodding to Aziz.

"Kemal, you are too wise to have not realized that Il Lupo's presence here has been no accident. He is not an official envoy of the Venetian Doge. He is here at my request and thankfully arrived in time to help crush this plot against me. I had called him here because there were stirrings and unsettling events within the walls of the palace. I did not tell you until I was sure I could trust the Count. I am now sure and can inform you that you should, and must trust him as well. You will work together with him and Francesca to determine the depth of the conspiracy and solve other palace intrigues. Do you understand?"

"Of course, Your Majesty. I willingly do whatever is necessary to thwart any plots against you or your family. I confess I had my suspicions about the authenticity of his role as an envoy. He appeared far too shrewd and educated to have been a mere envoy. Praise Allah he is here."

"Yes, and on these matters of the investigation, we will dispense with customary formalities, and the Count will have authority to conduct inquiries unfettered—wherever he is led. You are doing all at my behest. This is my command. Agreed?"

Each at the table responded with an audible, "Yes, Your Majesty."

"It has been a most eventful day. It is late. We have much to attend to tomorrow. Thank you for gracing our table, but most of all, for saving my life."

Suleyman rose from the table. "We will discuss these matters further tomorrow, Ibrahim. You may go and continue your own investigation."

Intending also to take their leave, Il Lupo and the remaining guests began to follow the measured and calculating Ibrahim from the room, a man whose loyalty, Il Lupo felt, was questionable. As they passed Suleyman, he pulled Il Lupo aside. "Please stay."

Il Lupo stepped back as the others left the room. "I will join you later," he shared with Kemal and Francesca as they moved toward the ornamented double doors.

As the guests departed, Suleyman turned to Il Lupo. "Let me get straight to the point. I wish to enlist your help in solving another mystery—not just that of the events of today. I had asked you to come here to help resolve concerns I have had and determine their causes and possible relationships. Obviously, we could not have known of today's events, but the latest intrigues could all be interrelated. Questions multiply. I fear I live amongst venomous ophidians, and we must find and burn their nests and extract their poisons. We must uncover the answers, wherever the search takes us."

"I am honored," Il Lupo responded. "I will do all I can to assist, but it will require a great deal of trust between us. You have brought me here to be suspicious of all potentially involved until the mysteries and puzzles are solved. Are you able to place me in a position of such trust?"

"As I have stated, you are to proceed unfettered. It is my instinct that I can trust you, just as I have instructed Kemal to trust and work with you. There is no question that well-placed and high-ranking officials within the palace must be complicit. Everyone has a potential motive. You have not had the time or the opportunity to develop such a motive yourself. Corruption usually takes time, not just inclination. I believed you to be above corruption when I sent for you, and am more convinced of it now." Suleyman was known for acting on instincts and being a good judge of character, which had served him well.

"You must not forget, Your Majesty, that I am Venetian and Venetians have made corruption an art form," Il Lupo laughed. Suleyman patted him on the shoulder. He had decided he liked this Venetian and, even more, he trusted him.

"I offer just one more concern. Ibrahim has been my friend since childhood—we were schooled together and as I rose, so did he. He is an unpleasant man, but I choose to believe he is loyal and serves only my best interests and those of the empire. I hope I am not wrong. This investigation may take you in many directions. I urge you not to overlook possibilities that the Grand Vizier has somehow been involved. I am not offended that the investigation may head in his direction. So be it. It is the truth I seek however painful the costs may be. If exculpatory evidence is found to vindicate him, I will be most relieved, even though he has failed in his responsibility to protect me. That, however, is an entirely different matter, which will be dealt with separately and privately. Go where you must to find the answers, Vincenzo."

"Rest assured that I will be relentless in the pursuit of truth," Il Lupo concurred.

"Yes, Vincenzo, I believe this of you. I feel you are a man of honor and rectitude. I am grateful for that and that you are here. Thank you."

"Yes, Your Majesty. I will do as you have instructed. The best judgment is patient and it waits until the facts have been uncovered and carefully scrutinized."

Suleyman nodded, extending his arm and leading Il Lupo to a door on the other side of the room. "Follow me."

Portentous Pricks

Traversing the Topkapi complex via a succession of dark, narrow hallways made accessible through elaborate doors heavily fortified with massive locks, Suleyman led Il Lupo to an underground passage. Wall-mounted torches with flames sustained by oil-filled cups provided illumination.

"The palace has been built over many years on top of the old Byzantine ruins. We are beneath the second courtyard. I am taking you to the morgue, which lies between the carriage gate and the Tower of Justice. There are tunnels and hidden passageways everywhere. Even I am unfamiliar with them all," Suleyman explained.

"Warning you in advance as we approach the morgue, there is an unmistakable stench of death. It will cling to the inside of your nostrils and your very person and is not easily washed away. You will know before we arrive that we are close. I must apologize, but it is necessary that you see for yourself what lies there."

Suleyman had not exaggerated the overwhelming fetor as they approached their destination. It was noxious and invasive, causing reflexive gags with each whiff of breath. Just before entering the morgue, Suleyman grabbed a cloth from a wooden vessel sitting on an entry table and handed it to Il Lupo. He took one as well and motioned for Il Lupo to tie the fabric around his nose and mouth. As he did, Il Lupo was relieved that the fragrance of the sandalwood-soaked kerchief considerably diminished the rank smell of death emanating from the room.

The morgue was large and unadorned. A series of luciferous transom windows lined the tops of the walls. Little air circulated and particles of dust floated freely in the air, illuminated in the moon light. The height of the windows prevented potential onlookers from observing the physicians at work. There were twelve slabs available to receive cadavers for examination and preparation for burial. Four were occupied: one with the body of Qais, one with the corpse of Roxelana's eunuch guard who had been killed with the bowstring. Two other slabs supported the mutilated bodies of unidentified janissaries.

Ordinarily, no anatomical procedures or autopsies were performed on the corpses. Absent suspicious circumstances surrounding their deaths, deceased members of the court were simply prepared for burial. Such preparations included the washing of the bodies three times and then wrapping them in clean white cloths with reverence and efficiency. For the dead lying here, there would be no clean cloths and basins of water to wash and enshroud the corpses, at least not until their bodies had undergone careful examination for clues regarding the causes of death.

The clues regarding the death of Roxelana's eunuch guard were evident – strangulation with an assassin's bowstring. The stricture marks on his neck remained visible and concrete proof of the cause and manner of death. Qais' cleaved skull from the blow of the scimitar was proof of the cause of his demise. Uncertainty surrounded the mutilated cadavers of the two janissaries found in the cistern beneath the Harem and near the *Has Oda*.

"This is our most eminent court physician, Abdullah," Suleyman said, introducing Il Lupo to the wizened man who was closely examining the body of one of the mutilated janissaries. On the next slab was the similarly butchered body of his companion. Across from him lay the body of Qais, Kemal's lieutenant, who had taken the lethal blow delivered by Mehmed's scimitar. Qais' brains were exposed within the gaping wound, unwashed and thick with dried blood.

"Abdullah, this is my friend, Count Vincenzo Lupo. He is known for his skill as a swordsman and as a detective. I requested his assistance long before I knew of the conspiracies against my own life and that of Roxelana. His services were requested because of the unrest within the walls of the palace and I wanted to determine the source, or sources. His expertise at solving mysteries precedes him. He has my complete confidence and you may share with him what you share with me." Abdullah and Il Lupo nodded respectfully to one another.

"Also, this morning I spoke to Kemal and asked that he attempt to identify the bodies of the two janissaries. I have learned from him, before coming here this evening, that they were both Beyliks, members of my personal guard, recruited by Qais less than a year ago. Kemal identified the bodies as those of Kareem and Jamal. Kemal mentioned that he had disciplinary problems with them and at least eight others. He made recommendations to Qais for their punishment. It is possible Qais used the severity of the disciplinary actions, and possible leniency in their execution, as a tool to recruit them for his plots, whatever they may have been. Now, at least, we have identities of these two. What are your findings so far?" Suleyman queried Abdullah, wasting no time getting to the point of his visit.

"May I look before you give me your analysis?" Il Lupo asked respectfully, anxious to make his own observations before hearing from Abdullah.

"Of course, take a closer look." Abdullah nodded and stepped back from the body.

"A closer look is exactly what I need." Il Lupo moved to the slab, grateful for his sandalwood-soaked kerchief.

"A close look is indeed what is required," Abdullah stated, realizing that Il Lupo had likely already discerned what it had taken him hours of examination to conclude.

Il Lupo moved from Kareem's body to Jamal's, closely examining their necks and mouths. "Look closely at the *neck* in particular, wouldn't you say?" he said, turning his face to Abdullah.

"One would want us to believe that the mutilation of their bodies was cause for their deaths. That may not be the case, however."

"Excellent! You see them too? It is not the mutilation of the bodies, but the pinpricks in their necks!" Abdullah's expression revealed he was elated with Il Lupo's validation of his opinion.

"Yes. Without the slight swelling of the area, the marks might have gone unnoticed. The fact that they are even slightly swollen means that they may have been alive for a few minutes before a toxin could take effect," Il Lupo surmised.

"Look here on Qais. The blow to Qais' head was the obvious cause of his death. However, did you observe this tiny mark on his neck? It is not swollen and that is likely because he was killed within seconds after receiving the pinprick. There was little to no time for much swelling to occur," Il Lupo deduced.

Il Lupo walked around the tables as he continued the examination of the corpses. Suleyman watched and listened intently, without interruption.

"I have not yet had time to examine the body of Qais," Abdullah explained, "but I see that you are correct. There is an almost indiscernible pinprick on his neck as well. Very interesting." Abdullah bent his head down, closely examining and comparing the marks.

Il Lupo studied the wound, deep in thought. "Despite attempts to have us conclude Qais was killed by the blow to the head and the janissaries by mutilation, I believe they were all first poisoned and the poison was delivered by the same method. We do not yet know the *type* of poison. It is astonishingly fast-acting. Based on the pinpricks, I believe a dart would be the only likely source of introducing the poison. It worked very quickly once delivered directly into the bloodstream," Il Lupo continued.

"Correct!" Abdullah exclaimed, his head bobbing with excitement over his agreement. "All three with pinpricks and ancillary wounds inflicted later! In the case of Qais, he may not have been killed directly by the poison, but if Mehmed had not cleft his skull, he would have succumbed quickly. This will take a great deal of study to understand the nature and source of the poison and how it was introduced into their bodies. The reasons for the mutilation of the bodies of the other two janissaries must be determined. The poison alone would have done its work. The perceived need for deception certainly remains unknown, but I agree entirely with what you have deduced," Abdullah concluded.

"Why would not killing simply by the poison have been enough? Why was there need to mutilate bodies or cleave a skull nearly in half?" Abdullah wondered aloud.

Il Lupo weighed Abdullah's questions and conclusions affirming his own theories as he paced the room inculcating each detail. "The mutilation of the janissaries was only a secondary cause of their deaths, Abdullah. I think we are in complete agreement on that point. The pinpricks tell us that. I would like to know how long after they received these wounds their bodies were mutilated. The swelling of these janissaries does tell us something because their neck wounds are considerably more swollen than that of Qais. Yes, very importantly, we must determine whether the mutilations were an attempt to cover up the primary reason for their deaths and if so, the need for this deception."

Il Lupo sought further details from Abdullah. "Were there any other significant objects recovered with the bodies of the two janissaries?"

"No, just their weapons and—oh, yes, I almost forgot. One of them had this small metal shaft in his hand and this small jar of a pasty white compound in his sash. I do not know their purpose or significance but they are not directly related to the cause of their deaths." Abdullah handed Il Lupo the shaft and jar.

Il Lupo opened the jar, sniffed it, and then dabbed his finger to the inside of the lid. "What remains in the jar is almost completely dry and tastes like mortar," Il Lupo concluded, having put his finger with the compound on it to his tongue. "Indeed, it is worth noting."

Just as he was ready to close the jar, Il Lupo paused. "Look here," he observed, tilting the jar toward Suleyman and Abdullah. "There appears to be an imprint of a finger. Can you see that? If you notice, in the middle of the imprint there is an indentation, as though the fingertip of the person who used the compound was disfigured."

"Yes, yes! I see that! How interesting," Abdullah was animated.

Il Lupo moved toward the mutilated janissaries. "Yes! Just as I suspected! Look here at Kareem's right index finger." Il Lupo lifted the hand of the janissary to show Abdullah and Suleyman. "It has a deep scar across the center of the finger, one that appears to have been a deep cut from a clean blade. It healed well, but left its identifying mark. And," he continued, "if you look closely, you will see the remains of the white sealant under his fingernail."

"Astounding! Your perceptions are astounding!" Abdullah complimented.

"Yes, Vincenzo, you are indeed quite observant. Remarkable!" Suleyman marveled.

"Kareem undoubtedly used this compound in some way, but exactly what he used it for remains to be determined. The purpose of the shaft is also yet unclear. They could be important pieces of evidence to resolve the mystery of their deaths and why they were killed. Abdullah, please store both the compound and the shaft securely," he instructed, handing them back to him.

"There were no other objects collected from the bodies of the janissaries or from the area where they were found that could have caused such a wound. I believe, Your Majesty, as I believe Il Lupo concludes, that the slashing of the bodies and possibly the cleaving of Qais' skull were deliberate attempts to divert attention from discovering any other possible cause for their deaths."

Il Lupo continued, "Whoever is responsible for the introduction of the poison was not prescient enough to realize that your esteemed physician Abdullah, or even I, would be conducting detailed postmortem examinations of the bodies."

"Indeed that is true. One would presume with such obvious wounds, the means of death for each of the victims were evident. The perpetrators did not consider the possibility that you both would together dissect the details," Suleyman, who had been quietly observing, interjected.

"Il Lupo, you mentioned *darts*." The emperor queried, "Was that the weapon? How do you know a dart has caused these pinpricks? Is there another instrument that could have caused the same mark? Is there any way to recover the objects that caused them?"

"Thank you, Your Majesty. As for the darts, it is with great certainty that I know how the poison was delivered and what is responsible for the pinpricks on their necks. Prior to Mehmed's blow, Qais was shot with this." Il Lupo pulled a handkerchief from his pocket and unwrapped a long, narrow feathered dart with an exceptionally fine tip from his pocket. There were audible gasps of surprise from both Abdullah and Suleyman.

"I retrieved this from Qais' neck just after Mehmed's sword strike. Do not touch it directly," Il Lupo cautioned. "I have it wrapped in my handkerchief because, if what I suspect is true, any residual poison on the tip of the dart could still be lethal even if not introduced directly into the blood stream. Please use extreme caution for it may have toxins that are even poisonous to the touch or if ingested. I think we should now examine the neck wounds to see if this type of poisoned dart could have been used on all three of them."

The three men gathered around the bodies and compared the wounds and the size of the pinprick that would have been delivered by the dart held by Il Lupo. They conferred and agreed that not only was it possible that each of them had been struck with similar darts, but it was probable that each had died, or in the case of Qais, would have died from the deadly toxin that had been applied to the tip.

"This is remarkable!" Il Lupo exclaimed, excited that all wounds did, in fact, match the implement. "All shot with uncanny accuracy and all striking the jugular. Masterful timing and precision by the assailant. The poison was introduced directly into the bloodstream, and at least in the case of Qais, an expert shot from some distance. I very briefly observed movement of a ghost-like apparition immediately before and after Qais was killed; I believe the dart was shot from the screened mezzanine above the throne."

"This is an astonishing revelation. You are both concluding that the two janissaries found in the cistern died from poison darts and not from the other obvious wounds they suffered? And that Qais was struck by the dart to his neck from the balcony above the dais? This would mean that someone within the palace has access to the poison and the darts! This is as astounding as it is horrifying if all true!" Suleyman was incredulous.

"Yes, and a further observation," Il Lupo continued. "Of course, the janissaries may have died from their wounds, just as Qais did. However, it is the poison that killed them. We should also note that the slashes that the janissaries suffered were done with much finer blades than that of the scimitar used by Mehmed on Qais. The deep, but very thin entry wounds, and slicing and filleting of the skin confirm this. Something other than a scimitar and likely someone or something other than Mehmed killed the other two janissaries."

"Excellent observations," Abdullah congratulated. "You are absolutely right. As an expert on blades, you would know those used in the mutilation are of the most superior quality. Also far finer than any raptor's talons."

"Yes, here the mysteries intersect." Il Lupo continued his dissertation on blades.

"In fact, there are similarities between the fine cuts made by the shredding blades and the types of cuts that can be made by knives in the collections I have at the academy. We insist on the finest quality and many I own have been forged by highly skilled Italian and Spanish metallurgists and crafted using the unparalleled quality of Toledo steel."

"This is as interesting as it is concerning. And poisoned!" Suleyman stood perplexed as he held the handkerchief containing the dart. "What kind of poison was used? I have never known of a poison that worked so quickly and was delivered in such a manner."

"I am uncertain, Your Majesty," Abdullah offered. "In my time, I have examined the properties of potions and poisons concocted by herbalists and designed to be ingested. I have examined bodies that have died from the venom of an asp. I have seen the effects of nightshade and monkshood and all the poisons used for centuries, each manifesting its own distinctive and often peculiar characteristics and side effects. However, I have never before seen anything that has matched the speed and deadliness of this toxin. This must be a *new* poison, one never before encountered. The kinds of poisons that have been used that I know come from many places, including Africa, but none is as fast-acting as I believe this to be. There is no change in the coloration of the skin, frothing of the mouth, or bulging of the tongue or eyes—all side effects of the poisons we know are fast acting. However none so fast and deadly as this. This is most lethal in my experience. I must do further study and research."

"Where were the bodies discovered?" Il Lupo asked.

"They were found by Aziz in the cisterns beneath the Harem near the *Has Oda* late last night. There are many hidden places and passages that even I do not know. There are many locked doors in the palace, just as those we passed through today. Some that have been opened lead nowhere—just a stone wall—parts of the palace meant to be completed but left unfinished. Some have been installed for aesthetic purposes only, intended to conceal unfinished construction. There is such a door near Roxelana's rooms in the Harem," Suleyman explained.

"Apparently, Aziz heard noises emanating from beneath the Harem. He broke the lock and found a passageway that led him to the discovery of the bodies of the janissaries under the *Has* Oda. Not wishing to upset Roxelana, he sent word to Kemal who notified me immediately. I sent Aziz with others to recover the bodies, and Kemal identified them here. According to Abdullah, the bodies had already gone through particular stages of change that we know occur in the dead. He deduced they had been dead for at least twelve hours, but not a full day. They were murdered in one more passageway I did not know existed. Secrets hidden, even from me. It is very unsettling." Suleyman spoke as he paced the morgue in thought, his concern etched into the deepening lines on his face.

"May I visit this area with Aziz? Perhaps now that we know what we are dealing with, there may be more discoveries left behind that were not found when the scene was initially searched."

"Yes, it will be arranged." Suleyman turned to Abdullah, "Advise me immediately of the results of your research. Solving these murders and mysteries is of utmost urgency."

"Yes, Your Majesty. Of course." Abdullah bowed.

Il Lupo turned to Abdullah and bowed to the astute court physician before exiting the morgue with Suleyman.

"Your Majesty, you must rest assured the pieces, the fragments, will come together and provide meaningful explanations, even if devastating in their implications. Some of what we find may be distractions, but I will not be deterred in finding the answers for the issues that plague you. I am thankful and humbled by your confidence and trust."

"Yes, Vincenzo. My confidence and trust? That you have. Good hunting, my friend, good hunting."

Dolts and Dunces

There was a quiescent hush in the palace gardens as Kemal and Francesca sat beneath an ancient olive tree awaiting Il Lupo's return. The hectic daytime pace of the palace had subsided and there were only a few guards patrolling the grounds. Passing the massive tree hollowed out from disease, Francesca marveled that it had miraculously survived by inosculating itself with another tree. The leaves of the conjoined trees flickered in the fragrant evening breeze and she was grateful as it refreshingly cooled her warm body. The moon was not full, but once again the sky was filled with illuminating stars. Restful aromas of incense lingered in the early evening air.

"What a magnificent tree. Somehow I never have taken enough time to notice the majesty in nature but since coming here, I seem to have become more aware." Francesca walked around the tree, caressing its trunk with the palm of her hand as she moved, musing to herself, puzzled by her elevated sensitivity to nature's grace.

"It is indeed marvelous! Almost as though the trees are standing in an everlasting embrace, sustaining one another to the end," Kemal reflected. Francesca was stirred by his words as she considered the symbolism of the intertwined trees.

"I have heard that trees like this, those that have joined together, each sustaining the other, are called 'marriage' trees." Kemal looked at her directly, gauging her reaction.

Francesca flushed. "What a beautiful description. It is as though they are held in an eternal matrimonial embrace. Perfect!" She turned away from him briefly, wondering if he had deliberately guided the conversation to intimacy or if he was simply sharing what he knew. She was unsure which alternative she preferred.

Kemal quickly switched subjects, his instincts telling him to reign in his growing desire to get closer to her, physically and emotionally. He was however, quite keen to know Francesca as a woman and not a young boy.

"Your men's clothing had me fooled, *kucuk uzman*! I must confess though that there were moments when I just could not understand how a boy could be as attractive as you! Your clothes could not completely disguise the curves of your body and your femininity," Kemal said.

"Your disguises were clever. You obviously fooled many. I was almost certain you were in disguise when the pitch of your voice changed when you attacked Aziz. Now *that* was a sight to behold! Astonishing for a boy—but for a girl—a remarkable feat! Once again, I am stunned! Poor Aziz. It was one thing to be defeated by a boy, but a girl—oh, the humiliation! I know I saw respect in Aziz's eyes. How could anyone not be impressed with your martial arts skills?" Kemal continued almost as if talking to himself.

Francesca laughed freely, with relief, pleased that deception would no longer be required, particularly with Kemal. "Make no mistake, Kemal. Yes, I am a woman, but never underestimate me. I am a match for any man. I do believe poor Aziz was slightly humiliated, but he has thankfully recovered. I had wondered, even from the beginning, if you actually believed I was a boy. Our conversations last evening . . . surely I revealed too much. It becomes increasingly difficult to hide the woman I have grown to be. But I must tell you that the disguise has delivered me from the drivel of many dolts and dunces!" Francesca asserted, unable to suppress a slight giggle.

Kemal was taken aback by her last comment and felt slightly hurt. He turned his face away from Francesca.

"Kemal! Forgive me! I did not mean you at all!" Francesca immediately attempted to soothe what was taken personally, as an insult, by Kemal.

"It's just that I cannot abide the antics of most men I observe as they play suitor. So often in my father's academy, men have made their intentions clear and most of them, while quite exceptional in the martial arts, were idiots and morons. Not the kind that would ever be of interest to me. Most men only want to win a woman's heart, or whatever else they may be interested in. I want a man to win my brain first, and *then* my heart. A man who will share my passions. The one who can win my mind will find that my heart will easily follow. As for the disguises, they have allowed me to be with my father. It has made life easier for me to be with him. I have found some comfort in my disguises," Francesca continued in an attempt to ease the discomfort inflicted by her unintended insult.

"You believe me, don't you, that I never intended that remark to be critical of you?"

Kemal, relieved and satisfied that she had intended no offense, turned to her. "Thank you, Francesca. Yes, I believe you! I can see that you are no ordinary woman and would settle for no ordinary man. As for your father, you obviously have enormous respect and love for him. The devoted relationship between the two of you is wonderful to behold, to be sure." Kemal's sincerity was apparent.

"*Mia Padre*," she murmured affectionately. "Yes, I love him very much, and while I live for his warm embraces of assurance and love, in some ways it would be easier if I weren't with him all the time. There are times when I do not know who feels more obligated to whom; I to my father or my father to me. We each want to care for the other and have been deeply close and loyal to one another ever since I was a child—ever since my mother's death. Men's clothing and my disguises have given us greater license to be together. As for my skills with the sword, he long ago gave up trying to prevent me from following in his footsteps. We work well together and our lives are quite challenging and exciting. Even with misfortune as I shared with you yesterday, I have a wonderful, adventurous life."

Kemal listened quietly. He could not help but feel a connection to her. They both had fought personal battles to overcome hardships. Kemal was realizing as he watched her speak, how beautifully etched her face was—like a delicate artist's rendering—and the curves of her profile especially exquisite. He wondered how an artist could possibly capture the fire in her eyes and the irresistible passion she exuded.

Realizing Francesca had stopped talking, Kemal snapped out of his momentary musing. She tilted her head slightly and looked at him quizzically, as he realized she was expecting a response.

"Yes, yes," he answered, hoping he had not missed a question during his moment of musing and that answering *yes* would keep him out of trouble. "I can see how your disguise would often be necessary to accompany your father. Your expertise with weapons was not enough. And now without the need for disguises, dressing in woman's clothing and having such talent with the sword, you should be able to learn a great deal at the side of Roxelana in the Harem. It has become a dangerous place."

"Tell me what you know about the attempt on Roxelana's life," Francesca inquired.

"Because I have spent my time with you and your father, I just learned tonight about the attempt on her life. As you heard, her eunuch guard was strangled with a bowstring. This is a method used by trained eunuch assassins. It is the traditional way a sultan's brothers are killed so they will not threaten his rule. The method of death is a clue in itself. We must be thankful to Allah that Roxelana was not there. She has many enemies within the palace because of the enormous influence she wields with the emperor. Some are extremely jealous of his great love and respect for her." Kemal's expression was again one of deep concern.

"I believe it was about six years ago that one of the sultan's children with Roxelana died. I was not in the palace at the time of the death and was not yet commander of the Beyliks. The child was a boy, Abdullah, and only about three years old when he died mysteriously in his bed. I have heard there was no fever, never an indication the child was sick, and even the great physician Abdullah, the child's namesake, was unable to determine a cause. It is still a great and haunting mystery and remains the subject of speculation as to the cause. The palace is rife with intrigue, Francesca."

"This is all important background information. It may be very useful to know as motives become clearer," Francesca replied. "We must agree to share and compare information. Make your discreet inquiries among the janissaries and give me the information and I will pass to you what I learn in the Harem."

"Yes, we will do that," Kemal quickly agreed. For Kemal the arrangement was ideal because rarely would he be able to obtain unbiased, reliable information about activities within the Harem.

No sooner had they agreed to share their information, Ibrahim approached.

"Come with me," he stated abruptly. "The sultan has been with your father, *Francesca,* but it is time to go," Ibrahim ordered, lifting the corner of his mouth in a sneer at the mention of her name. His anger with Francesca remained unabated. She deserved to be punished for her deception. "You too, Kemal. We will meet Il Lupo and I will escort all three of you from the palace."

Day Three

Üçüncü Gün

Indwelling and Constant

rancesca stood before a tall, ornately framed and gilded mirror in the foyer of the villa, studying her transformation. Never one to primp, she stared approvingly into the looking glass, nearly giddy with her reflection. She also found herself slightly discomfited by the change, having always been controlled and regimented - qualities required to ensure her successful deceptions. Despite feeling a slight awkwardness with her new appearance, she decided it suited her and complemented the new and elevated sensations that flooded her womanly body.

Life was now dramatically different. There was an inner emotional change that accompanied her outer metamorphosis. She asked herself if the person in the mirror was the woman she had longed to be—a reflection of her beautiful mother. For the first time in her life she felt free, not just from the restrictive bindings and voice controls required to complete her disguises, but free now to express herself unreservedly as Francesca. She was enticed by the unfamiliar and now omnipresent emotions.

Dressed as an odalisque, Francesca was beautiful even in the costume of a Harem chambermaid. The watermarked moiré fabric created the skirt and bodice of her garment and was layered with sheer chiffon covering her arms in shades of deep, lapis blue. Her breathtaking blue eyes shone just a few shades lighter than the color-saturated fabric. An intricately carved silver chain featuring a hammered center medallion encircled her small waist, coming to rest slightly above her hips. Her ears were adorned with silver chandelier earrings, and her neck was graced with a complementing looped chain with a lapis enhancer. She had added layers of hand-hammered silver bracelets sent from Roxelana to both wrists. Her shoes, flats with pointed toes and embroidered with silver silk threads, slid easily on her feet. While Francesca knew her attire was not nearly as elaborate or detailed as that of higher-ranking Harem concubines, she nevertheless reveled in her reflection, savoring the softness of the fabrics against her skin. Although her breasts were still somewhat constrained and elevated by her garments, she preferred the fit and look much more than the restrictive appearance and feel of her tight linen bindings that flattened her chest. The alluring exposure of her cleavage was quite pleasing, Francesca concluded, posing with her hands on her hips. She felt like a woman and relished her new role.

So engrossed was she in her image, Francesca had not noticed Kemal entering the room through a side door. Her eyes grew wide when she saw him also looking at her image in the mirror. He was mesmerized. She blushed, feeling great and unexpected pleasure in the realization that he was studying her. She wondered where his mind had taken him. Kemal, recognizing that she had read his expression, quickly recovered his composure. He hoped that she would not look back into his eyes directly, knowing they could reveal the depth of his growing emotion. In truth, Kemal was besotted.

"The dolts and dunces will be lining up!" he joked, attempting to conceal how transfixed he had been.

Fran threw her head back and laughed, recalling the conversation of the previous evening. "And you, sir, will have the job of keeping them from my doorstep!"

Kemal smiled. "This is quite a transformation. Who would have ever thought you to be a boy—not I to be certain! How could any boy be this beautiful?" Kemal continued, the playfulness in his voice disguising his admiration of her beauty.

"You are privy to deep secrets now, Kemal. And, thank you. I have never known until now what I would look like as a girl. Not bad—you think?" seeking a further compliment from Kemal, enjoying fully the effect she was having on him. Francesca felt new powers rising within her and it had nothing to do with her expertise with weapons.

"You are most welcome. However, I must correct you. Not only are you most assuredly not a boy, neither are you a girl. Girls in my world look very different from the *woman* standing in front of me. You play your part with exquisite flair!"

Francesca was grateful that her father appeared before she had time to reply. "Francesca—and indeed, you are now Francesca! You look beautiful! Now that this persona has made her entrance, there may be little room for Fran ever again." Il Lupo stared at his daughter.

Francesca wondered for a moment if her father was smiling or sad. Then, realizing his eyes were welling with tears, "*Mia Padre!* Why the tears?" she asked, hurrying to his side.

"Your mother. Your mother. I see her so vividly in you. Not just her beauty, but the way you hold yourself. It is regal, just as she was. I am stunned, a bit overwhelmed, a bittersweet feeling."

He stared at his daughter and was initially overcome with the astonishing resemblance she had to her mother, her striking blue eyes just as captivating. He remembered when he had first seen Gabriella Borgia, a stunning beauty. However, it was her spirit that had completely enchanted him. Now, standing in front of him was his beloved wife and little girl, morphed into a spectacular singular presence.

The weight of a universal problem, known to loving fathers, suddenly overwhelmed him. He felt a twinge of possessiveness and felt selfish for it. Il Lupo understood that he had to learn to distinguish between his own altruistic desires that she be protected and his own selfish desire to not let go. He remembered his wife's death, the agony of the final moments. Taking his beautiful newborn daughter in his arms, cradling her, he reassured the infant that it had not been her fault. She had come to represent everything in his life that was of import.

Francesca had been a primary reason for never remarrying— who could have filled the shoes of Gabriella and be the mother his daughter deserved? And so, he kept Fran, now Francesca, close to him and tutored her in the ways and disciplines of the only world he knew. He understood completely that his motivations for keeping her to himself were both noble and ignoble— protectiveness born from his great love for her and selfishness in his fervid hope that no one would ever take her from him. Her life had been one surrounded by men at his academy, and she had taken to it so completely, excelling beyond his wildest expectations. This reality had given him some comfort. However in this moment now nearly eighteen years later, the stark reality consumed him. Francesca was now a woman and he was ill-prepared to tutor her on womanhood.

Vincenzo Lupo's world was transformed just as quickly as his daughter had changed her clothing. They loved one another completely, but he knew the life he had given her had prevented her from growing into the woman she would have been had her mother not died. He had been both a father and a mother and felt completely unprepared to fulfill the role of the latter. He knew the possibility existed that a crucial time was coming when Francesca might choose to leave behind her disguises and the life of travel and intrigue she shared with him and lead a life more compatible with the times and her sex. He understood that she might find a different path and despite his own desire to keep her near, deeply wanted her to have the most fulfilling life possible. He did not know if she had yearnings and unfilled desires, for if she did, she had not shared them. Vincenzo Lupo did not know if there was a man who was righteous enough for her.

Kemal could not help but be touched by the intimacy of their relationship—the tenderness they showed toward one another. He felt the return of a deep internal longing for a life he did not have. There was a new urgency to his longing for his parents and homeland, and it pained him. He felt it just as much as Francesca was becoming ever-present in his thoughts, indwelling and constant.

"You realize, Kemal, that Francesca has one major flaw in her arsenal of disguises, do you not?" Il Lupo was ready to test the young warrior on his powers of observation.

"I do believe I know the weakness, and while it might impair and limit her disguises, there is no flaw. It is her eyes." Kemal had not needed time to think about his response. In fact, her eyes were unforgettable.

"Exactly Kemal! Our Shaolin monks have described them as an 'Elysium field of Himalayan blue poppies'. Exquisite description, do you agree?"

"I can only imagine," Kemal answered, realizing that the serious tone of the discussion had caused Francesca to blush.

Il Lupo, laughed, intending to lighten his mood. "Yes, you look wonderful, Francesca. In Venice, this is what we call an extreme makeover!"

Francesca, relieved that the conversation was at last, less serious, laughed, and like her father, attempted to lighten the conversation. She knew him well and could sense he was troubled and wanted to soothe him using their sparring, familiar way.

"I must tell you both that I am actually looking forward to the change! How bad can the wagging tongues of three hundred concubines be, particularly in the care of Roxelana? And, especially if spending time with you two is the alternative? Where is Aziz? Get me to the Harem!"

Kemal turned to Il Lupo. "I have also come to tell you that Suleyman urgently requests your presence. While we wait for Aziz, I will tell you both what I have learned.

"The leader of the janissary insurrection was Qais, my lieutenant. He was deeply offended and insulted when I was appointed Captain of the Beyliks. He assumed, because he was much older and had more battles to his credit, that he would be promoted to the position. Instead, the emperor chose me. There has always been animosity between us, but I would never have suspected it would go this far. I have also learned that he has even reduced the severity of punishments of those being disciplined if they swore allegiance to him. With me away recently from my daily interactions with the guards, the prime opportunity presented itself. It appears the plan had been longstanding, awaiting the opportune moment to strike." Francesca and Il Lupo listened intently as Kemal continued.

"Knowing there was unrest and dissent among the guards, Ibrahim rotated the guards closest to Suleyman. He had heard whisperings of a plot, but remains unsure of the identity of the ringleader. To his credit—and I hope that I am correct—he believed that by controlling the rotation, he might thwart any insurrection. However, yesterday, Ibrahim did not oversee the guard rotation because of the activities and plans surrounding ceremonial events that required his attention. Instead, in a highly unusual departure from protocol, Qais made the assignments. Since Suleyman rarely presides except at more important state functions, Qais believed yesterday was the most opportune time--not only his best chance to assassinate the emperor, but perhaps the *only* opportunity. Qais, of course, had his disgruntled janissaries by his side. We do not know how many others were involved in the plot. We must proceed with great caution, trusting few."

"So it appears the assassination attempt was a crime of opportunity, implementing their pre-existing plan. The rotation of the guards by Ibrahim was intended to prevent a well-planned and coordinated attempt on the emperor's life?" Il Lupo summarized, mentally putting the pieces together. "This could be a positive development in Ibrahim's favor, but far too early to eliminate him as a conspirator."

"Yes, Qais realized it might be months before he and his trusted co-conspirators would again all be assigned together in close proximity to Suleyman at the same time," Kemal responded.

"Unless, of course, Ibrahim was involved," Francesca opined. "I know you give him credit for the rotations, Kemal, but don't you find it a bit ironic and suspicious that he had other *more important* duties to attend to on the very day of the assassination attempt? Highly coincidental?"

"Perhaps… My instincts are telling me though that Ibrahim was legitimately preoccupied with his duties. I do believe that Mehmed was definitely involved. His attack on Qais was not to prevent Qais' from killing anyone else, but to prevent him from talking. If I am right, Mehmed is most definitely hiding something. I also may not like Ibrahim's manner, but whether he is guilty of treason is quite another issue entirely. He has of course, earned Suleyman's trust, a trust no doubt bestowed for good reason. We must remain circumspect and consider all the facts before jumping to final conclusions."

Il Lupo felt confident in Kemal's assessment. "I have more to relay to you, but that will have to wait. I see Aziz is coming."

Aziz arrived with news that he was to accompany the three of them to meet with Suleyman before Aziz and Francesca were to return to the Harem. He brought a full-length cloak with a hood to disguise Francesca's odalisque attire and the group departed Giovanni's residence.

Il Lupo turned to his three companions as they departed. "Beware of Mehmed," Il Lupo cautioned them all. "Aziz, you can trust us."

"I have also heard strange rumors today that a Jinn—an evil spirit—has been loosed beneath the Harem," Kemal told them, passing on further information.

"A Jinn? Perhaps one who kills with poisoned darts?" Il Lupo offered. "Let me take a moment to tell you of the findings yesterday in the morgue." Before mounting their horses, he spent a few moments describing the deaths, poison darts, his and Abdullah's conclusions, and the unresolved questions that required further investigation.

Treacheries Multiply

After dismounting their horses, two janissaries escorted Il Lupo, Kemal, Francesca, and Aziz to the repository of religious relics in the Topkapi Palace. Francesca had donned the hooded cloak given to her by Aziz, concealing her new identity. They entered the *Has Oda* where Suleyman awaited them. Sitting on the floor near him were two bound and gagged janissaries, terrified after having been tortured.

An infuriated Suleyman wasted no time in getting to the point. "After the discovery of the janissaries under the *Has Oda*, I became very concerned about the location of the discovery of their bodies. I had a sense that something was amiss with the relics, and so I sent Ibrahim to check the repository. My worst fears were realized and my suspicions validated. There has been a theft. Treacheries multiply. The security of the relics has always been critical. Thieves were somehow able to enter the repository, unseen and unheard, and steal the most sacred relics in Islam. Gone are the sword, mantle, and standard of the Prophet Muhammad. My father, Selim I, known to many as Selim the Grim, brought them to Konstantiniyye after his victory over the Mamluks more than a decade ago. You are all sworn to secrecy. If the clerics were to hear of this disaster, they would very likely incite riots. There would be chaotic unrest. Spiritual supremacy resides with the possessor of the relics. We have enough problems with our janissary dissidents. These are perilous times," he fulminated, pacing as he spoke. His expression was grave and his skin lacked the color of the previous evening; there was no reserve, no pretense in hiding his anger.

Pointing to the two bound janissaries, Suleyman continued, obdurate and furious, the terrified guards knowing they were at his mercy. "These guards who were on duty claim they neither heard nor saw anything. How is that possible unless the relics were stolen by an apparition? Ibrahim has questioned them and even under torture of having their thumbnails removed, their accounts of their time on duty remain the same. I have ordered their executions stayed until you have had an opportunity to question them," he said sternly, looking at Il Lupo.

Il Lupo removed their gags. "You were on duty the entire night?" he questioned, feeling the weight of their lives resting on his shoulders.

"*Effendi*, we were here the entire night! Neither of us left and we did not fall asleep! I swear this on the pain of never seeing Paradise. This is the truth! You must believe us!" the first guard pleaded.

"What he says is true, *Effendi*. The doors were locked when we arrived. We remained there all night and never slept. They were locked this morning and then Ibrahim came and unlocked the doors and we discovered some of the relics were missing. We would give our lives to defend the sacred relics of the Prophet. We are telling you the truth! I implore you—we are telling truth! By Allah we swear," pleaded the second guard as earnestly as the first.

Il Lupo assessed their credibility while his eyes moved up and down the walls and across the immaculate tile floor of the *Has Oda*.

"And the only means of gaining access to this room is through the doors where you both stood guard?" he queried, thoughtfully rubbing his chin.

"Yes, *Effendi*, yes. That is the only way anyone could gain entrance and they would have to kill us to do so!" the first guard answered.

"We swear it!" the second guard shouted, with deep conviction. *'Allah Al-Alim, Allah Who is All Knowing'*, knows we are telling the truth and that our hearts are pure! We live only to serve the great Suleyman and the dictates of our Islamic faith, which would include protection of the most holy and sacred relics!"

Il Lupo assessed the guards' demeanor and feeling certain there was no prevarication, dismissed any suspicions he had about their involvement. "They are likely innocent," Il Lupo said, turning to Suleyman.

"Take them away," the sultan directed his waiting guards. "You will be spared in custody pending completion of our investigation, but you must keep your mouths shut. Do you understand this order? If it is disobeyed, you will meet the executioner!"

"Thank you, thank you, and yes Your Majesty, we will be silent. No one could pry this from us. No one! Praise be to Allah! We are your loyal and devoted servants. Suleyman is the most merciful!" The distressed guards were led away.

Il Lupo had been surveying the room, tapping the floor with his sword. As he neared the corner in the back of the room, his sword struck an area that sounded hollow in comparison with the surrounding area of mosaic tile. Upon closer inspection, he noticed a slightly uneven white, pasty substance surrounding a section of the tiles. They gathered around the area. "Excavate the floor here," Il Lupo directed. The guards removed the tiles and sub flooring, revealing a large opening.

"This is where the thieves gained entrance and exited, applying a sealant after leaving in an attempt to hide where the floor had been raised. This is conclusive proof that the janissaries lying in the morgue, Kareem and Jamal, whose mutilated bodies were found just beneath this area, are the thieves! This paste is the same compound found in the jar!" Il Lupo concluded.

"Yes, this must be true. They are the thieves, but why, and at whose behest?" Suleyman hissed, angry. "I will order a thorough search of all these passageways and find the clues in this maze."

"Yes, Your Majesty. You should order a search. I must warn you, however, it is unlikely the relics will be found there—or at least any place that is not well hidden from us," Il Lupo cautioned.

"As soon as I learned of the theft this morning, I ordered extensive surveillance and searching of all cargo and persons leaving the city. Guards are everywhere. They have been told only that they are to look for things that might belong in a palace or anyone acting suspiciously. I could not reveal the true objects of the search for reasons I have stated to you earlier. I feel confident—I *must* feel confident—that these precious relics have not yet left Istanbul." Suleyman continued to pace, his hands clasped behind his back.

"Can a meeting be arranged with the palace architect, Your Majesty? Is my recollection correct that the Harem and this wing of the palace have been more recently constructed?" Il Lupo asked Suleyman.

"Yes, yes, these are newer additions. I will arrange a meeting with the architect."

As they left the repository, Il Lupo turned to Suleyman. "I agree with you, Your Majesty. There is an excellent chance that the relics have not left the city. I believe they will be held here until news of their disappearance and the searches have subsided."

"The searches will never stop until we have our precious relics returned. And those involved will regret the day they were born," Suleyman pledged.

"Knowing now who the thieves were, we must ascertain the identities of their accomplices and anyone involved in the wider plot. If you find who dug out the floor, they may talk. Indeed, time is of the essence since those involved may realize that Kareem and Jamal are dead. Their accomplices could be in great danger as well from unknown conspirators or even a mastermind, as well as your justice. We have a great deal of investigative work ahead of us, Your Majesty."

Fruit Salad

Aziz escorted Francesca to Roxelana's private chambers. The Harem, "the sacred and protected place," occupied a series of buildings housing several hundred concubines, guarded by eunuchs.

Passing one of the buildings, Aziz pointed, turning to Francesca, "These are the rooms where the Valide Sultan, Hafsa, lives. She is the sultan's mother. She always has two guards at her door. Roxelana's chambers are just ahead." He directed Francesca along the corridor.

"The Valide Sultan technically rules the Harem," Aziz continued. "She has abdicated her role to Gulbehar either because of pressure from Gulbehar or she has simply tired of all the squabbling. Everyone will acknowledge, however, that Roxelana is the most powerful woman in the imperial court. The fact that she is not the sultan's wife is of little import. Her power is manifest. She will not allow anyone or anything to stand between her and the sultan. She has many enemies.

"There is much intrigue in the court, Francesca. Not too long ago, Roxelana became violently ill. They thought she would die after eating desserts while dining with Suleyman. He had not yet eaten them when she became ill. Although Abdullah believes she was poisoned, he could not be certain. There is also continuing speculation about the death of Roxelana's third child, Abdullah, who died mysteriously at the age of three years. No one can be certain of the reason. Since that time, Roxelana has become even more protective of her children. We are constantly vigilant to ensure their welfare. Only her most trusted are allowed near them.

"The sultan has broken with many traditions. You may have heard this before, but I tell you now from what I, Aziz, Roxelana's most devoted and loyal servant, have seen and believe. Emperor Suleyman has nullified laws he considered unjust and enacted benevolent laws. It is believed he will break yet one more long-standing tradition, the tradition permitting only one wife. While he has not yet married his *Hürrem*, many believe he will do so. She has already born him a daughter and three living sons. It is also believed he favors his children with Roxelana over his only son with Gulbehar, Mustafa, who is Suleyman's natural and presumptive heir.

"Suleyman understands the means by which power is seized after the death of a sultan. When his own father died, he rushed to take power before his brother and gained the critical support of the janissaries. Thus, Suleyman sealed his position as the new sultan. Suleyman's love for Roxelana and their sons have greatly complicated matters. This uncertainty has caused extensive controversy and unrest within the Harem. If Suleyman had only one wife, there would be only the usual minor jealousies with no major potential debate regarding the inheriting son. Now life is more complicated. There is concern that Gulbehar will stop at nothing to ensure Mustafa's ascension to the throne. That would mean eliminating the threat posed by Roxelana and her children. Very worrisome!" Aziz candidly explained. "The recent murder of her guard by the bow string most certainly was a plot that was intended to end Roxelana's life. All of these events, and the theft of the relics, leave me extremely uneasy. I will do all I can to protect her. I would give my life without question." He smiled at Francesca. She decided that despite his formidable appearance, there was an innate virtuousness about him. She found him trustworthy.

Francesca was grateful for Aziz's candor because she knew the information could provide useful insight into the plots to end the lives of both Suleyman and Roxelana. She had noticed the day before that not only had Gulbehar not been invited to dinner but that Suleyman had handed the gifts given at the ceremonies first to Roxelana and not to Gulbehar, inconsistent with normal protocols and exemplary of Suleyman's preference for Roxelana. They continued walking, passing a series of doors and an open archway leading to an interior garden. Just beyond the archway, Francesca saw guards flanking a double door.

Francesca decided that she would not be the one to tell Roxelana, if she did not already know, about the missing relics. Roxelana had enough to worry about knowing there had been plots on both her life and that of Suleyman. Francesca did not know if Aziz would inform her. He clearly had not yet had the opportunity, having been with Francesca since the time of the theft. She would allow Roxelana to take the lead in discussing events of the day and to take her cues from Aziz. Her confidence in him was growing, and she sensed he would only act in Roxelana's best interests.

"We are here." Aziz motioned to the guards. As the doors opened, Francesca found Roxelana relaxing gracefully on a divan.

"Francesca! I am so glad you are finally here! I heard that you were detained this morning and were with the sultan, so I did not worry." Francesca removed the cloak that had enshrouded her identity from prying eyes. "And look at you! You are absolutely beautiful, Francesca!"

Roxelana embraced Francesca who was moved by her warmth. Despite her vivaciousness and youth, Francesca discerned that Roxelana was probably very lonely for true friendship and affection. She was likely envied, resented, and disliked by many in the Harem. Francesca understood it would be difficult for Roxelana to trust. Despite the luxurious quarters and life, Francesca knew it could not be a completely fulfilling and happy existence for Roxelana. She felt a twinge of sympathy and sadness for her. Francesca was acutely aware that Roxelana was indeed an exotic Bird of Paradise held captive in a lovely, filigreed and gilded cage. Roxelana's cage however—*The Golden Cage*—was the Harem, a place of treachery where she was forced to live with hundreds of witless, chattering chickadees and a pernicious and predatory vulture.

Roxelana's rooms were beautiful but not nearly as ornamented as the palace rooms Francesca had visited the day before and were quite understated in contrast. The lavish fabrics were draped and layered over the beds and divans, giving the room a sensual appearance. Where there were no mirrors on the walls, there was an artistic balance of ornamental mosaics in varying shades of blue and green creating a soothing environment enhanced by Kula kilims in subtly intertwined shades of reds and blues. Elaborately detailed tapestries hung in an adjoining chamber. Aromatic fragrances from gold and silver incense burners wafted through the chambers, all conducive to the art of seduction.

"It is my intention that we have fun today even as you must gather information that may help in solving the palace's great intrigues," Roxelana said with some gaiety, clearly pleased at the diversion Francesca's presence offered. "Come here. I am going to show you how to look even more beautiful!"

In Francesca's mind, Roxelana was putting up a brave front. It could not be easy for her to know that her life and that of Suleyman were in peril and to live with the constant threats. She was in need of a distraction, and Francesca was just what was needed.

Taking Francesca by the hand, she led her to a long marble table. "Let me show you all the concoctions I have for making us more alluring!" Roxelana was eager to share her secrets with Francesca. Sitting on the table, along with the rosewood box filled with perfumes from Giovanni, were dozens of little boxes, the majority made from carved wood with inset brass. Others were silver with delicate silver tassels and some were fashioned from onyx or other exotic stones. Each a beautiful examplar of Ottoman artistry. Francesca found their miniature size and appearance enchanting.

"I'm anxious to see what's inside but I am delighted just to examine all these little treasures. I love them!" Francesca exclaimed, surprised that she would find such pleasure in the little boxes.

"Then I will fill some with my dusts and give you others that will be empty so that you may put your own treasures in them," Roxelana offered graciously. "See here on this table, the little inlays of malachite and lapis? Some of what I will show you are dusts made from these precious stones and others, as well as herbs, flowers, and spices. Grinding the stones to dust is laborious, but the labor enhances our beauty," she smiled.

"Now look! Here are techniques and ingredients to brighten my cheeks, lips and eyes." Roxelana opened box after box filled with dusts of vermilion, cochineal, and madder—all used to add pinks and reds to the lips and cheeks. Other boxes contained kohl to darken the eyelashes and ground frankincense, malachite, and ochre for the eyelids. Sitting also on the table was a small, blown glass bottle.

"What is this?" Francesca asked, holding the bottle in her hand.

"This is special," Roxelana said, taking the bottle from Francesca. "I use it only when I have been summoned to see Suleyman. It is belladonna. It adds a little sparkle to the eyes. That is why I use it only when I see him. My eyes will sparkle for none other." She turned and smiled at Francesca.

"You must be careful how much you use. Too much and it appears very unnatural—as if all the stars in the night sky dwell and flash in your eyes. You want sparkle just enough for him to notice— not so much it will blind him! I will send some of this with you too. Perhaps you will want your eyes to sparkle for someone special. Perhaps sooner rather than later?" Roxelana giggled, nudging her playfully, letting it be known that Francesca's blushing and interest in Kemal, had not gone unnoticed.

"Oh my goodness," Francesca responded, feeling her face flush. "I think it will be a long time before I will ever need or want to dazzle anyone. Besides, who would ever be interested in a woman who dresses as a boy and has sword skills superior to most men? I am likely to have little need for the strength and protection of even a good man," Francesca replied, trying to make light of Roxelana's feminine sixth sense.

"Ah, my friend, there you could be wrong. Be careful, for it is not the need for a man's strength and protection that guides us, but rather for the fulfillment of the heart's yearnings. I am perceptive and practiced in assessing human motives and emotions, Francesca. I believe I have noticed one very dashing young man who finds you quite attractive. Just as you are expert with the knife, I am expert in love. I perhaps understand, even better than you do, what is plainly obvious. But I will not tease you any longer. Come let me apply some of my dusts, making your face even lovelier." Roxelana opened the first box containing kohl and applied it to Francesca's eyelashes.

"Why is it that men always have such fascinating lashes, and women must work for them? You have the lashes of a beautiful young boy. They need little to enhance their darkness. Now, I will add a little malachite to your lid and some vermilion to your checks and lips. Your eyes, Francesca, they are remarkable. I have never seen such blue eyes," Roxelana complimented, her long, nimble fingers gliding over Francesca's face as she continued working her cosmetic magic. She stepped back to admire the results.

"There, what do you think, Francesca?" Roxelana beckoned she look in the mirror.

Francesca was stunned at how much more elevated her cheekbones appeared and how the blue of her eyes was intensified by the striking coloration of her lids. The green of the malachite dust on her lids made her eyes sparkle. Francesca delighted in her transformation.

"Oh my! It is amazing!" Francesca stared at her reflection. She could see Aziz's reflection still standing in attendance in the room. "Do you like it, Aziz?"

Aziz wore a massive smile, indicating he too admired the results. "I stand watch over the two most beautiful women in the palace!" he exuded, the women accepting and giggling over his compliment. His fondness for Francesca was growing, and he was desirous of redeeming himself for having assaulted her, even though it was a ruse commanded by the sultan. Indeed, he genuinely believed he had never seen two more beautiful women.

"Yes, we are beautiful today," Roxelana agreed, as both she and Francesca stood admiring themselves in the full size mirror, posing seductively.

"I cannot tell you how much fun this is, Roxelana. Thank you for sharing these womanly secrets!" Francesca was elated and felt the lightness of the mood. She was grateful for the relief from the stress of the previous day and for their growing friendship.

"There are few greater personal pleasures for a woman than enhancing her beauty. I mean this not just to please a man—which is of course, important. It is also the personal pleasure we gain from presenting our best selves—even if we require a little enhancement! I feel a certain contentment and enjoy feeling good about my appearance. There is no shame in that. Be self- aware and use your assets to best advantage. Francesca, you understand that I do not just mean that a woman's outer beauty is important. That is simply a reflection of her inner beauty and the state of her mind. Although I will say there is the greatest pleasure in the subtle art of seducing and subduing a man, reining in the warrior in him. Well, perhaps not too subtly. Just enough so that they are unsure of just exactly what has happened." Roxelana laughed at her suggestion.

Roxelana struck a pose in front of the mirror. She had wrapped her arms around her waist and squeezed, her upper arms pressing against the sides of her chest, giving her breasts an added plumpness and accentuating her cleavage. Francesca was soaking in every moment of the lesson.

"And just to be certain there is no misunderstanding Francesca, I mean subdue them with your charms…not your knife! I caution you—your tongue should not be as sharp as your knife. You must believe me when I tell you that slowly is much more satisfying. There is a sweet torture for both of you that way!" Roxelana laughed. "You will learn these things."

"I am beginning to understand that women need every weapon at their disposal," Francesca quipped. "You are adding to my armory, Roxelana!"

"Now that I have taught you a little you must teach me the art of the dagger," Roxelana challenged. "There are times when fast is good, too."

Francesca retrieved a bag that Aziz had carried to Roxelana's rooms. She pulled out a leather belt of throwing knives. Roxelana stood in amazement at the assortment, each in its own leather sheath.

"There are many types of throwing knives. Some are the same as were used in ancient times. No need to improve upon a good thing. In my belt, I have a kulbeda, pinga, thrombash, khanjar, jambiya, stiletto, and kard. I brought several jambiyas and kards. The jambiya is usually not considered a throwing knife, but I love its weight and power and I have worked many hours to master its use. I have found a way to use the curve of the blade to my advantage. There are differences in weight and balance among the knives. Therefore, adjustments are required when throwing. For example, if I were to use the pinga, I would slightly change the angle of my wrist. When you are used to throwing many different types of knives, you know immediately what you have in your hand by the way it feels. Its use becomes instinctive. Expert proficiency takes years of practice. Two of my favorite blades are the khanjar and the kard for they are easiest to throw. I will show you how to use the kard today. Although not always the most deadly, it was the first knife I learned to throw. If necessary to inflict immediate death, I prefer the jambiya because of its weight. It is an Arabian knife," Francesca explained, handing each knife to Roxelana.

"I had no idea there were so many different kinds," Roxelana commented, keenly surveying the collection and holding each knife as Francesca described them. "Yes, I can feel the difference in weight and I can see the differences in their blades. Each is very finely crafted and amazingly sharp," she observed, running her finger along the edge of each blade. "Intriguing."

Francesca buckled her knife belt on her waist. Realizing the bracelets would interfere with her wrist action and accuracy, she removed them and instructed Roxelana to remove her bangles as well. Then quickly, in rapid-fire succession, Francesca threw each of the knives in her belt, skewering a line of pineapples and melons sitting on the adjacent table. Her motions were so quick and adept that Roxelana was left speechless, her mouth gaping.

"The throw and accuracy comes mainly from the wrist," Francesca explained, surprised by the effect her demonstration had had on the sultan's favored concubine.

Clapping her hands gleefully, the redhead commanded, "Aziz! More fruit! A great deal more fruit!" A girlish Roxelana emerged amid all the excitement. Raucous fun was a rarity in the Harem and Roxelana intended on taking full advantage of an opportunity to learn a new skill.

Francesca approached Roxelana. "Let me show you," she said, standing behind Roxelana, placing a kard in her hand and then taking Roxelana's hand in her own.

"Here, take this knife and hold it. Feel it first. Allow your hand to sense its weight by holding the knife and dropping your wrist. Your body will guide you and sense the balance required. Do not think. Now, let me guide you." Roxelana listened, dropped her wrist holding the kard and then allowed Francesca to take control of her hand.

"The trick is for the muscles to throw without the brain. Let me show you as I guide you through the first throw." With that and before Roxelana's brain had time to register the action, Francesca had manipulated Roxelana's hand and the blade was thrown, hitting a honeydew melon dead on center.

"Oh no…I have a diabolical idea—well, maybe not diabolical, but very naughty at least! Aziz, please fetch me my writing implements and ink." Aziz went to Roxelana's desk and brought back a pen case and a small bottle of dark ink. She opened the silver case delicately inlaid with mother of pearl and retrieved a bamboo writing stick, dipping it in the bottle of ink.

"I am going to paint the face of my nemesis Gulbehar on these two melons." She began drawing a caricature, its nose and ears greatly exaggerated and hair not neatly pulled into a tight bun, but depicted as sticks coming from her head. Roxelana tried to stifle her laughter.

Finishing, she proclaimed, "I do believe she looks better in caricature than in person! Now the real fun begins! I have added incentive." Zealously, she threw the kard at the first melon, splitting it neatly in half.

Francesca and Aziz, who covered his mouth briefly with his hand over Roxelana's audacity, watched with great amusement. Roxelana proclaimed, "I am having the best time! There is such satisfaction in destroying my enemy! Francesca, I need the jambiya. I will decimate the next melon!"

Francesca obliged, handing the deadly weapon to Roxelana, stepping back, realizing that if Roxelana hit her mark, there would be a great deal of melon spread over a large area.

She threw the jambiya with Francesca's assistance and hit a bull's eye, squarely in the middle of Gulbehar's caricatured smile, sending the ripened and sticky fruit all over the floor.

"There, I feel so much better!" Roxelana giggled, skipping back for another knife.

After an hour of practicing, both women were still giddy. Aziz had provided ample fruit for their continued target practice, and Roxelana indefatigably worked to hone her skills. It had been quite a rollicking shivoo, both laughing and engaging in slapstick antics. Their earlier, meticulously applied makeup was melting on their faces from heavy perspiration, and their beautiful silk garments clung to their sweaty bodies. They were frazzled—even their hair was frizzy and protruding from their heads at all angles in riotous disarray. Pieces of fruit strewn about the room were making the floor wet and sticky. Francesca had, however, succeeded in teaching Roxelana a few techniques, and she was satisfied that Roxelana, an adept student, could defend herself with some ease and agility.

They were still enjoying the target practice, deceased fruit littering the floor, when Aziz loudly hissed, "Gulbehar!"

Panic registering on her face, Roxelana looked at Francesca, eyes wide as saucers, and shouted "Oh no!"

"Please, help me clean this up!" Both in a frenzy, they laughed uproariously as the comedic clean-up of the previously elegant rooms of the sultan's favored concubine ensued.

Squealing so hard with laughter it brought tears to their eyes, the women grabbed fabrics from the beds and divans and began wiping the tables and floors with furious frenzy. They gamboled about the room in the slippery mess of their creation, emitting breathless giggles while attempting to hide the mess. Even after shoving many of the fabrics and Francesca's belt holding the knives under a raised bed, the room remained a spectacle of disarray. Huffing and puffing, they desperately tried to make some semblance of order out of the complete chaos, but time had run out. Gulbehar entered. She was accompanied by Mehmed, his personal servant, Omar, a retinue of eunuchs, and several concubines. Roxelana and Francesca were caught!

Rumors and Repartee

Gulbehar entered the room with a smile as false and insincere as the words that she would speak. Her lips quickly curled into a sneer as she slowly surveyed the room, focusing her minatory gaze on Roxelana. She lifted her pointed nose straight in the air, making no pretense of hiding her disgust. There was utter silence in the room. Gulbehar stalked towards Roxelana and Francesca, intent on registering her displeasure.

Francesca fervently prayed Gulbehar would not recognize her as the same boy who had helped save the sultan the day before. Knowing her eyes might be recognizable to the sultan's wife, she cast them downward, never looking directly at Gulbehar. She also threw a scarf over her head to cover the boyish cut of her hair. Francesca and Roxelana held hands behind their backs—their bodies quivering slightly as they struggled to contain their laughter—looking like guilty school girls. Gulbehar gave them a thorough once over and then pointed to the table and floor still littered with the corpses of skewered fruit.

"What is all this? A party? A party with fruit salad on the menu perhaps? Aren't we the messy eater, Roxelana?" Gulbehar offered her conclusion, unable to imagine what could have caused such utter disorder and lack of decorum.

Their bodies aquiver, Roxelana and Francesca were no longer able to contain themselves and burst out laughing. In this moment, the friendship between the two was sealed. Francesca could not help but notice that Aziz, standing behind Gulbehar and her party, covered his mouth to suppress his own laughter, his large body rocking slightly. Their giant protector was becoming more and more endearing to Francesca.

Gulbehar continued to display her disdain; there was nothing that Roxelana could ever do to bring a smile to the face of her rival. She abhorred Roxelana—despised her and her brat children. She detested the influence Roxelana had over Suleyman and the obvious love Suleyman had for his favored concubine. As far as she was concerned, Roxelana was the only reason Suleyman's affection for her had waned. Gulbehar never imagined her own coldness could have been the underlying cause of Suleyman's diminished attention. She turned, again raising her pointed, skinny nose to the air, and loudly sniffed.

"You really must do something about the personal hygiene around here, Roxelana. This one here," she said, pointing to Francesca, "smells of camel dung. Please tell your slave to reposition herself downwind." Gulbehar eyed Francesca suspiciously. Francesca, dutifully and immediately moved slightly away, grateful there was less chance her identity would be discovered.

"And, I must say, you are not looking your best either. I think you need a touch of cleaning up, my dear," her sacchrine insincerity seeping out through her pores. "Stressful day in the Harem? Who does your makeup? I would have the slave sent to the executioner's block. You just cannot find good help anymore. It's all so tiring."

Roxelana was not to be intimidated and maintained a controlled and polite smile, an artificial smile she reserved only for those she found truly distasteful.

"Oh dear, Gulbehar. You are so predictable—ill-tempered and sententious as usual. What possible reason could there be for your visit?" Roxelana was not about to allow Gulbehar to dishearten or demean her in any way.

Roxelana knew Gulbehar's intent was to stultify and diminish her as a woman, but more importantly, as her rival. Gulbehar was determined to dispirit her and Roxelana would not allow it. Francesca was impressed with Roxelana's directness and fortitude in the face of this woman. Francesca believed Gulbehar to be banal at best, and possibly deadly.

"I came here to remind you that Suleyman has only one wife. And Roxelana, I am that wife and the mother of his heir. You may bed with my husband and we may share sons with the same man, but there is a crucial distinction." Gulbehar strutted around the room.

As she did, she lost her balance as she stepped into a puddle of juices. Francesca and Roxelana exchanged glances, their eyes wide as they heroically attempted to suppress giggles; they watched the scrawny woman gyrate, completing a near pirouette, struggling all the while to keep from falling and maintain her haughty demeanor.

"We should need no excuses for exchanges of conversation based on our shared bond. I have no doubt that keeping the old man happy is uppermost in both our minds. Speaking of the old fossil, how is he doing? Recovered from the excitement of yesterday, I presume? I hear all kinds of rumors. Could there be more assassination attempts? What have you learned about yesterday's events?"

"I refuse to engage in piffle with you, Gulbehar. My lover is fine," Roxelana answered confidently. "We owe a great debt to the timely intervention of Venetian envoy, Il Lupo. And you, Gulbehar, his *devoted* wife, can surely rest easy. Should there be any further attempt on his life, and I doubt those rumors, he will survive. It is his destiny to overcome the despicable dealings of those who threaten or spitefully use him. The truth shall be known, and you can trust me when I tell you this. I am confident that you will find great comfort knowing that our beloved sultan will be here until he has lived a long and full life and is peacefully called to Allah where he will shine in the light of angels. His end will be just and righteous, as he deserves," Roxelana finished defiantly.

"Well, interesting. Glad you have such confidence. I am not so sure. And Il Lupo—yes, infidels are occasionally useful," Gulbehar muttered. "Men with balls do have a couple of good points. Too bad there are far too few around here. They are so much more pliable when they come fully equipped, and you can get them to think with their, ah…good points.

"Of course, except for Mehmed here. I just could not go on without Mehmed. He is ever so clever." Gulbehar strolled over to Mehmed and kissed him slowly on the cheek. Mehmed curled his lip at Roxelana, revealing one of his rotting front teeth. It was evident Mehmed knew his place—total loyalty to Gulbehar. Francesca could not help but notice that, in contrast to Aziz's strong and muscular physique and pleasant demeanor, Mehmed stood flaccid, his expression scowling and surly.

"Speaking of balls," Roxelana said, redirecting the conversation. "There is a rumor among the concubines that one of the eunuchs has not been completely castrated. You wouldn't happen to know anything about that, would you, Gulbehar?"

"Eunuchs don't have balls, Roxelana. The lack thereof defines their 'eunuchness,'" Gulbehar laughed loudly at her clever squib.

"They've been cut off before the sluts around here ever lay eyes on them. Most of them are cut even before they are old enough to know what the parts being cut off are used for. I do like hot rumors though. Keeps things lively in this boring place. I know, let us offer a reward for his capture! Any clue who that naughty prick is? Hmm...this could prove more interesting than I might have originally thought. Opportunities, opportunities." Gulbehar's sexual insinuation was noted by both women. Roxelana did not bat an eyelash, but Francesca struggled to keep from turning pink.

"In some cases the procedures are botched or incomplete and the eunuch is not impotent," Roxelana spoke with confidence, having read histories regarding eunuchs, how they were chosen, and the techniques used.

"Well, in any event," Mehmed interjected, "if he is discovered, he will be executed."

Francesca had noted several things during the course of the conversations. Her first observation was that Mehmed clearly held Roxelana in contempt. His slitted eyes exuded venom when he looked at her and his churlish demeanor, as a servant, was completely inappropriate. It was as though Gulbehar had given her blessing, perhaps even encouraging Mehmed's disrespectful and condescending behavior toward Roxelana. Francesca had no doubt that Gulbehar never uttered flattering words regarding Roxelana; she only hoped her utterances were not treacherous, although she had no substantiating proof to be certain.

The eunuchs Mehmed and Omar appeared somewhat discomfited by the conversation when it turned to unsuccessful castrations, understandably so, perhaps reflecting on the horrific experience.

Mehmed's expression softened somewhat as he addressed Roxelana. "My lady Roxelana, if I may, I have heard this rumor also and can assure you there are no uncastrated eunuchs in the palace. Abdullah conducts annual examinations, which even I am subjected to." Francesca thought Mehmed's attempts to ingratiate himself to Roxelana were particularly insincere and possibly mendacious. She did not trust him.

"Well, Mehmed, your 'eunuchness' has never been in question. Perhaps you are right and the rumors are merely idle Harem gossip. You would naturally be in a position to not only know but also report any irregularities. You know the penalties are harsh for not reporting any such breach within the Harem," Roxelana cautioned.

Watching Roxelana, Francesca sensed that she loathed Mehmed, perhaps even suspecting him of complicity in perfidious Harem intrigues. She decided to explore Roxelana's instincts regarding Mehmed later.

Roxelana did not relent. "Of course, if there is such a eunuch, persons who knew of his condition could manipulate him easily. I think we should not too easily dismiss the possibility. I believe this matter may need to be discussed with the emperor," she scolded, making it clear to Mehmed that she intended to investigate the substance and source of the rumors.

"I suppose we should look into it," Mehmed offered, lowering his head in reluctant deference to Roxelana. "But, I think this is sheer speculation and distracts us from other more important issues."

Gulbehar intervened. "Enough of the lewd and lascivious talk about men's sexual organs or lack thereof, for now. It is making me all…hot…Tell me about your children. How are they?" She asked, disingenuously.

Roxelana was aware of Gulbehar's motivations for asking this question. "I realize you have a most intense and unusual interest in the welfare of my children. As you well know, they are cared for in a manner befitting the children of the sultan and are under the watchful and protective eyes of those most trusted by Suleyman and me. They are amazingly strong, so very intelligent and robust. They are the epitome of health and happiness. You need not waste your time wondering after their vulnerability, just as I will waste no time worrying about Mustafa." She was determined that Gulbehar have no doubt that her children were thriving.

"Honestly Gulbehar, I need to get on with my day. I have so much to do, including finishing with my fruit salad and then perhaps, a nap or leisurely bath. Is there anything of any import that you wish to say before bidding us farewell?" Roxelana was defiant.

"Ah, yes, actually there is," a peevish Gulbehar responded, struggling mightily to contain her outrage at Roxelana's dismissal. "Just the answer I expected from an overly protective mother. Of course Mustafa is also strong and healthy and the sultan's oldest son. One day he will lead armies to quell insurrections on behalf of his father and in time, and by Allah's grace, in place of his father as the supreme leader and sultan of the great Ottoman Empire. It is only a shame that he is yet too young because it is time for a good conflict, which would quell the restless janissaries' thirsts for the spoils of war. A war would be good for many reasons. Prime amongst them would be that Suleyman would be required to get his ass off his divan." Gulbehar's shocking statement revealed her private contempt for her husband, rather than the love she professed so passionately in his presence.

Without waiting for a further humiliating response from Roxelana, Gulbehar moved to depart. "Well, I've taken up your time and far too much of my own. I should have known that I would get nothing but trifles from you. I, too, have many more important issues to concern myself with and it appears that you need to finish your lunch," she retorted, the sneer still lingering on her lips. "You must pass along the recipe sometime. Goodbye, my dear." With that, Gulbehar turned, swirled her caftan, and left with entourage in chase.

Francesca and Roxelana looked at one another in mutual disgust. The Russian concubine sighed, delicately rubbing her temples. "Isn't she lovely? She is my major headache. Allah! She infuriates me!"

Francesca opined. "Perhaps she is more than a major headache. Perhaps a deadly cancer or venomous serpent." Francesca was certain that while there might not yet be unequivocal evidence of Gulbehar's complicity in the plots against Roxelana and Suleyman, Gulbehar was well aware that if Suleyman were to die, her son, despite his youth, would take the throne. Unless somehow Roxelana's children gained legitimacy and were able to seize power with support from janissaries loyal to all or one of them, Mustafa was the sole heir to the throne. Gulbehar would have influence over a very young Mustafa, perhaps even acting as regent, and as a first order of business decree that Roxelana and her children be executed, and likely Kemal and Aziz as well. Gulbehar had much to gain from an untimely demise of the sultan and Mustafa's ascendancy to the throne. Suleyman's untimely death could only profit Gulbehar. Francesca thought her demeanor and words to be a witch's brew of malevolence, duplicity and perhaps even treachery.

Metamorphosis

"Now, let us lighten the mood." Roxelana turned to Aziz. "Bring the musicians."

"Let us enjoy ourselves and forget all the unpleasantness of that visit. Now, my dear, motherless friend, is the time for more lessons. You have done so much for me, including teaching me arts of the blade. I must give you further lessons in the arts of seduction and love. How you finish these lessons, "graduate," and apply them will be your own dance. You will create your own sculpture, with your own honesty, for your own man who has seduced your mind and invaded your thoughts. That man to whom you want to bring pleasure. I am merely a concubine with whom the sultan has found love, but I have the heart of a woman who understands love. We are confederates, Suleyman and I, united confidants who bring physical, emotional, and intellectual pleasure to one another. When you find this man, the one who drives you to uncontrollable distraction, you will need to be prepared," Roxelana sighed.

"The world will often bring him unkindness, harshness enough. Do not let it be you who brings more. When a man and a woman love one another, they treat each other equally. Do not cause vexation or allow bitter sarcasm and criticisms to fall from your mouth. You can be true to yourself and in this, respect is developed. Pettiness and discontent are tiring and weigh on love. Kindness allows forgiveness and forgiveness is not just powerful, but necessary. Do not let small slights taint your affections."

The novice was eager for more. "When I was first ordered to Suleyman's private chamber, I did not know what to expect. I was afraid—powerless and vulnerable. When he first took me in his arms, I submitted completely because as a concubine it was my duty to do so. I soon found that I quickly submitted willingly, because of his kindness and tenderness. Suleyman is an enlightened man who has never used his power against me. I realized that there was a great depth of soul within him and that if I were to be ever present in his thoughts, I would have to offer more than my body."

Roxelana continued teaching a mesmerized Francesca. "It is in this invasion of the mind that hearts are captured. You must be his refuge, the place he feels completely safe, and this, as well as great passion, cannot be feigned. Most importantly there is shared responsibility in your powers, and each must use it carefully and unselfishly. You must be his ally, unafraid to correct him, but understand what his position calls him to do, and also be able to accept his corrections if your path is crooked. I know too that men, despite appearances, can often be more vulnerable and naïve than women; the world expects much, so guide him to honorable goals. Do not engage in cunning and guile. Love cannot be coaxed. While the Koran offers and guides the way to heavenly paradise, we, Francesca, are in possession of the earthly gates to paradise. I am able to offer the divine to the man I love, but love is so much more than just seduction." Francesca was spellbound, Kemal's image filtering through her mind.

"Francesca, I wish to share with you something very sacred to me. I have not shown or shared this with anyone." Roxelana walked to a small writing table and opened a drawer, pulling out a carefully folded vellum paper. She tenderly ran her hand across its written contents, rejoining Francesca on her cushions.

"It is a poem written by my beloved to me. To share it with you makes it even more real because I hardly feel worthy of the beautiful words he has written to me. To know someone else—someone I can trust—has heard them, validates for me that they are real. Will you listen?"

"Of course," Francesca answered, still absorbing the lessons Roxelana had imparted. "I am honored that you would want me to be the person you share this with. Thank you, Roxelana."

Roxelana began reading Suleyman's love poetry, her voice expressive and gentle, almost murmuring the words.

My resident of solitude, my everything, my beloved, my shining moon
My friend, my privacy, my everything, my shah of beautifuls, my sultan

My life, my existence, my lifetime, my wine of youngness, my heaven
My spring, my joy, my day, my beloved, my laughing rose
My delight, my wine, my tavern, my light, my lamp, my candle
My orange and pomegranate and sour orange, my candle of night
My plant, my sugar, my treasure, my delicate in the world
My saint, my Joseph, my everything, my Khan of my heart's Egypt
My Istanbul, my Karaman, my land of Rum
My Bedehshan, my Kipchak, my Baghdad, my Horosan
My long-haired, my bow like the eyebrow, my eye full of discord,
my patient
My blood is on your hands if I die, mercy on me my non-Muslim
I am a flatterer near your door, I always praise you
Heart is full of sorrow, eye is full of tears, I am Muhibbi and I am happy.

Roxelana once again caressed the page and looked at Francesca, who was profoundly moved by the intimacy and beauty of the words written in love. She thought about the powerful man, Suleyman the Magnificent—the Lawgiver—the leader of the vast Ottoman Empire, his visage sometimes ineffable and sometimes stern, who had humbled himself before the woman he loved. With tears in her eyes, Roxelana kissed the paper and folded it, said nothing else, and rose from the floor.

She reached to a nearby table and attached *zils* to her fingertips with delicate silk ribbons. She snapped her fingers and the musicians, who had waited patiently, began to play. Tears still softly falling from her eyes, she slowly began to move her hips in a seductive, circling motion with arms raised over her head, her gauzy fabric draped from her fingertips as she pulled it over her face, exposing only her moist eyes. Moving with exquisite grace around the room, her motions intensified, matching the pace of the music. Roxelana's dance was rapturous. Francesca found herself utterly captivated by the beauty and sensuality of each nuanced movement of Roxelana's body. The tintinnabulation of the tiny *zils* on her fingers created a rhythmic harmony to accompany the baglama and drums as the timbre of the music increased in tempo and volume.

Roxelana beckoned with her delicate cymbaled fingers, tempting Francesca to join her, then drawing her in as she pulled her from her cushions. Francesca began, slightly embarrassed by her awkwardness, but soon fell easily into mimicking Roxelana's sensuous movements. Francesca's natural grace quickly overcame her hesitant movements, and ever the clever student, she matched, move for move, the circling of Roxelana's hips. Artfully and with inherent grace, she copied Roxelana's undulating belly, with hands held over her head and legs spread slightly apart. They spun around, swaying, throwing their heads back, whirling and twirling in a near frenzy. The pace of the music became furiously fast and reached a crescendo, their bodies matching the tempo with a controlled passion, shaking as the music finally climaxed. These two women of disparate lives—one a concubine, a mother, and an expert in the art of love—the other, an ingénue and novice—fell to the floor intertwined in an exhausted heap.

And thus, in this moment, Francesca Lupo acquiesced, releasing herself to experience the utterly irresistible metamorphosis of the girl into the woman . . . an exquisite transformation tenderly and profoundly touching her embryonic soul.

Seduction

"Welcome!" Giovanni exclaimed with his characteristic bluster as he cheerfully greeted Il Lupo and other guests once again gathered at his palatial villa.

"I am so pleased that we are able to share another evening of revelry and conviviality. Please, help yourselves to the fine French wine, courtesy of Antoine, and of course Gregor's peasant juice! I find I so enjoy vodka and confess I have partaken liberally today! However, I have not forgotten that I have a guest, intent on sobriety. Hassan, we have brewed a special tea for you this evening. There is much to discuss tonight. Dinner will be served shortly."

Turning his attention to Hassan, intent on learning as much as he could during the evening, Il Lupo inquired, "Will you be returning to Persia in the near future?"

"Yes, I am planning to leave in three days," Hassan responded, sipping his hot tea complacently. The teacup consisted of an etched copper sleeve into which a glass insert was fitted and completed with a matching copper saucer - the Ottoman equivalent of the French demitasse. They appeared fragile and diminutive in his large and prominently knuckled hands.

"You are Shi'a, are you not and the Ottomans, predominantly Sunni, correct? Please, can you elaborate on the differences?" In fact, Il Lupo was very well versed in many of the complexities of Islam, but hoped Hassan could offer further insights.

"Yes, I am a Shiite. In some respects, the differences between the Shi'a and the Sunni are comparable to the religious differences between Catholics and the new Protestantism, the reformation sweeping through much of Europe. There are further distinctions, such as Wahabists, Sufis, just as the Protestant movement has Lutherans and Calvinists. And we are as much separated by tribes and tribal loyalties as we are by our religious sects," Hassan answered, moving slightly away from Il Lupo, allowing Gregor, Lucia, Antoine, and Giovanni room to enter the conversation.

"It never ceases to amaze me," Gregor, ruddy faced, already falling under the influence of vodka, chimed in. "One God with so many different paths to him. I prefer the Russian Orthodox. Keeps things simple for me." Il Lupo continued to find Gregor's company engaging and thought him somewhat out of place among other dignitaries and diplomats whom Il Lupo categorized generally to be sycophants and gossipmongers.

"Ah, but without the divergent paths, what would we have to quarrel about? There would be no reason for war!" Antoine piped in. "All these wars in the name of God or Allah or your Russian *Bog*. And which king, or emperor, sultan, duke or doge, is the true representative of God on earth? It is all to no avail. There will never be an end to sectarian, doctrinal hostilities."

"Perhaps there are things worth fighting about. I can think of a few," Lucia added, waving a hand-painted chinoiserie fan with a pale blue background. It complemented the brocade skirt of her dress, which featured a medallion print in shades of blue, and a predictably heavily boned silk taffeta bodice, also of a pale blue.

"I will drink to that!" Giovanni toasted, hoisting his glass upward, not giving Lucia the opportunity to elucidate further on just exactly what she found worth fighting for. "And I will fervently ask that God make me wealthy in trade with free access to it—and I'll take whatever path to God needed to get it! As long as it is Roman Catholic, that is! And now, to the table! Dinner is served!"

Continuing their conversations, the guests moved toward the dining room. Il Lupo was immediately struck by the smothering heat of the room. The effect was suffocating, despite the opened windows. Servants attempted to cool the air by waving oversized fans made from the feathers of exotic birds, designed to capture even a momentary, elusive breeze. So many candles were required to light the chandeliers and table candelabra, efforts to cool the room were futile. Il Lupo noticed Lucia frantically fanning herself as he pulled out her chair to offer her a seat. Lucia grabbed the linen napkin from her table setting and dabbed her perspiring face.

Giovanni's table was, once again, elegantly and meticulously laid with softly colored peach and pink peonies and white magnolias in arrangements, set into crystal vases, low and down the center of the table. Ordinarily their fragrance might have been pleasant, but the heat intensified any delicate aromas into an overwhelming cloud of sweetness; the magnolias in particular carried the strongest fragrance. Three silver candelabra with tall slender bases were spaced at perfect intervals among the floral centerpiece as not to interfere with guests' views of one another. The china was of Bohemian origin with a delicately painted floral border, and the wine goblets of Murano crystal with masterfully hand-etched complimentary motifs. It was a beautiful tablescape for yet one more sumptuous feast.

"What do you think Suleyman's ambitions might be in Europe? Will he move on Vienna again?" Il Lupo began the dinner conversation by turning to Antoine, seated to his right.

"I think not. Suleyman appears to me one who has grown to understand the limits of his armies and his empire. He has burned Buda and I doubt he has inclinations for further invasions. I believe he will not attack unless provoked. God help those who provoke him though. The massive full force of the Ottoman Empire would be unleashed. No, I do not think that will happen. I have, however, been trying to forge a meaningful alliance between my King Francis and Suleyman but without any substantial success," Antoine offered candidly.

Lucia interjected "Why? Would not an alliance between France and Charles V and the Holy Roman Empire make more sense and be more beneficial to both nations? How could an alliance with Suleyman be superior or more lucrative or create any more stability? In my view, Suleyman is unpredictable and prone to breaking his word. His religion allows him to deceive in order to advance his agenda." Lucia's geopolitical knowledge and insights were noted by those in the group.

"Madame," Antoine's response was chilly. "Charles is egomaniacal and threatens our borders constantly. Suleyman provides a useful diversion. If nothing else, 'the enemy of my enemy is my friend'." He answered dismissively, unwilling to engage in political squabble with the woman he knew to have close ties to Spain. Il Lupo took notice that his friend, the marquis, apparently had little tolerance for Lucia or her political viewpoints.

Gregor's growing intoxication did not prevent him from offering his insight. "You may be correct about Suleyman's ambitions. He may be content to consolidate his power within the current boundaries of the empire, which he has expanded greatly through his military conquests. But this will do nothing to quell restlessness within the janissary corps."

Giovanni speculated, "There remain issues regarding the janissaries who I believe are unpredictable in their support for Suleyman. Perhaps a few intrusions into the continent to plunder and stir things up a bit are not out of the question?"

"You will have restive soldiers always. Suleyman is not a man to act on impulse. I believe he is judicious when it comes to military involvement. Consolidation of power within his vast empire will be his primary focus," Antoine remarked.

"I have heard from Giovanni that you were offered a rare opportunity to join the sultan for dinner last night, Vincenzo," Lucia pried, dismissing the slight received from Antoine. "No doubt for your heroic actions in saving his life. Was there any discussion at the dinner about the details and motives of the plot to assassinate him?"

Il Lupo turned smiling eyes to the woman. "Ah, Suleyman holds everything close." He was prepared for the question and equally to deliberately mislead the gathered guests. He would not think to betray Suleyman's thoughts and concerns or compromise the investigation. All eyes at the table were on him, and he knew this was of utmost interest to them all.

"I merely believe the dinner was intended as a gesture of gratitude from the emperor," Il Lupo continued in deliberate deception. "He is unlikely to share information he may have gained with anyone until the intrigues are resolved. I was grateful for his kind invitation. It was a beautiful dinner, but we discussed primarily literature and a touch of religion."

It had not gone unnoticed by Il Lupo that Lucia was incessantly staring at him. Earlier in the evening when he caught her looking, she would immediately divert her eyes. During dinner, however, she dispensed with feigned shyness. Her intense gaze and deliberate attempts to catch his eye removed all doubt that she was interested in him. He thought Lucia was quite beautiful. While she did not possess the classic beauty of his deceased wife, she was exceptionally alluring. He wondered what direction their flirtation might take.

Dinner had been heavy. It included roast lamb and chicken that had been prepared with an apple and honey-soaked bread stuffing, heavily seasoned with cinnamon, grilled eggplant and sautéed leeks, rice with saffron and raisins. Desserts of sweetened yogurt with cherries and peaches with cream followed. It was difficult to rise from the table with stuffed bellies in the sweltering heat; Il Lupo believed that it was not just he who was grateful when it was time to leave. Giovanni walked his guests to the front door. Il Lupo headed to the terrace for relief from the suffocating interior rooms.

"May I join you?" Lucia boldly asked. "I see you wish to escape the heat too. Do you mind?" Lucia fanned her eyelashes nearly as furiously as her fan.

"Of course. It would be my pleasure," Il Lupo answered honestly, although he was uncertain what direction he wanted his relationship with Lucia to take.

He was lonely and longed for female companionship. He decided, however, to exercise caution and discretion regarding interactions with Lucia, until he could better assess her motives. He did not intend to be deliberately aloof, only prudent. He had Francesca to consider and, not knowing Lucia well, there was uncertainty regarding her character and adaptability to his lifestyle should he wish to pursue a serious relationship. However, he decided that these larger questions could wait. For the time being he would be content for some lighthearted and welcome female companionship, and some time away from the weightier, more serious tasks that lay before him in the coming hours and days.

They were just stepping onto the terrace when Giovanni joined them, inserting himself deliberately between them. Apparently oblivious to the possibility of a developing liaison between Lucia and Il Lupo, he began speaking, gesturing wildly, wineglass in hand and spilling a little on his sleeve. It appeared nothing would stop him from enjoying every moment of the evening and listening to himself talk.

"What a night! I love dining with friends and enjoying such intellectual conversation. It would be so pleasing to spend more time entertaining one another. However, if you will forgive, I am tired and must go to bed." He threw his head back to down the remnants of wine in his glass. "If I ever leave Istanbul, at this rate, they will have to roll me *up* the gangplank to board the ship. I trust Vincenzo that you and my cousin will have no difficulty entertaining yourselves even without my charming presence. I will see you in the morning." Giovanni, amused with himself, winked at Il Lupo and in a flourish, waved his hands, bowed and tottered away.

"Where is Fran this evening?" Lucia's intent was clear to Il Lupo. She was not remotely interested in Francesca's whereabouts. Lucia was hoping to hear that they would have time alone and without interruption.

"Fran is with new friends and has made plans. I do not ask too much. Fran is capable and causes me little worry. No doubt happy to be with people other than my typical associates, probably especially pleased to have a break from me." He hoped his vague response was enough to satisfy her.

Apparently it was—she had only hoped to hear she had Vincenzo Lupo to herself. Lucia immediately changed the subject.

"That is good to hear. I mean, it is not good to hear she is not here, but that she has found a way to amuse herself," Lucia stumbled to correct an impression that she was not interested in Fran's well-being. "Of course, Giovanni and I have always known that she is a girl but respect your need for disguises. I surmise she must continue to conceal her sex?"

"No, in fact, her identity was revealed last night and was actually cause for delight at dinner." Il Lupo's answer was again, deliberately misleading, intending to reveal nothing about the circumstances or the true initial reactions, or her presence in the Harem.

"I suppose she will use her disguises as necessary. We will of course, have those discussions when I see her next."

"It must be very difficult for you to raise her alone, without a wife. But now she is growing into her own person and it will be easier for you." Getting directly to her agenda for the evening, she continued, "Why haven't you remarried, Vincenzo?" The tone in her voice was soft and caressing as she spoke his given name.

"Who would have an old warrior? A traveler—a vagabond. Always away from home," Il Lupo answered sincerely. He did not see himself other than as a father, and a man who was skilled in his crafts.

He was not proud or vain. He was confident, but did not see himself as a particularly suitable or interesting candidate for a husband. There was no false modesty, just his belief that his lifestyle would be most undesirable for a long-term relationship.

"Oh *Vincenzo*," Lucia chided, moving closer to him. "You underestimate yourself *greatly*! You are all the talk of Venetian women, unmarried and married alike. They swoon, they pine, they dream! You and your exploits are often the topic at dinner tables and afternoon teas. And you punish us all by making yourself so infrequently available. You are a wealthy, handsome aristocrat in the prime of your life. And, oh, how did Giovanni put it, 'The finest rapier in Europe'. Besides," she teased, "many married women relish their husbands' absences."

"Ah, true love. I have actually heard that may occasionally be true." Il Lupo knew its veracity based on the frequent and prevalent indiscretions and sexual scandals in Venice. "They say that even the truest of loves needs an occasional break. It would be particularly so in my case. Just ask Fran," Il Lupo reflected, recalling the faces and names of past loves knowing that whether or not unrequited, they would not be forgotten. He felt somewhat wistful.

"Not a good example, Vincenzo," Lucia continued, oblivious to his distant look. "She is devoted to you and a daughter—not a wife or lover." Lucia suggestively drew out her enunciation of the word *lover*. Lucia felt an urgency to the conversation, as though she had only moments to convince Il Lupo that he was in need of a wife and lover and that she was the perfect candidate.

Somewhat surprised by her directness, Il Lupo moved to change the subject. "Tell me. Giovanni seems very well connected with sources at the palace."

Perturbed that the conversation was, at least for the moment, detouring in an unwelcome direction, Lucia responded, her mouth moving from a seductive smile to a pout.

"Yes. If you ever seek palace gossip, Giovanni is your man. He has probably paid off half the officials in the entire empire. Money buys knowledge and power, and the acquisition of information, by any means, is a necessary business expense. Giovanni is a very good business man." Lucia turned her fan toward the house. "He has quite the collections and connections."

Having had enough discussion of Giovanni, Lucia decided she needed to take things into her own hands if her seductive overtures were to succeed. Stepping close to him, Lucia boldly took Il Lupo's arm and put it around her waist. She drew near to him, put her arms around his neck, and kissed him. Il Lupo did not pull away. He returned her kisses and their kissing aroused him fully. He wanted to take her there, in that moment and on the terrace, even if it was only to fulfill an overwhelming desire for his own physical gratification. But as he held her, her head to his chest, he felt a wave of queasiness come over him. He did not know if it was the profoundly sweet aroma of her perfume, or whether it was the odd and unusual smell of her hair. Had he perhaps eaten tainted food? Whatever the reason, his momentary and exhilarating thoughts of desire receded as quickly as they had risen. He pulled himself from her and held her by her arms.

"Lucia. Not now." Il Lupo looked her directly in the eyes, repressing his queasiness. "We are in your cousin's house. You and I both know this is a most inopportune place for us to enjoy one another. Fran could come home." Il Lupo searched his mind for plausible reasons to extricate himself from the situation.

"I am sincerely flattered that a woman, one beautiful as you, could find me attractive and desire me. However, we both know that there will be other occasions and settings better suited for fulfilling our interests in one another," he continued, trying to offer opportunities for her to save face over his rejection of her advances.

Lucia appeared briefly stunned by his rebuke, even as gracious as it had been. She quickly attempted to regain her composure after the sting of his rebuff and appear in total agreement. "Vincenzo! Of course I was not intending that this go any further beyond a few playful moments to get to know one another more intimately. Excuse me, sir, if for one minute you believed that I would have allowed this to progress beyond a few trivial kisses and innocent flirtations," Lucia defended herself, feigning outrage at the perceived slight to her character. She wondered if, despite the kindness of his words, he found her unsuitable. Becoming annoyed, she decided to turn the tables and behave as though Il Lupo had aggressed against her.

She softly slapped his face. "Had anyone else suggested that I would be so forward as to aggressively seduce him, you can be sure that his face would be stinging for days to come. I know you to be a gentleman and *I*, a gentlewoman. I have great affection for you. But never would I have compromised myself. I have made myself clear, have I not, and you do understand, do you not?" Lucia continued with a more serious tone, trying to recover the dignity she had earlier discarded.

Il Lupo, ever genteel, allowed her to express her anger over his rebuff. He had insulted her, and although unintentional and even unavoidable, she now needed to save face and he would allow it.

"Of course, Lucia," Il Lupo responded gracefully, knowing fully well she had intended to seduce him. "I know you to be a woman of integrity. I would never imagine you in any other way." Il Lupo nuanced his words carefully to ensure they appeared sincere. He sensed she accepted them. He would not expect a woman of refinement to have been so directly bold with him and he found himself somewhat uncomfortable and wary. There was something not right—an element of awkwardness in their embrace. Despite his strong sexual desire, he was ill-at-ease. He was relieved he had pulled away.

"Then this evening is ended." Lucia began walking toward the terrace doors. Il Lupo followed. "It is cooler now and we will be able to sleep better. Good night, Vincenzo. Perhaps I will see you before you leave tomorrow." She turned and walked away.

Vincenzo breathed a heavy sigh of relief, his nausea subsiding, as he watched her ascend the wide staircase. He returned to the terrace for one last breath of fresh air and assess the evening's events. She had failed in her attempt to ensorcell him, and he felt wise to have turned her away.

Minacious Umbra

"No, Francesca! Cease immediately! Stop! It's Aziz!" Roxelana bolted from her bed.

Francesca froze, her hand poised, holding a jambiya as she straddled Aziz. In the flickering light from Roxelana's candle, Francesca realized she had mistaken Aziz for an intruder—a shadowy figure she had seen in the dim light hovering over Roxelana as she seemingly slept. She dismounted quickly.

"Aziz! I thought you were an assassin. I am very much on edge. Please forgive me," Francesca apologized, offering Aziz her hand to help him off the floor.

Brushing himself off and straightening his turban, Aziz laughed, quickly recovering his dignity and sense of humor. "Francesca, are you sure you are not secretly a dominatrix?" He was again duly impressed with her lethal skills and wiry strength.

Francesca felt a slight flush, uncertain whether being labeled a dominatrix was a compliment or not. She decided Aziz was simply being good-natured.

"Aziz, I will try to be less obvious about my sexual proclivities with you in the future," Francesca offered, laughing in response.

"Francesca, we need to tell you what we have learned." Roxelana sat up in bed and began putting on a luxurious robe.

"Before I went to bed, Aziz informed me about the missing relics. He also told me some very disturbing news he received from your father via Kemal and had not shared because he did not want to alarm me. Very early on the morning of your arrival, sometime before dawn, Aziz heard noises beneath the Harem and broke through a locked door. We had thought that like so many of the doors in the Harem that lead nowhere, this door was just one more dead-end. However, it was not and it led to a secret passage beneath the Harem, where Aziz found two mutilated bodies of janissaries! The bodies were taken to the morgue and examined by our physician, Abdullah, and your father. Your father has suspicions that the mutilations were intended to cover up poisoning, possibly by poisoned darts. Apparently, during your father's examination of the bodies, he discovered clues and, coupled with the discoveries this morning, has concluded that the mutilated janissaries Aziz found were the thieves. There are apparently many pieces of information he has puzzled together, including the fact that they were found in a secret passageway directly beneath the repository for the relics.

"These accumulated facts are no longer speculative or hypotheses, but direct evidence of the plot to steal the relics. There are many other questions that must be answered and we must not discount anything. Each piece of the puzzle requires evaluation as to its relevance and possible connection to the proliferating mysteries. Something that may seem unimportant could be the very clue needed to solve these questions. You had just gone to sleep, so I thought I would wait to tell you of Aziz's discoveries in the morning. I had also told Aziz if he heard anything unusual in the night, to wake me. I assume, Aziz that is why you are here?"

"Yes, yes," he said with some urgency. "I came to wake you because I have heard more strange noises emanating from beneath the palace. I thought you should know. I followed the sound and discovered yet another secret passageway opening to a crypt, and perhaps leading further into the cisterns. It is near the path to the area under the *Has Oda*. It also intersects with another longer passageway that I did not have time to explore fully. I did not want to be gone too long and leave you unprotected, so I came back to inform you. Now that you are awake and can keep a watchful eye, I am going to investigate further and see where that path leads," Aziz informed them both, his eyes filled with anticipation and concern.

"No, you are not going alone. Francesca and I will come with you. Francesca, grab your knives and give me a couple. Give me that kard. It felt good in my hand. Your lessons could not have been better timed," Roxelana directed, handing Francesca a caftan to cover her night clothing.

They followed Aziz, cautiously venturing into the cimmerian depths, each carrying a lantern with just enough light to illuminate their way but not enough to be seen from too great a distance. They hoped to conceal their approach from anyone or anything lurking, hiding beneath the palace. Roxelana held onto Aziz's waist sash with one hand, knife in the other, while Francesca followed, frequently looking back to ensure they were not trailed. The path was narrow and the uneven cobbles caused them to stumble occasionally. Within a few minutes, they came upon areas dug into the wall that contained ancient sarcophagi, with inscriptions incised into them from a long bygone era and covered with cobwebs and dust.

Roxelana suddenly jumped back. "Look!" she exclaimed, pointing to a skull and mound of bones that had found their way out of the carved rock sarcophagus, its heavy stone lid ajar. "How grisly! What a desecration of remains. A hideous place! And the fetid smell! My stomach revolts!" Roxelana coughed, her gut retching.

Francesca surveyed the area, but did not believe the smell was emanating from bones long ago decayed and stripped of flesh.

They continued a little further and entered the cistern. They were now overwhelmed with the stench of death.

"Careful!" Aziz directed. "We are close to the edge of the water here. Step cautiously. Our path narrows." Aziz held his torch downward revealing they were less than two feet from the murky cistern waters.

"We are still under the Harem. I wonder how much further this goes?" he questioned, nervously, his voice exhibiting a slight trembling. Without warming, Aziz let out a sharp gasp.

"Oh Allah...oh Allah *Al Hafiz*, preserve us!" Roxelana exclaimed as she and Francesca saw the bodies of two festering and mutilated janissaries. Their rotting, decomposing corpses exuded a horrible stench. Dried blood surrounded the bodies and was so thick in one area that the dark, almost black, crimson pool had failed to dry.

"Ghastly. Look at their bluish-green lips and how bloated the bodies are," Roxelana declared, still choking slightly from the malodorous stink. "Do all corpses have bulging, blue-green lips?" she asked, looking at Francesca.

"No. Given the extent of their decomposition, they must have been here for at least a day. My father and Abdullah will want to examine them. We must return and report this immediately to my father and Kemal," Fran insisted.

"I agree," Aziz said, anxious to leave the ghastly scene. "Come, Majesty, we must go back. This is no place for any woman much less the sultan's favored."

Turning to leave, a fleeting wisp of wind caught their flames, nearly extinguishing them. Their attention was drawn first to an umbra, an insinuation, a sense that something supernatural was present. Suddenly the mercurial shape took form, transforming quickly into a hooded and cloaked creature, previously indistinguishable and blending into the wall of the cistern. Its back was to them and stood tall and menacing in the shadows cast by the torches. It had positioned itself over the bodies of yet two more janissaries, one completely mutilated and the other in the final throes of death, still writhing in pain. The creature—the Jinn—was finishing its fiendish work with the moribund janissary who, just as his brothers in arms before him, was being sent, mutilated, to his death. Abruptly, the Jinn stiffened and sensing the presence of the three onlookers, ceased in its demonic maiming. Turning its head slowly and deliberately in their direction, it focused its minacious gaze on them.

The three were transfixed by the terrifying creature that had materialized out of the darkness. It fiendishly hissed. Aziz stepped back, his arms outstretched in an attempt to shield Roxelana and Francesca. The Jinn slowly moved its fingers, wrapping them, one by one around a long, tube-like stick previously concealed within its cloak. In one motion, the tube was raised to the center of its chest. The three continued to watch as if in a hypnotic trance, when Francesca was suddenly seized with the enormity of the danger that accompanied the raising of the long tube.

"Down!" she yelled, pushing Roxelana to the stone floor and Aziz to the wall, just as a dart whizzed over their heads. They waited a few moments, bracing for an onslaught of darts, but there was silence. Raising her head cautiously, Francesca realized that the Jinn had disappeared. It had vanished nearly as quickly as it had appeared, but the sense of danger remained palpable.

"It is gone. We must find it," Francesca directed, summoning the courage to pursue the demon. "First, be sure these two are dead." She straddled the motionless janissaries, lifting each of their hands and checking for a pulse. "They are both dead. Quick, we must follow and attempt to discover where the creature went."

The three moved quickly but with great vigilance further down the path. No sooner had they rounded the first corner that they came upon a dead end. Francesca ran her hand over the ancient stones of the wall where the path ended. She searched for any give—any movement in the stones, but her hands felt nothing and her light was dim. The wall felt sturdy and completely intact.

"It's as though it has vanished into thin air." Roxelana stood shaking her head, continuing to be incredulous. "How could it get away from us? Where could it possibly have gone?"

Aziz backed up, terror on his face. "Only a Jinn could pass through such a wall. Or perhaps it has changed its shape and is watching us now. Please, let's leave," he pleaded unable to hide his growing trepidation.

"Remain calm, Aziz. There is an explanation for all this. Mark this spot so we are sure to find it when we come back with others and more light," Francesca directed. "Now, we must go back and see what clues these bodies may reveal." She turned and Roxelana and Aziz followed.

Returning to the bodies, Francesca examined them more closely. "Look, they both have darts in their necks! And this one here," she pointed, "his lacerations are not as severe as his mutilated companion—probably because we interrupted the demon. In his case, the wounds could not have been the cause of his death. It was the poison in these darts. Look, their lips are not bulging either like the victims we saw a few minutes ago over there." She pointed back in the direction they had come.

"I'm sure this is because these victims are freshly dead, unlike the others. It is good fortune for us that the demon did not have time to retrieve the darts after we caught it in the act."

Recognizing that the darts were tipped with poison and posed a possible danger if touched with bare skin, Francesca ripped a piece of fabric from her nightshirt beneath her caftan and carefully removed the feathered darts from the victims' throats.

"I recognize this janissary!" Francesca said, pointing down to one of the newly deceased bodies. "This is one of the janissaries that attempted to assassinate Suleyman. I recognize the scar on his face.

I think his dead companion must be the other janissary who was able to escape the scene after the failed assassination attempt, but I cannot be sure.

"We do not want to disturb the Harem. But it is imperative that first thing in the morning we get this information to my father or Kemal or both. Let us return to the Harem now."

Turning to leave, Francesca noticed something in the waters of the cistern. "Aziz, hold your torch down here," she pointed. Aziz complied and as he did, he recoiled, attempting to suppress a shriek.

"Ayyyyy!" he yelled, jumping backwards, "It is the Medusa!"

Roxelana, Aziz, and Francesca stared in horror at the ghoulish face roughly carved and eroded on the base of one of the collapsed, partially submerged stone pillars of the cistern.

"It is the head of Medusa!" Francesca exclaimed. "Imagine how horrible it must have been for these two dead janissaries. Look at the position of their bodies." She pointed to the swollen, distended bodies at their feet.

"The face of the gorgon must have been the last thing they saw in this life. How ghastly!" Roxelana shuddered. "We need to leave this unholy place of witchcraft and diabolical machinations."

With the light from their small torch nearly extinguished, they left the bodies and the stench of the caliginous subterranean graveyard behind them.

Endowed with Sapience

Back in the relative safety of Roxelana's chambers, Francesca was curious to learn more about the creature they had seen in the cistern. "Please tell me about this demon—the Jinn. Is it also called the Shaitan or the Ifrit? I have heard these different names for Islamic devils," she questioned, still recovering from the shock of the evening's discoveries.

Roxelana settled onto the divan, swaddling herself into her caftan, as if to give comfort or shield her from evil. "I learned of its mythology when I converted to Islam. I was Orthodox Christian; the closest comparison is the devil. In Islam, the Iblis is the archdevil. He commands lesser devils and whispers into the ears of humans and Jinn inciting them to perform evil deeds. There are five levels of the devil in Islam after the Iblis. They are the Madrid, the strongest, then the Ifrit, the Shaitan, and the Ghul—which is the Jinn—and the Jann, the weakest. The Jinn may take human or supernatural form. The Koran speaks of them as having been created from the 'smokeless fire.' From the earliest teachings of Islam, children are warned never to speak the names of these devils for in doing so, they will be summoned. The simple utterance of their name can cause catastrophe."

Roxelana continued. "They can interact with humans and are tactile and can be destroyed. They can be good or evil. A Shaitan Jinn is evil and must be what we have seen tonight. They are endowed with sapience, or wisdom, and are one of the three creations of Allah. Humans, angels, and jinns. They are known to inhabit dingy and dark places." Francesca listened intently while Aziz remained wide-eyed and in an apparent state of distress.

"They can appear in many forms—human, animal, and even dragon. They can fly in the air, look like snakes or dogs or tall creatures in cloaks. They can appear any way they choose—they are ghostly shape changers. They are believed to live on dung piles, have a horrible stench, and subsist on bones. I have always dismissed this mythology. After tonight, I am not so sure. For example," Roxelana carried on, "when I just mentioned that they live on a dung pile, I had forgotten that. I do not know if either of you noticed, but while in the crypts, aside from the wretched smell of death, I thought I also detected the smells of dung and a faint sweetness. The smells were incompatible with each other and I cannot be sure if the smells were intermingled or from two separate sources. Perhaps there is a slight saccharine smell emitted by a decomposing body? It is all so vexing and contradictory. I do not know."

"Yes, I noticed a faint sweetness also. It seemed so completely out of place near the rotting corpses. One smell in juxtaposition to the other —the two seemingly incompatible. This is perhaps something to remember and discuss later, but please continue—this is most fascinating. What does tradition say happens to the Jinn when they die?" Francesca's curiosity piqued.

"Just as we mere mortals, they go to Heaven or Hell. I think we all know where the Jinn we encountered tonight will go!" Roxelana answered with certainty.

"One more reason not to wind up in Hell," Aziz offered.

"Also, to avoid the Jinn, we are instructed to avoid graveyards. Considering all the bodies littering the cistern and crypts, the passages tonight were a graveyard, to be sure. Upon discovering this 'graveyard,' it would be a warning, signaling all to stay away. Most would heed that warning and avoid such an unholy and gruesome place."

"We can certainly all agree on that. One of the things that astounded me was the size of the Jinn we encountered. But, the dart was delivered from the chest area and not the area of the head of this demon. It is most perplexing," Francesca remarked, finding the discussion enlightening as she pondered her questions. "There is so much to analyze and report. We have no idea what tomorrow holds. Now it is time to rest."

"You will sleep inside the room for the rest of the night here with us, Aziz," Roxelana ordered. "We will all feel safer that way.

We will sleep in shifts. We need to be ready for any further trouble. Aziz, you take the first shift. Wake me in two hours."

Roxelana laid her head on the pillow, but lifted it a moment later. "Oh, and before I forget, be sure to make arrangements as soon as possible for Francesca to see her father in the morning. She may have been able to enter the Harem cloaked and disguised as a concubine, but I do not think we should allow her to leave dressed as one. I will take care of that and you make the arrangements, Aziz."

"Majesty, forgive me for this last disturbance, but in all the excitement, there is one more bit of information you and Francesca need to know. There is truth to the rumor that there is a eunuch that has not been castrated. I have heard this from a trusted member of my tribe—he is Daju—and would only bring me information if he knew it with certainty," Aziz informed, referring to his native home in the Sudan. "We do not yet know his identity."

All the candles but one were extinguished and the room was quiet except for the soft, fluttering sound of the fabrics catching the night breeze. They were exhausted, but finding respite for their restless minds would be challenging at the end of their most frightening and eventful day.

Day Four

Dördüncü Gün

Rapprochement

incenzo Lupo sat alone at the dining table of the palazzo's morning room, which was elegantly covered with a Florentine lace tablecloth, artistically hand sewn by nuns from the convent at Santa Maria Novella. Place settings of Dehua white porcelain plates known as *Blanc de Chine,* gold utensils and tankards adorned the table, ready to receive the food, sweet juices and warm beverages served with the morning meal.

The morning room of the Contratini villa had a visual lightness when compared with the formal evening dining area. The wall coverings were a delicate green chinoiserie paper depicting exotic birds with brightly colored plumage held captive in gilded birdcages. The rays of the sun caught the gold paint bringing it to a shimmer in the delicate morning light. Il Lupo knew that Giovanni traded heavily in the arts of the Orient and was always intent on displaying the most recent fashion trends and acquisitions. Standing against one wall was a beautifully detailed Dutch marquetry cupboard of flowing lines, delicately arched with a double-door upper cabinet topped with a graceful carved pediment and mounted on a three-drawer bombe base. A slender English mahogany sideboard held an eclectic mix of elegant silver service overflowing with breakfast foods, and a pair of rare, carved jade Chinese Foo Dogs prominently displayed and placed as if standing guard over the extravagance of wealth. Once again, each element in the room had been meticulously selected by Giovanni to be of the finest quality.

He breakfasted on baked eggs with rice and spices, breads with jams and chutneys, cheeses, fresh fruits and yogurt. Vincenzo was just finishing when Lucia walked in the room. Although she was in full makeup and her hair coiffed, she remained in her chemise, flimsy and nearly transparent, covered by an equally diaphanous caftan. The fabric was cream in color and embroidered with delicate gold threads leaving little to the imagination with regard to her sensual figure. Her slippers were gold. She wore no jewelry and, without the constraints of the structured and boned bodice of her typical daytime clothing, her breasts were unrestrained. Il Lupo could not help but admire how the fabric draped over and accentuated her voluptuous body. He felt another sudden twinge of desire. She was a beautiful woman but also an enigma. Il Lupo hoped her presence at breakfast could prove useful. She might provide valuable information, given her extensive travels, friends and rumored escapades in the royal courts.

"Good morning, Vincenzo!" she greeted him cheerfully. She walked over and kissed him on top of the head, casually and deliberately brushing her breasts to the side of his face, as if nothing had transpired between them the previous evening.

"There!" she said, matter-of-factly. "Does that not make things all better now after our little misunderstanding last night? We are perfectly fine and at ease with one another?"

"Of course, Lucia. I hope you understood my reasons and accepted my apology as sincere. I had no intention of putting you off. Perhaps we can resurrect the moment at a better time and place for us both." Il Lupo offered his best attempts at early morning diplomacy.

"Perhaps, indeed! Good then. Let us talk. It is a perfect opportunity because unless Fran is here, we are once again alone—except of course for the servants. Giovanni has already left this morning to inspect a shipment that has just arrived in port."

"Yes, I saw him just as he was leaving. He is a busy man with many business opportunities. He seems to make the best of them. However, Fran could arrive at any moment, so our time alone may be limited," Il Lupo responded. While he was certainly not anticipating Francesca's imminent arrival, he continued to remain uneasy and did not want a repeat of events of the previous evening—at least not for the time being and until he had resolved his unsettled feelings regarding Lucia.

Lucia remained a woman on a mission and was not to be deterred. "I thought about you so much last night, Vincenzo. Please do not be mistaken when I tell you how sincerely I care for you. I

was thinking about your tragedy—your wife dying in childbirth—
the worst of fates. To be on the verge of such complete happiness
and have it all stolen, I do not know how you have adjusted to the
tragedy. After all, to be a father and a mother—you have taken on
both parental roles rather than hiring a governess or remarrying.
You know, Vincenzo, Francesca needs a mother—even now. There
should be many fine candidates. But you must consider this same
woman would need to be your wife and capable of giving you all
that *you* desire," Lucia persisted.

She paused, now slowly stirring her hot tea. "You must know,
Vincenzo—surely you are not immune to my flirtations—that I am
more than suitable as a wife and mother. In fact I am well sought
after, as you may have heard. You would do very well...be the envy
of many a man. However, unlike the ingrained and boring mating
rituals of our society, *I* prefer to do the choosing. Will you at least
concede that you find me attractive?"

Il Lupo looked at the seductress sitting before him. "Lucia, I
am honored and flattered. Of course you are a beautiful woman
and extremely desirable. It was nearly impossible for me to restrain
myself last evening. However, do you not think this conversation
should be postponed until we have time to spend privately? Let us
wait." Despite his growing impatience with her directness, he knew
he needed to choose his words carefully. She could possibly provide
valuable information and he did not want to risk alienating her. He
tiptoed delicately. "Can we agree on this?"

"Yes, yes, of course!" Lucia responded, her spirits lifted by, and
seizing on, what she perceived to be his apparent encouragement. "I
absolutely agree that now is not the time. There is so much happening
and we have little opportunity for privacy, let alone intimacy. I can
assure you, Vincenzo, that you will not be disappointed," she flirted,
now playing seductively with a loose strand of hair.

"With that in mind, how long are you intending to stay in
Istanbul?" Il Lupo wiped his mouth with the napkin and placed it
on the table, signaling he was ready to leave.

"Originally I had only planned a short visit. Now, perhaps in
light of our conversation, I will say that my departure date has yet to
be determined," she answered coyly. "Do you have a busy day ahead
of you, or might I see you later in the day?" Lucia was hopeful.

"I doubt I will return before dark. I am unsure of my exact schedule, which will evolve as events unfold."

"Anything related to the rash of strange occurrences at the palace? Giovanni's sources are telling him that there are several janissaries who have been found murdered. Do you have knowledge about that?"

"Several? I had heard janissaries have been murdered." Il Lupo was surprised by Lucia's knowledge. "I see that Giovanni informs you and that he is kept informed. He seems to know more than I do." Il Lupo put on his doublet—his favorite—a well-worn and beautifully tanned, cognac leather.

He continued with feigned amusement, "Giovanni has proven himself to be quite resourceful. He pays more for his sources than I could afford. Please inform me if you find out any further information or rumors." Il Lupo decided it was time to begin using Lucia's attraction to him for his own benefit. He wanted to determine and assess just how much she and Giovanni knew and the source, or sources, of the information. Unwittingly, or perhaps willingly, she might prove to be an asset for his investigation.

In moving to leave the room, he brushed briefly against Lucia. Lucia, immediately responsive to his touch, stood up. Il Lupo took her in his arms and drew her close. "See if you can find out what he knows of Mehmed. My understanding is that problems seem to center on the Harem."

"Yes, I will do that," Lucia agreed, purring and pushing her body closer to his. "Women always get blamed for men's problems. It is the way of the world. I only want to be blamed for one man's problems—yours." She moved her hand along his pelvis, pushing her body into his, her morning clothing now loosened allowing her breasts to nearly spill from beneath the gauzy fabric, so thin he could feel her skin beneath it.

"You are right," he laughed, indulging her for the moment, trying to keep his mind focused and undistracted. "But in this case I am more concerned with the keeper than the kept."

Lucia pried, her hands continuing their exploration with the great expertise gained from vast experience. "Will you tell Suleyman of your findings?"

"I cannot say, for I do not know what discussions I will have with Suleyman or what questions he might ask." Il Lupo's answer was intentionally vague. He was sure that she must know more than she was revealing. Her interest was more than simple curiosity.

There was a momentary pause in their conversation and Il Lupo knew that she wanted to kiss him. "Ah! I see that Kemal has arrived," he remarked, looking over her head and breaking the mood upon hearing Kemal's voice as he entered Giovanni's home.

"I must go, Lucia." Il Lupo gave her a quick kiss on the tip of her nose, adjusting himself and his belt.

"It is good to see you, my friend," a relieved Il Lupo greeted Kemal as he entered the room. Kemal turned away when he saw Lucia so scantily dressed, his face reddening, slightly embarrassed that he had intruded unexpectedly on an intimacy.

Lucia grabbed Il Lupo by the arm and whispered in his ear, "I may just wait up on the chance you may want a most delicious dessert this evening and continue our explorations." Il Lupo smiled and waved goodbye. Lucia was self-absorbed and filled with conceit. She was worldly- anything but insecure- and confident Vincenzo Lupo would be unable to refuse her 'dessert' invitation.

Schmatte

A haggard female beggar sat on the cobbled street near the construction site of a new mosque. The foundation and framework complete, application of the exterior finishes had begun. The hag went unnoticed by the dozens of work men in the area; her head and body wrapped in layers of ragged, dirty hemp, with sandals tied to her feet by strings of leather. Her face and clothing covered in soot and grime - she was dressed in schmatte. She rocked back and forth muttering, holding her staff and a scarred, verdigris copper bowl in an outstretched hand.

She watched the workers in awe as heavily laden flats of tiles were hoisted to the high towers and installed on the minarets and onion-domed roofs. The tiles glistened like gold in the rutilant morning sun as the laborers toiled incessantly and devotedly to lavish their artistry on the magnificent structure. While appearing to watch the construction, her focus had actually been on two men nearby who had been conversing for some time. Stooped and decrepit, she finally approached them cautiously, nearing her targets in a deranged, circling pattern. Her demeanor would have raised suspicion in no one, blending so easily as she did with the masses. The beggar's motivation was not to beg but surreptitiously eavesdrop on their conversation.

"Il Lupo...." she heard from the man she knew to be Giovanni Contratini.

"Tonight..." she caught from the Grand Vizier, Ibrahim, watching as he accepted a leather pouch which she surmised, contained gold. Ibrahim glanced over and watched the old hag approach, his lip curling in disgust. His manner only confirmed the beggar's impression of him—she thought him despicable.

Moving closer she offered the cup in her hand, her walking stick used to support her hunched position. "Alms for the poor, your excellencies," the old beggar woman solicited, stooping in their presence and avoiding disrespectful eye contact.

"Leave, you old hag!" Giovanni demanded, attempting to kick her. She moved just quickly enough to avoid injury. "Get out of here!" Turning to Ibrahim, he laughed, "She's pretty fast for an old witch."

The hag acquiesced and bowed. "*Salaam Aliqum*, excellencies." Hobbling away, the beggar continued using her walking stick necessary to support her gibbous posture.

Once out of their sight, she quickened her pace, moving to the rear of the construction site where Il Lupo and Kemal were in discussion. The beggar circled Kemal mindlessly, muttering and shaking the cup up at him, her eyes cast respectfully downward. She watched the handsome warrior reach for a small pouch in his sash.

"It's all right, Kemal. Save your money. This old hag doesn't deserve a thing."

Kemal was taken aback, stunned, by Il Lupo's harshness and wondered if he had misjudged him, having thought he would be a generous and kind man. Il Lupo's callous attitude toward the needy woman was unsettling.

"Your gig is up, *Francesca*. Pretty convincing, would you not say?" Il Lupo chortled, turning to Kemal in obvious amusement.

Francesca looked up at Kemal. He immediatly recognized her blue eyes and then, beneath her dirtied face and disheveled appearance, her beauty. He locked eyes with the stooped beggar. Even with her disguise and dressed in rags, he again felt the reemergence of the deep longing so suppressed before his first moments alone with Francesca. She inspired him to hope. Dare he, he wondered? She enchanted him completely. After seeing her transformation the day before, he had returned to his room in the evening and written another entry in his journal.

Francesca. Francesca.
A word of sweetness on my lips
Skin warmed and honeyed by the sun
Elysium fields of Himalayan blue poppies in her eyes

Dare I recklessly reveal
The amorous truths so quickly and completely,
Spoken by my heart…
I am bewitched…

Kemal could not know that as she watched him, she had been touched by the act of kindness he had intended to bestow on an old beggar woman. She believed it a glimpse into this warrior's soul, intensifying her positive feelings about him. *Was this the exciting invasion of the mind that Roxelana had referred to?* Francesca wondered, her heart too, was full of hope.

"See what just one night as an odalisque can do for a girl?" Il Lupo laughed, snapping them both back to reality.

"Indeed, a few nights in the Harem should be a required finishing course for any young woman. It appears to have done wonders for you, Francesca," Kemal teased, deciding that his musings would have to wait.

"Yes, clothes really are a girl's best friend." Il Lupo could not help but laugh at the sight of his completely disheveled daughter.

"Well, they are clearly not yours—either of you. Those hats and tassels—so last century!" she parried.

"And those dresses over pantaloons and such clashing colors! Really gentlemen, you could not have chosen more garish combinations!" Francesca continued, laughing loudly.

"It appears Francesca is in need of yet more schooling. A little polish and perhaps lessons in diplomacy? Another night should do it," Il Lupo remarked, feigning disapproval.

"No more than a couple should suffice given the already considerable progress," Kemal opined, his eyes twinkling and playful. Il Lupo watched the two banter, realizing fully there was a strong attraction between his beautiful daughter and the accomplished paladin.

"Francesca has much to learn, but we should remember that she is expert in a few things—she is as fluent in Latin expletives as she is with the sword. Just like those birds Giovanni gave to Suleyman. If we are not careful and offend her, she will soon be hurling one and swinging the other in attempts to silence us. You may need to learn, Kemal—in fact it may be imperative—that Francesca does not like to be the object of ridicule," Il Lupo cautioned Kemal, who appeared to take the words seriously and raised his eyebrows.

"Enough drivel, you idiots. Do you two want news or not?" Francesca changed the subject, her patience with them waning. "I have learned much."

"Whoa! Yes, yes, of course, Francesca. No need to throw a conniption," Il Lupo offered, seeing that his daughter was becoming impatient to relate what she had learned from her time in the Harem and in her newest disguise as a beggar.

"Last night was very eventful. Just after we had gone to sleep, Aziz woke us. He had heard noises emanating from beneath the Harem and came to tell us. He was going to investigate further on his own, but Roxelana insisted we go with him.

"We followed Aziz through secret passages that run through the cistern and crypts. The cisterns obviously contain water, and the crypts are relatively dry especially considering their close proximity to the cisterns. I am not sure that this will matter, but I believe they were constructed at different times and further, that the cistern paths intersect in one way or another with the crypts. The cisterns appear to have been built block by block, but the crypts have been carved out of the earth; they are of different materials. It may be by design or simply accidental that they are connected." Kemal and Il Lupo listened intently as she continued describing her insightful observations of the previous evening.

"Aziz explained that when he investigated, he found that the main passageway intersects with a shorter one leading to the area under the *Has Oda*. He then explored what appeared to be a longer path, one that interconnects with the path beneath the Harem and perhaps led to an exit. He turned back before traversing it completely because he was uncomfortable leaving Roxelana so long, given recent events.

"First, we came to an area containing stone tombs and a pile of bones that frightened us all; this area was very dry. It was eerie down there. The passage through the crypts led to the cistern. The passageway narrows and at some points you must be observant to ensure not actually falling into the water. This is the area where the construction is of stone blocks. There is a virtually constant dripping from condensation of the water."

She continued. "Then, dreadful things happened. We were initially overwhelmed by a fetid, putrid stench. Within moments, we came across the rotting bodies of two janissaries—we knew they were janissaries because of their clothing. Their bodies and clothing were ripped to shreds. The bodies were bloated, especially their lips. We were just getting over the shock when we heard a noise, then a wisp of a breeze, so we went to investigate." Francesca was nearly breathless in her retelling.

"There—before our eyes—was a cloaked gruesome demon, standing over the bodies of two more janissaries! At least one of them was not yet dead. This creature, this demon, loomed so large and was just standing over them with its huge steel-like talons exposed. It was ghastly; the most frightening thing I have ever seen—impossible to fully describe. Does anyone have something to drink? My mouth is so dry." She stopped, accepting water from her father's leather canteen. She breathed heavily, pausing to regain her composure.

"Then it saw us. I think we were all so stunned at the sight. We must have been frozen in that spot. It had been staring down at the bodies—one of the janissaries was moaning. Very slowly, it turned its menacing head and looked at us. We could not see its face because it was shrouded in the hood of its cloak. It emitted a horrible hissing sound. Somehow, thankfully, I realized its hands were moving. We were dazed for what felt like hours, but what happened must have occurred within split seconds. This thing—this demon—drew a long stick from its cloak and moved it to about chest height—and that is puzzling. Why raise it to the middle of the chest and not to the level, much higher, where the mouth of the demon would presumably be? Puzzling and possibly pertinent?

"Fortunately, I realized this creature had a blowgun and I instinctively pushed Roxelana down and yelled to Aziz to get down. He is pretty quick for such big man. He reacted just in time to avoid a dart. We lay prone for just a little longer. When we realized the attack was over—at least for the moment—we impulsively followed the retreating demon. We jumped over the bodies and rounded the corner, but came to a dead end—just a wall. How could this creature have just ephemerally disappeared? Into thin air?" Francesca shook her head, incredulous. "There has to be an explanation."

"It's the Jinn—the Shaitan, which, however, I do not know," Kemal offered. "In our time together, I have told your father about Jinn mythology, since there have been rumblings that one is roaming in or near the palace. Jinns are dangerous and manipulate the nescient, uneducated, and superstitious into acting against their conscience. Terrified of the Jinn, they dare not disobey, believing they will suffer dire and deadly consequences. It can terrorize even the most pure at heart to commit criminal, immoral acts. Even some who are well educated believe in the Jinn's ability to work its wickedness, the myths having been so ingrained from childhood. To whisper its name is to 'call' it up. Most proclaim that, while they themselves could never be moved to act against their conscience, the malevolent demon can coerce others to do its evil bidding."

"Yes, I learned much the same from Aziz and Roxelana. We also discussed folklore of the Jinn when we returned to the room for the night," Francesca shuddered.

"Are the bodies still there? We need to study them," Il Lupo said urgently.

"They are, *Padre*. We will take you to them. One more thing—a very important element. When we interrupted the Jinn, I believe we stopped it from completely shredding the body of one of the janissaries. Yet he died anyway. It had to have been within just a few seconds of our reaching him. Based on that, I have concluded that in fact, it is the poison from the darts that killed at least this one janissary. The mutilations are intended as a deception to conceal the true cause of death," Francesca offered.

"Yes!" Il Lupo agreed, proud of his daughter's assessment. "This would confirm the other evidence. Abdullah and I suspected poison was the cause of death when we examined the bodies in the morgue. I was uncertain, but concluded, just as you have, that the maiming of bodies is intended to cover up the true cause of death. Were you able to retrieve the darts?"

"Again, yes, *Padre*. Here they are. I was able to retrieve them from the necks of the newly deceased and found two near the bodies of those who departed this world earlier and the one that was intended for us," she explained, cautiously unwrapping the darts bundled up in the piece of torn cloth.

"I wonder if the Jinn intended to take them and we interrupted more than a murder? It may have wanted to remove the evidence before leaving. Our presence likely foiled that," she speculated.

"Yes, this Jinn would likely want to eliminate all traces of the cause of death," Il Lupo responded with certainty. "But since no one had actually witnessed it shredding the bodies, we could not be certain. Your observations confirm our conclusions."

Il Lupo paced. "Remember also that, up until your discovery, only one dart had been found. The darts were removed from the necks of Kareem and Jamal before they were found. They now lie on slabs in the morgue. The area where they were found in the passageway under the *Has Oda* was also searched. And, there were no darts found in the bloated bodies of the janissaries. Was it the Jinn that removed them or another? Did someone else or *something else* manipulate it to perform these vicious acts or, at the very least, act in concert with it? Is there only one or are there more of these devils? And the obvious, larger questions are the motivations behind the demonic acts."

"But there is still more that I learned from Aziz and Roxelana. Aziz told me yesterday on the way to meet Roxelana that despite the fact that the Valide Sultan—Suleyman's mother—is nominally in control of the Harem, she has actually abdicated her responsibilities to Gulbehar. The Valide Sultan has chosen a quiet life and wishes to be free of Harem drama and duties. The mother of the sultan is technically the most powerful woman in the court.

"As a result of her abdication, Gulbehar wields the power in the Harem. Although Suleyman clearly loves Roxelana, and she is his favorite and confidant, she is not his wife, and under the laws, as they exist now, Gulbehar's son, Mustafa, would be in line to ascend to the throne. It appears unlikely that any of Roxelana's children would be considered a legitimate heir. Mehmed is Gulbehar's favorite, and he would do anything for her—*anything!* He knows his position is completely dependent upon her position of power within the Harem and court," Francesca explained.

"These factors are as fascinating as they are worrisome. They continue to provide valuable clues we must not lightly dismiss. It cannot be denied that both Gulbehar and Mehmed have obvious motivations to want Suleyman dead," Il Lupo observed.

Kemal, who had remained silent, added his thoughts. "To ensure Mehmed's continued authority, Gulbehar's son, Mustafa, must become sultan. Gulbehar and Mehmed will then retain their positions of power—even over Mustafa's wife when he marries. Gulbehar will become the most powerful woman in the court and would rise to the position of Valide Sultan as the mother of the sultan. You can rest assured that she would never abdicate her authority to anyone. You are right Count, these circumstances provide strong motivation to murder Suleyman," he concluded with growing concern in his voice. "His death would ensure her ascendancy."

"Right now, time is our enemy and we must make the best use of it. There is great urgency. The murders escalate and we do not know what continued danger the sultan faces," Il Lupo remarked, pacing again and immersed in thought. "There are many potential motives. We need more facts."

"I have more information to share," Francesca said. "Aziz told us last night that it is certain there is an 'intact' eunuch in the Harem— or at least one whose castration was botched—which is apparently equally dangerous. His existence was confirmed by another eunuch from Aziz's tribe. Someone must be protecting the eunuch from discovery."

"Whoever knows his identity would have great power and control over him. Of this, we can be completely certain. Is there anything else you have learned, Francesca? Your time in the Harem has proved most productive," Il Lupo asked.

"I have one final piece of information. Just before I met with you this morning, I saw Giovanni handing gold to Ibrahim, very likely a bribe."

"Very interesting. I suspected it already. It could simply be that they were 'doing business' as is the usual 'custom,' or it could mean something more sinister. I will speak to them without being specific about what you observed and overheard. Any clues ascertained as a result of speaking to them, independently, could lead to dismissing the bribes as business as usual, or something substantially more serious. Are they complicit in these treacheries?" Il Lupo watched as a young man in clean but simple clothing approached them.

"I am looking for Count Vincenzo Lupo. Is that you, *Effendi*?" the young man asked.

"Why do you ask?" Il Lupo queried him suspiciously.

"I have a message from Abdullah, the chief physician to the sultan. He said you would likely be in the company of Kemal, the Commander of the Beyliks. He also said you might be speaking with a beggar," he responded.

"Yes, I am Count Vincenzo Lupo," he laughed, "spending time with a beggar. What do you have for me?"

The messenger handed him a note. Il Lupo pulled a silver coin from a pouch and handed it to the messenger who thanked Il Lupo, courteously bowed, and left. Il Lupo read the message and turned to Francesca.

"Do you think Roxelana could determine for us if any of the eunuchs have lived in the New World before being enslaved?"

"Well, that's an interesting question. I will ask her when I return to the Harem," Francesca confirmed.

"I will tell you more later. Return now and see what else you can uncover. If you discover anything, including information regarding a possible eunuch from the New World, tell Aziz, and he will relay the information to me." Il Lupo turned to leave.

"Hmmm, I wonder how Abdullah knew we would be talking with a beggar. What do you think, Kemal?"

"I think someone was having a little too much fun disguising Fran this morning and word got back to Abdullah. I think Aziz and Roxelana are overly enjoying themselves. Dressing Francesca must have been a welcome diversion for them both," Kemal laughed. He watched in continuing enchantment, feeling the enormity of his growing affection, as the haggard yet beguiling beggar, walking stick in hand, disappeared beyond a stand of olive trees.

Contratini's Crate

Having cast aside their clothing, the naked stevedores scurried amid the trunks, crates, and barrels in the sweltering heat in the hold of the ship. Sweating heavily in the steamy environment, they worked to fulfill the orders barked out by their overseer above deck.

"Get me the damn crate for Contratini!" the chief stevedore shouted. The stevedore was clothed, as were all topside, in nothing but a thawb—a loose fitting, dress-like, ankle-length muslin shirt that allowed for the free flowing of air around their bodies. The only distinguishing feature of the garments worn by the chief stevedore was the black inset fabric on his muslin turban.

"This crate holds precious merchandise. Get it up here! I have waited too long already," Giovanni ordered, slapping the back of the chief stevedore's head.

"Idiots. You are all idiots. If my cargo is damaged in any way, I swear you will quickly see the end of your days," he threatened.

A muscular stevedore, his skin shiny and dripping from sweat, curiously examined a crate and yelled out, "I have located it. We will get it out now!" The crate was heavy and made from wide, wooden slats assembled with narrow gaps between. The stevedore grabbed the corner, catching his hand on a sharp, unfinished edge of a metal "L" bracket holding together one of the corners of the wood box.

"*Damn!*" he yelled, looking at the blood as it poured from a large, jagged gash, running from his index finger to his palm.

"*Bok!*" the stevedore continued swearing, wedging his bleeding hand between the slats for a better grip, and in so doing, wrapped it around something inside of the slat. It moved and he instantly pulled his bloodied hand from the crate, writhing and screaming in pain.

His sweating companions stopped and looked as, before their eyes, the quivering stevedore fell to the floor, grasping his hand as he died.

"What has happened?" the chief stevedore demanded. "What the hell is taking so long?"

"Araf cut himself and now he is dead!" one of the stevedores yelled up through the entrance to the hold. "We don't know what has happened, but *he is dead!*" he exclaimed.

"We will get to the bottom of it later. For now, get the crate out so it can be delivered!" the chief ordered, callously disregarding the death of his worker. "We have customers waiting!"

Uncharted Labyrinth

The Tulip Garden, located in the fourth courtyard of the Topkapi palace, was breathtaking in its splendor. In full bloom, the countless floral varieties were magnificent beyond measure. A native species of Eurasia, tulips were gathered from all over the Ottoman Empire and beyond—their rarity and cost of no concern for the landscape architects. Varieties included the Crimean, Balkan, Persian, Pamir, Aleppo, Damnara, and Siberian, ranging in height from a diminutive four inches to over two feet, their colors every imaginable shade and hue. The manicured and ornately designed beds were woven through the entire garden, encircling statuaries and fountains. The smaller, more delicate specimens provided gloriously colored edging for the pathways.

Amid the visual delight of the garden stood an imposing kiosk. Its roof and floor were designed with gold and turquoise-colored tiles. At its center was a large banquet table for al fresco dinners, one of Suleyman's enjoyments. On this day, the table at its center was being used for other purposes. Four men stood around it, with the area patrolled and guarded by janissaries.

Suleyman, Il Lupo, Kemal, and Sinan, the court architect, studied architectural plans of the palace. Aziz patiently waited for any instructions. Mimar Sinan was to become the greatest architect of the Ottoman Empire.

Suleyman noted, "As you have explained, Sinan, the plans you have seen do not disclose the existence of any crypt beneath the palace. Nor do they show passageways from the Harem to the cisterns. Roxelana has told me that in fact that there *is* access to the cisterns and the crypts from the Harem. She has been there, accompanied by Aziz and Francesca Lupo. There are connecting pathways and there are crypts—all beneath the Harem and *Has Oda*. The bodies of two mutilated janissaries were recovered from the area beneath the *Has Oda*. There must also be at least one exit other than the way they gained entrance last night."

"As you know, Your Majesty," Sinan began his answer, "the Topkapi and area beneath the palace has been built over Byzantine ruins over many centuries. During those periods it was possible to build underground passageways, some of which might have been documented, and some kept secret. It is impossible to know. Detailed architectural plans were not always maintained. After you first raised this matter with me yesterday, I consulted my colleague, Faisal. Apparently, he received a request some time ago to view plans of the Topkapi that might show the existence of such passageways. He responded to the inquiry by saying that he did not know of any such drawings, but that they might exist, and permitted the eunuch who had inquired to search the archives himself."

Sinan continued with his exposition, adding historical context. "We know the cisterns have existed since the time of the Romans for the storage of water, but it was not until the last century that they were discovered. It has only been a few decades since they have been excavated to an extent. During those times, it might have been possible to construct passageways and exits or even uncover preexisting passages that were original to the cisterns or the crypts. Their design and construction could have been accomplished secretively, with or without drawings to map their extent. They may have been created for nefarious reasons or simply by request of the sultan, with no record made, or kept, of their design and existence."

"Who sent the eunuch to obtain the plans? Was he recognized?" Il Lupo asked Sinan directly.

"Yes, it was Mehmed, the *Kizlar Agha*. He claimed to be acting on a request from Gulbehar," Sinan answered succinctly. "The request came some time ago; it was not as recent as even one or two months ago; Faisal could not remember."

"Do you know if he found anything, Sinan?" Il Lupo asked.

"I do not know exactly what was found, but Mehmed departed the archives with some plans. Faisal did not learn what was taken, and as far as he knows, they have not been returned. He did not feel that he needed to question Mehmed since he is the *Kizlar Agha* and the request came from Suleyman's wife," Sinan answered.

"There are no records indicating whether Mehmed returned the archive materials, which likely included architectural plans and drawings depicting the location of the underground passages and their entry and exit points. I apologize, Your Majesty, for this lapse in protocol and judgment. We will keep track of all our drawings in the future," Sinan offered, his head bowed as he spoke to Suleyman.

"Yes, that is for the future. For the time being, we need to focus on the present investigation. Vincenzo, what are your thoughts?" Suleyman inquired.

"I have told you about the passageways and discovery of four additional janissary bodies by Francesca, Aziz, and Roxelana last night. It is indisputable that persons have gained knowledge of them. Possibly, the janissaries that we found dead had learned of an entry point and negotiated their way via connecting passages beneath the Harem or perhaps even the *Has Oda.* Not one of the mutilated janissaries that we found had *exited.* It is difficult to believe they would exit the same way they gained entrance, that there could only be one way in and out. It would be too easy for them to be followed. Different entrances and exits would help them avoid detection. It is possible that some of the paths lead to one or more exits outside the palace grounds. Entrances also likely exist within other areas of the Topkapi complex itself, not just the entrance found by Aziz so close to Roxelana's chambers," Il Lupo offered.

"Yes, once one has knowledge, learning to navigate the passages would be quite simple," Sinan concurred.

"At this point, we are certain that two exist. There could be more. Knowing that one of the passages leads to the area under the *Has Oda,* one would only need to identify precisely where to dig in order to gain access to the repository containing the sacred relics," Suleyman deduced.

Il Lupo agreed. "Yes, perhaps just a marker...Suleyman! The shaft found in the hand of one of the janissaries from the passageway near the *Has Oda!* The shaft Abdullah has in the morgue! That shaft marked the spot so the janissaries—the thieves—knew where the floor had been loosened and where to raise the cistern ceiling and *Has Oda's* floor. The shaft must have been driven into the floor just far enough so that it would be visible in the ceiling of the passage. The shiny metal would have reflected off the torches carried by the thieves. It must have been driven through the floor by the conspirators who opened the floor for them to gain access!" Il Lupo concluded, "To confirm, we must identify and question the janissaries who were on duty earlier that day and even a few days before if necessary."

"All excellent points, but it is critical that we find the hidden relics. I had intended to tell you that we have already been searching for the janissaries who were on duty just before the thefts. We have located all but two who have been quite elusive. We will find them and they will be questioned, if they remain alive."

Suleyman continued, while nodding agreement with Il Lupo's hypotheses, "However, we can only hope that someone, other than those we have concluded are the dead thieves, knows where the relics were stashed for later retrieval."

"Once the perpetrators learned of the passages, it would be simple enough to remove stones from the walls to create secret vaults or small chambers. The mortar that holds them in place is centuries old and very likely disintegrating," Sinan suggested, after deliberating for a few moments on the type of construction used in the cisterns. "Exits, hidden niches, or even rooms could be created without much work. Under close scrutiny and with sufficient time, they could be found by meticulously examining the walls and floors for disturbed stones. There would be hollow areas between stones where the binding mortar has failed, creating spaces. One merely needs to know where to look. The plans Mehmed took could hold the answer."

"Yes, a thorough examination of these areas shall be made. Kemal, gather janissaries. Send someone to retrieve those plans from Mehmed, under my order. We will not wait for the plans. We will investigate these passageways in the crypt and cistern immediately," Suleyman commanded.

Turning to Il Lupo, Suleyman shared his latest information. "Aziz led a group of janissaries to the cisterns to retrieve the four janissaries found dead last night. The bodies were taken to the morgue. I also informed Kemal that two of the bodies were identified by Francesca as accomplices in the assassination plot against me. Kemal may later be able to identify them all by name. Abdullah will examine them and convey his observations to you. Perhaps you will need to examine these four bodies as well. Now we have six dead janissaries found in passageways beneath the palace.

"As you know, Abdullah is beyond corruption. He is also personally conducting an unscheduled examination of all the Harem eunuchs at this time. If any are determined to be 'intact,' the uncastrated imposter will either be found or he will run. In any case, he will be captured, tortured, and questioned."

"Perhaps the progress of our investigation will accelerate the thieves' timetable for retrieving and delivering the relics," Il Lupo speculated. "If that is the case, we can station lookouts in areas we suspect may be in the vicinity of the exits. First, we must investigate the area where these latest bodies were found. That location may suggest places where we should concentrate our surveillance."

As commanded, Kemal returned with the janissaries. Together with Suleyman, Il Lupo, and Aziz, who would take the lead, they made their way through the Harem and into the secret passages.

Kemal also brought news from Francesca and Roxelana. "Roxelana has made inquiries as you asked concerning the possible existence of a person in the Harem from the New World, Your Majesty. She has learned there are only two. Both were Spaniards captured by the Ottoman Admiral Barbarossa during a sea battle in the Mediterranean. One is a concubine, about twenty five years old, and the other a eunuch—a youth now in his late teens or early twenties. He appears timid and rather mousy. One would not ordinarily notice him. Roxelana does not think he could be involved in these crimes given his demeanor," Kemal reported.

Il Lupo cautioned, "Apparent demeanor is an insufficient reason to rule anyone out at this time. Remember, we cannot discard clues until we are completely certain they are of no value. We must always open-mindedly interrogate our assumptions.

"Aziz, first show us where to enter the passageway. Then return to Roxelana's rooms and instruct Francesca to follow if either of the two New World residents of the Harem leaves the palace," Il Lupo instructed. "You can rejoin us in a few minutes and lead us to the area where you saw the Jinn and the dead bodies. This time, we will bring torches that have been well-soaked in oil to light the way. Good illumination is important and will enable us to carefully scrutinize the areas of the walls at the locations where the murdered janissaries were found and this Jinn disappeared."

Feather

Anyone entering the secret passageways was not immune from its eerie, anxiety-inducing atmosphere. One could believe that the souls of countless thousands of slaves, having toiled in the subterranean caverns, remained embedded in the cold, carved stones along with the detritus of their crushed and broken bones. In somber silence, the group threaded their way through the labyrinth, adjusting the width of their column as the pathway narrowed, each of its members deep within his own thoughts and harnessing his fears. Kemal lead the procession of twelve janissaries—six in the front and six in the rear—with Suleyman, Il Lupo, and Sinan fully protected.

"Wait!" Il Lupo heard Aziz shout, as he caught up with the group, slightly out of breath. His torch held a full and bright flame and Aziz could not hide the relief he felt as he rejoined the group. "I have done as instructed. Francesca will ensure that the two from the New World will be closely watched," he informed Il Lupo and Suleyman. "Roxelana intends to call the New World concubine to her rooms and engage her in some way, thereby allowing Francesca to focus on the eunuch."

"Good, Aziz," Il Lupo thanked him. "Now, you and I will join Kemal at the head of the company so that you can point out exactly where the bodies were found."

"I will now join at the front as well." Not intimidated by the forbidding environment, Suleyman moved to the front with Aziz and Il Lupo to join Kemal. "Are we nearing the area, Aziz?"

"First we came here, through these crypts, and then found the bones. See here?" He pointed to the dusty heap of remains. "That frightened Roxelana badly."

As they moved forward, Aziz turned to Suleyman. "Yes, you can see it from here—just a few paces," Aziz pointed his flame in front of him.

They walked a few steps and Aziz exclaimed, "Here, here is the spot where we found the first two janissaries. They had been dead for some time, their flesh shredded—it was ghastly. Even now, with the bodies gone, the stench of their rotting corpses remains. Can you smell it?" he asked, holding his nose up in the air, sniffing and looking for confirmation.

"Yes, it reeks in here," Kemal confirmed, with all nodding in agreement.

"Now, show us where you found the other two bodies and saw the Jinn, Aziz," Suleyman directed. At the word 'Jinn,' several of the janissaries recoiled. There were murmured prayers to Allah for protection. The possibility of contact, much less an actual encounter with a supernatural Jinn, was known to reduce even ordinarily fierce janissaries to whimpering cowards, their beliefs in the supernatural so inextricably instilled in them. In the presence of the mighty Suleyman, however, they would not be cowed, and remained stoic, controlling their fears, their whispered prayers fortifying them.

"The next two bodies were lying here, turned in this direction." Aziz moved the squad a few steps further and demonstrated. "And one of them briefly remained alive, lying on the ground, moaning. The Jinn stood over them, cloaked and sinister." Aziz's eyes grew wide remembering the scene.

"We did not see it shredding the bodies—it was just standing there. And then it ominously turned—so menacingly slowly," Aziz emphasized, drawing out the word 'slowly.' "In the darkness we could not see its shrouded face, but we sensed it would be hideous.

"When it saw us, it made an angry, prolonged, hissing sound. It was as though it had all the time in the world to work its evil. Slowly. It stood just here," Aziz continued to demonstrate. "Here just before the path turns a corner. Suddenly, it drew out a long rod from the chest area under its cloak. Francesca recognized the blowgun and danger. She forced Roxelana to the ground covering her and yelled for me to get down. I did. I've learned I am faster on my feet when I am terrified," Aziz confessed. Now, feeling safe with the group, the telling of his tale took on a more relaxed, comedic tone. There was an entertaining bravado to his presentation, and the janissaries were impressed that the courageous eunuch had survived to tell the tale.

"And then, 'whizz'—over our heads—a dart just missed us. We stayed down for a short time, waiting for a second dart, but it never came. We first checked to see if the janissary was still alive. After Francesca determined he was dead, the three of us chased after the Jinn, but when we turned the corner, there was nothing but a wall. It is a ghost, I swear, this Jinn is a ghost! It vanished into thin air!" Aziz finished, hearing more murmurings from the janissaries, all of whom had listened with mouths agape and eyes wide in astonishment. Aziz found comfort in the numbers of the group, and had conquered his fears of the previous night.

"Kemal, Aziz, bring your flames closer," Il Lupo instructed, Suleyman and Sinan standing directly behind him. "Aziz, just exactly where did the Jinn disappear?"

"I cannot be exactly sure because when we turned this corner, it was already gone," Aziz admitted.

Il Lupo ran his hand over the wall, now fully illuminated by the torches, first side-to-side and then up and down.

"Here! Sinan, let us see if we might uncover one of those secret rooms or exits you think might have been built off these passageways." Sinan moved closer to Il Lupo and joined him as they expertly examined the cracks and crevices in the wall.

"Look here at these tiny cracks in the mortar." Sinan drew Il Lupo, Kemal and Suleyman closer. "Here, here it is!" Sinan moved his fingers into an area where the mortar was nearly non-existent and upon finding a latch, pulled on it. "Just as we suspected!" he exclaimed, nearly jubilant. The wall slid open after the architect gave it a firm and quick push. There was just enough room to allow one person to enter at a time by moving through it sideways.

Suleyman extended his arm in front of Il Lupo preventing him from entering through the opening. He motioned to two of the janissaries to come forward. "Enter, but with caution," he ordered.

Doing the sultan's bidding, the first janissary held his torch in front of him, scimitar at the ready in the other hand, and shimmied his way into the opening, with the second following closely behind. "There is only an empty room, Your Majesty," the first janissary reported.

Suleyman raised his hand and waved for Il Lupo, Sinan, and Kemal to follow him as he entered through the narrow entry into the small, hollow room.

"We should search these walls to determine whether there is an exit from this room. It would be a perfect place for a Jinn to hide and wait until it was clear and make its exit through another passageway," Il Lupo offered. "Let us examine these walls, the ceiling, and the floor and then we will know." With the room fully illuminated by torches, the men examined every portion of the space.

"There is no exit. It is a hideout only." Il Lupo began to follow Suleyman out of the room when he noticed an object at his feet. He reached down and picked up a large, black feather.

Puzzled, Suleyman asked Il Lupo, "A feather? What would a feather be doing in such a place? How could a bird somehow get in here?"

"I doubt that one did," Il Lupo answered with certainty. "At least not a bird with a long exotic feather such as this. I know of no ordinary black bird with feathers of this size. Its source and significance, however? At this point I am not certain."

After exiting the Jinn's hidden den, Il Lupo continued reasoning, the feather stashed carefully into his pocket. "This is a place where the Jinn could wait and surprise its victims, and make a quick retreat. It is highly unlikely that the sanctuary could be discovered for several reasons. First, few would suspect the den even existed, so they would not even know to look. Second, those who happen upon this area seem to end up dead. Those finding the bodies would be unlikely to remain in such a frightening place. Finally, it took Sinan's expertise and our concerted search with torches to locate the den. A perfect refuge for the Jinn, or one with nefarious intent.

"There is a further puzzle, however. More questions to answer. How and why did these four janissaries stumble upon this dead end? Were they lost in the maze of passages? Did they randomly choose this passageway only to find it impassable? Were they intoxicated and, or disoriented? I do not yet know the answers." Il Lupo paced, disquieted.

"Do you think we should post guards to keep the area under surveillance?" Sinan asked, turning to Suleyman and Il Lupo.

"No. If I may be heard on this subject, Your Majesty. To solve this mystery, I believe it is better not to do this. It is essential that whoever is involved not suspect that we have discovered one of the very important secrets of the crypts and the murders. We should not place anyone here directly at the scene. I believe it would be better to establish a general surveillance of the area and potential exits," Il Lupo urged.

"I think we passed the area that lies beneath the *Has Oda*. Am I correct, Aziz?" Sinan asked.

"Yes, we did. We passed that connecting passageway on our way here. It is where I found the first bodies. Follow me," Aziz, feeling empowered, ordered the group. "I will show you. But first, before we leave, look!" he said, pointing to the gruesome head of Medusa. The janissaries emitted startled gasps. "Do not worry! If she was the true gorgon, we would have all been turned to stone by now." Aziz reveled in his ability to shock and awe his audience.

Arriving at the site where the bodies of Kareem and Jamal had been found under the *Has Oda*, Il Lupo surveyed the area.

"See here, there is ceiling debris on the floor. This is the point where the shaft in the ceiling must have pinpointed the spot where the repository floor could be lifted. The thieves, Kareem and Jamal, came here, lifted the floor, purloined the relics, and retreated— replacing the floor and adding a sealant. It is imperative that we find the two guards from the previous shift who have eluded us and question them, for it is virtually certain that they are co-conspirators. They are surely the guards who excavated the floor and placed the rod while they were on duty to mark the location for the actual thieves. A very well conceived and executed plan. They too may know the identity of, or at least provide clues that could lead us to, the mastermind of the thefts," Il Lupo observed.

Suleyman further surmised, "The relics are only exhibited once a year—at Ramadan. Even I am only allowed to view them on the fifteenth day of Ramadan. Since they had just recently been on display, and returned to the repository for safekeeping, it is known they would be there for another year. That left plenty of time to plan and execute the theft. The thieves very likely took this into consideration. Pilfering them directly after Ramadan gave them time to dig, remove the relics, and have approximately a year to transport them out of the city before they would likely have been reported as missing.

"This gives me hope they are still in Istanbul. It is fortunate the thefts were discovered so quickly since their last viewing. Otherwise, the relics and those involved could have long since left the palace and the city. This is one more security protocol that will change immediately. *Daily* checks of the contents of the *Has Oda* henceforth," an angry Suleyman ordered.

"I see your point," Il Lupo responded. "The dates of Ramadan change every year?"

"Ramadan occurs once a year, but it generally moves back approximately twelve days every year based on the cycles of the moon. The date is determined by the first sighting of the crescent moon on the first day of the ninth month of the lunar calendar. Just as with your celebration of Easter, there is no set date," Suleyman provided a simplified explanation of the complex Islamic calendar.

"Ah, I see," Il Lupo nodded. "Yes, it is somewhat similar to the Christian Easter. Easter is based on the cycle of the moon also—the first Sunday after the first full moon occurring on or after the vernal equinox.

"We know that the janissaries involved in the theft obtained extensive knowledge of the crypts and passageways through the cisterns by some means," Il Lupo stated, returning his attention to the unsolved mysteries.

"We will presume, even though the examinations have not yet been completed, that it is likely that all of the janissaries were also killed by the Jinn, by poisoned dart. We have already concluded that Kareem and Jamal were the thieves. Now we have four more cadavers in the morgue, with two believed to have been involved in the assassination attempt. We need to determine if the other two corpses were the janissaries on shift earlier on the day of the theft and were those who dug out the floor. If they are, it will be detrimental to the investigation since we cannot question them and must find other means of ascertaining the extent of their involvement and the identity of their accomplices. We know from Francesca that all of the corpses have poisonous pinpricks to the neck and their bodies were mutilated to cover up the actual cause of their deaths," Il Lupo summarized.

"Questions remain as to whether the Jinn is simply attacking all it encounters in these passageways for evil and diabolical reasons, or whether it is rationally eliminating them because they know too much—whether it be knowledge of the thefts, or the assassination attempt, or both," Il Lupo pondered the mysteries.

"If the Jinn is somehow a collaborator in the theft, it would be logical that it might eliminate any accomplices to prevent them from talking or being subjected to interrogation and torture if captured," Suleyman speculated.

"Yes, Suleyman, silencing them permanently would be an excellent reason for the Jinn to eliminate coconspirators. Greed could certainly be a motivation. If the Jinn is eliminating accomplices who were to be paid for their work, and for that reason only, it possibly is being directed by someone who would profit directly, taking the shares of the dead. At this point, we just do not have enough reliable evidence. Who knows who may return to collect the relics, assuming they have been secreted somewhere in these passages—or have they already been removed?" Il Lupo posited his questions rhetorically.

Continuing, he summarized some of the remaining unresolved questions, "Were those involved in the assassination plot also involved with the thefts? Are there more than one group? Moreover, why would they remain in the area long enough to be killed, unless the Jinn knew beforehand exactly where those involved would be and when? And, if the relics are still hidden nearby, when will a conspirator return to collect them?"

Kemal theorized, "Perhaps the two unidentified janissaries at the morgue that were found more decomposed were those on the earlier shift who dug out the floor of the repository, as has been suggested. For some reason they returned to the passageway under the Harem. They would have been killed before the thieves that actually removed the relics from the repository. Perhaps just hours before—in the early morning on the day of your arrival, Count. The other two bodies found with them were newly dead and suspected in the assassination plot—Aziz knew one was alive moments before they got to him. We know of course, of the two bodies discovered by Aziz beneath the repository that were found just before dawn on the day of Vincenzo's arrival. Aziz heard the noises, and so they must have been alive until shortly before he found them."

"Excellent observations, Kemal!" Il Lupo was impressed with Kemal's reasoning.

"And perhaps the more decomposed bodies found by Roxelana, Francesca and myself were not moved as a warning to others to stay away! At least until the theft was complete," Aziz chimed in.

"Another sound observation and potential explanation, Aziz," Suleyman offered. Aziz beamed at the compliment given by his sultan.

"Precisely, Aziz! To send a message that no one should enter except for the purpose of executing and completing the theft. Stay away from graveyards or enter at your own peril! Excellent, Aziz!" Il Lupo agreed approvingly.

"A Jinn with a purpose. If these theories are correct, and I believe they are, I am heartened that the relics may very well still be here." Suleyman looked relieved at the prospect.

"Perhaps in another secret cache or chamber. One that existed or one that has recently been carved from the rock. This could explain why Mehmed collected the drawings for Gulbehar," Sinan rationalized. "One or both needed the drawings to learn of the passages and to determine the location of any secret chambers or where best to construct one."

"I agree. These are but two passageways in the crypts and cistern. There could be dozens, we do not know. Logic tells me that if the relics were hidden, they would be concealed close by to avoid detection. This is yet one more question without an answer. To find the relics, we need the help of any remaining unidentified thieves. It was difficult enough to locate the chamber where the Jinn disappeared. If Qais was involved—well, he is dead. Jamal and Kareem actually entered the repository and took the relics. They also are dead. It might be that the more decomposed bodies, which we are hopeful Kemal can identify, are those who dug out the floor of the repository, and they are dead. While we know that the two other corpses have been identified as participants in the failed assassination attempt, were they also involved in, or have knowledge of, the thefts? All with possible answers. Their lips sealed forever. Are there others? We do not know."

Il Lupo paced back and forth, shaking his head in frustration. "These mysteries proliferate like a hydra."

"Finding another cache or chamber where the relics may be concealed, I agree, would be like finding a needle in a haystack," Sinan acknowledged.

"I think perhaps the best way to find the relics is to implement our plan to have spies discreetly watch the area and report any suspicious activities. That may be the only way of locating them. Perhaps a surveillance will uncover someone retrieving the relics. This is what will be done! Time is of the essence!" Suleyman pronounced.

"Yes, an excellent plan, Your Majesty. It is my belief those involved will act quickly. We have stirred a hornet's nest and may have sped up their timing," Il Lupo replied, nodding his agreement.

"Kemal, first I think you should quickly stop at the morgue to identify the bodies just moved there. Then immediately after that, please go and assist Francesca. Aziz, go to her directly. At this point, she does not know everything we know and is unaware of all the dangers. It is becoming more perilous, and it is possible, she may require both your skills. We are dealing with a consummate evil and all of us must be exceedingly vigilant, always on guard, and have our wits about us," Il Lupo cautioned.

"I think it is time we depart this evil place. Once all the mysteries are solved, I will have it sealed forever," Suleyman asserted. "I will call for you, Vincenzo, when I have news. And you likewise, must keep me informed of any developments." Suleyman was solemn, his eyes penetrating and truth seeking, as they departed company.

Hammam

Il Lupo, Gregor, Giovanni, Hassan, and Antoine gathered at a Turkish bath, a *hammam*, recently designed by Sinan. They had first entered the *tepidarium*, a massive domed room with a large center stone where they were seated and engulfed in warm steam, eventually departing in full sweat. The ritual was followed by entry into an even hotter room known as the *sicaklik*, before submersing themselves in the cooler waters provided by underground streams where the *tellaks* soaped and washed their bodies with their *keses*. Just before finishing, they each received a massage, the rituals ending in the cooling room, the bathers completely relaxed. The *hammam* varied in some ways from the earlier Roman and Greek baths—those using hot, dry air rather than steam.

"Sinan has told me that the Hammam in the new mosque he has under design will be even more ornate and lavish. He has not yet completed the plans nor has he presented anything to Suleyman. Sinan is a remarkable architect," Il Lupo observed, as he admired the fine and detailed stonework of the cooling room. His remarks were met with complaisant nods of agreement from the men, now all feeling fully refreshed.

"Yes, Suleyman has a fine architect. His work is known throughout the Islamic world," Hassan complimented. "I believe he may equal Shirazi, who was the architect for the Goharshad Mosque in Mashhad, a mosque unparalleled in its beauty. Should any of you choose to visit and enjoy my country, I will escort you there personally, and comparisons can be made." Hassan offered his hospitality. "Then you will each be able to pass final judgment as to which of the architects is more talented."

Antoine was oscitant, his body tranquil and his head bobbing slightly and drooping over his chest. Dozing, but sufficiently awake to engage in conversation when necessary, he was unable to resist reflecting on French mores.

He sat upright and sighed, "Ah, why can't we be this civilized in France. Bathing is not a usual practice. In fact, we often find the use of perfumes offers an effective method for covering our distaste for frequent bathing. However, this—this is something different. I would bathe daily if I had such an option. This could become quite fashionable in France if they realized how luxurious bathing can be. Luxury is the ultimate opiate of the French."

"Yes, I have heard of this French custom of preferring the use of perfumes to bathing," Gregor chimed in. "Meaning no personal offense, Antoine, you know it is said that we know well in advance that the French are coming, whether it be in war or in diplomacy. We smell you—and your perfumes—from miles away." Before Antoine had the opportunity to respond, Giovanni, who was skilled in the art of talking and not listening, interrupted.

"That is rather like Lucia and she could certainly help you with that! You know she has a passion for creating new fragrances. She says she can't abide foul odors and is determined to bring new meaning to *eau de toilette*!" Giovanni chortled at his feeble attempt at humor. "She too proclaims that bathing is a waste of valuable time, agreeing with the French that it is more efficient to apply perfumes. She uses them so freely that they cling to everything in my villa when she visits. I believe she thinks that with her heavy new concoctions she will change the way everyone feels about the toilet and the toilette, with little difference between the aromas of the two."

Turning to Il Lupo, Giovanni broached the subject that weighed so heavily on Il Lupo's mind. "My sources tell me that you are helping Suleyman determine what is causing unrest among the janissaries. What have you learned?" he asked, presumptuously.

"Just exactly *who* are the sources you are referring to, Giovanni?"

"Oh, Giovanni has sources everywhere and I mean everywhere—not just Istanbul. We are all very jealous," Gregor interrupted, allowing Giovanni to avoid Il Lupo's pointed question. "We all do our best to pay off high court officials, but Giovanni has more money; and the more money you have, the more juicy the gossip and information one can buy."

"For example, everyone bribes Mehmed. The Harem information he provides is valuable, but I personally suspect that Giovanni also has Ibrahim in his pocket," Antoine added, turning his head to Giovanni. "Of course, that is just my own speculation."

"Vincenzo, it is our culture," Hassan began an explanation. "One does business by buying and selling favors. Perhaps it is a bit more sophisticated and circumspect in Europe, but we are all only doing what must be done to accomplish our work. Court officials expect payment for their information. We simply satisfy their expectations. In this culture, one generally should not assume nefarious intent regarding what is considered an ordinary cost of doing business."

"Well, as a ranking court official, I would expect that the *Kizlar Agha* has nearly the wealth of the sultan he serves. There is much information that comes from the Harem—it is the center for palace gossip," Gregor commented. "In fact, for all the rumors, I would doubt that a single syllable passes the Harem walls without Mehmed receiving a toll."

Antoine elucidated, "Wealth accumulated by Ottoman officials usually reverts to the state upon their deaths. The acceptance of bribes is one way, and perhaps the principal way, that an official can ensure his family will be cared for upon his death. It is known that even Ibrahim, for example, is enormously wealthy. Some, of course, has come from gifts and compensation from the emperor. However, his greatest wealth, it is widely believed, has actually come from the information he sells. By the way, Hassan, have you decided when you are returning to Persia?"

"I will probably leave a little earlier than anticipated—perhaps as early as tomorrow," Hassan answered Antoine's question directly.

"But didn't you arrive here right after Ramadan ended? It seems such a distance for such a short trip," Antoine asked, perplexed.

"Yes, I had thought I would stay longer, but I have nearly concluded my business. My primary purpose here was to receive goods from Europe, and everything that I have ordered has arrived faster than I anticipated. It will be loaded out of the port as soon as possible. I will don my nomadic robes and caravan my goods home to Persia. Other than the hospitality of my host country and communion with old and new friends, there is nothing else to keep me from returning." He closed his eyes and leaned his back casually against the wall.

"Giovanni, will Lucia be staying in Istanbul much longer?" Il Lupo asked.

"Anything is possible with Lucia. She is never sure of her plans. They are fluid—just as the gossip that flows from her lips. She can be off on a whim, but then another whim can keep her here. She has relatives throughout Europe and she enjoys travel. Perhaps you are interested in influencing her decision?" Giovanni's raised eyebrow insinuated there was something between the two of them. Lucia's demeanor around Il Lupo, and observing them alone on the terrace the previous evening, had given rise to Giovanni's speculations.

"Not at all, Giovanni. We have known each other for some time. But we are no more than mere friends."

"Ah, I see," Giovanni looked at Il Lupo skeptically, appearing unconvinced.

"Yes," Antoine piped in, "It was at court in France where I first met Lucia. She is indeed well-traveled, even as far as Russia." He turned to look at Gregor. "She would not share her secrets and has been uncharacteristically mute on the subject of her beloved Cossacks. She will only go so far as to speak of them in vague, but nevertheless glowing terms," he laughed, watching as his friend, Gregor, raised an eyebrow.

"Lucia comes from a very wealthy family on her father's side. Her father is a Spaniard—that is where she gets her sultry good looks. Her mother is my mother's sister and that is how we are cousins. We Contratinis had to earn our wealth, not have it handed to us. She can afford the luxury of extensive travel. She takes care of herself and is not a demanding guest. In fact, I rarely even see her." Giovanni was proud of the wealth he had attained and wanted to be certain there was no misunderstanding that it had been achieved solely by his own doing.

"Ha! Now that's a good houseguest—one you never see!" Gregor chuckled.

Fully rejuvenated, the group removed their *pestemal*—cotton cloths—from their waists and the wooden clogs designed to keep them from slipping on the soapy, wet floor. The group quickly dressed and prepared to go their separate ways. Il Lupo pulled Antoine aside.

"I need a few minutes with Antoine. I may soon revisit the court of Francis I and I need Antoine's advice regarding details of the trip," Il Lupo deliberately deceived as he waved to the others. "Please don't wait." While the others departed the baths, the Count and the Marquis paced back and forth, in deep discussion.

Surveillance

Fumbling to adjust his ill-fitting uniform, the eunuch hurried as he exited the Harem. Headed toward the Grand Bazaar, he succeeded on his second attempt to prevent his turban from falling off his head. His hand came to rest in the sash at his waist, a small package visible and bulging slightly from the cincture. Kemal and Francesca knew they would need to shadow him closely through the Grand Bazaar's maze of narrow alleys, often packed with goods from countless shopkeepers that overflowed into the alleys, making them so congested they were nearly impassable. Hawkers lined up in front of their shops, beckoning potential buyers as they smoked their water pipes—the vapors wafting and mingling with pungent, spicy, and exotic market aromas.

Although Francesca had once again donned her schmatte, Kemal still found her enticing. He wore equally filthy and tattered rags. He hunched over, circling playfully around Francesca, giving her the same deranged stare she had given him earlier. Despite attempts to appear serious and suppress her amusement at the mischief, she laughed.

"Kemal, stop it!" she commanded, feigning control. "This is serious business. No time for nonsense. We have to keep our eye on him. He will be easy to lose sight of," she chastised.

"Here, here," she jabbed at him. "Here, take this. It will give your disguise more credibility." She passed him the sturdy staff, fully equipped at the tip with a potentially lethal blade and a rapier that could be pulled from the handle. "This one is slightly upgraded—now you will be doubly lethal. Stay safe."

"Don't we look good together . . . meant for each other?" he flirted. He accepted the stick and examined it, impressed. "My, Francesca, you are one deadly derelict!"

"Sometimes I just don't know what to think about you! Come on, let's go!" Francesca ordered, both amused and irritated.

"At least you're thinking about me. Hold that thought," Kemal persisted, determined to make her smile. She offered him only a slight upturn at the corners of her mouth, although she was pleased by his persistence.

They followed the eunuch past a number of rug merchants as well as dozens more selling pottery, copper, and fabrics. Their target stopped abruptly after turning a corner, looking around furtively to ensure he was not being followed, then moving to a narrow alley between two shops.

"Look! Did you see his face just then? He is different than the other eunuchs. He looks like the natives I have seen from the New World in Venice. Kemal, I think this is the New World eunuch that was captured and brought to the Harem! Aziz told me that Roxelana said his name is Ali!"

"It has to be him. His skin has a different tone. It also appears he is in his late teens or early twenties." Francesca tried to keep her voice down despite her excitement.

"Yes, I see what you mean. I believe you are right. He does fit the description," Kemal nodded.

Assuming a kneeling position, as if begging, Francesca and Kemal watched as the eunuch again suddenly stopped and pulled the small leather-wrapped message from his sash. Looking around once more, he placed it in a hollowed space carved out of the stone wall and retrieved a burlap bag from the same opening. Ready to depart, he surveilled the area to ensure he had not been observed and departed quickly, walking past the two beggars who were still kneeling and huddled close together.

"Did you see that?" Francesca asked, looking wide-eyed at Kemal.

"Yes, whatever was in that parcel was moving." Kemal's eyes still following the stealthy eunuch.

"I wonder what the bag contains?" she speculated.

"Do you think we should follow him?"

"No. He will likely return to the Harem. I know my father said to follow him. But I think he would agree we need to wait and see who retrieves the message he has left," Francesca decided.

"You are right," Kemal agreed, putting his arm around her when she slightly lost footing in her crouched position.

"Uh, thanks." Francesca was flustered, and removed his arm. "I'm good now." She loved the feel of his strong arm around her.

"Francesca, did you know it is said that lovers read from the same book, but each writes their own page?" Kemal was suddenly a little more serious while they waited. He was increasingly struck by the elegance and intelligence of her face. He stared desirously, unable to hide the growing depth of his emotions and feelings for Francesca.

"No, I had not heard that. Kemal! Why are you talking like this? As for your statement about lovers, well, I for one would much prefer the showing of love to the speaking of it. I would also prefer the *doing* to the *writing*." Francesca was emphatic. "Deeds, not words!"

"Well then, we are in agreement! I am always for the showing and doing rather than the talking and writing." Kemal was serious, hoping she would infer his intent. However, his tone was lighthearted, attempting to lessen any timidity she might have over the developing change in their relationship. He could not be sure if her feelings paralleled his, or if he was simply imagining—praying—that the encouraging evolution was evidence she too, was interested in him.

"And I have to tell you, Kemal," she began playfully, "the pleasures of your stares do have their limits!"

"What? What do you mean? I haven't been staring at you!" Kemal retorted, knowing fully well that he could *not* stop staring at her. "I am merely observing our target's movements and your face is in the way!" he protested.

"Oh stop it! I have come to know that look! Surely you don't expect me to believe that there are no teary-eyed virgins ablaze with passion for you, do you?" She circled him as they waited, jabbing him playfully with her staff. "Melancholy maidens whose dreams and deliriums you suffuse," she laughed. "All those lustful, lovelorn ladies?"

Kemal was completely nonplussed as to how to respond. Mixed with her silly banter were some truths and one small snippet of information. Buried within her words was a glimmer of hope. She acknowledged she found pleasure in his gaze.

"I don't know what you are talking about! I doubt that any of the women I have known are melancholy, or lovelorn, or whatever other descriptions you have ascribed to them. In any event, there is no honor, Francesca, in a man revealing anything about past loves," he retorted.

"No insults intended, Kemal. You know that. I am only teasing—you cad!" she jabbed him once again with her staff, laughing loudly. For all her teasing and playful banter, Francesca could not help but feel a slight twinge of possessiveness and jealousy. What women had Kemal, the Captain of the Beyliks, held in his arms, caressed, or even made love to? Did he love or dream of other women when he laid his head to his pillow? Did they invade his thoughts as he had invaded Francesca's? Francesca could not bear to dwell on the possibilities.

Kemal broke the momentary silence perhaps sparing her from details she, in fact, did not want to know. "Oh! Look, look!" They watched as a man entered the small alleyway, and quickly retrieved the message from its hiding place. "We need to follow!"

Kemal and Francesca did their best to follow the quick pace of the second messenger, melding once more into the crowd, a task made more difficult because their disguise required them to remain hunched and crippled in appearance. Hurrying with the greatest alacrity allowed by their ruses, they stopped occasionally to resume their stooped and begging position, finally following him out of the bazaar and into less congested city streets. Closer to the Bosphorus, the messenger stopped and sat for a moment on a long, stone fence. After a brief pause, seeing no one suspicious nearby, he deftly removed a stone from the wall, placed the message inside, and then wedged the stone back into place.

"How many more intermediate dead drops will there be before we learn the final recipient of the message?" Kemal questioned, his handsome brow wrinkled in thought.

"I'm not sure, but we must wait," Francesca emphasized. "If the delivery process goes on much longer, I will begin to feel and look like I belong in these clothes. Staying crouched like this and hunched over takes its toll." She put her hand to her sore back. "I've been in disguise virtually the entire day. You are but a novice!"

"Here, let me take care of that for you," Kemal offered. Anxious to offer his assistance and alleviate her discomfort, he gently began to rub her back. He had the initial thrill of touching her, but it intensified when his hand registered the heat of her body through the rough fabric of her schmatte. With great delight, he continued with a neck massage, absorbing the feel of her strong body as his fingers played with the soft curls at the base of her neck.

"Kemal!" Francesca laughed nervously. "I have to admit that feels good, but you must learn to keep your hands to yourself. If you do not, I will have to tell my skilled and excellent swordsman of a father. He might not have any other choice than to make a eunuch out of you. Rendering you a eunuch might give him pause, because I do believe he has grown fond of you. But I have given you fair warning!"

Francesca reveled in the exquisite feeling that electrified her body when he touched her, leaving her completely confounded. She was experiencing the fear of falling without any assurance of rebounding to undiscovered new heights. She nearly shuddered with delight under his touch and felt so very much alive.

"All right, all right!" Kemal withdrew his hand reluctantly. "I am forewarned. You know *kucuk uzman*, there is not much I would not do for you, but becoming a eunuch is not one of them. Besides, I would be of no use to you at all then." He looked at Francesca, his expression pitiful and feigning innocent sorrow. The devilish twinkle in his dark eyes told another story entirely and was not overlooked by Francesca.

Another messenger arrived at the wall, alleviating any need for Francesca to respond. "There, I'm sure *this* one is going to move the stone." Her assessment correct, they watched as the latest messenger cautiously checked his surroundings before sitting. He positioned his leg so that the fabric of his garment hid the movement of the stone, but their sharp eyes confirmed that the courier had retrieved the leather-bound message, stashing it in his cloak.

"Let's go!" Francesca yanked on Kemal's robe and they hobbled off together, again stopping occasionally ensuring they blended with the crowd, but not long enough to lose sight of their quarry. They shadowed the third messenger as he walked the length of the stone fence until he arrived in a more familiar residential area.

"I have a feeling I know where he is going. I think his destination is the residence of Giovanni Contratini," Francesca proposed.

"I believe you are absolutely correct," Kemal answered as they watched the messenger walk through a side yard and toward the front door of Giovanni's palazzo. They moved to a position where they could watch the entrance. The messenger walked up the marble staircase and knocked on one of the two massive front doors. The door opened and Giovanni Contratini, the newly appointed Venetian Ambassador, personally accepted the message.

Pulsing Parcel

As dusk began to fall over Istanbul, the *Muezzin* began his *Adhan*, the crepuscular call to worship for the followers of Islam, from the parapet of the minaret of the revered *Hagia Sophia*. His first recitation was that of the *Takbir*, followed by the *Shahada*, its repetitious chant, called five times a day, evocative and beckoning. Its haunting beauty enveloped Il Lupo as he stood near the *Seraglio* overlooking the Golden Horn, the coruscant sunset waning, predictably coloring the clay tile roofs in a copper glow. He thought the call reminiscent of the simplicity and beauty of the Gregorian chants, their expressive echoes filling the cathedrals of Europe. The beauty of the setting delivered a pleasing diversionary relief, distracting his thoughts from the sorting of clues that had so engaged his keen mind. Experience had taught that it was in quiet times of reflection he was best able to bring clarity to his thoughts; now he puzzled together the myriad clues associated with the complex mysteries before him. While enjoying a fine, vintage wine, he had often found tranquil interludes most productive when at his home in Venice, as he now watched the early setting of the spring sun. Serenity often filled his mind and cleared his thoughts at eventide. He was grateful for the peaceful respite, even if fleeting.

His contemplation broken by the arrival of the two beggars, he recognized them to be Francesca and Kemal. His amusement at their bedraggled appearance could not be contained.

"Oh dear...," he greeted them. "I'm not sure if I should call a doctor or the wine steward," he laughed, holding his arms out as he beheld them in their inglorious state.

"Very funny, *mia Padre*," Francesca replied sarcastically. "We have much news. Don't you want to know what we have been doing?"

"I'm afraid to ask," he chuckled at the pair. "Go ahead, share your discoveries with me. There is an urgent need to get you out of your schmatte and back into your beguiling role as a chambermaid."

Ignoring her father's gibe at her current disheveled condition, Francesca began reporting excitedly. "We were successful in following a series of messengers who dropped off and picked up a message at dead drops. The message was sent from the Harem and ultimately delivered directly to Giovanni!"

Kemal continued, "We watched a young eunuch leave the Harem for the first dead drop—we both agreed it was the eunuch from the New World. Ali—oh, you may not know that his name is Ali—who delivered the message from the Harem to the first drop location. As Francesca said, it was ultimately delivered to Giovanni! What on earth would he have to do with all of this?" Kemal paused, but did not wait for an answer.

"While Ali was at the first drop, he picked up a package that was waiting for him. He left the message that was delivered to Giovanni. We could not determine if Giovanni responded with a message in return or handed him anything, but the messenger did not wait for him to write a response. Nevertheless, we did see something else! Tell your father, Francesca," Kemal urged, turning over the relating of their discoveries to Francesca.

"Yes, *Padre*, there was something else. This eunuch—Ali— retrieved a parcel, a burlap bag that he carried by his side. He walked right past us and the contents of the bag were moving!" Francesca's weariness vanished, replaced by renewed animation. "What, do you imagine, was in that bag?" she asked her father.

"I have my suspicions," Il Lupo nodded. "But for now, you say the message that was left by Ali was delivered directly to Giovanni— that it was placed in his hands?"

"Yes, directly into his hands," Kemal confirmed.

"I need to pay our host a visit. In the meantime, you return to the palace and report your findings to Suleyman. Also tell him I have reason to believe the thieves will act tonight to retrieve the relics," he ordered. "I will meet you at the palace after I return from my visit with Giovanni. It will be a long night for all of us."

Flora and the Fox

Il Lupo followed the course of the Bosphorous, driving his heels into the sides of his horse, urging it forward with a celerity impeded only by the unevenness of the cobbled streets. Just as he was dismounting at the Palazzo, the door was thrown open and he was greeted by Giovanni.

"You are in a hurry! I heard the clatter of hooves from a mile away, Vincenzo. What a surprise! Are you home for the evening?" Giovanni asked, puzzled. "If I had known you were coming, I would have had dinner prepared. I have just finished a few light courses myself."

"That is most generous of you, Giovanni, but I have another engagement shortly. I had not intended on such a hasty entrance, but occasionally I find I like the wind in my hair and a fast gallop for my horse. I find I can often better focus my thoughts when I feel such freedom.

"I found my way here so I merely thought I would stop in. I did not intend to disrupt your evening serenity," Il Lupo deceived. "I hope you have had a productive day. I see you have retrieved what you went into port for this morning." Il Lupo pointed to a large crate in the hallway.

"Ah yes! I did. No one is supposed to know, but Lucia and I have a very special project. We have agreed to keep it quiet, but Lucia is not here. She was here earlier when it was delivered, and spent some time, I believe, attending to its contents. I do not think she would mind me telling you about our project since she has confided her affection for you. Vincenzo, your status has risen above that of her favorite Cossacks! I believed she would never find anyone to compare. You, however—well, I suppose you should ask her . . . Come, let me show you." Giovanni began walking toward the terrace. "Come!"

Il Lupo was unsure of Giovanni. Had he simply opened the door and received a message so surreptitiously delivered, on behalf of someone else or was the message intended for him personally? His demeanor was casual and relaxed. Giovanni appeared completely transparent with nothing to hide.

They departed the house by way of the terrace and into the vast, landscaped gardens. Il Lupo followed while Giovanni led him toward the conservatory, a greenhouse on the edge of the property that Il Lupo had noticed previously but never had occasion to visit. Upon opening the doors, they were met immediately with stifling heat and overwhelming humidity created by the large braziers strategically placed throughout the large, glass room. The steam generated by the braziers clouded many of the windows, but ensured the verdure of the vast array of splendid tropical flora flourishing within its walls. Their fragrant aromas filled the conservatory, and their variety and colors were spectacular in beauty.

"Lucia had this built on her last visit. She said she got the idea from what they call 'hothouses' in the Crimea. I have had this home for many years as a central location to gather the goods I have traded from both Asia and Europe. It became most convenient when I was appointed ambassador. Lucia developed this idea recently—only within the last several months—and today is her second shipment of these new exotics. She thought this the best place to build the conservatory for her exotic imports."

"It is indeed magnificent. At some point I would love to be allowed to collect specimens—an avocation of mine; I enjoy collecting exotic flora and sketching them. Perhaps sometime I will show you and Lucia my albums. We can discuss that at a later time, however. Tell me, what is the purpose of nurturing all these plants— merely a pleasurable hobby?" Il Lupo inquired.

Wandering through the rows of plants and small, unpacked crates, some with foliage peeking toward the sunlight from between the narrow slats, Giovanni continued. "Yes, yes, in a moment, I will get to that. The key to their preservation are these braziers. They maintain the heat and humidity at the requisite levels to nurture these exotic flowers. Even when I made arrangements to have them transported here, special accommodations had to be made to ensure the stability of temperatures and conditions within the holds of the transport vessels. Most complex, I can assure you. And costly," Giovanni harrumphed. "We have lost many, but those that survive will make for quite an exhibition."

"Exhibition?" Il Lupo asked, confused.

"Oh, yes, that is what Lucia intends. Who knows? Perhaps she intends to have them exhibited to the sultan hoping he would develop interest in them. She could provide them, and perhaps earn a hefty profit. You know of the emperor's keenness for beautiful gardens. She has also said that she may have a grand exhibition for our friends and dignitaries," Giovanni informed.

"But truth be told, I really don't know what she intends. I allowed her to build the conservatory here. She pays for everything, and I am able to acquire what she requests because of my contacts. She also has many contacts in the New World—the Spaniards, you know. I know very little more." Giovanni waved his arms around at the walls of the structure.

"I see. This is most interesting. Do you know precisely where she gets her plants?" Il Lupo quizzed.

"She has gathered them from many places, but most recently, the New World. This crate was imported from the New World. As I explained, this is only her second shipment, although she has had several earlier shipments from the Orient. This one here, for example, is a peony. One of the few I know. I asked because I find it very beautiful. Lovely, isn't it?" Giovanni ran his hand across the face of the flower.

"Those," he pointed to a table near the entrance, "those came from the crate I picked up this morning and they are from the New World. She does most of the unpacking of the crates herself, not trusting others to handle the precious plants with the great care they require. She put a large cover over them to ensure they did not continue to lose heat before conveying them to the conservatory. When I last saw her this morning she was preparing to tend to them."

"Do you know what these plants and flowers are called?" Il Lupo asked, turning his attention back to the new arrivals.

"No, I know nothing about these. You would have to ask Lucia. She is the expert," Giovanni advised.

"Lucia has done beautiful work here in cultivating such rare species. Of course, one would expect no less from Lucia," Il Lupo stated.

"Yes, yes, she does have a flair for the exotic and flamboyant," Giovanni conceded.

"Giovanni, please forgive my abrupt manner, but I realize it is much later than I had thought. I see through the glass ceiling that darkness is fast approaching. Please forgive me, but I must leave in order to make my previous engagement. Thank you for the tour. Very educational," Il Lupo said, excusing himself.

"Of course, Vincenzo, I understand. You are a busy man. It was good to see you." Giovanni was jovial, swishing the wine in his tankard, as he escorted Il Lupo around the side of the house to the front. Il Lupo's horse was tied to the post, waiting.

"Thank you again, Giovanni," Il Lupo said, mounting his horse. "This exhibition—if there is to be one—do you know when it might be scheduled?"

"I cannot be sure, but I believe in a few weeks," Giovanni speculated. "Assure me you will tell no one of this. I do not think Lucia will be angry that I told you, as I have said, but I only ask you tell no one else so that her surprise is not spoiled."

"Of course, Giovanni. Worry about this no more," Il Lupo assured him, knowing that his visit to the conservatory would be shared with Suleyman. "Good night, Giovanni!" Il Lupo mounted his horse, its dappled coloring nearly blending with the silvery gray of an overcast, and darkening sky.

Arriving at the gates, Il Lupo was startled to see Lucia just entering. He pulled the reins on his horse and offered a greeting.

"Lucia! Sorry to just miss you!" he offered quickly, hopeful the dark shadows cast by the thick canopy of trees masked his surprise.

"Vincenzo!" Lucia smiled broadly. "What an unexpected pleasure— to see you even for a moment since you are apparently leaving. You've been neglecting me, but I will allow myself to believe you stopped here just to see me and are leaving feeling disappointed," she chided him, tilting her head and her mouth, forming a practiced pout.

"Yes, I have an engagement, but I've spent a little time with Giovanni. Do not be angry with him, but our conversation led him to share with me the splendor of your secret conservatory, but I promise I will tell no one," Il Lupo cajoled.

"My secret?" she asked, appearing puzzled, as she moved her slightly disheveled hair from her forehead. "What secret?"

"The beautiful flora you have been cultivating; you have created a wondrous collection, Lucia. I was most impressed. I particularly liked the peonies from China. Lovely—as are you. I am hoping that you will indulge me with a few specimens. I enjoy sketching exotic flora—an occasional indulgence." Il Lupo complimented, hoping to console her. Lucia beamed, enjoying the attention. Her vanity allowed her to believe any accolade was richly deserved.

"Giovanni! I will have to chastise him. That was supposed to be confidential; just between the two of us. He has been very naughty. I will have to devise an appropriate punishment for my dear cousin," she answered, her tone teasing. She did her best to appear bemused, but her initial surprise had not escaped Il Lupo's detection. "I intended to have an exhibition—a grand opening kind of party. Please, Vincenzo, do not spoil that for me," she fretted.

"Of course not," Il Lupo assured.

"Can you stay for just a bit? Perhaps for just a little of the dessert we spoke about earlier? Just a small taste of dessert?" Her eyes were wide and pleading.

"Lucia, I cannot. I am sorry, but I am already late," Il Lupo replied, anxious to leave.

"Perhaps later then? I *need* to see you," she continued seductively.

"Lucia, your invitations are nearly irresistible! Perhaps I shall see you later, but it would be much later." He was evasive, while purposefully intending to encourage her.

"Alright, then. I will hold you to it. Do not be bashful. Just knock," she murmured seductively, removing her shawl from her shoulders and revealing her cleavage. "Till then..." A relieved Il Lupo departed.

"Lucia," she admonished herself. *"This is the man known for solving mysteries of imperial courts. He is very clever and often impassive. Be cautious. Vincenzo Lupo is more a fox than a wolf."*

El Diablo Nino

The wood of the black walnut tree, common to riparian zones in parts of the New World, had recently been acquired by Suleyman. So impressed was he by its beautiful markings, he had commissioned the crafting of a table, which stood as the centerpiece of the council chamber in the Topkapi. Suleyman sat at its head, immensely pleased, his hands caressing the finely polished finish, marveling at the burled, book-matched top, so-called because both sides of the top of the table were joined in a mirror image, thereby giving the appearance of an open book. The technique was new, and his latest acquisition was unique to his collection. He turned to his assembled guests.

"Vincenzo, will the thieves act tonight?" Suleyman was anxious.

"Your Majesty, I cannot be certain, but I believe their likely knowledge of our investigation will cause them to proceed rashly," Il Lupo conjectured. "Rumors and gossip abound within the walls of the palace. Those foolish enough to have stolen the relics may also be foolish enough to act with haste and make mistakes."

"My concern is that our hallowed relics are recovered before word escapes that they are missing. Right now, only the people in this room know with certainty, and those who have stolen them. The dead do not talk. If knowledge of their theft slips out, it will spread like wildfire in the Harem and throughout the palace to the clerics and janissaries. Usually in a group of thieves—and I believe we can certainly assume numerous persons are implicated—*one* has a loose tongue. Word of their disappearance would cause havoc, particularly among the radical clerics and their followers." Suleyman was calm, but his patience was growing thin. He was angry with himself for not insisting on more rigorous safeguards for protection of the relics.

"I don't believe the relics have been removed and delivered to co-conspirators. Of this I feel most certain," Il Lupo assured him.

"Well, we all know what happened to St. Mark's relics. You crafty Venetians secreted yourselves in barrels of pork to evade the Muslim guards in Alexandria, Egypt. Those relics were stolen and now reside with your Doge in his palace. Over seven hundred years later they still have not been returned to their rightful owner." Suleyman was uncharacteristically brusque.

"That cannot happen here. By the way, Vincenzo, as a Venetian, I do not hold you personally responsible. The return of our hallowed relics will sufficiently atone for the sins of your ancestors." Suleyman's tone changed and he smiled, allowing all assembled to feel slightly more at ease.

"I will, of course, strive to atone for the sins of my ancestors," Il Lupo rejoined, smiling.

"As for the plot on Suleyman's life… Is there any relation to the theft, Vincenzo? What do you believe?" Roxelana interjected.

"Kemal has a theory that I agree with. Kemal, why don't you tell them?"

"It was a rogue action—a crime of opportunity, as suspected. When Qais and his rebellious squad were assigned duty on the day of the ceremonies, he realized he might not have another chance for months when both Suleyman would again preside and Qais would have control of the guard rotation. The connection to the theft is coincidental," Kemal concluded.

"Qais expected to be appointed Captain of the Beyliks. Instead, two years ago, his majesty," Kemal gestured in the direction of Suleyman as he addressed those at the table, "appointed me. Qais was furious and allowed his anger to fester. I often thought him a somewhat unpolished and perhaps unscrupulous rogue, but did not think him capable of this treachery. During this time, he personally recruited new janissaries to the Beyliks. By doing so, they felt ingratiated to him because to be a member of the sultan's most trusted and loyal guards is the highest honor. Qais recruited them with great purpose, consciously and carefully suborning them to insurrection and treason. I believe he had long been planning the assassination. He needed others willing to join him, and so he deliberately encouraged their restiveness and frustration and recruited them, knowing they were more loyal to him than to Suleyman. These same malcontent janissaries conspired with Qais and followed his command when the opportunity presented itself."

"I see," Suleyman nodded. "Qais and his cabal of restive janissaries were bent on fomenting rebellion, disorder, and my death. He was an anathema in this court. May his soul be forever damned for his treacheries. It appears we will need to be more careful in the selection and recruitment of our future guards."

"In addition," Il Lupo spoke to the assembled group, "the theft of the relics would likely spread further unrest among the janissaries, the clerics, and, as a result, even the general populace, threatening the survival of the empire, as well as the emperor's life. A plot with potentially far-reaching and devastating consequences."

"Do you have an opinion as to who planned and financed the theft?" Suleyman asked Il Lupo.

"Your Majesty, I cannot yet be certain, but I do have suspicions," Il Lupo answered. "I believe Mehmed was likely involved. I feel confident that this is the only way that the janissaries could have learned of the passages through the cisterns and crypts. Mehmed had to have helped them. The planning and the financing, however, are much more sophisticated. I am reasonably confident that the funding of the thefts came from outside the Harem. I believe Mehmed should be able to lead us to the instigators. I must continue the investigation, but we shall soon have more definitive answers," Il Lupo confidently concluded.

"Ah, then Mehmed's killing of Qais was intended to silence him and to protect his own interests, not those of Suleyman or the empire?" Roxelana questioned Il Lupo.

"Yes, no doubt that was his intent. What Mehmed did not know was that he did not need to act. The poison dart would have killed Qais. This single, unnecessary act by Mehmed has now brought him under greater suspicion. Mehmed was surprised by the poisoned dart. I know that he saw it, but believe he knows less about the manner of the janissaries' deaths than we do." Il Lupo twirled the feather he had found in the cistern with his fingers.

"So the actions of this Jinn, which are likely to be directed by another or perhaps others, are designed to ensure that the theft is completed and that all the thieves are now silent—is this part of your conclusion, Vincenzo?" Roxelana asked, confirming her understanding.

"Yes, I think this is what Vincenzo believes," Suleyman answered Roxelana. "If that is the case, Mehmed remains alive only until the thieves deliver the relics. He will no longer be of use."

"And," Il Lupo broke in, "He is likely in much greater danger than he realizes."

Roxelana attempted to stifle her fears, but her expression revealed that she was worried. "Do you think Mehmed is somehow involved in the attempts on my life?" she probed.

Il Lupo looked at her seriously. "I would not wager against it. Mehmed would lose all his authority if you replaced Gulbehar. His loyalty lies only with her." There was a palpable uneasiness in the room, as those gathered wrestled with the enormity of the ramifications had the assassination attempt been successful, including the potential execution of Suleyman's children with Roxelana.

"You can wager on his immediate replacement!" Roxelana slammed her hand on the table.

"He will certainly lose more than his authority if these suspicions prove true. Anyone found to be involved will lose all that they have," Suleyman avowed.

"But Mehmed is not a trained assassin. The strangulation of your guard, Roxelana, was undoubtedly committed by another eunuch. I do not yet know his identity. Yet one more reason to keep Mehmed alive and unaware of our suspicions for the time being," Il Lupo reminded them.

"However, speaking of Mehmed, has he been found?" Il Lupo asked, knowing that he was to be questioned regarding the drawings taken from the archives.

"No, he is nowhere to be found. Even Gulbehar does not know where he is, unless she is lying about his whereabouts. However, we did find the drawings when a search was done of his room. He will likely be terrified when he finds them missing, confirming that he is under investigation," Suleyman answered. "When we do find him, he has much to answer for!"

Abdullah entered the conversation. "While we are on the subject of the eunuchs, all of those examined were found to be completely castrated. However, one was not examined—the eunuch Omar. We have been unable to locate him."

"Why is that relevant?" Roxelana looked puzzled.

Suleyman looked at her intensely. "The eunuch Omar is a trained assassin with the bowstring, Roxelana."

"And he is another of Mehmed's favorites," she chimed in, the realization dawning on her. "They are frequently together. Omar is Mehmed's shadow, his personal servant. He has not been here long—at least I have not known him to be. The hunt for him continues."

"Before we deal with Mehmed, share with us the further information you have gained regarding the sources of the poison and the killings of the janissaries." Suleyman nodded to Abdullah.

"Before I begin, I would like Kemal to relate what he has learned of the identities of the murdered janissaries after visiting the morgue earlier today."

Kemal began, "I was able to identify all the janissaries we have found. Of course, you all know about Kareem and Jamal, found beneath the repository. Qais lies with them in the morgue. I was able to ascertain the identities of the two janissaries that were involved in the plot—the two that escaped—over whom the Jinn was hovering when Roxelana, Francesca, and Aziz came upon the scene. They were two Beyliks recruited by Qais within the past year or so. Their names were Farid and Nazim.

"I was also able to identify the other two bloated bodies found with them who had been dead longer. They were not Beyliks. I had help from Tadros, a janissary who keeps me informed of what transpires within the janissary quarter. He identified them as Baris and Adem. Tadros informed me that he suspected they had ties to Mehmed in some way and that they had been known to frequently return to their quarters late at night, intoxicated. It is rumored that Mehmed provides sensual pleasures in the Harem for favored janissaries over whom he would then wield considerable influence," Kemal elucidated.

"Further," he continued, "after I identified the bodies of Farid and Nazim, I checked and found that they were on the rotation for guard duty on the day of the state reception and no doubt participated in the assassination attempt. I also checked the schedules for the previous night. Baris and Adem were the guards on duty at the *Has*

Oda on the shift that ended just after midnight on the day of the thefts. That leads to the likely further conclusion that they excavated the floor and placed the identifying shaft in the ceiling for their conspirators—Karem and Jamal—to find. Doubtless, all were killed with poison darts, despite the post-mortem maiming of their bodies."

"Very good, Kemal!" Il Lupo complimented. "Your discoveries add a great deal to the unraveling of the mysteries before us! Your Majesty, I might need to steal your prized janissary captain for my own use! He has not just the skills of a warrior, but quite the inquiring and resourceful mind as well. I am impressed!"

"Not so fast, my new friend!" Suleyman retorted. "Trusted before, but now my most trusted, Kemal is indispensable to me!"

"I understand, Your Majesty, but it never hurts to ask." Il Lupo saw that Kemal was pleased by the compliments.

"There is more to discuss." Suleyman turned to Abdullah. "What else can you tell us?"

"First I must tell you that intoxicants were present in the bodies of Baris and Adem. They had apparently ingested a great deal of wine of some variety. They smelled of figs. There is apparently a make-shift distillery of sorts within the walls of the palace that is well-hidden. The interaction of the wine and the poison likely contributed to the severe bloating and discoloration of their lips."

An infuriated Suleyman slammed his fists on the table. "Forbidden by me! Forbidden by Islam! Of course they consumed the wine! It was required to numb contemplation of their heretical desecration of the sanctity of the holy *Has Oda!*"

Abdullah continued, "These past hours have been most chaotic, filled with research and discussions with those who might have the knowledge I needed. The inquiry led to a colleague suggesting that I question certain sailors serving under Admiral Hayreddin Barbarosa. I did, and the discussions were fruitful and most interesting. I have concluded, based on these inquiries that the darts used by the Jinn were likely tipped with poison originating in the New World..."

An audible gasp from those gathered interrupted Abdullah. "It is produced from the sweat glands of frogs native to the jungles of certain areas that were conquered by the Spaniard Pedro Arias Davila. Davila established colonies in the central areas of the Americas. In fact, he led the first expedition into that part of the world, and many of his soldiers and even some fellow administrators fathered children with women from the native tribes. Incidentally, during my discussions I have learned that Davila has just died this year."

"Fascinating, Abdullah," Suleyman interjected. "Admiral Barbarossa is a fine man and skilled seaman and warrior. I actually gave him the name '*Hayreddin*' —the good one—for his glorious conquests and devoted service. I knew that the importing of goods from these areas has greatly increased and the court has seen the luxuries—gold, fruits, marvelous and exotic things—such as the Toucans given to me by Giovanni! Continue, please!"

"Barbarossa's sailors learned of a story told by captured Spaniards returning from the New World. It involved a young boy, fathered by one of the Spanish administrators, whose proficiency in the use of poison darts and blowguns was almost legendary. He was trained by Davila to be an assassin. Davila was a terrible man—unscrupulous—and if the reports are accurate, even sadistic. The conquistadors were often infamous for being merciless and cruel in vanquishing and ensuring the subjugation of conquered native tribes."

Abdullah continued. "Because this child's mother was a native, he was able to easily penetrate tribal societies. Davila used him to assassinate chieftains that challenged his Spanish rule. This enabled Davila to avoid suspicion and have dissidents eliminated. The darts were tipped with poison extracted from the deadliest tree frogs native to the central Americas."

"Intriguing. How is the poison safely extracted from the frogs and how would it be transported here?" Suleyman asked Abdullah.

"As for the second part of your question, Your Majesty, I cannot be sure. However, I was told of the method for extraction. It is quite disturbing," Abdullah answered.

"The frogs are carefully skewered, making sure not to kill them in the process. They are then, slowly roasted alive. The frog, in an attempt to protect itself, releases the poison. The poison is collected in receptacles placed beneath the roasting frogs and pasted to the tip of the darts. Someone unfamiliar with handling them could suffer a most unpleasant death. They should never be touched without protective covering such as gloves. Once used, those contaminated gloves must also be burned. Since gloves were not available to the natives of the New World, I was told that the frogs are held in large leaves and then a thick paste was used to cover the skin of the handler, creating an impermeable barrier between human skin and the frog."

"Those frogs have obviously been shipped here—or at least the poison," Suleyman ruminated.

"Yes, in fact, there was an incident this morning at the docks, Your Majesty. There was a suspicious death of a stevedore, who was unloading a crate from the New World this morning. He cut himself. I can only assume, based on what I now know, that in the moving of the crate his open wound made contact with one of those frogs inside," Abdullah related the story. "In doing so, the excreted poison of the frog would have entered his bloodstream and that was his death sentence."

"We must immediately track down the recipient of the cargo and the vessel in question," Suleyman demanded.

"Your Majesty, I believe I can save you the time," Il Lupo offered. "The crate in question was delivered to the residence of Giovanni Contratini this morning. Even though this is my temporary residence, it is most prudent to have the house watched until the conclusion of our investigation. We do not want to disrupt any planned activities for they may lead to the answers we are seeking."

"Yes, yes, a good suggestion, Vincenzo. But why? This is the newly appointed Venetian Ambassador to my court. Why would he be involved with such a thing? I have just been the recipient of such lovely gifts from him." Suleyman was incredulous.

"I do not yet know. It is essential to uncover the extent of these odious crimes and the perpetrators. I am uncertain of his involvement, if in fact there is any at all. There are still many missing pieces to these puzzles. We have yet to untangle the knots," Il Lupo answered.

"Ambassador Contratini's gift of the birds to you may also account for the discovery of this feather in the cistern. This type of long, black and narrow feather is from a toucan," Il Lupo speculated, again twirling the feather between his fingers. "We do not yet understand its significance to our investigation, but I am beginning to develop better-substantiated theories, which I will, of course, share with you at the appropriate time. I must first, however, be certain."

Roxelana redirected the conversation. "Abdullah, let us return to this child who was captured by Barbarosa. Can you tell us more?"

"Apparently the child was returning to Spain on a galleon from the New World with his father, a Spaniard. It was several years ago, before the invasion of Rhodes. At that time, Admiral Barbarossa was returning from a raid on the Balearic Islands and encountered several Spanish galleons returning from the New World off the coast of Cadiz. Some of the ships were sunk and others seized, but not before many were killed. The ship carrying the child, who was probably about ten years old at the time, was also sunk. He was captured and taken prisoner, along with many others. His father was likely killed. I do not know whether the father was an administrator under Davila or merely a soldier. The captured child was then sold into the slave trade and rendered a eunuch. That boy would be in his late teens today, possibly twenty."

"And where, might I ask, is that eunuch today?" Roxelana asked, already sure she knew the answer.

"After his castration he was brought here. He is a Harem eunuch," Abdullah confirmed her suspicion.

"I knew it!" Roxelana shouted. "It is Ali! It is the eunuch Ali! I already conveyed my suspicions today to Aziz and directed that he inform Francesca. Ali is so different than the other eunuchs; I felt with great certainty it had to be him."

"You may call him Ali, the eunuch, Roxelana. Ali, the assassin, however, is known by another name as well. The Spaniards referred to him as *El Diablo Nino*, the devil's child," Abdullah noticeably shuddered as the group sat, looking at one another in astonished silence.

Barbaric

"Roxelana, before we leave, may I talk to you for a moment?" Francesca asked in a whisper, taking her aside by the arm.

"Of course! What is it, Francesca? You look bewildered."

"We don't have a lot of time before I must leave, so I'll just be direct. I need to know more about eunuchs. I broached the subject briefly with *mia Padre* and Kemal but they were reluctant, saying only that the boys are castrated at an early age, but they declined to offer detailed information. I understand what castration is, but what is an incomplete or botched castration?"

"Oh Francesca! As you know, the procedure makes it safe for eunuchs to be around women. Without their sexual organs, they can love but have no means of fulfilling any sexual desire. Because the procedure is performed at such a young age, they never develop fully into manhood. This is the reason they usually maintain the higher pitched voices of a young boy, a falsetto, and never develop body hair. Aziz and Mehmed are two of the very few eunuchs in the Harem that have deeper, more commanding voices, an anomaly among eunuchs. In other ways, the eunuchs appear to be men."

"Yes, the high pitched voices. In fact, my father and I once visited a monastery where the all-male choir had soprano voices. They are called *"castratos"* and my father thought it unconscionable that men were castrated simply to retain their beautiful, high-pitched singing voices. Despicable!" Francesca shared her limited knowledge on the subject with Roxelana.

"How is the castration performed? And what exactly, if you know, is an incomplete castration—there has been so much talk of that," Francesca listened intently.

"First let me describe the gruesome process," Roxelana answered, gritting her teeth. "Boys, usually between the ages of eight and twelve, are captured in war, or stolen, or sometimes taken simply because parents cannot pay their taxes. Did you know that it is against the laws of Islam for one Muslim to enslave another? This is why slaves are taken from other countries and are non-Muslims. The boys enslaved to be eunuchs are mainly from conquered areas of North Africa and the Balkans. Sometimes the castration is performed by those who take them, or sometimes they are sold intact and others perform the procedure. I have heard the Coptics are often involved, but I do not know if that is true or not. I was born Christian—my father was an Orthodox priest—so I don't like to believe Christians would do this," Roxelana continued, prepared to be honest with Francesca about the grisly details.

"Once it is decided that the child is to become a eunuch—mind you, the boy has no say in the matter—he is chained to a table, and in usually just four slices, and not necessarily from a sharp blade, the pudenda are removed," the beautiful concubine shivered in horror. "Just thinking about it makes me cringe." Roxelana stopped speaking for a moment in attempt to maintain her composure. "I cannot imagine the terror and pain they must experience.

"Enduring this process must be horribly painful. It is shocking that some actually survive. After the slicing is done and genitalia removed, a bamboo rod is inserted in the opening to allow for the flow and removal of bodily fluids and to prevent the wound from closing completely. The child is then buried in hot sand to seal the wounds. If they survive—and only about one in ten survives— they become eunuchs. The survivors are an extremely valuable 'commodity.' Only the most wealthy can afford them."

Francesca replied, tried to grasp the full meaning and consequences of the brutal disfigurement. "But what is an incomplete or botched castration?"

"Well, my understanding is that a botched castration—or as some call it—an incomplete castration—is when unknowingly a portion of the genitalia remains. The possibility of regeneration exists in some cases. There is speculation that such regeneration could result in concupiscence, leaving those guarded in the Harem vulnerable. It is imperative the concubines are under no threat of seduction from a eunuch, and so the eunuchs are periodically examined. This is really all I know, but it is terribly ghastly, don't you agree?"

"Oh my. Yes, Roxelana, I believe I do understand now. So sad. What an unconscionable thing to do to another human being—and a young boy no less." Francesca was contemplative.

"Yes, it is one more example of the perpetuation of the inhumanity of man; castration is an unjust cruelty, just as is slavery. From time immemorial, all peoples of the world have enslaved one another. These neverending cruelties are the way of the world. The Ottomans will perhaps go down as the worst, however, and in all candor.

"Francesca, I am a slave! As is Kemal! It is hard to imagine, but true! While neither of us would choose to leave, if we so desired, we could not. I was captured and torn from my family just as Kemal was. We are just two of the fortunate. Our fate has been different from the masses that are subjugated and ripped from all they love and know. Can you grasp the enormity of the idea that neither of us is free to leave? That if it were attempted, we would be hunted down and likely executed?"

Francesca shook her head, realizing she had never thought of either Roxelana or Kemal as slaves.

"The Ottomans enslave Africans and white Europeans equally. Africans war with each other and then enslave Africans. Chinese enslave the Chinese. White Europeans enslave other whites. It is said that Julius Caesar sent over a million Gauls into bondage. The word slave even comes from the word, 'Slav' because the Slavic people are favored as slaves by the Mongols and the Arabs. And the Jews—well, they have been the most enslaved and persecuted of all since before the time of Moses. It is all a tragedy, just as it is a tragedy to steal boys and castrate them. The cruelties man inflicts upon fellow man are endless and barbaric." Roxelana spoke so passionately, Francesca believed the concubine struggled to suppress her tears.

"I know, Roxelana. These things are beyond comprehension, and each brutal, bestial act creates an individual human tragedy, the consequences spilling into many lives." Francesca put her arms around Roxelana and they held one another for a moment of comfort.

Sapphire Blues

The small fire in the field behind the stables at the Topkapi Palace was barely visible in the thick, atramentous darkness. A lean figure hunched over the flames in a trance-like state, slowly stomping his sandaled foot in a rhythmic drumbeat, his shoulders and torso moving in cadence with his chant, mostly hummed, interspersed with a few audible but indistinct words. His long black hair was pulled back and tied at the neck, and short, cropped bangs framed his forehead.

Just as he had done after receiving his first delivery, Ali carefully removed the poisonous anurans from the burlap bag he had retrieved from the dead drop earlier in the day. His gloved hands held steady the skewers that were extended into his small fire, upon which the writhing, poisonous frogs—the most deadly Sapphire Blues—had been carefully impaled. Eyes bulged from their heads, and their previously beautiful, gem-colored skins were turning to a charred, crisp black during the slow roasting process of poison extraction. They wriggled on the long, thin wooden spears attempting to free themselves and emitted a hissing sound as their skin crackled in the intense heat. It was a sound *El Diablo Nino* knew well and mimicked as he performed his sinister and deadly work. He was an expert and knew how long it would take for each of the frogs to deposit a maximum amount of venom, drip by drip, into the vessel positioned beneath them to collect the lethal drippings. Placed strategically in the vessel in a circle, the fine points of the darts, decorated with the feathers of exotic birds, waited to receive the lethal, gooey trickle.

As he sadistically watched the desperate movements of the doomed donors, his mind returned to the New World, the place of his birth, and running naked through the jungles in which he spent his earliest childhood. His memory flashed back to a ceremony of chanting natives, arms reaching high in homage to their gods, their chieftain's voice rising above all others, his groin and head covered in layers of woven grasses and feathers. The eyes of the *El Diablo Nino* glazed as he remembered the feeling of the jungle floor on his belly, slithering and maneuvering as a serpent, hushed and silent, watching and waiting. The rhythmic tamping of his foot and chanting increased to a frenzy as he remembered lying within the thick underbrush of the jungle. He remembered as he pulled a long, five-foot blow gun to his youthful face, inserting a dart into the shaft and bringing it to his mouth, poised and waiting for just the right moment to strike. His disguise was a cloak, elaborately feathered and camouflaged, crafted to blend with his surroundings and finished with the protruding beak of a toucan. He vividly recalled his emotions, the feeling of invincibility—that no one could see him—a small boy dressed as a bird with black feathers and yellow breast and neck. Patiently, quietly, he waited for the opportune moment. Within an instant, that precise moment came and he masterfully shot the poisoned dart into the neck of the chieftain. He did not need to wait to confirm his demise, so sure was he of the lethality of the toxin. Instead, the boy slid away just as he had arrived, on his belly and as a serpent, invisibly and quietly, into the dense and protective jungle.

El Diablo Nino sat in recollection, and as he did, he continued to emit hissing sounds mimicking that of the roasting frogs, first rising and then diminishing to a low guttural wail. His utterances ended finally in a sigh of sated relief, as if in climax and complete satisfaction as he recalled the demonic kill.

Within moments, his chanting slowed, returning to a quiet hum, his foot again slowly, rhythmically tapping. The open seas, as far as his imagination and sight could take him, flashed through his mind, followed by visions of blood and fires on the deck of the ship, and the realization he was never to see those familiar to him again. He remembered being taken from place to place, his body sore and his mouth parched only to finally arrive at a place of barren sands, so unlike the lush jungles he had left.

His memory took him then to the darkest of places—to a table where he was laid, heavy metal chains strapped to his arms and widely spread legs. Three men with long black robes, all speaking a foreign gibberish, stood at the table. One, holding a crudely shaped metal blade, moved to the table and grabbed his genitals. With four strokes, all that could ever identify him as a male had been removed. His recollection took him to the moment just before he lost consciousness from the mind numbing and excruciating pain as a thin, bamboo rod was inserted into his gaping and bleeding anatomy.

El Diablo Nino began a frantic rocking back and forth, massive tears flowing from his eyes as he recalled awakening to a reality of being buried in hot and burning sand. He recalled the agonized and terrified looks on the faces of eight other boys, buried up to their necks nearby him. He choked at the still lingering smell of the men, their cruel and insensitive hands pulling the rotting, stinking bodies of six boys, who had not survived the ordeal, from the sand—eyes and tongues bulging from insect-covered heads. Exhausted, he was overcome with feelings of supreme sadness and overwhelming hatred.

He threw the fully roasted frogs into the fire, collected the vessel and darts, and stood up, his slim physique casting a long shadow in the enveloping darkness. He moved to the dung pile in a corner of the yard and retrieved a large burlap bag, and returned to the fire. He cautiously removed the two layers of protective gloves, throwing them into the flames before kicking the dirt to extinguish the remaining embers. His work here was finished. It was now time for *El Diablo Nino* to complete his mission and fulfill his destiny.

Chthonic Chimera

Hassan made his way through a heavy mist into the Jewish quarter of Istanbul, checking over his shoulder repeatedly. The obscure light of the early evening fog made him apprehensive and distorted his view, causing him to stop every few paces, pausing to listen for any quickening steps behind him. As he rounded a corner, he glanced back again. As he turned forward, a cloaked figure suddenly emerged from the darkness a few steps in front of him. Hassan put his hand to his mouth to muffle his gasp. Even with its shrouded face barely visible, its visage manifested pure evil. It moved slightly, lowering the cowl of its rancid cloak over its face. Hassan shook with fear. His mind was confused by the suddenness of its materialization; an image of a hideous demon emerging from a smokeless fire consumed his mind. *'Is this the end of my days?'* he asked himself just as it had on his previous encounters with the demonic fiend. He wanted to cover his ears to muffle the terrifying sound of its long and sustained hissing.

The macabre figure moved closer to him and he recoiled, stepping back. "Stand where you are," it ordered, as it threw back its hood revealing its grotesque face.

"Shaitan! It is you! I have carefully followed all your instructions!" Hassan, subservient, lowered his head in an attempt to divert his eyes from the frightening countenance. The Shaitan's face was dense with thick, wrinkled skin, its snarling lips revealing sharp, broken and decaying teeth. Its eyes flashed with a thousand flames—its black stringy hair streaked with white—and its beaked nose was large and offset. Hassan shuddered at the terrifying otherworldly apparition.

"You miserable little shit. You are late!" it shrieked, its spittle covering his face. "Did you bring the jewels?"

"Yes, of course, Shaitan." Hassan's trembling hands moved into his cloak for the pouch. "Here, they are all here, just as you ordered on our last meeting." He held out his hand while averting his eyes from the fiery, chthonic chimera.

"It was only because of a change of plans that my arrival here was delayed. Please, please forgive me! I would never wish to displease you! I did all that you have asked of me and will continue to do your bidding!" he begged.

The snarling Shaitan grabbed the heavy and bulging pouch of jewels and handed Hassan a folded parchment sealed with wax.

"You must follow the directions precisely if you wish to gain possession of the relics! Do not deviate from the plan and deliver your last payment to me on time or you will die. You will have the relics before I have received my final payment, but do not delude yourself, for *I* will be watching your every move. Once you have satisfied our agreement, you will not see me again, *unless* you attempt to deceive me. If betrayed, you, the relics, and your party will not leave the city and *I* will be the last thing you see before you die!" it growled, threateningly.

"Go! Do not fail me. Heed my warnings for I am the messenger of *Iblis!*" the Shaitan hissed its order, peering up and over Hassan's shoulder.

Hassan turned to look, but only observed empty streets behind him. He heard a faint rustling of the Shaitan's cloak. The Shaitan vanished as suddenly as it had appeared, leaving behind only its fetor, strangely comingled with a slightly sweet fragrance that hung thick in the air. Hassan, left to recover his wits and courage, scurried away, quivering and ready to once again, do the Shaitan's bidding.

Stealthy Assassin

Mehmed and Ali removed the cache of holy relics, wrapped them in a soft cloth, and placed them in a long, leather shoulder satchel. They worked for a few moments, spreading the loose pebbles that had fallen upon opening the secret stone chamber so they blended with the floor. They had taken precautions to ensure they had not been followed, but their attempts were insufficient. Watchful janissaries, clothed in black, blended in to the murkiness of the night and followed them into the caliginous cisterns. The janissaries were not alone. Omar, filled with a hatred for Mehmed and the abusive treatment he had been subjected to at the hands of the Kizlar Agha, also trailed them waiting for a suitable moment.

Carrying the relics stowed in the satchel, Mehmed and Ali departed the area beneath the *Has Oda* and walked through the passages. Their exit was well-known to Mehmed, the same used by Baris and Adem after partaking of Harem pleasures.

Just past the eerie, sepulchral confines of the crypts, they heard a shuffle, a slight, furtive movement. Alarmed, they barely took a breath, waiting to see if they heard it again. They did not wait long. Out of a tall, narrow indentation in the cistern wall, Omar was upon them—a stealthy assassin of the night. Bowstring in hand, Omar was on Mehmed in an instant, wrapping it around his tormentor's neck. Mehmed fell to the floor writhing, his hands clawing at the bowstring's tightening hold, unable to loosen it.

Stunned only briefly by the swiftness of the attack on Mehmed, Ali reacted, pulling a knife from his boot. He attacked Omar and severed his left Achilles tendon. Omar shrieked in pain, releasing his grip on the bowstring around Mehmed's neck, and lashed out with a knife to keep Ali at bay as he struggled to recover. Finally able to stand, he spit in Ali's face before hobbling away.

"I will take care of him!" Ali exclaimed, chasing after Omar.

"No! Wait!" Mehmed barked, still gasping for breath. "I will find him and deal with him later. There is no place he can hide! We have more important things to do. We *must* deliver the package on time!" Mehmed commanded, fearful of the consequences if he did not precisely follow the instructions of the wicked Shaitan.

Band of Beggars

"Look!" Francesca whispered, pointing to a passing group of janissaries. "They have Omar in custody! He is always with Mehmed. I wonder what happened. We must wait to learn more," she said, turning to her identically dressed companions, Kemal and Aziz, all attired in beggar's schmattes.

Kemal responded philosophically. "We shall find out soon enough. I am certain he will have tales to tell under torture."

As the janissaries disappeared from sight, Aziz motioned to their matching beggar's rags with disdain. "You know friends, I don't usually do threesomes—especially dressed like this," Aziz threw his head back in laughter. "But then for that matter, I haven't been doing twosomes for some time either. Well, make that never," he chortled.

"A bit of *eunuch* humor Aziz?" Kemal squibbed. "You have also maligned one of Francesca's favorite fashion lines," pointing to their three schmattes. "I do believe you have hurt her feelings." Kemal looked at Francesca, with a feigned sympathetic expression.

"Never," Aziz emphasized. "We never poke fun at Francesca. Whatever dominatrix wants, dominatrix gets! I love the outfits," he replied, a broad smile covering his face.

"Dominatrix? *Dominatrix?*" Kemal looked from Aziz to Francesca with eyes wide and brows raised. "Now that is quite fascinating! Who would have thought? What secrets have you been keeping from me, Francesca?" Kemal's interest piqued as he teased and watched her turn away to hide her reddening face.

Despite their friendly bantering, Kemal was keenly aware that he was falling in love. Even in the midst of chaos, he had discovered an unfamiliar delight, a heartsease, and inner, peaceful tranquility in her company. He sensed, he hoped, that she was developing a growing affection for him. He found himself daydreaming, immersed in the joys and pleasures of his new feelings. His desire to be with her had become a near torment. It was only the pressing concerns they faced that prevented her from being a constant image in his mind.

Francesca chastised, "Quiet, imbeciles! Am I the only one here that can stay focused on business? Boys! There is no time for frivolities. The only woman here and I must do all the work? Pay attention! Watch, there are only two ways we think that Mehmed and Ali could exit the cisterns. I will watch the area of that exit from the Harem," she pointed to an area approximately twenty yards away.

"The other possible exit," she shifted her gaze and pointed in the opposite direction, "is just around that corner. Kemal, you take watch there. Aziz, you wait at the corner with your little flute—you musician you—and I will wait here. Kemal, if you observe them exit, alert Aziz and he will begin to play the flute, alerting me. I will do the same if they leave from the Harem," she instructed.

"Kemal! Need I remind you once again that the pleasure of your stare has its limits. Now is not the time! Focus!" She looked at him sternly. He had furrowed his brow, bringing his eyes together and giving him a lovelorn look. She chuckled to herself and thought it quite endearing.

"No reminding needed, Commandant! I will do exactly as ordered!" Kemal answered, snapped back to reality and attention. He stood tall, saluting the self-appointed leader of their band of beggars.

"And me, Francesca, what about me and my flute? Should I do it like this?" Aziz responded, embracing his role as a flutist enthusiastically, while dancing in a circle.

"I don't care how you play it, just play!" Francesca told him emphatically. "We're not looking for a masterpiece destined for the ages, just a signal, Aziz, just a *signal*. But my vote is that you keep your day job in the Harem," she jabbed.

Within minutes of moving to their designated positions to monitor the two exits, Kemal recognized Ali and Mehmed as they emerged. Waiting until they had passed, he lifted his staff above his head and waved to Aziz. Aziz began playing his little flute, without much melodic success, but his feet moved in tune. Unsure of his disguise, Aziz kept his head low, appearing deferential, ensuring he remained unrecognized, as Ali and Mehmed passed by him.

"You expect to get paid for that?" Mehmed scoffed. They moved on laughing at the sight and the thought of bestowing any monetary goodwill on the pathetic and poorly playing beggar.

The three beggars tracked the two as they wended their way through yet one more seemingly endless maze of narrow alleys and cobbled streets. Finally, Mehmed and Ali reached their destination, a massive Mediterranean cypress in a clearing at the end of one of the streets. The two eunuchs carefully wedged the large leather satchel deeply into the thick foliage of the tree.

Pausing and satisfied their handiwork had gone unobserved, the conspirators departed the area heading back in the direction of the Harem. The beggars waited to see who retrieved the satchel that they believed contained the relics, now well-hidden in the boughs of the tree. There would be time to deal with Mehmed and Ali later.

Intending to barter with a local shopkeeper, Mehmed snapped at Ali. "You go on ahead. I will meet you shortly back at the Harem." Mehmed picked up a small, silver flask and began speaking to the vendor. Ali complied and walked on alone.

Admiring his newly acquired silver flask and congratulating himself on his bargaining acumen, Mehmed entered the cistern, following his memorized path through the narrow passageway. Rounding the corner near the entrance of the crypt, he stopped cold, fear encompassing his massive body. He had no time to react before a poison dart found its mark in the jugular vein of his thick neck.

"Ahh!" the brutish *Kizlar Agha* cried out. Grabbing his neck, the towering figure crashed to the ground with a colossal thud.

"It is the devil—it is the Jinn!" Mehmed uttered his final words.

Bleeding Jinn

Vigilantly waiting in the cisterns near the scene of the earlier janissary mutilations, Suleyman and Il Lupo observed firsthand the Jinn in the commission of the murder of Mehmed.

"Get him!" a waiting Suleyman commanded his janissaries, pointing at the Jinn, his voice booming and echoing through the subterranean passageway.

The janissaries moved quickly in front of Suleyman and Il Lupo, acting as a human shield as they pursued the dark figure. The Jinn, lithe and moving with great agility and fully armed with a deadly arsenal, fired darts in rapid succession. They missed their mark. With each shot, the forewarned janissaries stopped, ducking to avoid the lethal missiles, but giving the Jinn precious seconds to increase its lead. Recovering each time and once again in pursuit, they neared the cistern exit. Suddenly, the motionless and cloaked figure was before them. Standing with bows notched with arrows and poised to shoot, the janissaries froze.

"Wait!" Suleyman, who had followed the pursuit, commanded. "Take it alive, if possible. Caution!" Two janissaries moved forward, bows still notched. It did not resist.

Il Lupo stepped forward and lifted the empty cloak. In doing so its putrid odor was released. The assembled group stepped back, gasping from the stench of the repugnant garment. Il Lupo had revealed an elaborate costume, its interior made completely of bird feathers—the body black with yellow throat and head—and a ghoulish, demonic mask.

"Your Majesty, look here," he called to Suleyman. "These talons are made from the finest Toledo steel, just as I had suspected. The Spaniards are known for their blades. Here, also, the straps were used as armholes allowing the costume to be worn. And, the feathers!" He pulled the black feather from his cape. "They are an exact match to the one found in the secret room under the *Has Oda*."

"Extraordinary!" Il Lupo continued. "The costume has been designed to be nearly a head taller than an ordinary man. This hideous mask has been artfully created to sit on top of the head of the wearer, giving it great height and adding to its fearsome appearance. It would also account for the blowgun being raised to the center of the chest—exactly where the mouth of the person wearing the costume would be located. The darts were not blown from the area where the head is, where one would expect. Whoever it was that hid in that secret room, is also the Jinn.

"This costume is of ingenious design. Look at the back of it. Come here and help me hold it up against the wall," Il Lupo requested, pointing to one of the janissaries. He stepped forward to assist and together they held the large, sweeping cloak to the wall.

"While the costume of the Jinn is that of a toucan with the face of a demon, it is the back and exterior of the garment that allowed camouflage in the narrow passageways. You can see that the back of the cloak has been painted to replicate closely the walls here in the cistern. The Jinn could easily have faced the wall, arms outstretched with only the back of the cloak showing, thus blending so completely into the wall. The entire costume is unique and meticulously designed by someone who knew the passageways well. No one would think that a living being was standing in front of them. Only when it moved, perhaps only emitting a slight shuffling noise, was it likely to be discovered. Before and after the killings, it simply waited in the small hidden room, but at opportune times could monitor its victims, camouflaged and without fear of detection," Il Lupo explained.

"Remarkable ingenuity and creativity on the part of the mastermind of this diabolical scheme!" Suleyman observed. "And look here...our Jinn has been wounded! Even a Jinn can bleed."

Turning to the janissaries, Suleyman attempted to assuage their fears. "These are the disguises used by a human—not a demon or a ghost. The costume is intended to terrify while disguising the person committing the murders. Your bravery here is required. We have not recovered the blowgun and the murderer may still have a supply of poisoned darts. Follow me," he encouraged them on as he began to follow the trail of blood. There was a silence of palpable but controlled terror, the play of shadows created by their lamps adding to the disturbing and frightening narrowness of the passageway as they moved forward. Finally the passage reached a dead end, and the wicked and unholy Jinn was caught.

Wounded but not finished, the unmasked demon was crouched on the floor, blowgun in hand. At the sight of his pursuers, he raised it to his mouth targeting the sultan.

"No!" Il Lupo yelled, lurching forward to strike the blowgun from the mouth of *El Diablo Nino*.

"Down, Suleyman!" The quick response by Il Lupo diverted the dart from its intended target, but in doing so hit one of the janissaries. He howled and then, in an instant, was convulsing in the throes of death.

"You will learn nothing from me! The Shaitan has promised Spain! I will pass through Hell first!" *El Diablo Nino* hissed, drawing a knife from his boot. In one motion, Ali slit his own throat from side to side. His hissing ended in a gurgle as the blood gushed over his body and onto the floor and wall.

Grabbing the knife from Ali's hand, Il Lupo grabbed his shoulders, shaking him. "Who is the Shaitan?" Il Lupo continued to shake Ali, repeating the question.

"*El Diablo.* Your son returns," was the only answer Il Lupo received. Ali—*El Diablo Nino*—the Jinn born of the smokeless fire— descended into the fires of Hell.

"Your Majesty, there is nothing more I can do here, but as you are aware, there is much more work to be done elsewhere. May I borrow some of your janissaries?" Il Lupo made the urgent request.

"You twelve, go with Il Lupo and do exactly as he tells you! That is my command!" Suleyman agreed, fully understanding the pressing need to recover the relics. He and four remaining janissary guards watched as the Count and his men hastily made their departure. "Take the bodies to the morgue," Suleyman ordered.

Against All Odds

The beggars watched as another cloaked courier retrieved the leather satchel containing the relics from the dense boughs of the massive cypress. It had taken a few moments to find the satchel, groping unsuccessfully in several areas of the tree before making the discovery.

Kemal and Francesca stood north of the tree and Aziz to the south as the figure strode away with the relics. Aziz joined Kemal and Francesca and they trailed him quietly. The messenger entered an open square pacing back and forth, as he apparently waited for another. He stood near a fountain, finally taking a seat on its wide edge, then removing the large satchel from his shoulder and setting it on the ground next to him. The beggars became uneasy. The shops were closing down, and with crowds dispersing, the open area offered little place for them to hide. Doing their best to mingle, they attempted to appear preoccupied with begging so as not to arouse the suspicion of the messenger. Suddenly, the messenger abruptly stood up and handed off the satchel containing the sacrosanct relics to a tall hooded figure, with no attempt to hide their transaction. Kemal, Francesca and Aziz followed the departing recipient, careful not to lose sight of this latest courier.

"I think I should make an arrest," Kemal urged, watching the recipient walk away with the satchel.

"No, all these messengers will ultimately be identified. They are relatively unimportant, perhaps even lacking knowledge of what they carry. We must wait until final delivery is made. We need to stick together because we do not know what dangers await us," Francesca insisted.

"We are to follow instructions and act only if our lives are threatened. We *must* wait until the final delivery is made," she reminded him.

"Yes, you are right again, of course," Kemal relented.

Huddled together, they moved forward, occasionally dispersing when the shrouded figure paused, looking around for assurances he was not being followed. Beggars were a constant presence in the city and often followed people with hopes of a handout. Had their presence been noticed, they would hardly have been perceived as a threat, but the shrouded figure gave no indication that it was aware of their watchful eyes.

After weaving their way again via yet one more twisting route though Istanbul's streets and alleys, the hooded figure entered another open square. He joined some thirty warriors, several carrying torches as darkness approached. They waited on horseback, with additional pack horses fully loaded, prepared for a long journey. The assembled troops watched as the shrouded figure approached. His cloak flowing behind him as he hurried toward them, he removed his hood as the warriors dismounted and bowed, the flames of their torches illuminating his face.

"The Persian envoy! It is Hassan!" Kemal exclaimed, shocked.

"Yes, with a small army," Francesca acknowledged in a murmur, lowering her hand, urgently signaling all to keep their voices down.

"And ready to travel," Aziz chimed in.

"Not if we can help it," Francesca insisted, resolute.

"Who is *we*?" Aziz asked, the white of his eyes large and expressive in typical Aziz style. "Ten to one. Those odds are not so good. Did you bring any artillery?"

"Just these," Francesca pulled back her cloak to reveal her belt of deadly throwing knives and sling. She grabbed the jambiya with her right hand, keeping the staff in her left. "And *this*," she flashed the jambiya, "is the most deadly and my favorite for a time like this. I have three more of those in my belt."

Not to be outdone, Kemal threw open his cloak, revealing his bow and a quiver of arrows. "And these."

"And this," Aziz reached to the back of his sash beneath is cloak, presenting a huge weapon resembling an African war club–a juggernaut when wielded with Aziz's awesome strength behind it.

"I made it myself. Just like the one my father had. I watched him when I was a child as he made his," he boasted, holding the bulbous end and pulling a leather hood from the slender end, revealing a heavy, metal spear.

"Impressive, Aziz! I am relieved to see you both came equipped. My instincts told me you would. I prefer my friends always be prepared. If we can make the knives and arrows count, we've reduced the odds to five to one," she calculated.

"Those are odds I can live with—I hope!" Kemal offered with Aziz nodding his agreement.

They huddled together, honing their strategy. "I need to get in closer range. Aziz, you come with me. Kemal, I think you should concentrate your fire on that group to the right. Aziz and I will approach the men in the front. Once they are within reach of your club, I will take as many as I can in the center with my knives. It appears they are not fully armed—just swords and a few daggers— many of their weapons are still attached to their saddles. When I throw my first knife, take out as many as you can. We can only hope they will be so surprised, they will break and scatter. That may give you further opportunity, Kemal, but you must keep your focus first on that group to the right. Are we in agreement?"

"Yes, commander in chief," Kemal answered, surprised by her strategic planning. He would have changed nothing.

"Good. Let's go!" she directed. The hunched and pathetic beggars made their way to the group nearest them, in the center.

"Alms for the poor, alms for the poor," they all chanted, meeting with immediate rejection and laughter.

In unison, the three threw off their cloaks. Adrenalin surged, bringing a forcefulness and momentum to their attack. First killing two with knives thrown with precision accuracy, Francesca then used her staff to propel herself into the air, her feet quickly disabling two more guards knocking them unconscious. With great agility, Francesca had dispatched five before she ran out of knives, while Aziz managed to spear and bludgeon the three closest to him. With equal proficiency, Kemal dispatched seven, all arrows finding their deadly mark. There was a pause in the melee, and the three regrouped around each other.

"Out of ammo and they are not scattering," Aziz commented.

"Hardened warriors. Just our luck," Francesca smirked. "We have not yet begun to fight!" she yelled, pulling a rapier from her walking stick. Kemal grabbed a scimitar from the hand of a warrior with a jambiya protruding from his eye socket.

A second onslaught began and they propelled themselves with ferocity and determination into combat. Approximately fifteen Persian warriors and Hassan now on horseback remained and the two Francesca had knocked out were regaining consciousness. The three continued fighting valiantly, but they were surrounded. They were disarmed, and taken prisoner.

Hassan sat astride his horse and haughtily looked down on them. "Take them over there," he ordered, sneering, pointing to a stand of trees. "Kill them there. They will not be found so quickly and we can be on our…" Hassan was cut off in mid-sentence.

"Not so fast, Hassan," Il Lupo walked up, twirling his rapier. "You have spoken of the renowned hospitality of the Shi'a. Is this the way you treat beggars and derelicts?" he queried, pointing in the direction of Hassan's new prisoners.

"*Kill* him! *Kill* him!" Hassan screamed, pointing a thick, shaking finger in fury at a bemused Vincenzo Lupo.

"Hmm, I think not," Il Lupo responded, his demeanor a mix of boredom and humor.

Il Lupo surged forward, a second rapier drawn from the scabbard on his back. Holding a rapier in each hand, he jumped into the fray, slashing and stabbing with skillfully maneuvered movement. With remarkable speed, he created pandemonium and awe in equal parts as he dispatched two, and in a further display of extraordinary swordsmanship, somersaulted in mid-air and again to the center of the entourage, striking two on his descent and then killing, in an instant, three more.

Not one of the combatants had ever before beheld such a display of speed, agility, power, and deadly skill. In equal surprise and reverence, Hassan's astounded warriors gave way as Il Lupo stalked in a circling swirl dealing death, so swift they were unable to coordinate a unified counterattack. Even in their fear of the one-man lethal force, they could not help but marvel at what they had just witnessed.

Fully aware that the fight was over, Il Lupo turned and calmly addressed Francesca. "What, no help for an old man in distress?" He saw her smile, but did not wait for her retort.

"Enough, Hassan?" Il Lupo knew fully well that he had control of the scene. He whistled, signaling the janissaries who had been waiting in the shadows, to reveal themselves.

Understanding the fate that surely awaited him upon capture, Hassan made a last desperate attempt to escape. He galloped toward Il Lupo, raising his sword, ready to strike as he passed. Always prepared, Il Lupo unbuckled a mace and chain from his waist, swinging it into the air as the galloping horse approached. Ducking to evade Hassan's blow, he wrapped the chain around Hassan's sword arm and yanked Hassan from his saddle. Hassan flew head first, arms and legs flailing in the air as his riderless horse galloped by Il Lupo.

Il Lupo, disgusted, walked over to a moaning Hassan who lay in a humiliated heap on the cobbled street, "If you reveal all about Shaitan, your death will be quick."

"I will tell you nothing!" Hassan spewed, blood pouring from the empty sockets where a few teeth had once been.

"Ah, Hassan, another bad choice."

Turning to the janissaries, he ordered, "Take him to Suleyman. His soldiers too. And all the goods on the horses. Who knows what treasures we may find? I suspect the sacrosanct treasures of an empire. Bring me the satchel." The janissaries complied, tying Hassan and the few remaining soldiers together in a column and one horse to another for the trek to the palace. There the prisoners would be delivered to the infamous torture chamber within its walls.

"How did you know that it was Hassan who was to receive the relics?" Francesca asked, curiously.

"I was not certain until tonight. He had suggested he might be returning to Persia earlier than had been originally planned. The knots unravel, Francesca. He mentioned 'weeks' originally which suddenly was reduced to a few days. There were too many discrepancies in his plans. His departure was all too coincidental given the recent thefts. As you know, I rarely believe in coincidence. So, I went to Hassan's villa to speak to him. I was informed by a servant where Hassan was to meet his warriors this evening. That led us here."

Il Lupo looked a bit tired, but enormously relieved that his trusted instincts had once again served him well and he had arrived in time to save Francesca, Kemal, and Aziz and rescue the sacred relics of the Prophet Muhammad.

Gardener's Harvest

In the early evening hours, Ahmet Manragoz—*the Bostanic Basha*—the head gardener at the Topkapi Palace—was summoned to the dungeons where the torture chamber was carved deep into its subterranean walls. As mandated by decree, his duties as head gardener required that he become expert in the macabre arts of torture and execution. Over the centuries, the men who nurtured life in the palace gardens also became the deliverer of pain, torture and death—all according to the customs and traditions of the palace. Some lesser gardeners also served as civil servants or even police. The gardener's newest undertaking would require his greatest skills, a responsibility requiring creativity to extract information crucial to resolution of the mysteries plaguing the palace.

The *Bostanic Basha* had perfected many procedures for inflicting and prolonging pain and death and was equally expert at beheading with one, perfectly placed stroke of the sword. He worked with deliberation, little-by-little and sometimes piece-by-piece, in attempt to gain the desired outcome—extracting information. He hummed under his breath in an attempt at distraction—his own—but the incongruity of the hummed tune increased the prisoners' terror, thinking it proof the gardener enjoyed his gruesome tasks.

This early evening was no different for him. He had been delivered two men and his job was to uncover their knowledge of the thefts and assassination attempt on the Sultan Suleyman Khan as quickly as possible, deliberately avoiding death for his victims, until his employers were satisfied they had all they needed. There was a special urgency this evening—time was of the essence. He would employ whatever tactics and devices necessary to obtain what was required and with the greatest efficiency. Unless instructed otherwise, the ultimate choice for their deaths would be his and he chose according to the seriousness of their infraction, their status, and the degree of the accused's cooperation.

Within the chamber were all manner of draconian torture devices, each delivering different forms and levels of intense and excruciating pain, including the Judas Cradle and Chair, the latter having been a favored form of torture during the Inquisition. The chamber had originally been an oubliette, but was later enlarged to incorporate a wide staircase and entry doors. It was equipped with the rack, the breaking wheel, a Spanish donkey, impaling stakes, and the iron maiden, a preferred continental torture. Scattered over several tables were hand-held tools of his trade—knives of all sizes and sharpness, the heretic's fork, the lead sprinkler, pilliwinks, breast rippers, crocodile shears, ropes, neck torture rings and the tongue tearer. Some of the instruments looked simple—almost innocent—with little hint as to the pain each could inflict. Others were conspicuously fearsome. Prisoners watching the torturer's selection process murmured prayers that the torturer would not select those from the table.

Creative techniques that could be employed for extraction of information required no tools, rather ingenuity using live animals or water, or honey and milk—scaphism—and other methods such as burying alive, freezing, burning, dunking or strapping the victim to the ground, cutting holes in their stomachs and introducing starving rats into the cavity. The *Bostanic Basha* could employ any of these, the Five Pains, or drawing and quartering. He knew them all. He had every tool he required and was also in possession of an imagination and zeal that ensured he would never be subjected to any of them. He considered himself an artist in his way, albeit he abhorred the "creative process," in his quiet, reflective moments.

It was late evening when the coxcomb, Ibrahim, was summoned to learn the detailed information the *Bostanic Basha* had gleaned from his victims. Ibrahim arrived, his foul mood elevated. He heard the protracted and piercing screams of the victims as he descended into the chamber. He had already witnessed the heads of Hassan's soldiers wheeled out on a cart to be displayed atop pikes outside the Imperial Gates. Their deaths had been easy—beheading—they were only enemies carrying out orders from a higher authority—Hassan. They had met with swift justice and shown mercy—a quick death. If the *Bostanic Basha* did not know already that Hassan and Omar would be shown no mercy, Ibrahim would make that abundantly clear. Before they met their slow demise, he wanted all they knew extracted from their dying carcasses.

Hassan and Omar had both been strapped to tables that faced one another at an angle. Ahmet wanted to ensure that each saw the infliction of pain the other would endure. Their faces were bloodied and swollen beyond recognition; Ahmet had already removed their noses. He was in the process of flaying Hassan when Ibrahim entered the room. The Grand Vizier watched as Ahmet sliced pieces of skin from the upper thigh and placed them carefully in neat and tidy rows between the two tables—just as if he were planting rows of exquisite flowers in the garden. The screams were terrifying and shrill.

"Shut them up!" Ibrahim demanded, devoid of any sympathy. He eyed the victims as skin was stripped, exposing muscle and oozing blood. "Stick something in their mouths! Just be sure to keep their tongues until they talk. No using of this yet." Ibrahim picked up the tongue tearer and then threw it back among the other implements of torture. Ahmet ripped a bloodied cloth he had used to wipe his hands and tore it in half—stuffing each of their mouths.

"Let me tell you what I have learned," Ahmet said, turning his attention to Ibrahim.

Hassan and Omar were grateful for the respite from their torment as Ahmet paused in his work and shared his knowledge. Ibrahim listened intently, nodding his head from time to time, whispering instructions to Ahmet regarding further needed information. Unable to scream, their mouths stuffed with the filthy cloth, both prisoners continued whimpering in pain as they watched the conversation, dreading the moment the torture would resume.

"Good work, Ahmet," Ibrahim complimented, grudgingly. "I will report this to Suleyman immediately. Further action may be required this evening based on what you have told me. Keep on working to find out as much as they know. I am unsure if they are lying about some of the details or surprisingly nescient. If you have more to report, send a messenger immediately. Now, what more do you have planned?"

"I had started with the Five Pains—you can see I removed their noses, but have decided against pursuing that method further. I...I think I will continue the flaying, but ultimately I think will administer death by compression of the testicles. It is a very slow death, causing gangrene and poisoning of the blood. It seems most fitting—especially for that one," he pointed at Omar, who despite his charade as a eunuch remained in full possession of all his sexual organs. His gag only muffled Omar's shrieks when he learned the means of his ultimate demise. Hassan was now motionless, having fainted from the excruciating pain and the dread of more to come.

"Yes, it does sound most fitting. But whatever your choice, Ahmet, kill them *slowly*," Ibrahim directed as he turned and left the chamber. Guilty of heretical acts of desecration, they were deemed unworthy of swift and merciful deaths.

Vir Intactus

Suleyman was initially startled by the entrance of three beggars into the luxurious palace chamber. He stepped back, registering a degree of shock and concern. His hand went to the dagger at his waist, but he quickly recognized the three, as Francesca, Kemal and Aziz removed their hoods, revealing sooty, dirty faces to a now amused sultan.

Turning to Il Lupo he quipped, "I think they need a raise. Allow them to afford more suitable clothing, not to mention a week in a hammam!"

"That's Francesca's new fashion line. Already two customers," Il Lupo quipped. "Upon our return to Venice, you can be sure she will get remedial hygiene training."

With one exception, the gathered all enjoyed the lightness of the moment after their melee, including Il Lupo and Roxelana. It had become apparent to all there was little that would amuse Ibrahim. He knew that Il Lupo would never join the circle of sycophants that obsequiously genuflected before him, seeking favor. Ibrahim was without influence over Il Lupo and the conduct of his independent investigation. Ibrahim realized he needed to be wary and remain above suspicion and not dragged into the web of deceptions that had so carefully been spun by the perpetrators of the thefts and assassination attempts. The powerful and pretentious Ibrahim remained stone-faced, still harboring a festering resentment for the preferential treatment bestowed upon the infidels by Suleyman.

Suleyman continued, "It appears Allah has not been merciful to you, my three beggars. But, I will tell you that according to Ibrahim, the Almighty has been much less merciful to Hassan's soldiers. Their heads now sit atop pikes at the Imperial Gates. You, however, need beg no longer. You shall be rewarded," he promised. "But first there is more to do."

"Praise be to Allah," Aziz shouted. "These clothes, designed by her majesty, Francesca, queen of the beggars and gypsies, are one thing. But their critiques of my beautiful flute symphonies... unacceptable!" Aziz tipped the flute lightly to his lips, playing a few notes and giving his large body a klutzy twirl. "Obviously, they have no taste," Aziz joked, at ease with his audience.

"Beautiful indeed, Aziz. You can entertain us at the palace anytime!" Suleyman laughed. "But now—work! Ibrahim has just returned from the torture chamber. Share with us the information that has been extracted from Hassan and Omar," Suleyman adjured, his stern tone redirecting the conversation.

"Our *Bostanic Basha* has been most resourceful and we have learned a great deal in a short time. I will begin with information gained from Omar. He said that he was captured during the siege of Buda two years ago and was selected by Qais to be trained as an assassin. Omar was sinewy and stealthy—both requisites for an assassin. I also suspect that Qais wanted to train Omar for his own purposes—the assassination of Your Majesty—although of this I cannot be certain. Even though he now had a fully trained assassin at his disposal, as we know Qais conceived other plans regarding your assassination. Consequently, Qais turned him over to Mehmed to further their joint interests and enterprises." Ibrahim was haughty in his presentation, but grateful to be the center of attention once again.

"I see," Suleyman's expression was grave. "Continue."

"Omar was only turned over to Mehmed a few months ago. He lived in Mehmed's quarters, and it was assumed that he was merely Mehmed's personal servant—which, of course, he was. However, he was not integrated into the eunuch population for obvious reasons— he remained a fully functioning, *vir intactus*, an 'intact' male. This suited Mehmed perfectly—he had complete control over Omar's destiny. Omar complied with Mehmed's every wish simply to remain unexposed and alive.

"As such a recent arrival and under Mehmed's protection, he had not yet been subjected to the inspections conducted by Abdullah and there was never any reason for anyone to suspect that he was anything other than a eunuch. We are only certain that two people knew—Mehmed and Qais. Perhaps Gulbehar knew. It is unlikely Mehmed withheld much information from her. Aside from that, there is no reason to believe that any others knew." Ibrahim continued relating his findings to his attentive audience.

"Omar also confessed that he had been ordered by Mehmed to kill Roxelana. He admitted to strangling her eunuch with the bowstring and would have murdered her in the same way had she been in her chambers." Ibrahim watched Roxelana as her graceful hand fluttered upward, toward her neck, alarm draining the color from her cheeks.

"Why?" Suleyman was incredulous. "To what purpose?"

"We can only be certain of Omar's purpose. He simply followed Mehmed's orders or be exposed. What Mehmed wanted, Omar did—no matter what the bidding. More complex of course, are Mehmed's motivations. Was Mehmed, acting alone to ultimately elevate his own status, or perhaps on Gulbehar's command? I believe had Omar known, those details would have been extracted by the *Bostanic Basha*.

"Finally, a few more interesting bits of information. Omar also revealed that Mehmed was quite enterprising. He was running a prostitution ring out of the Harem. Mehmed of course, only used discarded concubines and provided the services only to a select group of janissaries—disgruntled and loyal to him and to Qais. It has been verified that Mehmed also distilled the fig wine, which the janissaries imbibed on their visits to the Harem. Omar knew of the secret passageways. He and Mehmed studied the plans Mehmed had taken from the architect. Once again, he did not know whether Mehmed took it upon himself to get the plans or whether he had been ordered to do so. Omar said that Mehmed was ordered by someone who terrified him, to turn over the plans to Ali. The plans were returned to Mehmed after a few weeks. We can conclude that Ali, and perhaps others, used them to thoroughly study the passageways and know where to hide and what routes would be used. We do not know if the mastermind, or whoever it was that ordered Mehmed to release the plans to Ali, ever entered the labyrinth. Knowledge of the maze beneath the palace and how and where the passages could be entered and exited were essential for the thefts to be executed. Omar overheard Mehmed speaking to Qais and janissaries on several occasions and believed those could be the same janissaries involved in the theft. Of this, he could not be completely certain. He was not privy to the details of the theft."

"Ah! Forgive my interruption, but this information clarifies other information we now have," Il Lupo began.

"Mehmed shared the secrets of the passageways within the crypts and cisterns with selected janissaries initially for the purposes of entering the Harem and corrupting them. They had been recruited by Qais and were passed on to Mehmed. Later their knowledge of the labyrinth was essential to successful execution of the theft," Il Lupo offered.

"Yes, and undoubtedly they were promised bounty as well—many reasons Mehmed and Qais were able to control them and their tongues," an infuriated Suleyman added.

"Corruption breeds more corruption. We have spoken of this before, Your Majesty."

Zealot

"Ibrahim, now share what information has been extracted from Hassan," Suleyman directed.

"This is interesting and disturbing because we have some answers, but not enough to resolve many questions regarding the thefts," Ibrahim began.

"Hassan, it appears, is—or perhaps I should now say, was—a radical and determined advocate for the Savavid movement in Persia. He was bent on annihilation of the Sunni, as well as the infidel. He was instructed some months ago, that he was to travel to Istanbul. Once arrived, he would be summoned to receive his instructions. He was funded by the Mullahs within the movement and provided with three pouches of jewels, each containing one hundred gems, all weighing over three carats each—a veritable fortune. He was to bring one pouch to the first meeting, where he would then be given his detailed instructions. He had no idea who he would be meeting, just that the first payment was to compensate the mastermind and planners of the thefts and provide an initial payment for the services of those who were directly involved in stealing the relics. It was the mastermind, with whom Hassan would meet. At the second meeting, he was to deliver the second payment apparently intended as a final payment to Mehmed, Qais, and their four janissary co-conspirators after successful completion of the thefts. Also, at the second meeting Hassan was given the final details required to effect delivery of the relics to him. The final payment, after Hassan received the relics, was to pay the mastermind.

"Hassan did as instructed and met on two occasions with a cloaked and masked demon known only to him as 'Shaitan.' In his first meeting, the Shaitan mentioned 'others' and Hassan came to suspect that Shaitan was alluding to Mehmed and his cabal of janissaries, perhaps Qais as well. He described these three encounters with Shaitan as terrifying. He firmly believed that had he not followed instructions precisely he would be killed in some grisly fashion. He was petrified and would never have acted against the demonic Shaitan. He intended to meet Shaitan again later at midnight to transfer the final payment, but instead was intercepted by the beggars and Il Lupo as he was readying his troops and caravan to return to Persia. Even under torture, he wished to die rather than face the promised wrath of the demon.

"Hassan does not know the identity of Shaitan, I am certain. The *Bostanic Basha* has been resourceful and it is unlikely that under torture, Hassan would not have revealed its name if he knew. He firmly believed this Shaitan was a supernatural being, not a human. He could only say that it had a gruesome face, and its body always cloaked and shrouded during their late night encounters. It had had wildly flashing and fiery eyes, a putrid, rotten and yet contradictory faintly sweet odor. He said further that it had a commanding, hissing voice that he had not heard before.

"Hassan knew the plot would cause immediate instability and, as a true religious zealot, found comfort that his action might have provoked a war between Persia and the Ottomans. He would have done whatever was within his power to undermine the Ottoman Empire and the Sunnis. As an envoy, he often had to mask his beliefs. Possession of the relics would validate and legitimize the Savavid Shiite 'true believers' in Persia. While fearful, he realized the powerful political value of the plot and found no difficulty involving himself in any treachery that would precipitate further divisions within Islam. He is obsessed with the annihilation of the enemies of the true Shi'a faith. Even as he attempted to conceal his beliefs for diplomatic purposes, he despises the Sunnis. He did, however, remain fearful of the Shaitan, even if its evil plots coincided with and furthered his goals, beliefs and the Savavid movement in Persia.

"We also learned that Hassan was to meet the Shaitan prior to departing the city tonight. It was tonight, as I said at midnight, that he was to make the final payment. This Shaitan told Hassan that he and the relics would only be permitted to leave the city if that payment was made in full. If the final payment of jewels was not made—if he attempted to deceive Shaitan—Hassan felt certain that the Shaitan would make good on its threat to expose and kill him. He fully intended to keep his end of the bargain and meet with the demon tonight before departing with his entourage for Persia." Ibrahim appeared fatigued and stopped, pausing as he moved to take a seat.

Il Lupo felt a twinge of sympathy for the man he had come to believe was petty and vain. The revelations he was sharing of the egregious breaches in security and protocols were his responsibility. The ultimate consequences Ibrahim would face would likely be severe. Despite Il Lupo's dislike for the man's pretention and pomposity, he knew it was unlikely Ibrahim would escape the wrath of Suleyman. Il Lupo watched as Suleyman viewed the Grand Vizier with a sharp and penetrating gaze.

Ibrahim added, "Hassan knew nothing definitive of Mehmed's or the janissaries' involvement or any of the specific details concerning the assassination attempts or execution of the theft. He was ordered merely to take possession of the relics, make the payments and transport the relics to Persia. He took satisfaction in the knowledge that the theft of the relics would cause great unrest and harm to Suleyman and to the empire, while further legitimizing and advancing the interests of the Savavids."

"So there are political motivations behind the theft. We are all followers of Islam and our differences longstanding. This Savavid movement is indeed radical! But to steal relics—to steal anything— violates fundamental tenets of the Islamic faith and the teachings of Muhammad! How could this be justified for any reason? I am stunned that such duplicities would occur in order to elevate one sect above another," Suleyman was incredulous.

"Hassan confessed his reasons. Possessing relics of the Prophet Muhammad would give greater authority to the Shi'a movement in Persia. Hassan believed it would rally the Shiites to win an inevitable war with us, not just the empire, but all Sunnis. His motivation, again, was purely religious zealotry. The motives for others involved likely would have been merely the money, possibly including Shaitan, but we cannot be sure. We must consider that this Shaitan perhaps had greater motives than just mere greed. We will only know the answer to these questions once the identity of the Shaitan is known, Your Majesty." Ibrahim continued in his exposition.

"Further, with regard to the timing of the theft, as you and Il Lupo have speculated, it was indeed planned so that the relics would be taken shortly after they had been displayed during Ramadan. He was informed by someone privy to our lax policies that they were locked away and not displayed again until shortly before Ramadan next year. That would provide ample time for the relics to be stolen, secreted from the palace and transported out of the empire with discovery unlikely," Ibrahim concluded.

"I agree that the motive of Mehmed and the janissaries was likely money," Il Lupo offered. "Perhaps there is some possibility that they also hoped the loss of relics would provoke a revolt against the emperor. Your overthrow would likely have elevated Mehmed's standing in the court, as has been discussed, and should not be overlooked as a potential motive. The thefts would perhaps inflame dissident clerics as well. Whether Mehmed was directly involved in the rebellion is of little consequence. If he was only on the periphery of the conspiracy and simply knew about it and did nothing, he was complicit. Rebellious janissaries might have precipitated a widespread insurrection capable of toppling you and the empire." Il Lupo continued grimly, "Also, a fall from grace and power for everyone who supports you—Roxelana, Kemal—those you trust and care for the most. This includes, Your Majesty, your children." There was a loud gasp from Roxelana.

The room became very still as Il Lupo's words were slowly and completely absorbed. Suleyman then spoke. "These treacheries are complex and interwoven, although the individual perpetrators perhaps have only minimal knowledge of the overall schemes, only the isolated roles they played. It appears that neither Mehmed nor the janissaries knew that it was Hassan who would receive the relics. They undoubtedly did not know his motivations. However, I also believe they did not care as long as they were paid for their duplicitous acts." Suleyman was vexed as he attempted to piece together the details of the conspiracies and motives of the conspirators.

"How would fear be instilled in the janissaries to act with such treachery? We know about the corrupt janissaries involved in the assassination plot with Qais, but that is somewhat of a settled issue. It is in the thefts where the mysteries remain. Did this Jinn act to instill fear? Was Mehmed induced by fear or greed or desire for more power or all of those?" Suleyman's questions raised more concerns.

Troubled, he continued. "Is the Shaitan, whoever this creature is, supernatural or human, the instigator and planner of the thefts? We now know Hassan and his mullahs were the financiers. The Shaitan masterminded the details, passed along instructions and served as a facilitator to Hassan and Mehmed and the thieves. Those who had contact with the Shaitan would likely have experienced the same overwhelming fear of this insidious and loathsome devil, even if they were not motivated by zealotry."

Il Lupo noted. "Yes, vexing questions remain, but in our scrutiny of the facts as they gradually unfold, we are finding answers. First we must separate the crimes—the assassination attempt, the theft, and the murders. We have at least one answer and that is we know the assassination attempt was unrelated to the thefts and was a crime of opportunity. There could be other peripheral issues that are related to both the thefts and murders as well. Analyzing the crimes separately we may be able to find their commonalities and interrelationships to the extent they exist.

"Shaitan used an elaborate network of messengers and dead drops that prevented the conspirators from learning each other's identity. It was quite complex and required detailed planning. Our discoveries, as insignificant as they may have seemed at the time, play a role in the deciphering of these mysteries. We must now determine Shaitan's perhaps more sinister motives." Il Lupo paced, sharing his questions and speculations.

Briefly pausing in thought, he continued, "A Shaitan, Hassan said? We shall see, we shall see. We know when the meeting was to occur, but did Hassan say where?"

"Yes, he did," Ibrahim nodded. "They were to meet at midnight at the Justinian Bridge."

"We may yet have time!" Il Lupo looked at his Nuremberg timepiece. "Your Majesty...," Il Lupo turned to Suleyman, his face and voice registering great urgency.

"Take the janissaries," Suleyman offered before Il Lupo had even finished his sentence, understanding fully that taking immediate action was key to solving the mystery.

"Thank you, Suleyman, but I'd prefer my motley band of beggars, if you will allow it. Any sign of janissaries and the Shaitan will flee," Il Lupo cautioned.

"Yes, I see your point. Of course, take your curious crew with you. Downwind please. They can bathe later." Suleyman managed a smile. "Godspeed. This Shaitan is treacherous and dangerous. Once again, good hunting, my friend."

"Sans the flute?" Aziz raised his eyebrows and tilted his head with a hopeful look on his face.

"Yes, leave the flute, Aziz. But bring that club!" Francesca encouraged, having witnessed its deadly impact.

·Dȧy Fivė·

Beşinci Gün

Justinian Bridge

incenzo Lupo and his band of beggars arrived at the Justinian Bridge a few moments after midnight. Built in the 6th century, the bridge stood at the western end of the old city near the Theodosian land walls and was Constantinople's first bridge. Constructed in typically Romanesque style with massive stones, semi-circular, and double-vaulted arches and towers, it endured a heavy daily traffic, rendering it frequently in need of repair. In the early 16th century, Leonardo di Vinci had presented plans for a 790 foot, single span bridge to be built over the Golden Horn, but the plans were never implemented by the Sultan Bayezid II.

Unlike the Justinian Bridge, which did not connect the two continents upon which the city was built, and to ease foot traffic congestion in the busy ports, Suleyman had ordered that barges be placed side by side linking the European and Asian continents. The bridge, thus built, offered easy passage for merchants, as well as soldiers and their armories of weapons. However, it was congested and even in the late evening hours, unsuitable for clandestine meetings. Now shrouded in thick fog, the ancient Justinian Bridge was the perfect venue for the Shaitan's final covert meeting. Il Lupo hoped that they had arrived in sufficient time.

"Kemal and Aziz, you are to stay near the area where I enter to cross the bridge. Francesca, you will follow slightly behind me to the middle. Act only as a passerby without acknowledging me and proceed a bit further toward the other end. Just be certain, all of you stay within sight of me," Il Lupo shared his plan as they approached the bridge. "We will part company just ahead. Be vigilant! We all may be meeting the devil itself!"

Il Lupo stood in the middle of the bridge, wearing Hassan's distinctively deep-blue cloak and hood, his position offering him the best vantage point to watch approaching activity from either direction. He felt unsettled, the cool mist of the swaddling brume so dense he was unable to see but a few feet in front of him. Il Lupo's instincts were heightened and he sensed that as soon as he had stepped onto the bridge, he was under surveillance. The persistent murkiness prevented him from noticing barely perceptible movement from under the far archway of the bridge, but he sensed danger. He suppressed a shudder, knowing the Shaitan was likely nearer Francesca who waited, crouched in her beggar's pose.

The mysterious and amorphous figure waited, observing its subject as he paced back and forth. The Shaitan too was on a heightened sense of alert sensing an imminent danger, wondering if Hassan had brought guards with him or, perhaps worse, betrayal. Determining the risk to be greater than the reward, the Shaitan suddenly aborted its plan. Returning to its hiding place under the ancient bridge, the Shaitan did not know that Il Lupo had caught a momentary glimpse of its shrouded figure and had followed.

Quickening his pace, Il Lupo signaled to Francesca to join the pursuit, ensuring that between the two of them the Shaitan was not lost in the shadowy night. Il Lupo no longer required his disguise and cast aside Hassan's regal cloak. Francesca knew to stop once her father passed her.

As they passed, Il Lupo cautioned his daughter. "This is becoming very dangerous. I know that Kemal and Aziz cannot be far behind. It is imperative that you not be seen in the chase. Where did it go?"

"Just there," she pointed as they stood behind a small kiosk. Resuming her beggar's posture, she shadowed him closely. "Be cautious, *mia Padre*. We are right behind you," Francesca reassured her father, hoping they would not lose the ghostly apparition in the opaque darkness.

Il Lupo followed as the phantom made its way through the quieted, inky-dark streets. Frustrated by limited visibility, he occasionally stopped, attempting to ensure he did not reveal himself. He had noticed that his target had a pronounced, distinctive gait. Listening to the footfall, he used the sound to gauge distance and follow with his ears, even more than relying on his eyesight in the bleak dreariness of the night. Confounding his pursuit was a small caravan of men with donkeys and two camels, slowly making their way through the streets, interrupting the chase and causing disorientation as to the direction the shrouded figure had taken. He wandered for a few seconds before heading down an alley.

As he exited the alley, the Count was suddenly and forcefully seized from behind, the gleaming blade of a stiletto, flashing before his eyes, its point coming to rest on his jugular. He immediately stiffened.

"My god, it is you! You frightened me to death! Are you alone or is that Fran who is following you?" Lucia withdrew the stiletto from his throat. "I was supposed to meet Giovanni here this evening, but he never came and I became concerned at being alone out here. I decided he had missed our appointment and was just now returning to the villa. I sensed I was being followed. I am not usually out at this hour—at least not unaccompanied. You gave me quite a scare," Lucia explained.

"I wouldn't worry about being out alone, Lucia. You are obviously quite capable of protecting yourself and appear quite practiced!" Il Lupo answered, irritated that she got the better of him. "I am impressed," he said in admiration of her skills while avoiding the questions regarding Fran.

"I carry a stiletto with me at all times when I am alone. Just safer that way. It can be used to ward off attacks from beggars, if necessary. Haven't you noticed all the beggars around tonight?" Her small gloved hand pushed her hair back under her dark hood.

Il Lupo could not be sure, but thought he detected Lucia had another covering of some kind under her cloak. She had pushed it back into the confines of her hood when adjusting her hair. She was carrying a woven *heybe,* or camel satchel, over her shoulder. "Why would you be meeting Giovanni here and this late?" Il Lupo asked directly.

"Well actually, it was he who asked me to meet him here at this time. I have no idea why he would ask, but he is my cousin, so I assumed there must be a good reason and I came," she explained matter-of-factly.

"I waited for some time, but felt uneasy—as though I was being stalked. I was, it appears, but by you." Lucia looked at him suspiciously. "What, may I ask, are you doing here on this bridge?"

"I was certainly not stalking you, Lucia. Rather, a puzzling aspect of my investigations brought me here. Our meeting was apparently purely coincidental," he answered coldly.

"Just as I am at many things, I am very, very good at solving puzzles, Vincenzo," she moved closer to him, seductively.

"May I help you solve this one? You have given me so little opportunity to entertain you with my *other* talents," she cooed, setting her satchel down and reaching under his cloak to put her hands around his back. As she did, Il Lupo was once again overcome with the contradictory presence of a rancid stench mingled with her strong perfume.

"Lucia, you have managed to enlighten me on many matters—great and small. On this matter—this matter of solving the puzzle—you have once again enlightened me, perhaps without even realizing your contribution. You are not far from the villa, and I would ordinarily feel obliged to offer to escort you. However, I now know you are completely capable of making it there on your own. I assume you are able to carry your satchel that far. By the way, where could you have been shopping at this late an hour?"

"Oh, it is not heavy. It only contains a few trinkets and two small prayer rugs that I am putting in a trunk to send to relatives in Spain. It is not heavy at all."

"Where would you have managed to buy these things so long after the final evening prayers when all the shops are closed? You are, as usual, most resourceful, Lucia!"

"I bought them previously and they had been accidentally left behind at the home of my cousin, Phillip Carillo, with whom I had dinner this evening. I retrieved them from his villa. He, just as Giovanni, is a successful merchant and has a conveniently located home here in Istanbul. You have surely heard me speak of him or may yourself, know him? He is from the House of Trastamara and is descended from Alfonso Carillo, the former archbishop of Toledo. I intended to leave his villa after dinner but stayed when I remembered I was to meet Giovanni. His home is closer to our appointed meeting place. They were generous in their hospitality to me, and I enjoyed the extended visit."

"Ah, yes, Lucia, I see," Il Lupo cut her off, eyeing her suspiciously. "Well, I have much work to do. I must bid you good night." He bowed, turned, and left a stunned and frustrated Lucia alone in the fog. Lucia noticed that he joined a band of three beggars who had been observing the conversation between the two of them. No doubt, she surmised, the band included Fran in disguise, just as suspected.

Lucia watched Il Lupo until he and the beggars disappeared, consumed by the darkness. A surge of uneasiness fell over her. Breathing deeply, she turned in the direction of the palazzo, understanding fully well that Vincenzo Lupo's intellect and insightfulness represented a grave danger to her diabolical and well-laid plans. Il Lupo—perspicacious and discerning—posed a threat to her life as well as her plans.

As they receded into the darkness, Il Lupo said, "Kemal, can you arrange to have Giovanni's villa watched as soon as possible? It is urgent; we will need a report of any unusual activity!"

"Of course, yes," Kemal replied, understanding the critical nature of the request.

"Good, then go now and make the arrangements. Please also report to Suleyman that all the mysteries are nearing a solution. Also, explain to him that it would be most desirable to schedule a meeting in the morning. I will tell him more then, and I apologize for not meeting him this evening. I feel it will be worth the wait. I need to make at least one more stop—perhaps two to confirm my suspicions, and then I will return," Il Lupo instructed.

He wanted to share more of his thoughts, the puzzle pieces beginning to fit neatly together, but felt that by waiting for the matutinal meeting he would have time to gather more corroborating facts and the ultimate answers.

"Aziz, accompany Kemal, and Francesca, you come with me. I may need your assistance." They dispersed into the unabating and thickening fog of the night to complete their separate missions.

Jambiya Justice

Seated at his newly acquired walnut burl table, Suleyman waited with Aziz and Kemal standing guard directly behind him. Roxelana and Francesca were seated to his left. Il Lupo, seated to the right of the emperor, spoke. "Forgive me, Your Majesty. I have taken it upon myself and invited four guests to join us. These mysteries and plots are so multi-layered that their resolution required I work into the early hours of this morning to piece together the fragments. Yesterday was most eventful, filled with a near avalanche of information and clues. Our guests will assist us in understanding and clarifying the details, complexities, and motives underlying the intrigues."

Roxelana put her hand on Suleyman's. "Dearest, before they are escorted in, would you permit Vincenzo to share more about what has been learned?"

"Is it as I believe that the purpose of the Jinn killings was to facilitate concealment of the thefts?" Suleyman asked, looking at Il Lupo.

Il Lupo nodded in agreement. "The thieves, including Mehmed, might have talked. Of this, we can be certain. Qais' death at the hand of Mehmed during the assassination attempt was intended, most assuredly, to prevent him from revealing the thefts. Had Qais survived he would have been tortured, and Mehmed believed he would disclose all he knew concerning the plans. They both had knowledge and were to benefit greatly from both the theft and your demise, Your Majesty. It became too dangerous for anyone with knowledge to live. They were doomed even if each individually lacked full knowledge of all the details surrounding the theft's execution.

"Initially, the Jinn attempted to frighten the janissaries and even Mehmed from entering the crypt. It was unknown if others, unconnected to the schemes, knew of the labyrinth. The Jinn's presence ensured no one lingered or even entered the areas near the *Has Oda*, other than those necessary to the success of their criminal enterprise. Anyone traversing the passageway under the *Has Oda* likely would have been discovered by the Jinn and killed. Once the participants fulfilled their part in the overall plan, they were eliminated one by one. Those first to meet their demise were Baris and Adem, the drunken janissaries and excavators of the *Has Oda* floor. While found shortly after their deaths by Aziz, Kareem and Jamal were the next victims of the Jinn after they stashed the relics for safekeeping. The four deaths all occurred within an interval of only a few hours in the early morning on the day of my arrival in Istanbul.

"The two janissaries who escaped following the failed assassination attempt were killed because their escape route took them into the secret passageways guarded by the Jinn, a misfortune for them. I believe they were unfamiliar, or at least less familiar, with the maze within the cisterns and crypts, simply became lost, and encountered the watchful Jinn.

"And then, of course, the main conspirator, Mehmed. He had to be killed. He was too deeply embroiled in the plots. Although he had no direct involvement with the assassination attempt, he still knew of Qais' plans. He was certainly involved in executing the theft, directing his corrupted janissaries to do their work, directions he received from the mastermind, who I will discuss shortly. Mehmed was executed following the final delivery of the relics to be collected by Hassan. Thus all participants in the theft have died, their tongues forever silenced. Only the mastermind behind the thefts remains alive. I believe that mastermind to be the Shaitan. Having eliminated all of its co-conspirators, it retained for itself the lion's share of the king's ransom in jewels paid by Hassan. Greed has been a great motivator for this Shaitan, who is no supernatural apparition. Perhaps the Shaitan had additional motivations yet undiscovered, but the primary motive was greed. I now believe I know the identity of the mastermind, but not all its motivations."

Francesca offered, "Whoever is involved and whoever this Shaitan is, it is well-versed in Islamic folklore able to use the religion's fear of the supernatural, jinn and demons to its advantage."

"But why use poison darts?" Roxelana asked, curiously.

Il Lupo elucidated, "*El Diablo Nino* would never have succeeded in killing the janissaries without them. He likely would have been overpowered by any janissary. He used surprise and inspired great shock and fear, his presence unexpected, and his costume so hideous, large and rancid. Additionally, the Shaitan knew that the discovery of mutilated bodies would inspire even greater fear among already terrified thieves because they fully understood the consequences of being caught. The Shaitan directed the Jinn to kill them. The mutilated bodies sent just one more message to ensure their silence and keep others out of the passages except as necessary to perform their roles in the theft.

"I will very soon be able to inform you about the why and how of Ali's involvement. The answers lie with our invited guests."

Angered and struggling fully to comprehend, Suleyman wanted answers. "We understand Hassan's motive. What would be the motive of the Shaitan? Why would the Shaitan want the relics secreted out of the empire? It is most perplexing."

"This remains our most elusive question," Il Lupo answered. "Greed is obviously one motivation, but further investigation may reveal additional motivations. In my experience, the detailed planning of the thefts is far too complex to have been motivated solely by greed. It is puzzling, but the answers will be found. Hassan paid Shaitan, who paid Mehmed—at least once, perhaps twice—who then paid the janissary co-conspirators at least enough to satisfy them until they received a promised larger and final payment. Of course, none of those involved will receive any final payment since they are all dead—leaving a bounty for the mastermind. Undoubtedly, the Shaitan retained a large portion of each payment for itself. We do not know the amounts given to Mehmed, or the amounts he distributed to his janissary co-conspirators. However, I believe there are other motives. Once the Shaitan's identity is confirmed, we likely will understand such further motives," Il Lupo detailed his reasoning. "Perhaps, and with your permission, Your Majesty, it is now time to bring in our guests?"

"Aziz, have the guests escorted in," Suleyman directed, curious and anxious to see those Il Lupo thought pertinent to the resolution of the multifaceted, intricate puzzles that had occupied them for the past days.

Il Lupo stood as Ibrahim, Giovanni, the Marquis Antoine Valois, and Lucia entered the room. He took Lucia's hand and bowed.

"Lucia, you look exquisite as usual. Perfection in so many ways." She was stunning in her dress, an embroidered bodice made from a soft taupe dupioni silk. Her skirt was chatoyant, its layers of aqua silk changing shades as the fabric moved, and finished with a matching embroidery border at the bottom.

"Why, thank you Vincenzo. I see that you continue to have excellent judgment," Lucia replied, looking at him slightly askance, hoping his compliments were sincere. Knowing she was to meet with him, she had taken great pains to ensure that she was in her most attractive attire, eager to rekindle Il Lupo's interest. She wanted desperately to assuage her fears that Il Lupo was suspicious of her. She flashed him a lubricious smile, in hopes that all would be forgotten and they could, once again, start anew.

"And look at you Francesca! I am amazed at how handsome a young boy can be! You are astonishing," she gushed, attempting to ingratiate herself.

Francesca ignored the feigned flattery. "Thank you, Lucia. It's been fascinating and instructive to view things from the perspective of both a woman *and* a man," she retorted politely. Roxelana also had decided, despite Lucia's obvious beauty, she did not like her, taking her cue from Francesca who more than once rolled her eyes at the spectacle. Ibrahim remained smug, his froideur of acerbity constant and unchanging. Giovanni was patently apprehensive regarding the reasons for their most unusual audience with the emperor. The guests were seated around the end of the table.

Suleyman began. "There has been a theft from the palace recently, and Vincenzo has informed me that you may be able to assist us with the investigation. I am heartened that you may have information that can help solve our mystery. Vincenzo…" Suleyman directed Il Lupo to preside over the meeting.

"Giovanni," Il Lupo began directly, "Lucia has perhaps told you that we had quite a coincidental meeting last night. She was out very late and when we came across one another, I was concerned that she was out by herself. I have since learned, however, this is nothing I should concern myself with—she is quite capable on her own." Il Lupo paced back and forth.

"Lucia informed me that you were supposed to meet her, but you did not arrive. Is that correct?" Il Lupo questioned.

"Yes—well, yes and no, Vincenzo," Giovanni corrected. "Lucia has scolded me this morning for not meeting her. I have explained to her, however, that I did not recall asking her to meet me there. There was no reason for me to make such a request. I apologized to her. It has caused me consternation and to reflect on whether I am becoming an unsound of mind. A dotard in full dotage. But I am not yet senile and simply have no recollection," he insisted, shaking his head in puzzlement.

Lucia abruptly broke into the conversation. "Cousin! Your mind is indeed feeble and forgetful. Why would I have any purpose being out so late and at peril in the streets of Istanbul? I could have suffered great harm from thieves and miscreants! You were reckless in asking such a thing of me and not showing up as planned!" Her face tightened into a grimace, her eyes narrowing as she spoke.

She turned to face the attentive Il Lupo. "What difference does it make anyway, Vincenzo?" she demanded. "Obviously, we had a frustrating misunderstanding," Lucia said, attempting an explanation.

Before he had time to respond, Giovanni again interjected, desperation on his face. "Lucia! Why do you insist on this? I would have no reason to meet you! Why must we continue this ridiculous pettifogging over an issue that I have apologized for, even though I believe there is no reason for apology. Again, I simply had no reason for wishing to meet you on a bridge, late at night in Istanbul." He was completely aware of Suleyman's intense gaze and disturbed by the unknown purpose and consequences of Il Lupo's perplexing inquisition.

"I will answer your question about why all this matters in due time. Thank you, Giovanni, for your recollections. I am thankful, that despite your disagreement about the meeting, Lucia returned to the villa safely," the Count replied calmly.

"We cannot just yet provide you all the details of the theft mentioned by his majesty, but suffice it to say that Mehmed led the thieves and delivered the stolen items to Hassan. Both Mehmed and Hassan are dead. Before they died, we were able to learn much valuable information. However, questions remain."

Turning back to Giovanni, Il Lupo asked, "How well did you know Mehmed?"

Giovanni reddened slightly. "I suppose it would be honest to say we had occasional, even substantial, dealings," he replied cautiously.

"Did those dealings involve the exchange of money?" Il Lupo questioned, an undertone of suspicion apparent in his tone.

"What are you asking, Vincenzo? Of course! At times I gave him money. He sold useful information and here in this city, everyone pays for information and favors. As I recall, we have discussed this previously. It is customary and not at all unusual." Giovanni stiffened defensively, shifting his gaze to Ibrahim who was grimacing. Ibrahim was aware that Suleyman was also scrutinizing him. He attempted to retain a calm composure, understanding fully the ramifications that the events and revelations of the previous few days could ultimately have on his future.

"Including ambassadors!" Giovanni blurted, staring directly at Antoine. "Anyone who attempts to do business in this city must pay!"

"Not the amount involved in this theft. Now, we are talking a king's ransom. The problem is, Giovanni, that all of the evidence leads directly to the steps of your extravagant palazzo!" Il Lupo stressed, deliberately intending to make Giovanni uncomfortable.

"Vincenzo! What are you saying—accusing? I am the newly appointed Venetian ambassador and you are implying that I am a corrupt scoundrel—a deceiver—which I am not! I have had excellent relations with the Ottomans here, and throughout the empire. You surely cannot believe that I would risk all that I have worked so hard to achieve, can you?" Giovanni blustered in disbelief.

"I would like not to believe it, Giovanni," Il Lupo answered, assessing Giovanni's demearnor. "Moving to another subject, I must ask you to tell us about your tropical gardens." What Giovanni did not understand was that Vincenzo Lupo was convinced quite early on, that while Giovanni was boastful and bombastic, Il Lupo had dismissed him as a potential conspirator. Indeed, he thought Giovanni to be intellectually incapable of conceiving or implementing such complex and devious deceptions. However, intent on eliciting further valuable facts and information, Giovanni was Il Lupo's momentary scapegoat and foil; Il Lupo was already convinced that the treacheries lay directly at the feet of another in the room.

"The hothouse garden? What about it? It is not complete yet. I must confess, while I would like to claim credit for its beauty, it is Lucia who has done the planning and the gardening. I have simply procured and arranged for transport of the items that she has requested. She has money enough to indulge her fancies. She is the one who deserves the credit," Giovanni explained, still unable to grasp the direction Il Lupo was headed.

Il Lupo noticed that despite the cool, morning breeze that filtered through the open windows of the chamber, Lucia had begun furiously waving her fan, embroidered with miniature, tiny flowers, replicating exactly those on her bodice and hem. Realizing all eyes had turned in her direction, she slowed the fan to a forced, lazy flutter.

"This has been a hobby of mine for years," she drawled casually. "I actually have a lovely garden in Venice as well as a hothouse where I grow the most beautiful and exotic plants. The plants require a great deal of care to preserve them in transit. While many are lost, I almost always manage to salvage the seeds. I also use the petals to experiment in the creation of new perfumes and oils. Some of those I found most delightful were included in the bottles presented by Giovanni to the emperor, Roxelana and Gulbehar. I also import exotic birds—six have been recent gifts to the palace. In fact, the birds were at the villa for some time. Rather than keeping them for myself, as was my original intention, I offered them to Giovanni to present to the emperor. So, indirectly, those lovely birds were a gift from me and *not* Giovanni, Your Majesty. I had intended to let him take the credit, but now that I appear to be the subject of criticism in front of the sultan, I will take credit where it is due," Lucia sneered, looking at Giovanni, who stood shaking his head in disbelief at his cousin.

"Do you also take credit for their offensive language? Perhaps a result of your tutelage? As to your exotic collection of plants—is it not true that you have collected them from all over the world?" Il Lupo queried

"Yes, I do," she offered freely. "I have the money to obtain those species I wish to acquire and am fortunate enough to have someone I trust who can procure them for me." Lucia now decided to smile at Giovanni, who remained disconcerted.

"I suppose even contacts that have permitted him to procure plants and seeds from the New World?" Il Lupo continued his cross-examination.

"Actually," Giovanni interjected, insisting on clarification, "To be very clear, those contacts are Lucia's. She made the arrangements through her relatives in Spain and some in the New World. I merely ensure the proper crating and care for the specimens based on Lucia's specifications and provide the shipping when it is requested."

"Yes, Giovanni, I believe you," Il Lupo agreed, believing him to be innocent of any duplicity. Giovanni emitted an audible sigh of relief and nervously wiped the sweat from his face with a lace-trimmed handkerchief.

"I am indeed satisfied, Giovanni. Quite satisfied, in fact. You may be at ease." Addressing Antoine, Il Lupo continued, "I asked Antoine to make discreet inquiries on my behalf through his connections at the court of Francis I. He informed me of what he learned late last evening. I invited him here this morning to share his knowledge with you. Please, Antoine," Il Lupo invited Antoine into the conversation.

"I learned that Lucia has a cousin who is married to a Spanish count. You may know him Giovanni. His name is Eduardo de Bobadilla. I will be speaking of relatives from her father's side. Lucia and Giovanni are related through their mothers—they are sisters." Lucia eyed Antoine suspiciously.

"We have also learned that Lucia has been a frequent visitor to the court of Charles V. Simply by her presence, Lucia draws attention and it was not difficult to learn that she was often seen with Charles himself. In fact, I have been told, that before her last visit to Giovanni in Venice, she had been in Charles' bed. This fact appears undisputed and is not considered idle court gossip. She and Charles have been lovers."

Moving closer to Suleyman, Lucia snarled, "How is it that a lady should be so treated and subjected to malicious gossip and vile innuendo here in your palace? Totally uncorroborated, unproven, and despicable hearsay," she ululated, her voice shrill with spittle attached to nearly every word.

"It is true that I have many cousins in Spain. Indeed, many friends throughout Europe. But I have never—*never*—set foot in Charles' court, much less in his bed! I will not stand for these slanders—these scandalous canards!"

Il Lupo intervened. "Lucia, my presence here as a Venetian envoy has been a ruse. I was brought here to investigate the recent mysteries and unrest of the Imperial Court. My sole purpose in my role and in my service to Suleyman is to bear testimony to the truth. You have made it your profession to beguile and bewitch, but I have not fallen victim. Nor, in my search for the truth, would I, frivolously waste time. It is not our intention to impugn your reputation as a lady which, quite frankly, is of little consequence to me. You will never hear false or scurrilous accusations from me.

"However, Lucia, lady or not—and I think not—*you, Madame, are the Shaitan!*" he accused, pointing at her, his eyes narrowed and brow furrowed with conviction.

Il Lupo extended his hands to Francesca, and she handed him a woven camel bag and a large leather satchel. All watched as he carefully withdrew the contents of the leather satchel, revealing the relics. Lucia stood by, her eyes wide and mouth gaping.

"Praise be to Allah," Suleyman clasped his hands together. "The relics! Praise be to Allah!" Suleyman and the others watched eagerly as Il Lupo continued his exposition.

Il Lupo reached to his side and produced the second woven bag. "You are found out, Lucia!" Il Lupo exclaimed, throwing out a hooded cloak and bestial mask from the second bag. The Shaitan's foul odor had so permeated the garments that everyone gagged at its sulfurous stench.

"Your ruses are exposed! Last night, after our meeting on the bridge, I visited your hothouse and searched but could find nothing. As I was leaving, I remembered our momentary embrace and the smell of your hair the other night. Your smell. Your effluvium. I was unsure that night what the odor was; bathing in your perfumes could not disguise it completely. Your hair smelled of dung. So, I thought I would locate your dung heap used to fertilize those precious specimens from the New World. I found the Shaitan's cloak and mask in this bag, the one you were carrying last night when I saw you. When the costume and cloak of the Jinn were found in the cisterns, we later discovered they, too, had been hidden close to the dung heap behind the palace stables, which accounts for their stench. Your perfumes had even permeated them to some degree; when you handled or transported them to the Jinn, your trademark fragrances clung to the costumes." Il Lupo was mindful of the gasps from his audience at his revelations and Francesca's stunned expression.

"My suspicions have been confirmed that you had the Jinn's raptor—like talons, made in Spain of Toldeo steel. And these," he continued, pointing to the contents he had removed from the burlap bag, "these are the other reeking discoveries I made. The means, the tools, used by you, to control and frighten those in your conspiracy. I will admit it was very clever of you to have stored your cloak near the dung in order for your Shaitan to be most authentic—born of the smokeless fire and living on a dung heap. That would account for the smell on your hair and the smell that lingers with anyone who came into contact with the Shaitan."

The Count's masterful recounting of the details of the planning and execution of the thefts continued. "The workmanship of the mask I also recognize. It was made to fit your face and greatly exaggerate your height by the finest costumer in Venice—the same one who created the masks that were given as gifts to the emperor. This mask, as hideous as it is, is artfully designed. Even the mouth was made from a malleable fabric that allowed for movement of the lips. The gloves are tight fitting, like a second skin, and also masterfully finished with thick, talon-like fingernails. The cloak and costume of the Jinn were also finely tailored by the same artisans to your precise specifications. Its head is not simply that of the toucan, but a large and hideous hybrid, a chimerical countenance, designed to terrorize its victims. You were even clever enough to have the Jinn's costume painted to match the walls of the cistern you most assuredly visited with Ali." Il Lupo's accusations were methodical, commanding, and authoritative.

"And, finally, the belladonna." The Count removed a small flask from the bag. "You knew that to use more than a drop or two created a river of fire within the eyes, a bright and erratic flashing of lights—another frightening characteristic reported by Hassan, completing your transition into the fiery beast, Shaitan.

"You, madam, are indeed Shaitan! The mastermind of the theft!"

Il Lupo pointed his finger at the Shaitan. "You, '*Die Teufelin,*' the she-devil incarnate! You made an unholy bargain with your recruited conspirators, each of you motivated by greed and hatred of Suleyman and then bound them to you by schemes steeped in fear, superstition, and Islamic folklore. Your greed and actions precipitated multiple murders. We know that you have been well paid by the

Persian, but when searching Mehmed's room this morning only a meager fifteen gems were found! What happened to the remaining gems and what other sinister motivations did you have, Shaitan? All this will be uncovered. Nothing will remain hidden!" Il Lupo charged.

"Lucia! What Vincenzo is saying, this cannot be true!" Giovanni stammered in disbelief, breaking his stunned silence. "What...what have you done?"

Even as Giovanni was expressing his confusion, Lucia—the Shaitan—revealed its voice—so horrifying and other wordly, that it seemed inconceivable that it was emitted by a human throat. A growling, guttural, hissing, sounding as though it had been formed in the depths of hell, flew from her mouth, spewing hatred. "I should have slit your throat when I had the chance!" she screeched at Il Lupo, pulling a deadly stiletto from the boned structure of her bodice.

Her face grotesquely transformed, Shaitan, turned, taking aim at Suleyman, shrilling, "Join me in Hell, Suleyman!"

With prescient instincts, Francesca was ready. She nudged and alerted Roxelana who, instinctively and immediately understanding the need to protect the sultan, threw her Kard, hitting the Shaitan in the wrist, knocking the stiletto from Lucia's hand. With a strong and expertly executed flick of her wrist, Francesca launched her favored jambiya. The knife found its mark in the throat of Lucia. The Shaitan, the messenger from Iblis, fell to the floor bleeding heavily, gasping for her last breaths, before dying.

"Lucia, the evil Shaitan, must have forgotten that she and I share the same tailor in Venice. I knew the moment she began adjusting her bodice, she was not interested in enhancing the presentation of her décolleté," Francesca announced glibly.

Il Lupo, standing over the body of the beautiful woman filled with demonic and deadly intent. "Good work, Francesca and Roxelana."

"Have her head and that mask placed on the Imperial Gates reserved for traitors!" Suleyman commanded, janissaries scurrying to remove the body. His tone changing, he turned to Il Lupo.

"Praise Allah! Once again I am in your debt, Vincenzo. How can this ever be repaid? You have saved me, the relics and in the doing, perhaps an empire. I must find rewards that will truly display my gratitude. I assure you it will be uppermost in my thoughts."

"Emperor! Do not forget that *this* humble servant who loves you so dearly also played a role in saving your life today. Aren't you impressed with my new skills?" Roxelana laughed in nervous relief. "I hope you give equal thought to a gift you may consider bestowing on me. After all, I am not merely the mother of your sons but rather accomplished with the blade."

Even Ibrahim, the sour Grand Vizier, begrudgingly smiled. He understood full well, however, that his practice of being paid for the selling of information of the Topkapi Palace had forever come to an end.

"I have many details still to gather to make better sense of these happenings which have been so intricate and confusing, Your Majesty. I hope you will allow me the time to finalize my conclusions. I will do my best to fully understand and explain these treacheries, the complexities of their relationships, and the motives of the perpetrators."

"Yes, yes...of course, Vincenzo. I will be most anxious to hear your conclusions. Take whatever time it is that you need—you and Francesca remain my honored guests. As of this moment, I have much to be grateful for, and I will plan a celebration to which you will all be invited! I so order it," Suleyman exclaimed, beaming. "Yes, festivities unmatched by any other!"

A
Few Days
Later

Birkaç Gün Sonra

Celebrations

uleyman the Magnificent, the Kanuni—the Lawgiver—kept his word. The celebratory festivities of light and feasting were enjoyed by prominent officials and dignitaries from throughout the empire and included many court favorites. The fete was extravagant, with entertainment that included music, acrobats, jugglers, and belly dancing. During the belly dancing, Il Lupo caught a glimpse of Ibrahim with perhaps the faintest of smiles upon his lips enjoying their provocative and sensual movements. Il Lupo pondered whether the smile was simply registering pleasure that life in the palace was once again peaceful or if Ibrahim was lusting after the belly dancers. Ibrahim acknowledged Il Lupo with an enigmatic smile and gave him a respectful salute. At that moment, no one could have known the tragedy that lay ahead for the Grand Vizier. In less than three years, *'Makbul Ibrahim Pasha'* – the favorite - would become known as *'Maktul Ibrahim Pasha'* – the executed.

Among those attending were Gregor and Nadia, Antoine and Colette, and even Giovanni for whom Il Lupo and Francesca felt a growing fondness. Suleyman and Il Lupo agreed that Giovanni's offenses had been venial and in pursuit of his own selfish objectives but without nefarious or malicious intent. He had been foolish, but not a treacherous charlatan as had initially been suspected. Suleyman permitted him to retain his post as ambassador, deciding that Giovanni's public chastening would now make him a most trustworthy ambassador, ever wary that any further missteps would not be forgiven. A new humility possessed Giovanni. While still loquacious and affable, he abandoned his former bravado and bluster.

While the celebrations continued, Suleyman's thoughts were focused on how best to reward those who had saved his life and secured the return of the relics. Since the death of the Shaitan, he and Il Lupo had spent hours together—these two men of such disparate backgrounds— engaged in quodlibets, deep discussions not only of the philosophies and religion, but books, culture, and politics. They challenged one another to lengthy games of chess. Both were zealous in their pursuit of increased knowledge and understanding, engaging in scholarly debate as friends often do and, even on occasion, with voices raised, as each passionately advocated differing views and beliefs.

Often seen wandering the exquisite gardens, carefully designed and planted by the ever creative and meticulous *Bostanic Basha,* they walked, hands clasped behind their backs and heads bowed together, engrossed in conversation that was occasionally punctuated with extended laughter. Each of them gained new insight from the depth of their prolonged exchanges, leading to a growing trust and friendship.

Night Table Nightmare

When not engaged with Suleyman, Il Lupo spent hours piecing together the intricacies, fragments, and layers of the plots and deceptions as he formulated his final conclusions. Even though he intended to provide his findings orally, his conclusions were summarized in a written conspectus to be presented to Suleyman.

Il Lupo had arranged the sequence of events chronologically, linking the seemingly unrelated clues, and analyzing them in their chronological context. At one point, he asked Giovanni for access to Lucia's rooms, anxious to find an answer to the final message intended for Lucia that had been delivered to Giovanni. His discoveries were equally stunning and chilling.

In one of her locked trunks, he found a pouch of gems containing one hundred and seventy-five of two hundred she had been given by Hassan; the pouch of the remaining one hundred she was to receive had been found with Hassan and the relics. Lucia's lust for wealth was astounding. Her six co-conspirators, including Mehmed and Qais, had been paid only a paltry twenty-five gems for their risks in executing the theft.

It was, however, a small leather parcel he found in the night table next to her bed, that shocked and numbed the normally unflappable Count. Cautiously untying the strings and peeling back the layers of cloth packaging, he was stunned to find two feathered darts. He was at first bewildered, wondering why Lucia would have any need to possess the dangerous darts. Accompanied by a wave of nausea, the realization was upon him. It was the location of the discovery that provided the answer. It occurred to Il Lupo that her attempts to seduce him were prompted by her suspicions that he knew too much concerning her masterminding of the thefts and murders. He discerned their intent—Lucia had intended to use one of the darts on him. It would have been so easy. While sleeping, she could simply have pricked him in a most inconspicuous place, perhaps the area of his genitals, a place unlikely to be examined. He would have awakened to the pain, but doomed to helplessness, watching her taunting and twisted smile. He imagined that her demonic utterings, the growling, and hissing, might have been the last earthly sounds he would hear as he died. There would have been an examination of his body, but the likelihood of finding such a small mark in an inconspicuous place, was minimal. His death would have been treated as an unfortunate and untimely tragedy, struck down by a stopping of the heart during the act of lovemaking. Lucia would have acted the part so well, feigning embarrassment over others' knowledge of her intimate affair with the famed Count. She would have spoken of it at dinner parties and social gatherings, wearing it as both a crown of glory that it was she who had enticed and enchanted the renowned Il Lupo into her bed, and as a crown of despair deserving of pity at the loss of her beloved Vincenzo.

However, it was not this thought that concerned him most. There were two others who would have been the likely targets for the second dart. Reserved perhaps for Suleyman or the unthinkable—for Francesca. Il Lupo sat in silence contemplating the cruel and ghastly implications of Lucia's possession of the poison darts. Once again, he found himself grateful for his intuition, thankful that it cautioned him against engaging in intimacies with Lucia and the associated incomprehensible and devastating consequences. Lucia was ruthless, brimming with cunning and guile.

Il Lupo shared his discovery of the darts, as well as his conclusions, privately with Suleyman. He did not want Francesca to know that either of them had been in such mortal peril. Perhaps, long after the conclusion of their mission and back in the safety of Venice, he would tell her. It would be a ghastly disclosure, but perhaps enlightening for her to comprehend the depths of depravity and wickedness to which even those who appear to be most enthralling could sink.

Felicity and Fuzuli

Francesca spent time with Roxelana who continued the dispensation of womanly advice to her grateful and attentive student. Kemal was absorbed in the restoration of stability and order within the janissary corps. Acutely disappointed by his absence, she was filled with anticipation as she waited for this day to arrive when she would see him again.

Francesca could only hope, but did not know, that he too longed to see her and that she had been the subject of the writings in his journal. Kemal's thoughts, though many and often filled with torment and desire—even conflict—had been reduced to a few, deeply passionate written words. On the last evening they had seen one another, Kemal poetically wrote:

> *Enchanted, my heart receives her voice*
> *Golden silk, murmuring treasures*
> *Held captive in circumspect choice*
> *Felicity.*
> *Mirth.*
> *Beyond measure.*
> *I am lost….*

Kemal found it difficult to focus on the tasks he had been ordered to undertake by Suleyman. During his fifteen years in the Ottoman court, he had trained himself to suppress any feelings that would interfere with his ascension in the eyes of Suleyman. He was devoted to the sultan. A man of discipline in every aspect of his life, he now found his mind pre-occupied and wandering. A rising frustration consumed him over his loss of control as the needs and desires of the soft underbelly of his soul ineluctably surfaced and consumed his thoughts. His mind would not allow the longings or his passionate desire for Francesca to remain secreted within his heart.

In the evenings, Kemal would sit by the illumination of the small, clay oil lamp that sat on a chest next to his bed. He would carefully retrieve two of his treasured possessions—gifts from Suleyman—a book of poetry by *Fuzuli,* the pen name for Muhammad bin Suleyman, and his book of Persian miniatures by the master illuminator Kamal ud-Din Behzad. Kemal's strong and capable hands carefully held the delicate, pulchritudinous book of miniatures, examining each exquisitely drawn detail and their depictions of life—a life outside his and not within his reach. To further the pain of his magnificent obsession with Francesca, he would read the words of love so beautifully woven together by Fuzuli. The words were constant in his mind, continually confounding him even in the midst of an important task. He found himself often reciting the memorized words of Fuzuli and then following them with his own prayers to Allah for release from his torments. As Fuzuli poetically wrote

> *"Oh God, make me acquainted with the affliction of love!*
> *"For one moment make me not separated from the affliction of love!"*

Kemal, so inspired, prayed,

> *Allah, Ar-Rahim, Allah, the Most Merciful, release me, Kemal Bey, from the torments, the agonies that plague my weary heart. I, your humble servant, ask for this one small gift of beneficence. By your Grace and Mercy, release me so that I may give the love that I have and receive the love that my heart so desperately requires. Allow my unworthy soul to embrace the ecstacies – the raptures – that are contained within Your ultimate gift of love. Praise be to Allah, Most Merciful.*

Yearnings

Francesca also filled her days adventuring into the alleyways and bazaars, sometimes with her father and sometimes alone. She again donned her disguise as a boy to better enable her to move among the crowds and bargain with the shopkeepers. She did not seek material goods but purchased items that brought her delight or piqued her interest because of their artistry, particularly the art of Islam. She indulged herself with the luxury purchase of a very fine, Ushak rug. It was predominately turquoise and copper—colors she had grown to love since arriving in Istanbul, associating the colors with her first memories of Kemal. She marveled at the minute and careful craftmanship and thought back to the day of her arrival when she watched those little children so skillfully and nimbly weaving the precious treasures. She collected items that would remind her of her time in a city that she found fascinating and of a time when she awakened into womanhood. She sought to gather *impressions* rather than things…pondering and relishing each as if it were some sort of delightful potion, a concoction of enchantment and mystery… immersing herself in the joys of the past few days with Kemal.

Even in the midst of the activities with which she filled her time, Kemal was ever-present. Little else invaded Francesca's thoughts, just as Roxelana had predicted. She attempted to discuss them with her father, but found him reticent, stating he was her father and not her matchmaker, while seeking forgiveness for his inadequacy as an advisor on the subject of love. Affairs of the heart had not been kind to him. Francesca was overcome by the sadness her father experienced and that her mother was not here to guide her and love them both.

Francesca had once firmly and adamantly believed that she had little or no need for the strength and protection of even a good man, but that had all changed. She needed Kemal and knew she loved him. Her heart told her this was not a juvenile diversion, some flighty fling or passing infatuation. It was real and divine. Still, she was filled with the trepidation of all new loves—the fear of rejection and the fear that her feelings were more intense than those of the object of her greatest desire. Fear that her love would not be reciprocated and that she might face rebuke from the accomplished and fearsome janissary, rather than offered an invitation to love, tormented her. She fretted that he cared for her only as a young friend, his "kucuk uzman," and that he would find her passionate adoration silly and childish. However, as much as she worried, she equally indulged in the glorious possibilities that were embodied in Kemal Bey, Commander of the Beyliks, elite bodyguards to the Sultan Suleyman. How could they ever come to pass? She found the perceived obstacles to their love daunting but not insurmountable. They could be overcome, but only if her love was returned and not unrequited. If love was requited, she would not be deterred. Francesca Lupo dreamed her improbable dreams.

Denouement

A few days after the festivities ended, Suleyman assembled a small group to reward those who had saved his life and the Ottoman Empire from predictable and devastating chaos. Preferring an intimate gathering, he invited only Roxelana, Il Lupo, Francesca, Kemal, and Aziz to the private meeting held in the Tulip Garden, now in full and luxurious bloom.

"Before reaching the reasons for my gathering you here, there is more information that we should discuss. Lucia's motives have still been of great concern to me. Il Lupo has come prepared to discuss these lingering questions with us. I understand that you have reached conclusions following the investigation you have accomplished at my behest," Suleyman began.

"My final conclusions, Your Majesty, are predicated in part on answers to more questions. I have come to know you and believe I know your answers, answers that will support my findings. However, I need to hear your thoughts. First, had Hassan's efforts to transport the relics out of the empire and into Persia succeeded, would war with the Persians have ensued? If so, would that war not have diverted the empire's armies and focus to the East and away from Charles V in the West?" Il Lupo queried.

"The answers to both questions are very likely yes," Suleyman responded. "Even without war, the loss of the relics would have caused dissension and discord within the empire once their theft became known. During the Ramadan celebrations, the relics are displayed to a very few, but those include the most influential clerics in Islam. Knowledge of their loss would have undermined severely my authority."

Suleyman continued. "Even with restoration of the relics, it is possible there will still be war with the Persians. They seek, as we have discussed, the annihilation of the Sunnis. They are intolerant and intent on keeping learning and knowledge from the people. They believe that any who believe differently are heretical necromancers in league with the devil. I will share that I have contemplated an invasion. Their destructive and dogmatic intolerance does great harm to Islam and to the empire. It is not to be endured and is against all I believe to be good and righteous."

"Yes," Il Lupo agreed. "We have seen the far-reaching effects of zealots, for in our times, they are omnipresent."

"Still, this does not explain Lucia's motives," Roxelana stated.

"I must respond by stating that this investigation has been fraught with uncertainty and complexity," Il Lupo began. "My conclusions are based on what the facts support and seem most logical. One can never be completely certain—incontrovertible truth as well as proof, is rarely present.

"I believe that these mysteries have their genesis in the corruption of Lucia. Keep in mind, however, that all the intrigues have some intersection also with Mehmed.

"I have decided that Lucia had multiple motivations. The first was greed." Il Lupo threw two emerald green, velvet pouches onto the table. "These are the jewels found in her room or with Hassan—intended as final payment to her for the relics. You can see they are from Persia. Each of the pouches is embroidered with the sun and the lion, symbols of the Savavids. The total number of gems here is a count of one hundred and seventy-five in the pouches found in her room. She had only distributed twenty-five of the first two hundred she had been given. A paltry twenty-five gems to be shared by six people—Qais, Mehmed, and the four murdered janissaries involved with the theft. She also would have kept the remaining one hundred gems she was to receive from Hassan to herself. Each gem has a weight of at least three carats and so she would have amassed gems of over eight hundred carats in bounty, at a minimum. Your Majesty, I present them to you," Il Lupo offered.

"I have gems enough to fill my coffers. Keep them Vincenzo and divide them as you deem appropriate."

"Thank you, Your Majesty. I am grateful and once again, overwhelmed by your unprecedented generosity. I will be sure they are fairly divided among those without whose assistance my conclusions could not have been reached.

"My investigations, along with information provided by Antoine and in further conversations with Abdullah and his associates have enlightened me greatly. Initially, I had thoughts that perhaps greed was her sole motivation. However, my investigation has led me far beyond that now. I have made the most disturbing and elucidating discoveries, the first being that it was her cousin's husband, Eduardo de Bobadilla, who fathered Ali when he was in the New World and serving the Conquistador Davila. Bobadilla was returning to Spain and was killed in the skirmish at sea with Barbarossa. Ali, then a child of about 10 years old, survived. Ali was Lucia's second cousin. She did not learn of his fate until after Ali had already been castrated. Lucia, ever resourceful, found a way to pay and arrange for his entry into the Harem here at the Topkapi Palace and then pay Mehmed to ensure he was looked after. She was often in Istanbul on visits to Giovanni and hoped she might occasionally be able to visit Ali. There was no initial intention of using him for nefarious reasons. However, that changed, and brings me to her other motivation.

"Lucia was in love with Charles V and did, in fact, bed him—the rumors of their intimacies we all now know are true. She believed that she could become his 'Roxelana' and not only have his love but also the influence and elevated status she so greatly desired. It occurred to her that one way to accomplish this goal would be to manipulate those she could to wreak havoc within the Ottoman empire, which she knew was an obsession with Charles. If her scheming proved successful, she would curry greater favor with her powerful lover. She devised a plan to steal the holy relics. She was only left with finding a co-conspirator—or conspirators," Il Lupo communicated to his captivated audience.

"Hassan Pahlavi was a frequent visitor to Istanbul in his role as envoy. He was frequently at the home of Giovanni. She knew of his zealotry and his fervid support of the Savavid movement—which he often artfully disguised in diplomatic settings. She could have had no more willing an accomplice than Hassan, but she dared not share her plan with him. She knew that the Savavids were desirous of the relics—possession of them elevated their status and credibility. Through some means that will forever remain a mystery to us, I have determined she somehow initiated contact with the Savavid court and proposed her plan. It was accepted and Hassan was instructed to travel to Istanbul and meet his destiny. Lucia was known to him and need not have used her disguise as the Shaitan, but Lucia would never allow herself to be compromised. Hence, the Shaitan disguise which also served her well in her dealings with Mehmed."

Il Lupo paused to quench his thirst, drinking from a small cup of tea. "In fact, she was so careful that the relics were never in her possession. They passed from the thieves to conspirator after conspirator, before their ultimate delivery into the hands of Hassan by the messenger who retrieved them from the boughs of the Mediterranean cypress. This occurred on the same night he was captured. The Shaitan most assuredly instilled enough fear in him that there can be no doubt he would not have left the city before making the final payment. That was the purpose of meeting Shaitan on the Justinian Bridge. Lucia was not waiting for Giovanni, as we all now know, but to receive final payment from Hassan."

Il Lupo paused. "As a side note, and so I don't forget to share my suspicions, I believe the expletives hurled at you by the birds in her care, Your Majesty, were simply words spoken by Lucia in conversation with others or merely in loud mutterings to herself. She despised you, since it was by your orders that Barbarossa took the ship, killed her relative and enslaved Ali. It is reasonable to believe that she is responsible for teaching the birds such foulness, although perhaps not deliberately. It is possible that Giovanni might have had a few issues with the Doge. Perhaps, expletives hurled at the Doge from those birds originated from the tongue of Giovanni.

"This plan must have required a great deal of time to evolve because it was so well conceived and executed," Il Lupo continued his exposition. "She began importing her exotic flowers and frogs from the New World. She took the time to design the costumes of the Shaitan and the Jinn —having decided the time had come to use Ali. Lucia had the costumes made in Venice. She had heard the tales of Ali's skill for extracting poison from the frogs and his great proficiency with the blowgun from her family, which suited her plan perfectly.

"What were the intended results of her duplicities and diabolical machinations? To foment chaos and disruption within the Ottoman

Empire and thereby elevate her in the eyes of Charles—not to mention the additional wealth added to her already abundant coffers.

"And so, she began to implement her devious deceits. She first recruited Mehmed. She sent a message to him to meet and when they met, she arrived as the Shaitan. He surely must have been horrified and submitted willingly to the orders of the Shaitan. She instructed him to recruit and corrupt janissary dissidents, provide access to Harem 'angels of love' and fill the conspiring janissaries with wine. It was also by direction of Shaitan that Mehmed visited the offices of Sinan, requesting information regarding the underground passages and cisterns. I do not believe he was sent on that mission by Gulbehar. Mehmed gave the plans of the passageways to Ali who shared them with Lucia. Together they studied—also tasking Mehmed to reconnoiter routes to the repository and out of the cisterns. In turn, Mehmed would educate the few selected janissaries regarding the passages. It was imperative that both Shaitan and Ali also knew those routes. Together they orchestrated and implemented the murders and determined the best places to ambush the janissary conspirators after each of their tasks was completed.

"Once under the Shaitan's power, Mehmed ordered the corrupted janissaries to desecrate the holy *Has Oda* and steal the relics. I believe Lucia also appeared before Qais as the Shaitan, demanding he cooperate with Mehmed's requests. There is no evidence that Lucia was aware of Qais' own assassination plots, however. These clandestine meetings, where instructions were passed, transpired over several weeks, leading into Ramadan and gave her time to appear before Hassan as the Shaitan, receive payments and provide final instructions to him." There was not a sound from Il Lupo's audience as he took another drink of sweet tea. His perspicacious account of the events left little doubt as to the veracity of his conclusions.

"I think we can all agree that she would have been a most unlikely candidate as the Shaitan. Lucia masterfully protected her identity, always allowing plausible deniability for her critical involvement and masterminding of the conspiracy should anyone become suspicious. Persuading the Savavids to finance the thefts was also likely not difficult. Zealotry is a powerful motivator.

"She directed Ali to kill the janissaries who were co-conspirators after each had fulfilled their part in the thefts. The janissaries who were involved in the assassination attempt were simply unlucky in their selection of an escape route. Wrong place, wrong time when they met their demise at the hands of the Jinn. At some point Lucia decided that the fewer the number involved, the greater her monetary reward—she would not have to pay them their shares. Her callous disposal of them came with benefits. More importantly, however, I believe, it is likely she ordered their deaths to ensure her own protection. She simply had them killed because she believed they could not be trusted and under torture might reveal clues that could lead to knowledge of her involvement.

"As I have told you there are questions that remain. For example, I cannot be sure that King Charles knew of her schemes. Perhaps the seeds came from their discussions and Lucia simply developed her own plan independently. Or perhaps, together, they jointly developed the plot, anticipating the ensuing turmoil it could cause within the empire and likely precipitate war with Persia, diverting Ottoman focus and armies to the East. We cannot know with certainty, just as we surely cannot know the journey of the soul of another," Il Lupo concluded honestly.

Everyone quietly listened and absorbed Il Lupo's hypotheses. Francesca was mesmerized by her father's skill at marshalling and dissecting the evidence and tying it together. He had confirmed her instincts that Lucia was an anathema, embodying all she despised— greed, vanity, cruelty, and dishonesty.

"Well, what about the assassination attempt on Roxelana? Did Mehmed act on his own when he ordered it done?" Francesca asked, not yet having heard the explanation from her father.

Il Lupo looked to Suleyman to offer their shared conclusions. "We cannot be sure, *Hürrem*. There is no clear proof that Gulbehar ordered Mehmed or that she was directly involved. It could be that Mehmed acted alone and solely to ensure that he would remain in his powerful position. With Gulbehar established as the most powerful woman in the Harem, aside from the Valide Sultan, my mother, who has apparently chosen to abdicate her authority, Mehmed could remain her favorite and retain his influence. What Gulbehar has failed to realize is that while she has stature in the Harem, her position with me is very different. If she had acted based upon those suppositions, she would have acted for naught. My feelings toward her would not have changed or been rekindled in Roxelana's heartbreaking absence. In fact, I would likely have become more suspicious of her than I am now. I would have grown to dislike her rather than merely ignore her, as I do now. She will soon learn of my displeasures. We are to make changes, and I will discuss all of this in a few moments time.

"Kemal also has important news based on the time he has spent these last days with the janissaries. Please tell us, Kemal," Suleyman instructed. Francesca sat up straight in her seat, appearing serious, but Kemal caught her gaze and understood it connoted more than just mere interest in his forthcoming comments.

"Yes, I have made some notable discoveries," Kemal began. "Initially, for his purposes—the assassination of Suleyman—Qais recruited janissaries who were disaffected and in fact, he encouraged their restiveness. He apparently spent time lending a sympathetic ear as a counselor, so to speak, and feigned empathy for their plight. Those who he found to be the most disgruntled and manipulable were reserved and recruited for his own treasonous assassination plot. Other perhaps less pliable dissidents, those not simmering with hatred for Suleyman, Qais made available to Mehmed to corrupt and enlist to participate in the thefts. Those involved in the thefts did not necessarily know about the assassination plot. Qais and Mehmed knew of both but acted independently. If all had gone according to their individual plans, each would have been able to attain what they desired. Qais was the chief recruiter. He likely would have been appointed to command the Beyliks under the new sultan, assuming it was Mustafa. Mehmed would have remained the most powerful and favored eunuch in the Harem. And, of course, both would have attained far greater wealth.

"I have also learned something very interesting about Omar. He hated Mehmed because of Mehmed's hold over him, knowing he was a fully functioning male. His attempt on Mehmed's life was simply revenge. Mehmed had been merciless in his torments and Omar knew he would soon be found out and executed. He wanted to ensure Mehmed joined him in Hell," Kemal was pensive.

Kemal's audience was fascinated by these further details of the plots. They looked at one another, better appreciating the valuable individual roles each had played in the remarkable events of the previous few days and in saving the emperor and perhaps the empire.

Beneficence

Suleyman paused and paced for a few moments, his hands clasped behind his back. "So we have much to ponder, but understand what has happened and why. Our thanks to the shrewd and discerning Vincenzo Lupo. Now it is time for other matters. As promised, I have spent a great deal of time contemplating how best to demonstrate the depth of my gratitude to each of you," Suleyman addressed the small group.

"My decision required that I do what my heart dictated, even if in one case, I must reject my own selfish desires and best interests.

"First, for you, Aziz!" Suleyman smiled, returning Aziz's broad smile, whose eyes shone with anticipation. "For you, our ever faithful and most honorable eunuch, I appoint you the *Kizlar Agha*, the 'Keeper of the Girls.' This was not a difficult decision. You have earned my respect and it is my honor to promote you. Roxelana knows and has agreed, although I might say slightly begrudgingly, since she is so fond of you. She only asks that you visit her daily. I ask that you rid the Harem of any scoundrels— castrated or not. We shall have peace in the Harem henceforth."

"I am deeply humbled, Your Majesty," Aziz, the new Chief Black Eunuch answered, unable to hide the pride he felt having been bestowed this great honor. "Your Majesty, if I may, I had planned to tell you that I have already learned that the Harem eunuchs are much relieved to have peace and stability restored. They lived in great fear of Mehmed's corruption and bad temper. I thought you would want to know," Aziz reported. "So, it is peace . . . and perhaps, music lessons in the Harem henceforth.

"If you wish to remain popular with your new charges, not to mention the peace of the concubines, I would rethink the flute lessons," Suleyman advised with a laugh and pat on the back for his new Kizlar Agha. "And those birds! Be sure they learn some manners and diplomacy! May you be so blessed that these are the greatest tasks you have before you.

"And now, my dearest Roxelana. You have my heart, you know. But now, you shall have more. I have decided to send Gulbehar to Manisa, with Mustafa, where she will govern. I do not want her here any longer. As of today, she will leave the palace. And, you, my dearest Roxelana, my *Hürrem*, will rule the Harem as my wife. I will break with yet one more tradition because I can no longer deny my heart its desire." Roxelana was at his side in an instant, and their joy, so evident and complete, was reflected in the faces of each of those present.

"Is that a command of a sultan or a proposal of a man in love?" Roxelana teased. "Either way, the answer is of course, *yes*, my darling! I will say it a thousand times! And my love, we will also celebrate with a birth, for I am again with child. I ask that for a wedding gift I will be allowed to select the name. If it is a boy, I hope for the name Cihangir, which means, 'conqueror of the world.'"

"My sweet *Hürrem*! This is most wonderful news and yes of course, you have chosen a good and strong name. You are my treasure!" Suleyman was joyful.

Turning to Il Lupo and Francesca, Suleyman began, "I have nothing more to offer you that would ever be worthy of expressing the depth of my gratitude. You will, of course, be paid handsomely for your services and in gold Sultanis, as promised! There is always a home for you here whenever you choose to visit Konstantiniyye. Rooms will be set aside and made ready always for the family of Vincenzo Lupo. More than saving my life, Roxelana's life and the life of the empire, you have bettered me. I value deeply our debates and our strong friendship," Suleyman offered, his heartfelt emotions evident.

"Your Majesty, it is we who are grateful and humbled. You have showered Francesca and me with gifts of unimaginable beauty and value. You have listened to us and trusted us. And we too, humbly offer our friendship and hope that we are worthy." Il Lupo bowed and Francesca, dressed again as an odalisque, gave a slight curtsy.

"Then it is settled! Friends for a lifetime we are," Suleyman roared in expression of his complete pleasure. His gaze swept the room and stopped on Kemal, who was standing and smiling as well.

"Kemal, I have intentionally saved what I have to say to you for last. For me, my reward to you is most difficult. You see, in the rewards I have provided others it is I who have gained—a new Kizlar Agha, my beloved in matrimony, and dear friends. But in order to reward *you*, I must give up something that I want most desperately to keep." Suleyman stopped in an attempt to gain control of his emotions.

"In you, I have such faith and trust, and to imagine what it would be to not have you with me is most painful. In order to give you joy, however, I am learning that I must sometimes give up something and endure pain that accompanies the loss. Even an emperor must endure and be grateful for the heartfelt and even heart-wrenching emotions that are attached to my gift. My gift to you, my loyal and courageous Kemal, is your freedom." Suleyman could not hide the tears that welled up in his eyes, managing only to keep them from cascading down his cheeks.

"Allow me to explain," Suleyman continued to his astonished audience. "Over these past few days I have asked myself what, of all things, is most valuable to me. The answer is simply love. The love of my woman. The love of my friends. The love and respect of my subjects.

"And then I thought of you and how the love you had known was torn away from you as a child. We can be a brutal people, we Ottomans. I have loved you as a son and want what is best for you and without regard for the pain it might cause me. You are free to return to Palestine and find your mother and wipe the tears from her face. Find your father and taste his breads of which you have often spoken. Let him see your strong hands and know your wonderful mind. And then you must kiss the land and find love to release and fill the longings that must certainly have been stoically sealed within you. You may keep your Arabian stallion and you will be provided with horses, ample supplies, weapons, and gold to last you a lifetime—everything you will need for your journey." Suleyman paused again attempting to suppress his deepening emotion, a feeling unfamiliar to this ruler of an empire.

"However, I ask only that before you leave, you carefully solicit those janissaries that are most ardently loyal to me and give me advice as who to select as my captain. You will be impossible to replace,

but it must be done. My heart is filled with gratitude, Kemal."
Suleyman held out his arms to Kemal, seeking an embrace. Humbled
beyond words and unable to hide his tears, Kemal moved forward in
bittersweet acceptance.

The eyes of all gathered were moist. Il Lupo stood in awe of the
generosity of the Sultan Suleyman, the Magnificent, the Lawgiver
and found that in this single act, he was worthy of his titles and
namesake.

Francesca was filled with a joyous anticipation that now, perhaps
with Kemal's freedom, a way could be found for them. Roxelana
moved also beyond expression, reached over, and squeezed Francesca's
hand, understanding the promising implications for Francesca and
Kemal. Even Aziz looked at Francesca and smiled, giving her a
cheerful wink.

"I am so humbled. There are no words capable of expressing the
gratitude I feel, Your Majesty." The tears of the gentle warrior wetted
the great emperor's caftan. Breaking their fraternal embrace, with
hands holding each other's forearms, they smiled, acknowledging
their admiration and undeniable love for one another.

"One other proviso, if you ever decide to return of your own
volition, I will find a place for you at the head of one of my armies.
There is always a permanent and prominent place for you at my court!

"In conclusion, Kemal, you will know this. That I have forever
changed how I will treat the janissaries that are loyal and constant.
They will never want. When wounds or old age prevent them from
protecting me or the empire, they shall find respite wherever they
choose. If they wish to stay here, a place shall be made where all
their needs will be met until they are called to Paradise. We must
remember the debt that is owed to those who have gallantly served
the empire. Perhaps it will inspire our warriors to be even more
dedicated in their service."

"Your Majesty, your magnificence is exceeded only by your
magnanimity!" An astounded Kemal bowed.

"You see, Vincenzo, I have learned a great deal since you have
arrived at the court. I have learned to reconsider many of the things
that are common protocols within the empire and some needed
change. I am in your debt for the enlightenment you have provided."
Suleyman crossed his arm to his chest and nodded to Il Lupo.

"Come!" Suleyman clapped his hands, "It is time for another feast!" he summoned, gathering them around the table set and waiting in the kiosk. "Let us break bread together and give thanks to Allah for his beneficence and the many kindnesses he has bestowed upon us all!"

Esperance and Enshallah

There had been a lighting of the torches after dinner, but they were no competition for the dazzling display of the brilliant evening sky. Istanbul had once again delivered a breathtaking spectacle of glittering stars tossed across the deep sapphire blue night and showcased a clinquant crescent moon.

Vincenzo Lupo watched as his daughter and Kemal wandered toward the garden after yet one more celebratory feast. He too, was filled with bittersweet emotions. He was well aware that the affection between the two had grown quickly and deeply over these last days, leaving no doubt of their romance and love. His protective father's heart was at peace and accepting.

"I don't think I have seen them so bright, so early in the evening," Kemal remarked as he and Francesca made their way through the paths in the garden. "But then, the skies have appeared so much brighter every night since you have been here, Francesca. I know it is not just my imagination."

Francesca looked up, enraptured by the late evening stars. "That was most kind, Kemal. Thank you and yes, I agree, the skies have been particularly lovely, not only tonight but since our first evening on Giovanni's terrace." Francesca guided Kemal to a small stone bench near a beautiful Persian Silk tree.

"These trees are amazing. The first time I ever saw this variety was that night we spent on the terrace at Giovanni's. Here, we can sit here," she pointed to the narrow seat, sitting and patting the spot next to her.

"I have something for you!" She moved behind the tree and pulled out a wriggling beggar's cloak, ends tied together so as to form a bag. "Here!" She offered Kemal the package Aziz had placed for her just moments before, carefully following her instructions regarding its fragile content.

"What? Poison frogs? Surely I am not deserving of those! I have made great attempts to behave myself!" he howled, playfully.

"No, Kemal! You will be pleased, I promise!" she pleaded, convincingly.

Kemal took the schmatte, in itself a memento of their adventures together, and carefully unwrapped the squirming package. Then he heard a "yip," and hurriedly finished undoing the layers to reveal a puppy. He lifted the wiggling puppy high in the air, its tail wagging and ears flopping as it squirmed in his hands.

"He is very cute and small now, but I think that he will grow to be a very strong dog. Look at those massive paws, and the hair in between his toes! I have never seen such size and furry paws in a puppy!" Kemal exclaimed.

"It's called a 'Spinone'. They are hunting dogs commonly bred in regions near Venezia and are very devoted and loyal to their masters. They are known for their intelligence. I brought him with me on our caravel, the *Splendida*, intending to keep and raise him myself. Instead, I want you to have him. He really seems to like you. Do you like him? Just think, now you will have a traveling companion and constant reminder of your friend from Venezia!"

"Thank you, Francesca! I love his big ears and feet. He will grow into those! Today has been quite a day for gifts!" Kemal smiled, feeling slightly overwhelmed, lifting him from his lap onto the ground, allowing the puppy to play and laughing as it stumbled over its enormous feet.

"I shall have to think of a name that evokes good memories of our adventures together. Hmmm —how about Aziz? Look, he has big feet, just as Aziz! Remembering him will make me happy." Kemal smiled at his choice and Francesca smiled in response, reassuring himself of his choice. "Yes, Aziz, it is."

"Well, I am certain he will be honored—even if it is a dog!" Francesca laughed and their eyes locked. Kemal stood up.

"Perhaps you should keep him as protection from people like me," Kemal suggested, somewhat seriously.

"Ah, but Kemal…would that the world be filled with people like you."

He turned and looked at her seriously—the way a man with intentions would look at the woman he desires. "Yes, but if there be just one, could I be that one?" he asked, desperate to hear her say "yes"—that he could be that one to her.

Francesca continued to struggle to read his face, to understand herself as much as him. "Kemal, what's wrong? Please come and sit," she urged, unsure of his change in demeanor and not answering his question—unsure of its full intention. Her mind raced. *Of course I would want you to be that one person in the world that is meant for me! Are you saying that you wish for me to be that person for you?* Knowing herself now as a woman, with a woman's feelings and desires, she fully understood she was still a novice and not skilled in interpreting the language of love. She could think only that it felt lovely and divine to be a woman. *Did he feel what I just felt when our eyes met? Could he have the same feelings inside of him that I am experiencing?* Her stomach jumped.

Kemal did not want to sit. He wanted to stand and take her into his arms, absorbing everything about her that he desperately desired to know. He wanted to smell her hair, her skin, and her neck. He wanted to feel that extraordinary delicate touch from the woman who was so fearsome with her sword. He wanted to put his hands on her waist, feeling their curves, and draw her to him. He wanted to kiss her, to memorize her, and to know her. He never wanted to wonder again about his needs being fulfilled, or experience the melancholy that tore through his body and spirit. He felt his heart beating rapidly, just as it had felt before entering into battle, filled with fear, anticipation of the unknown, and adrenalin. He silently prayed that she too, was filled with the same trepidation and glorious desire that consumed him. *"Please Allah! Make it so!"* Kemal's prayer played repeatedly in his mind.

"Francesca," Kemal held out his hand to her. "Please, Francesca, come here to me." Kemal's epoch as a janissary was over and he was about to hold his dulcinea within his arms—the woman who perhaps represented the beginning of another new and glorious era, a restoration to a man on the verge of freedom in body, mind, and spirit.

Francesca looked at him and in that moment understood it had not just been her imaginings. He wanted her. Her emotions had run wild, her worried thoughts that his desire was a mere fantasia, and her hopes only the musings of a lovesick child. Now it was all changed and she wanted him. Only a few days ago she had admonished herself, cursing for feeling like a woman, resenting her shape and her desires. Just a few days ago she had been an ingénue, new to the world of love. That had all changed. This new world stood before her and she was captivated.

Drawn together by shared passion, spirit and need, it seemed only fitting that Kemal and Francesca, from separate continents, should find one another in Istanbul, the city connecting those continents. Surely, it had been a conspiracy of the fates that had brought them to this moment. . . Kismet. A magnificent moirai. The warrior and the ingénue. Unknowingly, their trouvaille, their seeking, had brought them here to end their shared and deep abyss of hunger and ache. One nearly motherless, the other completely so. The enslaved and the free, lives so divergent and yet so similar in their passions and talents. Their emotions ineffable, they did not speak, for there were no words capable of expressing their feelings, their desires, and their dreams in this moment.

Instead, they would find eloquence in their gaze, the touching, and the coming to innocent knowledge. She moved to him easily and eagerly as he pulled her close. The yearning, so long repressed, began to feel sated as he moved his hands—just as he had imagined—over her slim waist as he drew in her scent. He felt intoxicated, his senses nearly overwhelmed as he bent to kiss her—first her forehead—and moving carefully and deliberately to her beautiful mouth, desperate to reach it. Francesca felt the urgency of his need against her firm belly as he was overcome by the responsiveness of her perfect and sensual body to his touch. These fearsome warriors still innocent and naïve lovers, found themselves nearing a place of such supreme knowing. Kemal's mind felt a sense of release, all those years of emotional suppression culminating in this moment. She was no longer orphic, instead now known to him not yet completely in body, but in mind.

Roxelana's words to Francesca played in her mind… "he will invade your mind and you will need him in spirit and in body"… She responded to his kisses and ran her hands over the beautiful cloth of Salonica covering his back, imagining the moment when she would know the pleasures of his bare skin against hers. This lovers' odyssey she was about to embark upon left her nearly breathless... "the Koran offers the way to heavenly Paradise, but in the art of love, we possess the earthly gates to paradise. We are able to offer the divine to the man we love"...Francesca finally understood.

She put her head to Kemal's chest, listening to his steady, strong heartbeat. She held onto him tightly, as if to draw his body into hers, insinuating themselves into each other. His heart surged in response, pulling her in as he continued to kiss the top of her head lying just under his chin. Enraptured, she learned she was desired. She reveled in it—the sensations of pleasure overwhelming and enveloping her as her desire and love were fulfilled. She struggled as much to breathe as she did to prevent herself from crying from happiness, unable to control the depth of her feelings.

"Kemal, you are a free man." Francesca felt his continued kisses. She was almost afraid to look at him, fearful he would see the worry in her eyes—worry she felt about his journey and what it would mean for them. She was deeply and genuinely happy for his great good fortune, but afraid and uncertain about what it boded for her and them.

"This is the most wonderful gift you could have been given by Suleyman," she said softly. "Now you will begin yet another journey, one that will take you back to Palestine. You must be very happy," she murmured, not letting go of him, unsure of how he might answer. She understood that Kemal needed to return, however difficult it might be for her. She loved him and wanted him to go because it was part of his healing. She could not imagine a parting and the loneliness she would have to endure without him, but knew she had to encourage him.

"You know that my father has offered you a position at the academy should you ever find yourself free. You must surely know how ardently I want this also. Never could either of us have imagined you might be free to make this choice now," she whispered, her hands tightening on his back as she spoke.

"Oh Francesca," he responded softly, embracing her as closely as he could. "Yes, I cannot imagine a man so fortunate as I. Indeed, it is the most magnificent of gifts from the sultan. It has been a longing to see my mother again, to dry her tears, and see my father. I pray to Allah that they are alive and will accept that I have been raised in the religion of Islam!" Kemal laughed softly, trying to lighten the moment, but he understood the import of Francesca's words.

"And your father's generous offer. I am a janissary, a warrior, so it would provide me with opportunity to teach my skills, of course. A fortuitous opportunity. It would be a pleasure to fight alongside you! I will be able to teach you to ride and become an archer rivaling any janissary. In return, you can enhance my skills with blades and other weapons. But, Francesca, I must first do other things."

"Of course, Kemal. Of course you must. I understand. I understand this is an act of love you must first complete for yourself and your parents."

He pulled her closer again, hoping to offer reassurance. He wanted to go with her immediately to Venice, but his heart needed the healing and fulfillment that could only come from seeing his parents and homeland once more, a free man. He knew this was their dilemma. Their journeys must soon take them in separate directions.

"Francesca, today I have gained something even more important than my freedom. Just as Suleyman, I have given something away," he began. "Within a few days, I will begin my journey to Palestine and you will set foot back on the *Venetian Splendida,* the place where I first saw you, to begin your return voyage to Venice. We must not let this momentary separation be the end for us. Today, Francesca I have found a way to fulfill my longings. I have also on this most auspicious day, given you my heart. You are *in* my heart. I hope you will have it and be faithful and kind to it."

"Kemal, yes, of course. My dearest Kemal! Of course! I want this to be a beginning, to know this is just our beginning. There is impermanence to our separation. I know this now and my heart rejoices. How long will you be gone? Are you certain you will be able to find me?"

"Francesca, my beautiful, precious *kucuk uzman,* how long I will be gone, I do not know. I hope long enough to give comfort to my parents and sit and listen to the wise words of a rabbi and learn to make the sweet challah. And then, when I see you again, I will make it for you and bring it warm to you from the oven, for you to savor. I will tell them of you and know their hearts will be glad. And how will I find you, you ask? I hope one day that you will never leave my sight. But I promise you that you will never be so far that you will be lost from me. You are here." He gathered her hands in his and pressed them to his heart.

"You are here, Francesca—you reside here. And, when I come to you again and if you will have me, I will ask your father for your hand. Then Francesca, I will take you to my bed and lie with you, and we will have adventures and journeys. We shall have it all, Francesca. Enshallah, Francesca, Enshallah. God willing."

Releasing his hands from hers, he sweetly and reverently put his hands on her face, lifting it to him and kissed her again, allowing the longings to be delivered out of their bodies. In the profound quiet of the moment, their earth stood still as they held one another, their embrace expressing an exquisite and tender esperance—deep, inviolable, and indwelling.

And so, in the moment just after midnight, within the walls of the
Topkapi Palace and beyond the ancient
cobbled and cacophonous streets of
Istanbul, Kemal Bey, sat on the edge of his bed. His mind embraced
the fortuitous events of the past days and
the torturous, painful evolution
of his life. He found gratitude even for the hardships he had endured,
for without them, he could not have reached
this moment. He had come
full circle – excruciating pain to sublime
happiness – understanding finally
that in his suffering was salvation and necessary to become
the person he was intended to be and to find peace.
His fervent prayers, his pleadings for understanding
and mercy had been answered. He envisioned
the exquisite promises of
the future. So overcome was his heart that
he was unable to control the
outpouring of emotion. The powerful and fearsome warrior put his
hands to his head and wept. Spent, he then
dried his eyes with his shirt, made
from the beautiful cloth of Salonica, and thought of Francesca…his
Francesca. Picking up his journal, he wrote one final entry:

I AM FOUND.

Epilogue

As the light dimmed,
Kemal seldom thought of El Diablo Nino,
the Jinn or Shaitan. The many wars and battles
he had fought had
become fading, distant memories. Honors
bestowed upon him by the
great Suleyman seemed less important
and even his many wise words
mere whispers wafting on the winds of his years.
No…Kemal's last
visions would be the flow of the sweet waters
of two continents
mellifluously merging and sparkling in
the fading sunset… the passion
and love in a beautiful woman's eyes…
and the predestined life,
journeys, and adventures promised by,
and embraced within, the bliss
of a first kiss so many years ago.

Afterword

Having read our tale we hope you will relish further adventures and journeys with Count Vincenzo Lupo and his daughter, Francesca, to strife-ridden venues and royal courts of the tumultuous 16th century, those requiring their masterful skills and acumen. Perhaps others, those who assisted in the resolution of the mysteries in Suleyman's court, will join them? Perhaps a venture to locales steeped in superstition, deep in the darkest of Europe's primeval forests? Even as we write, the lives of our dramatis personae are evolving. As the intrigues that will summon them develop, their stories become richer and more enticing than ever. A sequel, perchance, awaits.

Robert Peacock
Sara Cook

The authors wish to acknowledge the creative and dedicated artistic and editorial contributions to our story made by Sara's daughters-in-law, Katelyn and Rebecca. We also thank Aynur Kadihasanoglu and Semra K. for their special counsel regarding the proper use of Turkish translations, and Ovidiu Bacini regarding the Romanian language. Latin translations of prose and expletives have been made with the assistance of Phoebe Peacock.

Special Acknowledgements from Sara Cook

I wish to thank and acknowledge the following, for anything of worth that I have ever accomplished belongs, in whole or part, to them. I am humbled and most grateful to:

God, for His inestimable blessings, inspirations and the gift of peace.

My parents, for their swaddling love and encouragement.

My brother, Robert, who trusted me with his wonderful and enticing story.

My husband, John, with whom I share 45 years of friendship and love and who has selflessly given up some of his dreams so that I could achieve mine.

My courageous, decent and fine sons, Zachary and Joshua...I marvel upon each sight of you and you fill my heart with joy...and their wonderful wives – our "dear little Kat" and "Becka blessing", who have so enriched our family and brought their special talents and artistry to this endeavor.

My closest and dearest friends Nancy, Lorraine, Kin, Ann and Phil...who have collectively given me two centuries of love and friendship.

And finally... to those who have left impressions and shared moments, enriching my earthly experience and who are now cause for nostalgic reminisce.

Annex

The Jinn and the Sword Art Credits:

TITLE PAGE: https://www.123rf.com/photo_13605126_traditional-arab-dagger-isolated-on-white-background.html?term=13605126&vti=nb2folu4af8qzxwrid-1-1

PREFACE: https://www.123rf.com/photo_86212870_vector-vintage-wedding-invitation-ornate-frame-for-design-template-eastern-style-elements-luxury-flo.html

PROLOGUE ART: https://www.123rf.com/photo_86541647_vector-vintage-card-ornate-frame-for-design-template-eastern-style-element-luxury-floral-decoration-.html

INTRODUCTION: https://www.123rf.com/photo_77891370_vector-vintage-card-ornate-frame-for-design-template-eastern-style-element-luxury-floral-decoration-.html]

DAY ONE: https://www.123rf.com/photo_30046846_red-background-in-persian-style-template-design-for-wedding-invitation.html&https://www.123rf.com/photo_39513927_vintage-

invitation-cards-with-lace-ornament-eastern-floral-decor.html?
term=39513927&vti=nwlh5i6inkdz1fdmfd-1-1 (lace border only)

DAY   TWO:https://www.123rf.com/photo_54108538_stock-
vector-vintage-greeting-card-with-swirls-and-floral-motifs-in-east-
style-bright-background-in-persian-style.html?fromid=Zy80SjF3
MFFNWXFzTG5BNWs3Z29VZz09

DAY THREE:https://www.123rf.com/photo_74652388_wedding-
or-invitation-card-vintage-style-with-crystals-abstarct-pattern-
background.html?term=74652388

DAY   FOUR:https://www.123rf.com/photo_74652369_stock-
vector-wedding-or-invitation-card-vintage-style-with-crystals-
abstarct-pattern-background--vector-element-e.html?fromid=
UjhmL3hnWk1IOFYwdU5uSHJmcTBXZz09

DAY   FIVE:https://www.123rf.com/photo_67851449_banner-
with-round-floral-abstract-ornament-circle-elements-card-vintage-
decorative-pattern-hand-draw.html?term=67851449

A FEW DAYS LATER:https://www.123rf.com/photo_56914141_
arabic-calligraphy-design-of-text-ramadan-kareem-for-muslim-festival.
html?term=56914141&https://www.123rf.com/photo_8014504_
eastern-background.html?term=8014504 (background for verso)

EPILOGUE ART: https://www.123rf.com/photo_86541658_
vector-vintage-decor-ornate-floral-frame-for-design-template-
eastern-style-element-luxury-floral-dec.html?term=86541658
&vti=lhvu8ch62mil9h9b3j-1-1